A Terrible
Fall of Angels

A Terrible
Fall of Angels

LAURELL K. HAMILTON

HEADLINE

First published in the USA in 2021 by
BERKLEY
An imprint of Penguin Random House LLC

First published in Great Britain in 2021 by
HEADLINE PUBLISHING GROUP

Excerpt from *Duino Elegies* by Rainer Maria Rilke. Translation by David Young.

1

Cataloguing in Publication Data is available from the British Library

Hardback ISBN 978 1 4722 8534 8
Trade Paperback ISBN 978 1 4722 8533 1

Offset in 12.22/17.18 pt Adobe Garamond Pro by Jouve (UK), Milton Keynes

Printed and bound in Great Britain by Clays Ltd, Elcograf S.p.A.

Headline's policy is to use papers that are natural, renewable and recyclable
products and made from wood grown in well-managed forests and other
controlled sources. The logging and manufacturing processes are expected
to conform to the environmental regulations of the country of origin.

HEADLINE PUBLISHING GROUP
An Hachette UK Company
Carmelite House
50 Victoria Embankment
London EC4Y 0DZ

www.headline.co.uk
www.hachette.co.uk

This one's for everyone who made the world a better place
this last year when everything seemed lost.

Thanks to all of you who did anything large or small to save,
to help, to be there for someone else.

You are all my heroes.

Who, if I cried out, would hear me among the angels'
    hierarchies?
and even if one of them pressed me against his heart:
I would be consumed in that overwhelming existence.
For beauty is nothing but the beginning of terror, which
    we still are just able to endure,
and we are so awed because it serenely disdains to
    annihilate us.
Every angel is terrifying.

—RAINER MARIA RILKE, *DUINO ELEGIES*

A Terrible
Fall of Angels

CHAPTER ONE

There were angel feathers in the dead woman's bed. They looked like huge white swan feathers, impossibly large, but then they were supposed to propel something the size of a tall man skyward. I didn't have to see the angel to know that he'd be tall; they were all tall, some close to eight feet, but average was between six feet and seven feet. I was six feet, three inches, a big guy by most standards, but angels always made me feel small, even when they were close to my own height. It wasn't about physical inches when you were in the presence of angels.

I stared down at the feathers scattered across the tangled bedclothes like soft ivory, lacy cream curling with their edges moving as the window air conditioner blew directly across from the bed. The bed was shoved up against one wall, with most of the small off-campus apartment taken up by the desk and enough floor space for the yoga mat that was leaning in the other corner.

The forensics team had finished in the bedroom, though I could hear them in the bathroom that this apartment shared with the one next door. I clenched my hands in the plastic gloves, booties over my shoes so I wouldn't contaminate the crime scene. My detective shield was around my neck on its lanyard. My FN 509 nine-millimeter was in a side holster under my jacket. I had its little brother, the 503, at home. Some of the other cops had given me a hard time about not carrying a Glock, until I invited them down to the shooting range to try an FN. Then they asked price. There were other cops around, lots of them; there always were at a murder scene, because that's how it was called in first. A murder scene with angel evidence on-site, and they bumped the call up to us. The Metaphysical Coordination Unit was our official title, but the other cops and most of the media called us the Heaven and Hell Unit, because we didn't just solve crime on one side of the spiritual divide, we worked both sides of the street—someone had to keep the peace between beings that could tear the world apart if they ever went to war again.

If the angel feathers hadn't been here it would have been listed as a rape homicide and been given to Sex Crimes. I stared down at the feathers; they'd started to gleam as the light faded outside the small window. I wasn't certain if they glowed with holy fire or I was seeing the light inside my head where I saw spirits and visions. The largest feather was so white it looked ghostly in the dying light. The others were less pure in color, more off-white, and they had flecks and edges of faint color to some of them. Not all angels had snow-white wings, but that was the color that most people expected, so that was the color the angels had chosen for the largest feather that they left behind. They had wanted to make certain the human police officers first on the scene would call in the Metaphysical Coordination Unit and send for me, because I was the angel expert.

I stared at the largest feather as if I was trying to read it, but it just lay there whiter than the sheets it was lying on. It was as long as the bed, carefully placed on the edge, a huge primary flight feather. There was no way for anyone to have gotten out of the bed without disturbing that feather, yet it lay ruler straight. The other feathers weren't anything that would cripple a wing, but this one would if angels flew like birds. The feathers were all on top of the sheets, not under them, not on the floor, not scattered like they'd be if the rapist had been an angel as the feathers seemed to imply. I knew angels didn't lose feathers when they had sex, not even if it was rough, because for most of them the wings weren't that solid. For those whose wings were solid, no human being was strong enough to tear them apart, not barehanded. Either the angels did it themselves, or something powerful enough to injure them did it, which meant it wasn't the victim. I'd have bet any amount of money that they'd been placed on the bed after the crime had been committed, but why? Why did the angels care enough about this one undergrad college student to incriminate themselves? God might know when every sparrow fell, but the angels didn't show up to catch the bird before it hit the ground. Of course, they hadn't saved the woman. She'd been found nude, beaten to death, and with enough dried bodily fluid on her body that rape was almost a certainty. Until forensics confirmed it, it wouldn't be rape, but it was a sexually motivated crime; we were only waiting on the medical examiner to give us a list of exactly what had happened to Megan Borowski. Thinking her name made it almost impossible not to picture her body, the beating her face had taken, her body left on the floor of the room like the murderer had just gotten up and walked out after he was done with her. There were no signs of remorse, no attempt to cover what he'd done to her face, or her nudity. It made it more likely to be a stranger, or someone who didn't feel regretful about what he'd done. We were all assuming the attacker was male, because of the bodily fluids on the body and the strength needed for the beating.

I had to try to think of Megan Borowski as just the victim, a body savaged by attacker or attackers unknown, because it could have been two men. That might explain why she hadn't screamed for help. Had one threatened her in some way during the rape—*I won't kill you if you just do what I want*—and then they'd killed her anyway? Evil, it was evil, even if it was just men who did it, but was it Evil with a capital *E*? Was that why the angels had been ordered to leave their feathers at the crime scene, so we'd know it wasn't just a human-on-human crime?

I had one of the few quiet moments I'd ever had at a scene like this, where some trick of duty or assignment had sent everyone somewhere else, so I had a moment to stare down at the dead woman's bed all by my lonesome. I didn't believe it was an accident that I was alone. The crime might not have been planned, but when every other person working a suspicious death leaves the prime crime scene to just me, well, I was waiting for whatever the Big Guy wanted me to see, or hear, or experience. Maybe there'd be a clue that only I would find, or needed to find. God worked in mysterious ways, and so did all His messengers, that much I knew. I heard one of the crime scene techs curse, as if something wasn't going to plan in the hallway. Celestial beings were involved; nothing would go according to human planning, I knew that much. In all the years I'd worked angel detail I'd never seen a single feather left behind unless the angel was fighting for their own safety.

If there'd only been one smaller feather, I might have thought the victim had an angelic lover, maybe. Angels were funny things and could affect people in ways that neither the human lover nor the angel could see coming. Because we were the wild cards, we humans, once angels got a taste for us, they could screw up both their eternity and our lives—screw it up all to Hell. Of course, one small feather might have been overlooked in the initial investigation. Realistic evidence of an angelic lover wouldn't have been spotted right away. It wouldn't have made anyone call us yet. I wouldn't be standing here if the angels hadn't gone all-out to grab my attention.

The silence got that weighted quality to it, and I knew that even if one of the techs came back into this room in the next few minutes, they might not see a damn thing except me. If they were one of the gifted and could see the unseen, they were about to be in for a Heaven of a show.

The angel manifested just in front of me, between the foot of the bed and the window. The hair on my arms stood to attention, but the skin on my neck stayed calm, so I knew it was an angel, but not one of the angels that had left the feathers. They wouldn't be able to manifest like this anymore. Once the spiritual got solid enough to leave DNA behind, they couldn't just conjure themselves out of thin air. The figure hovering before me wasn't even solid enough to stand on the carpet, because "it" was made mostly of light.

The angel glowed before me, all white and gold-yellow light; even its eyes were full of yellow fire, but there was no heat. Angels don't give off heat, no matter how fiery they look; if you ever see a glowing angel and feel heat come off it, it's not an angel, exactly. One of the first things you need to understand if you work angel detail is that fallen angels are still angels, and demons, well, that's another problem altogether, but the rule is, if it gives off heat, run; if you can't run, pray.

The angel's wings were barely hinted at; "he," or "she," was mostly just light with a humanoid figure in the middle of it, and a shimmering hint of wings, and flowing robes, but mostly just that full-bodied halo, the aurora.

The voice sounded male, but honestly angels this shining are sexless, they just are. "We are pleased that we do not have to manifest fully for you, Detective Zaniel Havelock."

It wasn't the opening I'd expected; if angels seek you out personally then it's with an extremely specific message like in the Bible: *You are pregnant with the Son of God*, or *Flee now, enemies are coming*. The personal conversational style was how they spoke to Angel Speakers, *Angelus Dictum*, which means "the angel said" to make it clear that the person sharing the message from the angel is not an angel but only their mouthpiece. Angels did not speak like this to people on the outside, but once I'd been inside and I fell back into the same rhythm, an old habit come back to haunt me. "You can lose the humanoid stuff altogether if you want. I do appreciate you trying not to drive me insane by manifesting in your pure energy form, but it's okay, I don't need the baby steps."

"Very well," it said, and the human pretense went away. I was left staring at light, or flame, or something in between the two. It filled nearly all of that half of the room, but it gave off neither heat nor formed shadows. Again, if something says it's an angel, and glows at you, but it causes shadows around it, it's not the good kind of angel, or maybe it's not an angel at all.

The light turned its "head," and I could read the body language of that glow; most people wouldn't have been able to. "You asked for me to drop the physical away, not for my comfort, but because you wished to see if I cast a shadow."

I shrugged and fought not to let my shoulders tighten. You couldn't wrestle an angel in this form; it wasn't "real" enough, but the body tenses, preparing for fight or flight, even though neither will help you. You can't hit pure spirit, and you sure as Heaven can't run from it, because spirit-level angels can just appear anywhere, in multiple places, at multiple times, and it's all real, all them, because when they're this pure, time doesn't mean to them what it means to most of us. They can simultaneously be in several places at once, at the same time for us humans, but different points of time for the angel itself. Time is way more flexible than the human mind can comprehend. It was a good thing that the pure spirit didn't commit crimes, because we would be beyond fucked trying to prove it, solve it, or catch them. When this guy was finished glowing at me, he'd go back to God, maybe even be absorbed back into that ultimate light. Witness protection had nothing on the pure spirit angelic. They could literally be reabsorbed and made pure and new again when they made their next earthly appearance.

"I know you are one who has walked through the flame and survived, but I did not understand what it might mean."

I remembered standing in the middle of flames that did not burn, and cast no shadow, and surrounded me on every side. If my faith had not been pure enough, I would have been consumed by holy fire. I blinked the memory away and faced the much fainter light of the angel before me. "And what does it mean?" I asked.

"That you do not think as others do or see as other flesh sees. You are the only *Angelus Dictum* to ever finish your training and then turn your back on it."

"I am not an Angel Speaker, I'm a cop."

"You are a police officer, but that does not mean you are not also an Angel Speaker; otherwise how could I be here?"

I couldn't argue with the angel and I very much wanted to, so I let it go. The conversation was getting too weird, and off topic. I was here to solve a crime, not dissect my past. "Maybe I was meant to be a police officer, and work with the angelic like this."

"Perhaps." Again, it did that "head" turn, but this time it was listening. The fact that it had to listen to hear God's voice meant it wasn't pure spirit anymore, or it wasn't going to be for long. This one was at the beginning of a path that might lead it to be as solid as the angel we were seeking. They sent down pure spirit, but every time they talked to anything of flesh, they stopped being quite so much spirit, and a little more . . . flesh. This one had come down to talk to humans before, several times before. The next time I saw "him" he'd probably be male, or closer to it. The voice is the first clue, the first move in choosing a "gender."

"What have you come to tell me, angel?" I asked.

"Can you not discern my name?"

"I probably could, but I'd rather not."

"Why not?"

"You want me to name you, and you display curiosity about something that has nothing to do with the message you were sent to deliver. You haven't been around flesh enough to be this distracted from your task, angel."

"What does that mean?" it asked.

"It means that you may not be cut out for being a messenger to Earth. I think you'll corrupt faster than normal. I think that God might want to rethink your job description. You might be better off polishing a star off somewhere away from things of flesh."

"You judge me, Detective Zaniel Havelock. That is not your place."

"You haven't given me the message that God sent you to deliver."

The cold flame made a movement that rippled through its shining light. At a guess, it was a stumble, or a startle reflex, as if it hadn't realized how distracted it had gotten. "You are right, my apologies. The message is this: The woman was not intended to die here like this. She had many years ahead of her here on Earth, before being called home."

"So why did she die here like this, if she was supposed to live?" I asked.

"I don't know." A contraction, instead of the full words, another sign of degradation.

I wasn't upset that the angel didn't know; they were given messages to tell us, but beyond the message they often had no other information. "Why was this woman important enough for the angels to leave their feathers at the crime scene?"

"She wasn't important," the angel said.

I tried again. "So, if she wasn't important, then what was important enough for the angels to leave this many feathers behind?"

"You must find the murderer, Detective Havelock."

"The regular police could have found her murderer if it's another person," I said.

"If they find the murderer without you there, they will die and there will be more outrages."

"Do you mean rapes?"

"I do not understand," the angel said. I knew he meant it; any angel that was this much spirit and so little flesh didn't understand matters of the flesh, not sex, or hunger, or bathrooms. Nothing that "real" made sense to pure spirit.

"What do you mean by outrages?"

"Things that are not supposed to happen."

I tried to think how to ask a question that might actually help us find the murderer. Then I realized I was treating the angel like I was still nineteen and an Angel Speaker, and not a cop.

"Where is the murderer now?"

"That is hidden from us."

"Hidden? How can anyone hide from the angels?"

"You are an Angel Speaker; answer your own question."

"I am not an Angel Speaker. I am a detective."

"Then why did you keep your angelic name, Zaniel? Why did you not go back to the name you had before?"

"I'd been Zaniel longer than I'd been any other name by the time I left. It was how I thought of myself." I realized I was trying to justify myself to the angel, which I didn't need to do. "I completed my training; the name was mine to keep or not, as I chose, so I kept it, simple as that."

"Is it simple, Zaniel?"

"Don't call me by my first name."

"Should I call you by your other name, the one that all the humans use? Should I call you Havoc?"

"No," I said; somehow having a fiery angel say the word *Havoc* was unnerving, as if it were part of the message and there would be havoc on Earth. It was my nickname from the army, that was all.

The angel looked at me, and its face was less flame and slightly more human, not in the pretense of humanity it had shown at first, but like it was deciding on a real face for when it became more solid. This one was in real danger of losing some of its pure spirituality. If I had truly been an Angel Speaker, I would have reported it to those who were supposed to have the ear of God. Now all I could do was warn the angel itself, which I'd done. They didn't have free will, but the more time they spent on the mortal plane the closer they got to it.

"Very well, Detective Zaniel Havelock, have you answered your own question yet?"

It took me a second to remember it. I was getting too distracted by the angel. It had been so long since I'd been near one in this raw a form. I could admit to myself that it felt good to be near the power, like I'd been cold for years and suddenly I could warm my hands.

"The adversary can sometimes hide its minions from the angels."

"Yes," the angel said.

"If a demon did this, the entire apartment would feel evil, and it does not."

"It does not, but it should."

"So, the murderer is a demon," I said.

"No, but it should be."

"I don't understand," I said.

"Neither do we."

I stared at the angel, wishing there was a face so I could read its expression, and the wish was enough that the face began to shape into cheeks and fiery hair, and . . . I forced myself to stop thinking about the angel's form. I stopped my imagination in its tracks because flesh could influence spirit. My training as an Angel Speaker didn't make it easier for me to force the angel into a shape of my choosing; the training enabled me to stop before it happened. It was partly a safety measure so that when angels appeared to humans, they didn't drive us insane, but it was more complicated than that. I took a breath and let go of my need to see human features on the fire shape in front of me, and it settled back into something even less human. Good.

"Are you saying that you, the angels, do not understand what the murderer is?"

There was a sensation of it moving again, and I could feel it listening again. I had a second of thinking that if I listened hard enough, I could hear the music of spheres, the shining language of creation that kept reality running. I fought off the urge because I knew how dangerous it would be for me and for . . . others.

"The murderer is something that should not be."

"What does that mean?" I asked.

"The thing that should not be has changed the fate of the woman. If this is allowed to continue, more fates will be changed and God's plan could be disrupted."

I blinked at the glowing angel and swallowed past a sudden lump in my throat as my pulse sped up. "Only free will can interfere with someone's fate, and nothing can interfere with God's plan," I said.

"Some humans have fates so tightly written that free will is not completely possible." It completely ignored the part about God's plan, but I stuck to what it was willing to talk about, because if an angel decides it won't talk about something, it won't. Human imagination can change their appearance, but it can't give us any insight into their thoughts.

I shook my head. "I know you have to believe that, but I don't."

"And that is your free will, Detective Havelock," said the angel.

"It is," I said, "but are you saying that this woman, Megan Borowski, was one of those people whose fate is so tightly written that free will shouldn't have been able to change it?"

"I am."

"So how did she end up being beaten to death and ruining her fate?"

"That, Detective Havelock, is an excellent question."

"Do you know the answer to my question?"

"I have been told that you must be elsewhere to find your answer."

"Where is elsewhere?" I asked.

"I will help you find your way to where you need to go."

"How?" I asked.

There was a gasp behind me, and then fellow detective George Gimble said, "Holy motherfucking God, it's a flame angel! Holy shit!"

The angel looked past me at Gimble, and then it just vanished. Maybe it had given all of its message, or . . . I turned around to see Gimble standing gaping at the space where the angel had been. His skin was so pale every freckle stood out on his face. His green-brown eyes were too wide, set off by short auburn hair that was almost red. He was barely five foot four and looked baby-faced, so he was always being carded; no one ever believed he was over twenty-five, let alone that thirty was his next birthday. He was the youngest detective in our division, and one of the reasons they'd bumped him up was that he could see spiritual beings. He could see them, but he didn't have my background with angels; no one else did who held a badge. The angel had said it: No one with my training with the angelic had ever left the College of Angels and not stayed to be an Angel Speaker, which was really a glorified secretary in some cases. You took messages, conveyed information to those who came to the College, read temple, and asked questions of the Angels on behalf of the petitioners, or sometimes a message from above was so hot you hunted down your recipient like Jonah; you couldn't escape your fate, not if God wanted you bad enough. Of course, Megan Borowski had escaped her fate, or someone else had stolen it from her, along with her life.

"Gimble, what did I tell you about cursing in front of Celestial beings? Especially using blasphemies that involve Heaven, God, God's Mom, or any other saint, Deity, or other spiritual being?"

He closed his mouth enough to look embarrassed. "Cursing using Heaven, God, God's Mother, saints, Dieties, et cetera . . . can cause beings of high spiritual content to dissolve, or otherwise flee a crime scene, not because they are guilty, but because your language causes them discomfort."

"Exactly," I said.

"Jesus . . . Jeez, Havoc, I'm sorry. I just never saw anything like it.

You know, they don't even show up on film in that form, so it's just been drawings and stories until now."

I sighed, and then I had to smile. "It is a Heaven of a thing the first time."

"How old were you the first time you saw something like that?"

"Thirteen," I said.

"Jesus, I mean, jeez, weren't you scared shitless?"

I nodded. "Yeah, yeah I was."

"What did you do when you saw it the first time? The angel in its pure form, I mean." What little color was left in his face drained away. I was already moving forward when his eyes fluttered back into his head and he started to fall. I caught him around the waist, but the height difference made it easier to just pick him up.

"I fainted," I said.

CHAPTER TWO

Gimble didn't wake up in the ambulance. I knew that because I rode in the back with him. He could come to like normal, just his usual cheery self, or there were other options. The kind that had made me insist on staying by Gimble's side even though the paramedics had assured me that I could follow in my car to the hospital. I'd stayed with Gimble no matter how many medical professionals tried to get me to step outside the little curtained area in the hospital, too. I had let hospital security take me back so I could put Gimble's weapons in a locker, which both I and the security person signed off on. When the security person suggested I could put my own stuff in a locker, I told him that what attacked Gimble might be coming back for him, which absolutely was a lie, but there was no way I was giving up my gun or anything else unless I had to, and I didn't think I had to.

Gimble and I were finally upstairs on the very top floor, which housed the Metaphysical Injury Unit. He was still unconscious in the bed, and I was trying to answer the doctor's questions. Dr. Paulson was a couple of inches taller than me, at least six foot five, positively willowy in his nice white coat. I felt like a muscular bull in the proverbial china shop standing next to him. "Are you seriously telling me that an angel did this to him?"

I took a deep breath and let it out slow. I'd told the story to the paramedics, several nurses, and at least one intern who had hunted up the doctor on call. Apparently, the intern had felt that an angel-induced coma was above his learning curve.

"Detective Gimble seeing an angel in its pure form caused him to pass out, but the angel didn't do it on purpose."

"I thought angels didn't do anything by accident," Dr. Paulson said.

"Short of God, no one's perfect," I said.

"Angels are," he said, as if it was true.

I smiled and tried to think of how to explain how very wrong he was, without pissing him off or oversharing with him. He was the doctor in charge of this area, so if he disliked me enough he could make me leave Gimble's side, and that wasn't happening.

"Maybe the angel thought that Detective Gimble could handle it," I said, though I knew that wasn't true. The angel hadn't been thinking about Gimble at all; it had thought about its message and getting it to me. Angels with a mission are very narrow of focus.

"You're both with the Heaven and Hell Unit; shouldn't he have been able to handle it?"

"The Metaphysical Coordination Unit handles things besides Heavenly and Hellish incidents, so not everyone in the unit is equally good with angels."

"But you're fine," the doctor said.

"I'm good with angels."

"Are you sure it was an angel and not something just masquerading as one? That would explain why your colleague has been harmed."

I took in a deep breath and let it out slow. The doctor didn't know my background, so he didn't know he'd insulted me. Heavens, there were people in my unit who didn't know all my background, so I really couldn't get upset with the doc, so why was I?

"I know the difference between an angel and the things that pretend to be angels."

"I've had patients in the ER that talked of winged demons, Detective Havelock."

"There are more things above and below with wings than just angels, Doctor, and most of them have little or nothing to do with any of the Abrahamic faiths."

"Abrahamic faiths? Oh, Christian, Jewish, and Muslim," he said.

"Yes," I said.

"I haven't heard them referred to like that since med school when I took the required metaphysical medicine courses."

"I take it you aren't a religious man, Dr. Paulson."

"My sister and I joked that we were raised Jewish light." He smiled as he said it.

"And nothing you've seen in your medical career has made you more religious?"

He shook his head. "I've seen miracles and curses and they both worked. I've seen spells from white witches and black, and everything in between. I've seen too much to want to follow any of them."

I wanted to ask him what he did when he dealt with illness that only faith would cure, or dangers that only belief would protect him from, but I didn't. He'd made his choice; if the Big Guy couldn't persuade him to join the fold, then nothing I said was going to change that. I know I'm supposed to want to convert everyone I meet to the one true way; trouble was I wasn't sure it was the only way into Paradise. I hadn't been sure since I was about nineteen.

"I respect your choice," I said at last.

"I take it that you are religious," he said.

"You could say that."

He looked at me as if he expected me to say more. I just smiled at him.

"What, you're not going to try to convert me to your path of faith?"

"Me talking about my personal belief in God isn't going to help Detective Gimble."

"Don't you mean personal belief in Deity, Detective Havelock?" said a deep voice from outside the curtain.

I smiled and said, "Sorry, Lieutenant Charleston, I forgot my political correctness for a second."

A large, dark hand parted the curtain and my boss, Lieutenant Adinka Charleston, stepped through. The rest of him matched the hand. He was as tall as the doctor but built more like me. He'd gone to college on a football scholarship and played pro as an offensive lineman for two years before injuries took him out. He was a little thicker around the middle than he had been in the NFL, but not by much. Other than the hair going gray he looked pretty much like the pictures in his office when he was in uniform for the Denver Broncos.

"Don't forget again, Detective. We wouldn't want the doctor to think we were insensitive." His voice sounded serious, but I knew that he thought the new PC vocabulary regulations were a crock of shit, which was what he'd called them when he was forced to give us the lecture about using them. I didn't know why he was pulling the doctor's chain, or maybe mine, but I knew he was.

"Yes, Lieutenant," I said, but I gave him a sideways look to see if I could figure out what was up.

He looked down at Gimble, who looked even smaller lying in the bed surrounded by the three of us. All traces of the smile faded from Lieutenant Charleston's face. "So, what are you going to do to wake up my boy here?"

"If he truly saw an angel, then he shouldn't be in a coma, but he is, so if we can figure out what did this to him, then we can put together a course of treatment."

"Did the angel touch him?" Charleston asked.

I shook my head. "No, if it had he'd be dead."

"I thought angels healed with their touch," the doctor said.

Charleston and I both shook our heads. "You explain, Havelock, you're our angel expert."

"If they are sent from God to heal, they can, but angels that are pure spirit like the flame we saw, they mostly follow orders, and he wasn't there to heal."

"What was he there for?"

"To deliver a message," I said.

"To the patient?" the doctor said.

I shook my head. "No, not for Gimble."

"Doc, I need to talk to my detective alone for a few minutes." Charleston smiled at the doctor as he said it, but it didn't quite reach his eyes. They showed that he was smiling for social convention and nothing else.

Dr. Paulson seemed to understand, or maybe he had other patients with less complicated complaints; whatever the reason, he gave us the room.

Lieutenant Charleston's smile faded until his expression matched his eyes, sort of unfriendly and taking no shit. "So, the angel had a message for you?"

"It gave me the message," I said.

"Don't play word games with me, Havoc. One of my detectives is lying in a bed unconscious and no one knows why, or how to wake him up. Answer my damn question."

I told him what little information the angel had given me. It sounded even less helpful than it had at the crime scene.

"So, the murderer isn't a demon, but it's somehow part of the Devil's plans?" Charleston asked.

"The Adversary, yes."

"That's just another term for Satan, right?"

"It's what I was taught to use at the College of Angels," I said.

"Just making absolutely certain we're talking about the same being."

"It's the same," I said.

"Could the murderer be possessed?"

"The angels are aware of what a possession is, Lieutenant. This was something new, or unusual, and whatever the murderer is, it's something that the angels don't understand, and that is powerful enough that it can hide its movements from Celestial powers."

"If it's not a possession, then the hot lead I was going to tell you about just got colder."

"What lead?" I asked.

"There was a security video in the parking area across from the apartment building. The camera caught a man leaving the building at the right time to be the murderer. Looked like there might even be blood on his clothes, but if we're looking for something supernatural this kid isn't it."

"Kid, so you have an ID?"

"Mark Cookson, nineteen; his grades have fallen in the last semester enough that he's on academic probation at UCCA, University of California, City of Angels. He got some complaints by female students for being overly persistent in his attentions after they'd made it clear they weren't interested; nothing violent, nothing illegal, just socially awkward and bordering on stalking. He's definitely a creeper. One of the students that had complained about him was our victim."

I looked at him and felt that eager rise when everything starts to fall into place on a case. "Did you find him yet?"

"He's not in his dorm and his roommate changed schools midsemester so no new roommate to question."

"Is there anything in the dorm room that says he's into black magic, or demonology?"

"Had to send someone else to see the dorm room and try to find any friends he might have, because I got a call that one of my detectives was in the hospital." He gave me a look.

"Sorry, Lieutenant."

"Mark Cookson sounds like he could be good for this, Havoc, but your angel makes it sound like we are looking for someone a lot more dangerous than a horny teenager with bad social skills and no criminal record."

"If they find things in his room that say he's been messing with black magic, then he may still be the guy."

"But if he is, then we're looking for him right now. He's from an upper-middle-class family, he's not going to know how to hide from the police. We will find him, probably soon, which makes me think he's not it, because if he was, why would we need a message from the angels?"

"I don't know. The angel shouldn't have given the message to me at all, Lieutenant. It should have gone to an Angel Speaker at the College, then they would have given the message to their handler, they would have given it to the administrative assistants, and they would have contacted the prophet on duty."

"How long would all that have taken?"

I thought about it. "Hours, maybe a few days."

"This is a murder investigation, Havoc; maybe God knew we needed the information sooner rather than later."

"The Big Guy can do anything He wants to do."

The lieutenant sighed. "Then he sent the message to you personally, because he knew we needed to know sooner."

"Perhaps, but in the twelve years I've been gone from the College I've never had a message given to me."

"You've never had another angel speak to you since you left?"

I looked away then, not sure what my face would show. I chose my words carefully, because Charleston wasn't just a good cop, he was a Voodoo Priest, and I knew he worked his own brand of magic to give him better insight into people when he needed information from them.

"I've worked my brand of magic with the angels since I left the College, but I've never had them seek me out to tell me some message as if I were still an Angel Speaker."

"You're an Angel Speaker and a detective on the case; it sounds like you're the perfect person to receive a message about the crime."

"I'm not an Angel Speaker."

"Maybe not officially, but you can talk to them without ending up in a coma, or worse."

I let out a long breath because I'd been trying hard not to think about worse. "If any part of the holy fire had touched Gimble he'd be dead."

"Or insane," Charleston said.

"If he wakes up, that's still a possibility, sir."

"How serious a possibility?" he asked.

"He could wake up with no memory of it happening, or wake up screaming, or violent, or blissed out."

"Blissed out, what does that mean?"

A deep breath from the bed made us both look down. I put a hand on Gimble's shoulder so that if he tried to get out of the bed and hurt himself, or us, I could keep him down until he could be restrained.

He blinked up at us. "Hey, Havoc."

"Hey, George," I said, and smiled because he looked normal.

"Hey, Lieutenant."

"Hey, Detective, how are you feeling?"

"I saw an angel, did Havoc tell you, I saw an angel?"

"He told me."

"It was beautiful, so beautiful, like looking at the sun just standing in a room, except it had wings, but they were made of fire. It was amazing, wasn't it, Havoc? Tell the lieutenant how amazing the angel was." He touched my hand, which was still on his shoulder. "Tell him, Havoc; I don't have the words." He held my hand and started to cry softly, but his face was full of wonderment and awe. I'd seen that look before on other Angel Speakers, and in the mirror. It was like being born again into God's chosen faith.

I held Gimble's hand and looked across at our boss. "This is blissed out."

CHAPTER THREE

He stopped crying and just lay there glowing with happiness. If it had been because of true love, or a new baby, or any of a dozen things I'd have been happy for him, but I'd seen the same angel and I wasn't glowing. It did feel good to stand near him, though, as if waves of happy contentment were flowing from him to the rest of the room. The nurse on duty came in to check his vitals and stayed talking to him, smiling down at him as he smiled up at her. Of course, Gimble was smiling at everyone; the whole world would be his friend while the afterglow lasted.

Lieutenant Charleston took me outside the room and spoke low while Gimble made friends with another nurse. "How long is this going to last?"

"Hours, days, months." I shrugged.

"Are you telling me one of my detectives is going to be like some charismatic preacher for months?"

"Or it could fade in an hour," I said.

Two other nurses came down the hallway and entered Gimble's room. We stepped back to look in on him, but he was beaming at the four nurses and telling them about the angel. There didn't seem to be any medical emergency that warranted that many nurses.

Dr. Paulson came down the hallway frowning. "Where the hell are my nurses?"

We both pointed at the room behind us. Paulson strode through the door. "We have other patients on this floor, ladies and gentleman."

They made sounds of apology and seemed a little embarrassed or confused about why all four of the nurses on the floor were in one room when there didn't seem to be much wrong with the patient.

Dr. Paulson shooed them out of the room like they were children being sent outside to play. He didn't seem affected by the angelic bliss spilling off Gimble; neither were Charleston and I, but we had training in resisting metaphysical interference, and the doctor didn't. So how was he unaffected?

He looked at both of us, the irritation in his eyes bordering on anger, but his voice was still controlled and even. "The religious mania is fine, I'll have someone from psychiatric look at him, but why is it affecting the nursing staff?"

I answered, because as Charleston liked to remind me, I was the unit's angel expert. "Sometimes people come away from angelic visitations trailing clouds of glory. Being that close to God can make them high, but it can also make them shine to other people. People are naturally attracted to things that bring them closer to God's presence."

"I know that seeing an angel in pure form can drive a person insane or give them amnesia, so they don't remember the incident at all, or even this type of evangelical experience, but there's nothing in the literature about it being contagious."

"It's a rare side effect," I said.

"I've never heard of it either," Charleston said. He joined the doctor in giving me unfriendly looks.

"It may be because Gimble is psychic in his own right, so that his powers are combining with the protective story his mind built for him."

"What protective story?" Charleston asked.

I looked at him as if to say, did he really want me to give out this much detail in front of someone who wasn't one of us? But he said, "Dr. Paulson is the doctor in charge of Gimble's treatment, Havelock. He needs to know enough to make that treatment effective."

"Point taken, Lieutenant," I said, and turned to the doctor. "I saw the same angel and it wasn't all light and choral singing. It was special and awe-inspiring, but it wasn't the way Gimble is describing, at least not to me."

"Are you saying that he saw something you didn't?" Paulson asked.

"I'm saying that there is some debate on whether spiritual beings look different from person to person. The theory is that it's the same reason that we can see spirit, but it doesn't always show on film, so we may be seeing it with the parts of our minds that see dreams, or daydreams, rather than concrete reality."

"So, you're saying that what you saw and experienced may not be what the other detective saw."

"Yes."

"So why is that a protective story?"

"It could be that he saw exactly what I saw, but it's too powerful for his mind to deal with, so in order not to go crazy his mind has given him a wonderful vision instead of the scarier truth."

"You mean like a trauma victim remembering things differently," Paulson said.

"Yes, in either case the mind is trying to protect the person from something that was overwhelming to them mentally and emotionally."

"Don't forget spiritually, Havelock; maybe what's happened to Gimble is that seeing an angel in person has given his religious beliefs a kick in the head," Charleston said.

"Maybe, but most of the time this kind of shiny happiness doesn't last long enough to change a person's religious habits. I pray that it doesn't last for Gimble."

"Why?" Charleston asked.

"Because this kind of belief can lead people to quitting their jobs, giving away their possessions, and devoting the rest of their lives to charity or something."

"Is that so bad?"

"It is when it's the mind protecting itself from trauma instead of a deeply held religious belief."

"If a person leads a good life, does it matter what motivated it?" Charleston asked.

I looked at him. "What would your wife say if you came home tonight and asked her to sell the house, empty out your savings, give or sell everything of value you had so you could give it to the poor, and then you'd spend the rest of your lives helping the homeless, or something like that?"

Charleston looked at me for a moment, then laughed. "She'd think I'd lost my mind and wouldn't do any of it with me. She'd probably try to have me put on a twenty-four-hour psychiatric hold."

"It's that kind of abrupt change, Lieutenant. It's not a person soul-searching for years to find their place in the world or in Deity's plan, it's like a lightbulb that gets turned on one day in a room that was already bright and sunny. It's not bringing people out of the darkness into the light of spiritual growth, it's shining so much light on a person that they become blind to the joy they already have."

"Okay, but why is it impacting the nursing staff?" Paulson asked.

"Like I said, I think it's because he's psychic."

"What kind of psychic is he?"

"Empath mostly," Charleston said, which was my clue not to add anything else. If my boss didn't want the doc to know everything Gimble could do, then that was okay with me. I didn't like oversharing with civilians.

"Is he a receptive or a projective empath?" Paulson asked, and that meant he paid more attention than most civvies did to gifted Americans. Most people didn't even know that there was more than one type of empath, or that their power could be more than just picking up emotional impressions from others.

"Mostly receptive," Charleston said, which again was my cue to not overshare.

"But he can project, too?" Paulson said.

Charleston made a head movement that could have been a nod or a shrug. Paulson took it as a nod. "Then could he be projecting his emotions onto my nursing staff?"

I nodded before I could stop myself, but Charleston conceded it. As if on cue the male nurse came back down the corridor and tried to go into the room, but Paulson stepped in his way.

"What is it, Gonzales?"

"Time to check the patient's vitals, Doctor."

Paulson shook his head. "No, it's not."

"Are you sure?"

The anger flared in Paulson's eyes again. "You took his vitals less than ten minutes ago, I'm sure."

"Maybe he pressed his call button?"

Paulson sighed and ordered the man to go back to his other duties. One of the other nurses was walking this way and passed Gonzales to reach Gimble's room.

"What is it, Prescott?" he asked her.

"The patient pressed his call button."

Paulson leaned back into the room and asked, "Did you press your call button?"

"No, but I'd love some company." I could see George's smile while he said it; he was a very social guy. I wondered if that was part of it; was he literally projecting his social need on the nurses? Had the angel somehow increased his psychic abilities? That would be a first.

"Check on your other patients, Prescott, this one is fine." She went farther down the hallway, and I saw the last nurse peeking around the corner at us, as if she'd go into Gimble's room as soon as the coast was clear.

"I can't have the entire nursing staff on this floor ignoring the other patients."

"Understood," Charleston said.

"Then what are you going to do about it?" Paulson asked, one hand on his hip, so the white coat swept back from his scrubs as if he was going for a weapon almost.

"What's your background with the gifted, Doctor, if you don't mind me asking?" I said.

"I do mind you asking." He turned back to my boss. "What are you going to do about his disrupting this hospital?"

"I'll make some calls. I'll leave Detective Havelock here until we can come up with a more permanent solution."

"How is the detective supposed to help the issue? I mean, if he could help, then why isn't he already?"

Charleston smiled at the man's anger, trying to be pleasant. "Maybe he can help shoo the nurses out."

"I cannot guarantee that their fascination with this patient isn't compromising their ability to care for the other patients on this floor. Your detective isn't the only one here who was negatively impacted by a spiritual experience. I need my staff to be able to care for all of them."

"I understand that, Doctor, and I will find someone whose gifts help the situation a little more actively than Havelock here, but until I can find the right person for the job Havelock is one of my best people."

I fought not to react too much to that last statement. Charleston wasn't much for that kind of compliment in front of civilians. Of course, maybe he was just reassuring the doctor. Either way I tried to look worthy of the compliment; some days I'd have believed Charleston was right, but Gimble was compromised because I had told the angel that it didn't have to pretend to be human for me; if I hadn't invited it to show itself in pure form it wouldn't have done it in a public area. So it was my fault that Gimble was blissed out and projecting happy social messages to the nurses, and if he gave away all his belongings and became a monk that would be my fault, too. I prayed hard that he got over this—I didn't want another person going insane because I couldn't protect them from the angels. One was plenty.

CHAPTER FOUR

The lieutenant started to make his call just down the hallway from Gimble's room, but I saw him look at the rooms on the other side of the hallway and then he looked at the door in the middle. He wrapped his hand around something that was under his button-down shirt. I knew it was a small bag that he wore around his neck. As long as I'd known him, he'd worn it constantly. He lowered his hand from the bag and came back down the hallway to me. "Ask the doctor what is in this room. I don't mean just metaphysical patients, but exactly what's wrong with them."

"It's going to fall under medical privacy, Lieutenant. He can't tell us without a warrant or unless he knows that us not having the knowledge threatens lives, and even then, it's his call."

"You're probably right, but ask him anyway." He gave me the room number as if I hadn't seen him point, but it was always good to be precise.

"I'll ask, but can you give me a reason why? Because the doctor will ask."

"Tell him I'm not sure that everything in this hallway should be this close to each other, and ask him if it's typical to have almost every room on the metaphysical injury floor full."

"Since you're the one that sensed something, it might make more sense coming from you. He's just in the room behind us."

"I need to ask for specific unit members, and some of the energy I'm feeling on this floor will not only hear the phone call, but they could sense things through the phone I don't want them to know."

I leaned closer to him, lowering my voice as if that would make a difference to something that could hear both sides of a phone conversation from another room. "What are you sensing, Lieutenant?"

"I'd have to do more spell work to be sure, and I'd have to get a warrant or the doctor's permission for that, too."

"Since I'm the one on point, give me a hint."

"Demonic, maybe, or something masquerading as one, and then just black magic—the kind that compromises the soul of the person who casts the spell."

I raised my eyebrows at him. "Did you feel it the first time you walked past the rooms?"

He shook his head and put his hand back over the bag under his shirt. He closed his eyes for a second. "We need backup. I'll request people from our unit and then put the word out that we have an officer down; that'll give us all the manpower—sorry, person-power—we need."

"Gimble didn't get injured on the job, he fainted. If the other cops hear that he'll never live it down."

Lieutenant Charleston flashed me a grin that was very bright in his dark face. "Tell them he wrestled with an angel and lived to tell the tale, or tell them he's a big pansy-ass and fainted from seeing his first metaphysical badass." He gripped the bag a little tighter and the smile faded.

I could feel it now, like something thick and dark trying to crawl down my throat, but it was as if it had to knock on the door of my mouth; I had to give it permission to enter me. I thought, *By free will and the grace of God I hold fast against the darkness.* The thick feeling eased back, pulling backward to the open door of the room.

"Make those calls, Lieutenant. I'll hold the fort."

"Get Paulson to talk to you, Havelock," Charleston said as he moved down the hallway, the phone already to his ear, and his other hand tight on the bag under his clothes.

I watched him until he rounded the corner for the elevators, gave one glance down the hallway at the other rooms, and went back to Gimble's room to try to get Paulson to tell me what in Heaven or Hell was in the room across the hall.

CHAPTER FIVE

N o, Detective Havoc, I won't reveal personal information about patients just because your boss has a bad feeling."

Gimble looked from me to him and back again like it was a verbal tennis match. He was still smiling and beaming at us, but at least he was letting us talk about something besides the angel at the crime scene.

"It's Detective Havelock, not Havoc."

"I heard your lieutenant call you Havoc."

I nodded. "That's a nickname; my last name is Havelock."

Gimble chimed in with, "Don't feel bad, Doc, I thought his name was Detective Havoc Havelock for months, because it's all anyone calls him at work. I don't know why he doesn't use his first name; Zaniel is a great name, better than George. George Gimble, with a name like that I have to work so much harder to charm the ladies."

I frowned at him and he just kept smiling up at me. We'd had to keep the nurses out of the room twice since Charleston left. He hadn't been gone that long.

"Zaniel, I don't think I've ever heard that name before," Dr. Paulson said, frowning at me as if he was trying to decide if I matched my name.

"I've never met another one, but George is right, I don't go by it much at work."

"Whatever you call yourself, Detective, I can't share confidential information just because your boss got spooked."

"Just tell me if someone on this floor tested positive for demonic contamination."

He reacted to the question, a slight startle. He tried to hide it, but I'd seen it. Charleston was right. "No matter how you ask the question, Detective Havelock, my answer will remain the same."

"Don't you usually try to isolate demonic-contamination patients from the rest of the metaphysically injured?"

"I can't . . ."

"I'm not asking you to divulge confidential patient info, I'm just asking a general protocol question."

Paulson seemed to mull that over and then said, "Yes, we do try to keep them a few empty rooms away from the others. If it's a full-blown possession then they go to the nearest religious institute of their faith, not my hospital."

So I now knew it wasn't a possession for certain; that didn't leave many other options when it came to real demons. "They aren't demon touched, are they?" It was a polite term for someone with demonic ancestry. It didn't always mean they would be bad people, or even that magically talented, but when they did have problems, they were big ones.

He narrowed his eyes at me. "Stop fishing, Detective, because I'm done rising to the bait."

That could be a yes, or he was just tired of the word games. "Why did you break protocol and put the patient next to another darker-energy patient?"

"How do you know . . ." He sighed, and the anger darkened his eyes again. "You didn't know until I just told you. Damn it, Detective, I can order you out of this room and have security keep you off my floor. I will do exactly that if you ask me one more leading question."

"Sorry, Dr. Paulson, but there's something wrong out there in the hallway. Something wrong in at least one room. My lieutenant felt it, and then I could feel it, so whatever it is, it's getting stronger."

"How do I know you're not lying to try and get me to give you more patient information?"

"If you step outside this room, farther away from George's aura, you may be able to feel it for yourself by now."

"No, I won't, my psychic shielding is impenetrable."

"If you can shield that well, then drop a tiny bit of your protection and you will feel it."

He shook his head. "I can't drop my shields, it's a natural skill. The metaphysical practitioners at the medical school weren't sure what would happen if they broke my shields down to teach me to control them, so they gave me a choice. I chose to leave them intact, which means I'm almost a psychic null except that I'm even more impervious to psychic attack than a true null."

I tried not to stare at him as I processed what he'd just said. "Thank you for sharing that with me, Doctor."

"I shared it because if there is a metaphysical problem that turns . . . dangerous, I need you to know that you don't have to protect me. I have the perfect defense against everything."

"Appreciate knowing that," I said.

"I also want to be clear that I will be useless for any metaphysical offense. I can protect myself, but no one else."

I nodded. "Good to know," I said.

"Yes, most people with my ability to shield can flex it outward to protect others, but I can't. I didn't want you to count on me to do something I am incapable of."

"Thank you, Doctor."

"You're welcome." He studied my face as if he would memorize me. "You aren't lying about what you're sensing on the floor, are you?"

"No, Dr. Paulson, I'm not."

"Then you need to know that this is the first time I've seen the metaphysical unit completely full. That's why we had to put patients next to each other that we normally would have separated."

"Was it one incident that left a lot of injured?"

"No, Detective Havelock, they're all from different incidents. In fact, there's not even a theme. It's not a shape-shifter gang war filling the ward, or fairies getting drunk on energy at Solstice, or even spells going wrong at the dark of the moon and sending us a whole coven. There's no pattern."

"Is it all"—I tried not to say *evil*, since the new, more sensitive vocabulary meant we couldn't call anyone's religion evil, but—"negative energies, except for George here?"

"No, we have three that you would call purely negative, two that are somewhere between good and evil, and the rest are neutral. Literally just injuries from magic gone awry. We've even got one teenager with a broken wrist from a poltergeist."

"It's rare that a poltergeist will hurt someone badly enough to be hospitalized. Are you sure it's not something more malignant?" I said.

"The injury isn't that bad, but the witch on duty suggested we keep him overnight in a warded room so the poltergeist wouldn't be able to feed off the teenage energy until a more permanent solution can be arranged."

"Aren't all the rooms on this floor warded against magic?" I asked.

He looked at me as if I'd said something stupid and then pointed at a small flat box set into the wall beside the door. It was blank and innocuous looking, but I knew if I looked at it with that other part of my vision it would have holy symbols on it.

"Of course, the new ward panels that got installed last month. Sorry, they're new enough I keep forgetting," I said.

He nodded, face softening, as if I'd redeemed myself a little. "Yes, even someone with a small talent could touch the ward panel and they would be invoked."

"Can you activate the ward panels?" I asked.

"I haven't tried, but I'd go on the assumption that it's like all magic and would require my shielding to be more porous, but I assume you have talent in that area, so the panels should work for you."

"Does it keep things in, or out?" I asked.

"What is inside the warded area remains, what is outside can't cross, or that's the theory."

"Theory?" I asked.

"It's very difficult to make a generic warding spell that a magical practitioner can use that will stand against all energies, Detective. I cannot work magic, but I've seen enough of it trying to get in and out of these wards to tell you that it's good, but it's not a perfect system."

"No mystical system is perfect," I said.

"There are a few priests assigned to this hospital that would disagree with you, but they aren't here right now, and I agree with you."

"Are the wards turned on in the two rooms with open doors, and the closed one across the hall from them?"

"No on the open rooms, yes on the closed one."

"I know you don't want to give me details, but with demons isn't it protocol to put up any wards you have?"

"Not in the case of possession, because we want the demon to leave the patient. If we put up magical walls to contain the demon, that means it's less likely to be able to leave the human host even if it wants to."

"I thought you said it wasn't a full possession."

"It's not, but it's similar enough, and when the wards were invoked the patient's vital signs became erratic. We tried everything else but only the wards being deactivated saved the patient's life."

I fought not to give him a look similar to the one that he'd given me just minutes ago. "Don't you think that was suspicious of demon possession? They have been known to almost kill their hosts to try to prevent priests from exorcising them."

"It was one of my colleagues who made the decision. I haven't had a chance to complete my rounds on the floor because you and your friend here have caused me to have to herd the nursing staff."

"So you haven't looked into any of those rooms yet?"

"I was just stepping in to do my own evaluation when another patient needed more immediate attention and then there was you."

"Do you have an exorcism team on call tonight?"

"If you mean priests, then no, but we have a Wiccan high priestess on call. She's also a nurse so she can help triage after the supernatural emergency is over." Something in his tone made it clear that he found her more useful than any of the priests who cycled through the hospital. I couldn't argue that most of them didn't have medical training.

"Don't most exorcism rituals take days to perform?" he asked.

"Yes, and if we need that kind of help tonight, we're going to need something quicker acting."

"We have angels," George said, smiling up at us from the bed.

"We did see an angel," I said, and smiled back, because how could I not with his eyes full of such perfect trust? George was an optimist, but he'd been a police officer long enough to make detective, which meant perfect trust had been left behind years ago. I didn't know any detectives who still believed in the ideals that they'd started with.

George's face crumpled a little, like he was thinking very hard about something, but it wasn't his usual grinning cynicism. It was like a glimpse of what he might have looked like at age five when the world was new and explaining yourself to grown-ups was hard.

Nurse Gonzales went past the door, not running, but like he had a purpose. He never glanced in at us; maybe whatever effect George was having on the nurses was fading.

Nurse Prescott rushed past the door next. It made me look down the hallway in time to see her go into the open door that Charleston had been worried about.

I stepped farther into the hallway and the moment I did I felt . . . evil. There was no other word for it. No politically correct term covered the sensation of it crawling over my skin, raising the hair at the back of my neck and along my arms.

Charleston texted, "Elevators not working. 20 floors be there ASAP."

A woman screamed and then Nurse Prescott stumbled backward out of the room; she fell on her ass in the hallway, but it was like she couldn't look away from whatever was in the room. She started backing down the hallway on her hands and feet like the crab walk they used to make us do in gym class. I was moving to help her before I'd even thought about it. I was a cop—we ran toward the sound of screams, not away from them.

CHAPTER SIX

had my gun in one hand as I grabbed her arm to pull her to her feet and get her away from the room. I couldn't see anything in the room but the bed and someone under the sheets. She screamed and batted at me with her hands. I pulled her across the floor by her arm as I said, "Police, I'm police, you're safe."

She stopped slapping at me and got to her feet with my hand steadying her. She shook her head too fast and too often. She gasped. "Ray, oh my God, Ray's . . ."

"What's wrong with Gonzales?" Paulson said from just behind us. He hadn't stayed in the room where it was safe, point for him, but he was an ER doctor—they tended to run toward trouble, too.

Her breath came out as a sob as she said, "It tore him apart."

"What tore him apart?" I asked.

"The patient, but a person couldn't do that." She finally looked away from the doorway to stare up at me. "He can't be human." Her voice lowered and I watched her try to get control of her expression, so she didn't look shocked. She did her best, but her eyes held all the horror she was trying to keep off her face. I gave her points for trying and changed my gun to a two-handed grip as I moved toward the room and whatever was inside.

"Mark Cookson is a nineteen-year-old college student, you can't just shoot him," Paulson said.

I stared at him. "What name did you say?" I wanted to make sure I'd heard correctly before I got too excited.

"Mark Cookson, do you know him?"

"Not personally, but he's the person of interest in a rape homicide last night."

"You just want me to let you shoot him," Paulson said.

"I'm telling you the truth, and I can't handcuff or Taser something that can tear a grown man to pieces. I'm out of options."

"He's not human," Prescott said.

"He's possessed; if we can get the demon out of him, he'll get a chance to be an ordinary college sophomore. He'll go back to his family and have a life unless we shoot his body full of holes that I can't fix," Paulson said.

"College sophomore is young for being a sorcerer," I said.

"He's not a sorcerer," Paulson said.

I looked at him but kept the door in my peripheral, because I didn't want any more surprises. "You don't conjure a demon real enough to tear people apart unless you're very well versed in the occult arts."

"He didn't conjure it, he *is* it," Prescott said.

"You mean he shape-changed into another form?" I asked.

She shook her head, her fear fading because she was having to think and explain things to the cop who was asking stupid questions. "No, the demon was inside him. It crawled out of him like he was a Halloween costume."

I was suddenly more hopeful.

"That is not funny, Detective."

"Absolutely not," I said.

"Then why are you smiling?" she asked.

"Sorry, but demons don't crawl out of people like that except in movies. Physical possession can manipulate the human body but not to that degree."

"I saw it!"

A deep bass voice called out, "Come see for yourself, Detective."

I ignored the voice and turned back to the nurse in front of me. "What does the room look like? What does the body look like?"

She looked at me like I was crazy. "Blood, blood everywhere." She said it angry; her eyes started getting that haunted look again, but that couldn't be helped.

"On the floor?" I asked.

"Of course, on the floor!" She was just angry now because anger feels so much better than fear.

"Then why isn't there any blood on your shoes? Why aren't you leaving bloody footprints down the hallway?" I asked.

"She did not step far enough into the room to be covered in the blood of my victims," the deep voice said.

"Why would she step into the room at all if she saw her coworker dead?" I asked, and by talking directly to that voice I opened myself up to it, but it was a calculated risk. If it knew intimate details of my life just from talking to me, then we were in serious trouble, but I was hoping it wouldn't know me, betting it wouldn't.

"She's just a stupid bitch."

I almost said out loud, *Was Megan Borowski a stupid bitch, too? Is that why you killed her?* But it wouldn't have helped anything. In fact, it would have just given the demon something to play with, and there was a chance that Mark Cookson had committed rape and murder under demonic influence. Depending on how the demon got hold of him, he might be innocent. We'd have to see.

"I couldn't see Ray from the door," Prescott said.

Paulson asked, "Was the body in the bathroom?"

"No, no, it was beside the bed like he'd gone in to check vitals and it killed him.'

"Prescott, you can see the bed from the door. You wouldn't have had to walk inside to see it," Paulson said.

She stared up at the doctor and then at me, frowning. "I don't understand."

"Come in and play with me, Detective."

Why was it still in the room? Why hadn't it attacked us by now? "The nurse activated the wards in the room before she ran," I said.

"It's protocol to hit the panel on the way out," Prescott said beside me.

"Nerves of steel, Nurse Prescott."

"I couldn't let it hurt anyone else." She said it as if anyone would have taken the seconds to touch the panel and activate it before running for their life.

"You come out and let me send you back where you came from," I said.

"You have no idea where I come from, Detective."

"Who are you?" I asked.

"Why, I'm Mark Cookson, they've named me several times."

"What's your real name?" I asked.

"Now, Detective, that would be far too easy."

"Was Mark Cookson ever in this hospital?" I asked.

A deep, rumbling bass chuckle spilled out of the doorway; whatever was making that noise sounded bigger than a human being. "Maybe he was, maybe he wasn't."

"What have you done to my patient?" Paulson asked.

"Your patient? Don't you give a damn about what I did to your nurse?"

"Prescott says he's already dead; I trust her judgment, so I'll move on to someone I can save."

"Very pragmatic of you, Dr. Paulson."

Had we said Paulson's name out loud? Up to that moment the demon had only repeated what he'd heard us say in the hallway, but we hadn't said the doctor's last name, so how had he known it? An Infernal that repeated things was small fry; one that *knew* things it had no way of knowing was a bigger fish and, Heaven knew, more dangerous.

"You can't get out of the wards, which means you didn't use a human as a costume. If you had that kind of power, no insta-ward would contain you."

"I don't have to come to you, Detective; you'll come to me to save the lives of the civilians in here with me."

"All I have to do is wait for backup; you killed your only hostage."

"Did I?" There was a scream, and I knew it was a man's scream.

"They are both dead," Prescott said. "I saw them dead."

"Demons can mess with your mind and make you see things that aren't there," I said.

What little blood had come back to her face drained away. "Oh God, did I leave Ray and that boy in there with a . . . demon?"

"You thought they were dead," I said.

The scream sounded again, higher pitched this time.

"God help me, I thought they were dead." She was hugging herself tight enough that her skin was mottling with the pressure.

"It could be the demon imitating the voice," I said.

"You're just saying that to make me feel better."

"No, it's the truth. He fooled you into thinking he was Mark Cookson; using the voice is nothing compared to taking over the whole body."

She gave a small nod, but her arms loosened their desperate hug, so that she could let go of herself and stand straight instead of hunched over her guilt.

I started to move toward the room with my gun up. Paulson said, "Don't shoot my patient."

"I'll do my best," I said, but I didn't change my shooting stance as I eased toward the room.

"The demon turned Mark Cookson into a weapon. He had no more control over what he did than the gun in your hand."

That made me pause for a second, because there was a chance that it had been the demon that turned Mark Cookson into a rapist and murderer. Had he been a terrified passenger in his own body watching the demon do horrible things? Except I knew that demons couldn't force us to do things that weren't already inside us. They could manipulate us into acting on them, but it had to be a thought, maybe a dark fantasy we never intended to act on, but it had to be inside us somewhere for the demon to find. They didn't create horrors without our help. I kept moving to get a better look inside the room. My gun stayed in both hands, tucked up tight to the front of my body with me able to sight down it to shoot if I needed it. It would have been great to save the teenager, but just because he was young didn't mean he was innocent. I'd had more teenagers shoot at me than adults, and I still had the scars from the eleven-year-old who stabbed me with a kitchen knife, because I thought he was too young to be dangerous. I'd lived through that mistake and I never made it again.

CHAPTER SEVEN

I didn't have to move far to see Mark Cookson's body standing just inside the doorway. I say *body* because the look on his face was all demon. The evil rolled off him in a wave that made my chest tight, but the body was still tall and thin with too much leg showing around the white hospital gown. If I didn't look at the face, then his body seemed younger than I'd been told, like early teens when boys get their big growth spurt but before the rest of them catches up and fills out. I'd have thought he was in high school, not college, and then I looked at his face again. Whatever was looking out of his face was ancient and evil and happy about it.

"You still in there, Mark?"

"Mark's not home right now, but leave a message and I'll be sure and tell him before I take him to Hell with me." The voice sounded like it needed a chest three times as wide as Mark's narrow one; it was weird that the voice coming out of the body was more jarring to me than the rest of the possession. You never know what will bother you most until it does.

"The human host doesn't go back to Hell when we cast you out of him. You know it doesn't work like that, but Mark doesn't. You're talking so he won't fight to be free of you. You've told him that if you go, he goes," I said, and my voice was calm.

"Stupid cop, you don't know shit about Hell."

"I'm a detective with the Metaphysical Coordination Unit, I know a lot about Hell and Heaven. I know you can hear me, Mark; fight free, we can save you."

"Liar!" the demon roared, and then he stumbled. For a second the expression on the face matched the rest of the body. Mark Cookson was in there and he'd been able to get to the surface for a split second. Paulson was right, Mark was an unwilling weapon. I'd worry how a nineteen-year-old college student got messed up with a demon later, after we'd saved his life. I holstered my gun, because if I wasn't willing to shoot the body it wasn't the right tool for this fight.

Charleston and security would be up here as soon as they walked up twenty flights of stairs. All I had to do was stall until backup got there. It was no coincidence that the elevators had stopped. The demons had started getting better at messing with modern technology lately. Proving that you could teach old demons new tricks.

"You put up your gun, does that mean you don't want to shoot me?" the demon asked in that voice that seemed too deep for Mark Cookson's body.

"I'd love to shoot you, just give up the boy's body and let me see the real you."

"The sight of me unfettered to flesh would drive you mad. I would enjoy watching you gibber and moan while your reality cracked and bled out your ears."

I glanced around to make a hundred percent certain that no one else had a sight line to the room, just in case the demon changed form. I didn't want another accident like Gimble because a demon in true form is madness, death, or in rare cases possession.

"I think you're just some poor errand boy from the nether regions that saw a chance to get inside a little boy. Is that it, you like children?"

"He's nineteen, old enough to make his own choices and to choose the way he will fall from grace."

It was funny how even demons didn't like being accused of being pedophiles, as if that were the lowest rung even in Hell. "But you didn't deny the errand boy part; you're hiding behind the boy because your true form isn't impressive enough to scare anyone."

The demon reached out to touch the wards. In the movies they sparkle, or fizz, or something even more dramatic, but the only thing I saw was the hand pressing against the air. He pressed against it as if there was something much harder and more solid than the clear air of the doorway. It wasn't dramatic, it was just solid workmanship. I made a mental note to ask them who did their insta-wards, because you didn't find magical craftsmanship that solid often.

"You can't get out," I said.

"I had to try," the demon said, shrugging, and the gesture matched the body. I knew that angels could become more humanlike the more they dealt with us, but I'd never thought the same might be true of demons. Angels could begin to adapt to fleshly ways just by being near us; how much more impact would it be if the spiritual entity were actually inside us? Was that why it was rare for a demon to stay in the same host body by its lonesome? If it was a possession of long standing you had hosts of Infernal spirits inside them. One demon at a time was usually quick in and out like an Airbnb; regular possessions were like renting to own except it was almost never just one demon. Long-term leases were group events for demons, because they wanted to trash the "house," not actually live in it. That one gesture meant either that the demon had been in the body longer than Mark's family or college noticed, or that this demon had been on possession duty before with other hosts. It wasn't that he was picking up Mark Cookson's gestures, but just human gestures in general.

"How long have you been inside Mark?"

"A direct question, really, Detective? As if." The look on his face was eloquent and a strange mix of the demon's "personality" and Mark's, just as the sentence seemed a mix of them both. Was it the boy fighting back or another sign that the demon was contaminated with humanity? Though saying the college student was contaminating the demon sounded backward and made me wonder what habits Mark had already picked up from his Infernal infestation. But I'd worry about that later, after I figured out a way to stop the demon from hurting anyone else without having to kill Mark.

Paulson's voice answered from a little farther down the hallway. "His parents found him passed out on his old bedroom floor at home. He'd showered but left bloodstained clothes. That's when they called the ambulance. Does that help you get a timeline?"

"He's been on academic probation for a semester, so the demon has been in him for about three months, maybe a little longer."

"Guesses are free," the demon called out in a singsong voice.

I thought things were going well; all I had to do was keep the demon interested in talking to me until Charleston and the rest of my backup finished climbing up the twenty flights of stairs. The lieutenant was in good shape, he'd be here soon. The demon was contained. I got my phone out and hit the button for Charleston to let him know what he was about to walk into, but I heard a groan, and it wasn't me, and it wasn't Paulson.

The demon turned its head and looked to the side of the room I couldn't see. "Oh, you're not dead yet, my bad," the demon said, and walked out of my line of sight toward what had to be Gonzales.

I called out, "Alive he's a hostage, and you have something to negotiate with; dead he's just collateral damage."

The demon's deep voice sounded pleasant, happy, as it said, "The wound closed around the needle, let's fix that."

I yelled, "Don't touch him!" As if the demon would give a damn.

Charleston was on my phone yelling, "Havoc, Havoc, what's happening?"

"Demon possession with violence, one hostage. Mark Cookson is the possessed." Then I had to hang up, because I might need my hands free for my gun, or wrestling demons, whichever came first.

CHAPTER EIGHT

M ark Cookson's fragile-looking body dragged the much larger Gonzales into sight of the door. The bigger man was holding his hand against the side of his neck, trying to stop fresh blood that was welling crimson around his fingers. He was a nurse, he knew how to hold pressure on a wound; that meant that the wound wasn't going to be stopped by just the pressure of a hand. We had minutes to get him more medical help or he was going to bleed to death in front of us. Heaven help us.

A look of hatred snarled across Cookson's face. "I guess I don't need muscles after all." He lifted the nurse upward by a handful of his uniform. It made the blood pump faster and cut off his air. The only thing that saved him was the cloth tearing so that Gonzales fell back to the floor, gasping for air and choking, but this time there was blood on his lips. What had the demon done to him to make him cough blood?

Paulson said, "Let me save him."

I wasn't sure if he was talking to me or the demon. The demon replied first. "Why should I let you save him?"

"He has a family."

Mark's face gave him a look of almost pity. "You really don't understand what I am, do you, Doctor?"

"You can't appeal to his better nature, Doctor; demons don't have one," I said.

"Mark, if you're in there, Gonzales's son is only eight. Do you want him to grow up without a father?" The comment showed he'd been paying attention while I talked to the kid. He'd noticed what I'd noticed—that Mark seemed to still be in there.

"We don't care," the demon said.

Then the body kept talking. "Of course, he has a family, he's tall and good looking, exotic. I bet he dated around and fucked everything in sight before he married someone beautiful." The voice was still deeper than the thin body, but the tone and whine of the words didn't sound the same. Mark was in there all right, but he wasn't a sympathetic ear. Heaven help Gonzales.

"Let me treat his wound and then you'll have two hostages," Paulson said.

"Sure," demonic Mark said.

"The more the merrier, Doctor, just cross the wards and come on in," the demon said. The fact that they were using the same body to talk didn't seem to faze the doctor any more than it did me. Apparently, we'd both seen similar shows before.

"No, Doctor," I said.

"I will not tell his wife and child that I stood here and watched him die and did nothing."

Gonzales's eyes fluttered, his hand slipping away from his wound as he passed out from blood loss. We were out of time. I looked down the barrel of my FN 509 and steadied my breath. Things seemed to slow down as if I had all the time in the world to aim at center body mass. The hospital gown was too baggy around him to aim anywhere else, and I wasn't confident enough for a head shot. The head moves a lot more than the chest.

Paulson didn't beg for Mark Cookson's life this time.

Demon Mark said, "You wouldn't shoot an innocent college kid."

I didn't bother to answer because there was nothing left to say. I didn't even look up at his face as I aimed at his chest. I just squeezed the trigger. The demon couldn't pass the wards, but bullets could.

CHAPTER NINE

got two shots into the chest before he started to fall. The only sound I could hear after the shots was the blood in my own ears, or maybe it's something else; whatever the sound is, it's what's left after the rest of your hearing goes away for a while.

I saw Paulson out of the corner of my eye rushing toward the room and the wounded, but I shouted at him, not sure he'd hear me, so it was probably more scream than yell: "No! Not yet!"

I glanced at him just enough to see him looking at me with wide eyes. He was pale, but he nodded, letting me know he'd heard me. I went back to staring at the room and the two men on the floor. Cookson's body had fallen backward against the bed and then slid to the side of it. His pale, thin legs were tangled up in the large hospital gown so I couldn't see much of his body. The gown was big enough and he was small enough that his breathing might not have been that easy to see. I couldn't even see if he was bleeding from here; there was already too much blood on the floor from Gonzales. I would have to get up on the target before I could be sure he—it—was dead.

The energy of the wards sat across the open doorway like an invisible sheet except this sheet vibrated with energy, but it wasn't meant to keep me out. I stepped through and didn't even hesitate as the warm rush of it passed over my skin. I'd stepped through stronger wards than this on the job; I was still impressed that it had contained the demon.

I stared down my gun at the body. There was blood where the two bullets had entered the body but none out the back. He looked even smaller and less finished from this angle, as if I'd shot a child. I swallowed hard, and my eyes burned, which was stupid. I'd had no choice. I kept the barrel of the gun steady on the body as I pushed it with the toe of my shoe. Why not kneel and check for a pulse? Because if the demon was faking, I didn't want to be that close to its hands. The body rolled in that boneless, empty way that no living person can fake. I didn't need to check a pulse to know that Mark Cookson was dead.

"He's dead, save Gonzales," I said. I repeated it louder to make sure that Paulson heard me. He and Nurse Prescott came in with another nurse whose name I never got. I moved into the hallway to give them room to work. My part was done; I'd taken a life so they could save one. I prayed that they would be able to save Gonzales, because if he died, too, then it was all for nothing.

I felt movement down the hallway like the brush of angel wings felt before they're seen. I aimed down the hallway and it was Charleston with his own gun out and pointed at the floor. I aimed my gun in a safe direction as I saw the hospital security in uniform at his back, and uniformed police. The tightness in my gut eased, because with Charleston I knew I had serious backup. The rest of the men and one female uniform were unknowns. You hope every cop you meet is good backup, but you never know until the bad thing happens, and then they either rise or fall.

My hearing was back enough for me to hear Charleston say, "We heard the gunshots. What happened?"

I started to explain, but Paulson and one of the nurses came out with Gonzales on a gurney. He was hooked up to two different IVs and they were moving fast, probably to surgery. The metaphysical floor had a complete operating theater, so if anything went really pear-shaped the hospital could still operate on the rest of the patients with a little less magic in them.

I wanted to ask if he would make it, but the way they were running, they didn't know yet and doctors won't lie about that, so I didn't ask.

"Is that the hostage?" Charleston asked.

I nodded.

"Jesus, that's Gonzales," one of the male security guards said.

"Is he going to be all right?" the female security guard asked.

"Did you say there was a demon?" one of the uniformed officers asked.

"It was a possession, not a full manifestation," I said. I glanced into the room to find Nurse Prescott kneeling beside the body that I'd shot. It was one of the bravest things I'd seen in a long time, her staying in the room where she'd been so terrified.

"What does that mean?"

Charleston looked at him. "Miller, is it? If you don't know the difference between a possession and a manifestation, then you shouldn't be up on this floor."

"We just answered the call for backup, Lieutenant Charleston. Neither of us has ever worked metaphysical detail," Miller's partner said, coming to his rescue.

"Possession is a human being ridden by a demon; manifestation is a demon appearing in full corporeal form."

"Corporeal?" Miller asked.

"It means *body*," his partner said.

Prescott looked up as if she felt me looking at her. I smiled and gave her a little salute. She smiled back and nodded. More nurses or orderlies, and a new doctor wheeled a second gurney through the door. One of them hesitated at the wards as if he was more sensitive to them.

"I didn't think demons could do that, appear on the earthly plane in their actual form," Miller said.

"Can I take these damn things down?" the orderly asked.

There were nods. Nurse Prescott said, "They trapped the demon just like they were supposed to." But she stood up and touched the ward; it seemed fitting that she was the one that deactivated them.

Charleston said, "It's incredibly rare for a demon to have physical form on this plane."

I added, "They can appear for a few minutes in their true form, but most human imaginations can't bear the sight of them and will change it from their original form, even if they manage to manifest."

"What do you mean?" the first security guard asked.

They had the body on the gurney now. Prescott stood near the ward panel, letting them cover what was left of Mark Cookson. The demon was back in Hell safe and sound. He'd left the kid to die, like a rat fleeing a sinking ship.

"Infernals take on the appearances of the human imagination nearest them," Charleston said.

"What?" Miller asked.

"What he said," the female security guard said.

"It means they look like what the nearest human thinks they should look like, but they won't appear in their true Hellish form, not here on Earth, except maybe for a second, then it changes," I said. I didn't add that a second could be enough for insanity or death for the human seeing it, but our minds protected us from so much, including demons. If a person could survive that second, then what they thought changed what they saw; demons used it to appear as our worst nightmares, but even that was usually less soul-destroying than the demon's original form.

"So, they don't have horns and tentacles and shit?" the male guard asked.

"Only if you think they do," I said.

"If you see a demon, think really happy thoughts," Charleston said.

"So, if we thought they looked like a red-skinned Ryan Gosling, that's what they'd look like?" the female said.

"Fantasize on your own time, Belinda," the male guard said.

"It's possible," I said.

"I'd rather have Ryan Gosling with horns than tentacles," Miller said.

We all agreed on that as we watched them wheel the remains down the corridor. They were going in the same direction that they'd taken Gonzales except that no one was running. The dead don't need to rush, they have the rest of eternity to get where they're going.

The orderly pushing the gurney acted like he'd been stung. He stepped away from the gurney. The man on the other side said, "A little help here."

"Didn't you see it?"

"See what?"

I was already moving toward them when I saw the body bag twitch like a fish that wasn't as dead as you thought.

CHAPTER TEN

The demon burst out of the body bag like an evil butterfly, because someone in the hallway had thought it should have big black bat wings. It was the wings that saved all the medics around the gurney, because the wings were too big for the hallway. The spikes on the wings caught on the sprinkler heads and got stuck in the drop ceiling. It gave them time to get out of reach of the huge muscular arms, because the body had to be over seven feet tall, muscled like some cartoon superhero. It was still wearing the hospital gown except that now the gown strained across the chest and biceps. It hung down long enough to cover the groin, and I was grateful for that. The long black horns got stuck in the drop ceiling as the demon tried to stand up and free its wings. One of the other humans in the hallway had seen Disney's *Fantasia* a few too many times, so that the demon was almost as trapped in the small hallway as it had been inside the wards. It was only a matter of time before the demon figured out how its new body worked. Once it did that, people would die—if not in this hallway, then in another part of the hospital, so we had to stop it here.

"Demons are your area, Havoc," Charleston said. It was his way of asking me for a plan. I had seconds to come up with it. No pressure.

The demon's deep voice matched the massive chest now as it rumbled, "What the fuck? Wings? I didn't ask for wings."

It was the demon's voice, but the word choice, the cadence of it sounded more like Mark Cookson. He was still in there, but now instead of the demon being inside him, he was inside the demon. That was impossible; humans couldn't possess demons, it just didn't work in that direction.

"I warned you that the other humans could impact your desire." That was the demon. They were both still in there—what in Heaven was going on?

"Oh yeah," demon Mark said, and even at a bass deep enough to make James Earl Jones proud, the two words sounded uncertain and younger than the body that was trying to stand in the hallway.

One minute he was fighting to get the wings and horns out of the ceiling and walls and the next the wings were gone, and the horns had shrunk by a foot so the demon could move its head without getting stuck in the ceiling.

"That's better," demon Mark said, and he stood up, careful to keep his head bent low enough so that the points of his horns aimed our way. The hospital gown sleeves started to split as it stalked toward us, swinging arms that made me think things like movie Thor or the Incredible Hulk.

"Proud of you, boy," the demon said.

The demon's face grinned, pleased; they were both still in there. It wasn't possession—it was a partnership. I stopped worrying that it was impossible and started thinking how to use the impossible in our favor.

I drew my gun and aimed at the center of the biggest chest I'd ever aimed at.

"Demons are bulletproof," Charleston said.

"Illusions are bulletproof, but illusions don't get caught in the ceiling," I said.

He nodded and drew his gun to move up beside me and aim down the hallway. "How solid will it be?"

"Unsure."

"Then watch your backstop, Havoc, we got civilians on the other side of this beastie."

"Roger that, boss."

The uniforms unholstered their guns and said, "Where you want us, Lieutenant?"

"You heard me say watch your backstop and the civvies, right?"

"Yes, sir," both said.

"If Havoc and I empty our guns, then you move forward and fire while we reload; until then stay back, the hallway's not that big."

"Bullets don't work on demons," the demon said. There was a ceiling tile stuck on the tip of one of its horns.

"You sure about that?" I asked, and pulled the trigger.

CHAPTER ELEVEN

M y bullet hit the demon in the middle of the chest. Charleston's bullet hit beside mine. The demon lowered its head like a bull charging. We raised our guns as if we'd practiced the move and aimed for the head. If it had been a human-sized target, I wouldn't have risked it, but the demon's head was as oversized as the rest of it, bigger than the chest on an average man. I knew I could hit that, and I knew my boss could, too.

What we didn't think of was that a skull hard enough to hold horns would be harder than normal skull. One of the bullets ricocheted right past us and into the wall. We ducked and I went to one knee. I yelled, "Top of skull is too hard."

I had time for one more shot, so I aimed at a leg. It was a big enough target to risk taking the shot. If we couldn't kill it before it reached us, maybe we could bring it down to us.

Charleston was emptying his magazine into the body that he could aim at around the horns and that hard head. I hit the leg because the demon stumbled and slowed down enough for me to have time to shoot it in the foot. I thought, *A foot with the horns and claws, it should be a hoof,* and just like that it was a hoof. But the other foot was still a foot, and hooves and feet don't move the same. The demon fell right at us, horns and all. Charleston and the others ran, but I was still kneeling, so I tried to roll out of the way. I almost made it.

CHAPTER TWELVE

T he demon fell on me and it was even denser than it looked. The breath was knocked out of me and if it hadn't raised its torso off me the weight would have slowly suffocated me. I had a second to try to catch my breath as it used one hand to raise its torso off me, its lower body still pinning my legs, and then I felt claws at my stomach.

"I'm going to wear you like a puppet," the demon growled.

Its talking let me catch my breath and raise my gun. I fired once into its chest; the claws tore my shirt away. "I like to see what I'm doing," he said.

The other cops were firing into its body and the bullets were hitting it. The demon was too solid to be bulletproof, but it was like shooting a side of beef for all the harm it did. It wasn't even bleeding.

The demon looked down at me. "I hate guys with great abs," it growled. I felt the claws start to pierce my skin; I knew better than to look, but I couldn't help myself.

"Yes, Detective, watch as we tear out all that hard work at the gym."

I yelled, "God!" and thought, *A hand, a hand to match the foot,* and the claws vanished, just like the hoof had appeared. It wasn't possible to change the shape of a spiritual being that easily, not once it had settled into a form, but it had worked anyway. I prayed, *Thank you.*

"You have to focus, boy, you're taking away our weapons," the demon said, staring at its hand. There was blood on the fingertips from where it had cut me, but the claws it'd used were just gone.

"I didn't do that, or the hoof." The demon said that, too, but the cadence of the voice was different. Mark Cookson wasn't possessing the demon: They were sharing.

Charleston must have reloaded because he came in and put his gun against the side of the demon's head and fired point-blank. The demon brushed him away with one big arm, sending him flying. The claws were gone, but it was still dangerous, and I was still pinned under it. *If only the damn thing would bleed and take damage from the bullets*, I thought. That was what we needed, we needed it to bleed.

Blood dripped down on me as the demon shook its head, and then it shook harder, spraying blood around the hallway. "Why isn't your blood burning like acid?" it asked.

The next drop of blood that hit my bare stomach sizzled and burned like acid. Someone else screamed, "It's acid!"

I thought, *No it's not, it's ordinary human blood*, and the next drop that hit me was red and harmless.

The demon looked down at me with its scary movie eyes. "You . . ."

I aimed my last bullet into its eye and thought, *I want the bullet to pierce the brain and kill it.* That was totally impossible, you couldn't kill a demon, but maybe we could kill this body.

I squeezed the trigger and the demon rolled off me, moving in a blur so fast that I couldn't stop the trigger pull and put a bullet in the ceiling where its head had been.

I got to one knee, popping my empty magazine out and reaching for my last spare magazine as I moved. The other two cops were aiming into a hospital room near me. Charleston was lying against the opposite wall where the demon had thrown him. He wasn't moving, but even as I wondered how badly he was hurt Nurse Prescott was there. I was going to owe that woman flowers or a case of something expensive.

I turned back to the open doorway and the demon that was hiding inside. A woman screamed inside the room. I paused and wished the room would be empty. She screamed again. It had been worth a try. I pressed myself against the wall near the open door and called out, "Discorporate now, you know the priests are on the way."

"Fuck priests!"

The demon's voice changed again and said, "Now that's a great idea."

The woman screamed words this time. "Don't touch me!"

I was not going to stay out in the hallway while they raped another woman. I prayed for an idea that would help us save her in time.

I thought, *I want the demon to be small and helpless.* I pictured something like Mark Cookson except red skinned, but weak. "You cannot work your magic on us without seeing us, Detective."

I tried to move closer to the door so I could get line of sight. The door shut as I tried to throw myself toward the opening and get one last look at the demon. I wasn't sure that I could even change it from big to small; that was harder to do to spiritual beings even when they were less solid. Small changes, though, small was easier.

There was a crash of something heavier than a person being thrown against the door. They didn't have a gun, so I could stand in the doorway without worrying about cover. I pushed on the door; it moved a few inches and then it caught on something solid. I put my shoulder into it, but I couldn't get it to move more. They'd wedged something in the door.

The woman screamed again.

Miller came over and put his shoulder with mine. We tried kicking it. The door wouldn't move.

The woman's scream turned to one word: "No!"

Her fingers found the crack at the edge of the wedged door. "Help me!"

I touched her fingertips, leaning in so I could see that she had brown eyes. Her fingers curled around mine; the opening wasn't big enough for anything more. I didn't know why the demon hadn't dragged her back yet.

"What's your name?"

"Kate, I'm Kate."

I held her fingers in mine. "I'm Detective Havelock."

"Detective what?" she asked. Her eyes looked too big for her face. She looked young and innocent and I wanted to keep her that way.

"Havoc," I said.

"Havoc, get me out of here, okay?"

"What's against the door, Kate?"

"The bed."

"What's the demon doing?"

Her eyes darted back into the room, then came back to look at me. "Just standing there."

I didn't know what the demon was waiting for, and I didn't want to wait to find out. "Kate, can you move the bed away from the door?"

"I don't . . . I don't know."

"Can you try? Please."

I'd thought she was holding on to me tight, but I'd been wrong, because now she squeezed harder. Her skin paled with the pressure of it.

"I'd have to get closer to it."

"I'm sorry, Kate, but the bed needs to move so we can get you out."

"She's too weak to move the bed." The demon's voice held that whining note that was Mark Cookson.

"Will you let her try?" I asked. I didn't know why he hadn't hurt her again, but I was going to use it.

"Sure," he said, as if he was being magnanimous.

"Kate, you can do this." I was more saying that she was brave enough to let go of my hand, than move the bed. If we couldn't move it from this side, I wasn't sure she could do anything on that side, but trying was better than giving up.

"Are you really going to let me try to move the bed?" she asked, and I realized she wasn't asking me.

"I said sure."

She squeezed my hand one more time, and then she left the small opening. I was left looking into the empty half of the hospital room. I could hear her moving around. I felt the door move under my hand and for a moment I thought she'd done it, but the door didn't open. I could feel the vibrations of her trying to manipulate the bed and whatever the demon had done to wedge it against the door. She wrapped her hands around the opening and pulled; I put my shoulder against it and pushed. Miller joined me. It moved a few more inches, but that was it.

I could see more of her now, her body lost in the oversized hospital gown, but her face was oval with a sprinkling of pale freckles; her lips were full, the kind that always seemed half pouting, the real deal that all the fake duckfaces on the internet imitate. Her eyes were big and brown with dark lashes and eyebrows arched just right in that way that women care about more than any straight man I'd ever met. She could have been missing an eyebrow and she would still have been lovely. Her hair was dark, curly, and just long enough to touch the tops of her shoulders.

Her hand and lower arm were small enough that she reached through the open doorway and held my hand. She could get her arm to the shoulder through the opening, but at the shoulder her body was too wide. She was still trapped.

"That's it, I can't move it any more," she said.

I heard the demon stir in the room. I couldn't see what it was doing, but I could hear it doing something.

"Havoc, don't leave me, okay?"

I squeezed her hand in mine. "I won't leave you, Kate."

She smiled, just a little, and squeezed back.

"I'm taller than he is," the demon said. "I've got more muscles, but I'm still not good enough for you."

Kate glanced into the room at him, then back to me.

"Look at me, bitch."

She shook her head and gave me some of the best eye contact I'd gotten from a woman in a while. If it had been a date, I'd have been thrilled. I put my other hand around her wrist, so I was holding her as tight as I could.

"Look at me, you fucking cunt!" the demon yelled.

"No," she said. Her eyes were so wide. She clung to me and I wanted more than anything to be able to protect her from what was about to happen if we couldn't get this door open in the next few seconds.

She looked away from me to something in the room that I couldn't see. Her hand tightened around mine. Even in profile I could see the terror on her face as she looked at the demon. I could see her arm rise as if she was trying to push something away, but I couldn't see her hand or what she was motioning at, but I knew. It was the demon and she wasn't going to be able to push it away like a date that got out of hand.

"Come on, Katie, give us a kiss," the demon said.

"It's Kate, not Katie, and I said no." Her voice quavered, but she said it like she meant it. I held her hand and marveled at her presence of mind. Damn, she was brave.

Her body jerked and I knew it had grabbed her other arm before she said, "Let go of me!"

Kate held on to me and I held on to her with both hands and the demon still dragged most of her out of sight behind the door. Miller went to one knee and shoved his face into the opening so he could put an arm through the narrow opening and shoot the demon some more;

maybe if we put enough bullets into him it might actually kill him. Kate plastered herself against the door and I saw her other arm trying to cover one ear against the noise. The demon had let her go.

I yelled, "Miller, get back!"

He started to pull his arm out of the doorway, but suddenly he lurched forward. His gun fired once more and then his shoulder was wedged into the opening of the door. If he hadn't been kneeling and Kate standing, there wouldn't have been room for them both, but more of her was against the front of the door, only her arm was outside. Miller's body shook as if the demon were shaking his arm like a dog with a tug rope.

Miller yelled. Kate screamed. She was looking down at something I couldn't see. I heard a wet, tearing sound. Miller screamed. He fell back from the door, blood spraying out of his shoulder where his arm used to be.

CHAPTER THIRTEEN

I tried to pull away from Kate to help Miller, but she held on so tight that I looked back at her. "Get me out of here!" There were spots of blood on her face now, competing with the freckles. Her eyes were wide with terror and I couldn't blame her, but I couldn't let Miller bleed to death either. The spray had slowed to that thick pumping that will bleed you out in minutes. Prescott was there kneeling beside Miller; she started packing the wound to try to slow down the blood.

She yelled, "Help me move him!"

I wasn't sure who she was yelling at until another male nurse came and helped drag Miller to safety, or as much safety as he could have now. I prayed that they'd be able to save his life.

"Your turn, cunt," the demon said.

Kate looked at me with her pale, blood-splattered face and said, "Havoc, help me."

I don't know what I would have said, because her body jerked in my grip. The demon had grabbed her other arm. I almost let her go—

I didn't want to see her arm torn away like Miller's—but she dug her fingers into me.

"Don't you dare let go!"

The demon pulled harder, but I held on and she held on tighter than both of us. The demon and I were playing tug-of-war and there was really no way for me to win.

CHAPTER FOURTEEN

braced my foot against the doorframe to help me hold Kate's arm outside the room. I could feel her fingernails beginning to cut into my arm through my suit jacket. It reminded me of how my wife had held on to me when our son was born. Now I held on to Kate and she clung to me not out of pain and life but out of pure terror; the pain would come later.

She screamed and I jumped because nothing had changed that I could see. That one second of lost concentration let the demon pull her farther into the room, so that my knuckles banged on the doorframe. I prayed that the Big Guy would help me hold on, that he would help me be strong enough to save her, and I fought to gain back a few inches.

"My shoulder," Kate said, "dislocated."

Still hidden by the door, the demon said, "You're strong for a human, Havoc; may I call you Havoc? I like the name, by the way; are you sure you're not one of ours? Kate here is made of sterner stuff than the cop was, but if you hold on tight enough to pretty Kate here, we'll tear her apart, too, and that's fine with me. You can keep one arm while we fuck her. It takes time to bleed to death; she'll still be warm when we finish."

"I thought demons had more stamina than that," a woman's voice from behind me said.

I felt Kate move toward me, as if the demon had lost concentration this time.

I didn't turn around to see Detective Lila Bridges, but I knew the voice and the attitude. She was a real ball buster and I half loved her for it in that moment.

"Bridges, thought you'd never show up," I said.

"Hey, Havoc," she said, and then louder, "Demon, you in the room, are you telling me that all that hype about demons being fantastic fucks is a lie? Hell's bells, there go all my teenage fantasies. Satan take you back to Hell if you disappoint us that much."

The demon hesitated again, and I gained a little bit more arm outside the door, but even if I got Kate back to the most of her out the door, the opening still wasn't wide enough to get her out of the room. We needed an opening big enough to get her out.

"I heard you weren't bulletproof, demon; what kind of demon isn't bulletproof, for fuck's sake?" Bridges said.

"I will tear the woman apart and fuck the pieces!" It pulled harder and I braced against the doorjamb and the door.

Kate whimpered as the demon pulled on her dislocated shoulder; most people would have been screaming by now.

"Where's the famous seduction of demonkind? Is that just a lie like the whole bulletproof thing, or are you just not that powerful a demon? Is that why they let you out of Hell, because you're just so fucking weak?" Bridges said, her voice thick with scorn.

"I am not weak!" the demon screamed this time, and it was more whine than roar. Kate screamed as he pulled so hard I had to give ground or pull her apart.

"Come out and prove it to me, demon, or are you just another weak-ass creep? I bet you're Hell's version of that creepy guy who lives in his mom's basement and whines online that he can't get a woman to fuck him. Oh wait, that is what Mark Cookson is, except he lived in the dorm."

"Shut up, you fucking bitch!"

"Tough talk, brimstone boy, come out of the room and make me shut up, if you're demon enough to do it."

"No," the demon said, but he didn't yell it.

"No, you're not demon enough to do it. Good on you admitting it out loud."

"She is baiting us," the demon said; he wasn't talking to any of us.

"I have the body of a god!"

"With a tiny little penis," she said, her delivery so dry that it almost made me smile, except I was looking at Kate's face going paler by the second. Things were breaking in her arms and shoulders from the tug-of-war; if she passed out from the pain, I wasn't sure what would happen.

Kate swallowed hard enough for me to hear it, and whispered, "I like her."

"We'll all go out for drinks later," I said, voice tight with the effort to hold her and not hurt her more than I had to.

The deep voice growled, "Let go of her, Detective, or I will pull her arm off as I did to the other police officer."

"What will you do to her if I let go?" I asked.

"Fuck her, better than she's ever been fucked before! Just like I did to that bitch Megan! I showed her." The rhythm of the words was different again; it was demon Mark.

"Don't let go," Kate said, her voice hoarse from pain and screaming.

The deeper voice said, "I will tear you apart, girl."

"Then do it," she said.

"You don't mean that," I said.

She looked at me, and she was having trouble focusing on me; shit, she was going to pass out, which meant she was in more pain than she was letting on. *Please God, help her.*

"I would rather die quick than let that thing kill me slowly."

"She's no fun," demon Mark said; I'd never known that a voice that deep could whine like that.

"You won't even come out and play with me, you're the most un-fun demon I've ever met," Bridges taunted.

I looked into Kate's face and said, "You sure?"

She nodded. "I'm sure."

"I'll fuck her and then you're next, cunt!" Demon Mark's whine again.

"Big talk from a demon that has to hide behind doors because he's afraid of bullets," she said.

The demon screamed, roared, and the sound made some of the cops behind me cry out, because you can't hear the wails of the damned for the first time without it haunting you.

A red-skinned arm went around Kate's waist. I had a second to decide if I'd hold on and force the demon to tear her in half while I was still holding her hand. I let go.

She screamed and clung tighter to me. "Don't let me go!"

"Stay alive, we'll get you out."

"NO!" she wailed, and her nails cut into my skin through my sleeve, and then carved bloody streaks down my hand. I had one last glimpse of her pale face and then she was around the door out of our sight. The screams started, and I screamed with her, "God help us!"

CHAPTER FIFTEEN

e will," a voice said. I turned to find Gimble standing outside his room. He looked even shorter and younger in the oversized hospital gown. He smiled at me, face still soft and shining with the memory of his first angel sighting. It hadn't made me this happy even at ten when I'd met my Guardian Angel. For a second I resented him his joy. How could he smile with Kate's screams filling the hallway? The sound made me want to start yelling for SWAT or explosives, anything to get through that door.

"You've got an IV hanging from your arm, Gimble," Detective Lila Bridges said.

He smiled at her as if nothing was wrong, and I wanted to hit him. "Stop smiling, Gimble, stop smiling while she's screaming," I said; my voice was thick with wanting to yell, to strike out at something, anything.

"No one is screaming, Havoc," he said in that happy, relaxed voice.

He was right, shit! "Kate! Kate! Answer me!" I yelled it with my hand on that damned stuck door.

"I'm here, Havoc. I'm . . . okay," she said; her voice was scared, but it wasn't a scream.

"Where's the demon?" I asked.

"I am still here, human." But there was something in the tone of the voice that had changed.

"What's happening?" demon Mark asked.

"Tell her to come to the door," Gimble said.

"It's stuck shut," I said.

"Call her to you, Havoc, it'll be all right." He smiled that beatific smile at me.

I started to ask the demon to let her come to the door, but Gimble laid a hand on my shoulder. The power thrilled over my skin like being hit with the warmest, coziest blanket while someone stuck your finger in a light socket, so that it felt better than anything and hurt all at the same time. No wonder so many humans who worked with angels ended up being masochists, because that's what it was: angelic power.

"How?" I started to ask, but Gimble looked at me and there was something older than him looking out of his hazel eyes, something achingly older than he would ever be.

"Do not ask the permission of the enemy, Havoc. You do not need it, just act, do, they cannot stop you." The word choice wasn't even his, as if he were as possessed as Mark Cookson.

Gimble's face frowned at me. "You know better than to equate this with the monstrosity in the other room."

I thought, of course, but I didn't really believe it. I'd gotten adept at thinking one thing and feeling another when angels were in my head.

The face frowned again, but it wasn't any expression I'd ever seen on Gimble's face. "Oh, Havoc, how sorrowful you have become."

I wanted to tell the angel to get out of my head, but I wanted Kate saved more. "Help me save her."

Gimble smiled at me, so happy. "That's why we're here, we heard your prayer for her."

I swallowed, trying not to be afraid for Gimble. I'd never seen this happen outside of the College of Angels and only to Angel Speakers, those of us who interacted directly with the angelic. It shouldn't have worked like this for Gimble from just seeing one in its true form. It didn't work this way, but I stopped questioning it and let that power flow over me, through me. The less I fought the better it felt, like sliding into a bath that was just suddenly the perfect temperature, not too hot, not too cold, just right, except it was power that I let cover me, a power I'd sworn I'd never allow near me again. I tried to think of it like finding a weapon that could save Kate and not like a spiritual magic that had almost destroyed me once.

"Kate, come to the door."

"Don't you fucking move, bitch!" Mark's demon voice again.

The power flowing from Gimble's hand to me pulsed. I felt it flow into my hands where they touched the door and I prayed again, silent this time, but I knew that God could hear me, and the angelic being using Gimble as its doorway would hear it, too.

St. Michael the Archangel, defend us in battle. Be our protection against the wickedness and snares of the devil; May God rebuke him, we humbly pray; And do thou, O Prince of the Heavenly Host, by the power of God, thrust into Hell Satan and all evil spirits who wander through the world for the ruin of souls. Amen.

"Ask for your own safety, too, Havoc." This was Gimble's voice, his frown jarring in that freckled face of his.

I added out loud, "Keep me safe as I save this woman. Help me defeat my enemies and those that harm the innocent."

Gimble smiled at me stupidly happy, and for just a second I saw stars in his eyes. "Tell her she will be safe, and it will be so." And that wasn't his voice again. It reminded me of the demon and Mark Cookson, but I kept that from the front of my thoughts and the angelic energy didn't remark on it, so I could still hide my thoughts even now. I guess I hadn't lost all my skills, even the ones that I wasn't supposed to learn.

"Kate, come to the door so I can see where you are."

"Don't you move!" the demon roared.

I heard her whimper.

"You cannot touch her," I said.

The roar sounded again, and then it was Mark's voice. "What's happening? Why can't we touch her?"

"We're outgunned." The demon's voice was disgusted.

"You're a demon! Do something!"

"Kate, come where I can see you."

"Why?"

"We're going to open the door."

CHAPTER SIXTEEN

———■ ■———

You said the door was stuck," she said.

"We have . . . we can open it now, but I have to see where you are so the door doesn't . . . so opening it doesn't accidentally hurt you." I shut out the image that went with that warning. I shoved it back down into the dark hole of my soul, where all the sins and horrors I'd experienced stayed.

I heard movement and the demon's two voices started arguing. The younger one wanted to grab her, fuck her, or kill her at least, and the older one, the real demon, was trying to explain that the girl was off-limits in this moment.

Kate appeared at the door, one arm trying to cover as much of her body as she could; her other arm was held awkwardly at her side, not moving much with the dislocated shoulder. The demon had ripped the hospital gown off her. I hoped that was the worst he'd done, but one problem at a time. Save the life first, save the rest later.

"Step that way, stay along that wall," I said, motioning with my head, because my hands were on the door. I felt that pulse of power as

Gimble laid his other hand on me, so that a hand sat on both of my shoulders and suddenly I felt them—wings. Wings so tall and huge that they went through the ceiling and through the floor, spread out around my human body like I was a child trying to wear my father's clothes. They rose up white and shining, edged with silver and shot through with gold, so beautiful. If they'd been a physical weight it would have dragged me over like a turtle stuck on its back, pinned to the earth by the weight of the glory at my back. Tears started down my face as I put my hands against the door and pushed. I knew the door would move for me, I knew it would open, because for this moment I had been granted the strength of the angel whose wings rose like a halo around me. Nothing so fragile as a door could stand against me. And just like I had at sixteen, I pushed too hard.

The door cracked, splintering, over half of it spinning into the room. If Kate had still been on the bed or just behind the door, she'd have been in its path and she would have died. I shoved the memory of another moment like this down, back into the hole inside me where all the sins lived. I could not let them weaken me now. A sinner for-given by God cannot be anything but strong. The wings at my back flared, flexing as if we would fly with them, and I reached my hand out to Kate. Her hand wrapped around mine and I pulled her out of the room with Gimble at my back as if he held the angel wings in place like a costume that wasn't fastened down yet.

Kate threw her undamaged arm around me, but there wasn't time. The demon rushed the splintered doorway. I pushed Kate into the hallway behind us. I felt the thrill of power as she stumbled through the wings. She reached up as if she felt something and then I planted my foot and braced for impact. The demon filled my physical vision, but the inside of my head was full of shining light laced with gold and silver finer than any that would ever hold a ring. My fear was gone, washed away by the light.

"I command you to leave this body in the name of God and all the angels." I said it confident that the words with the power at my back would stop the demon.

The demon hesitated and then it laughed, staring down at its taloned hands as if surprised they were still there. "Too late, angel boy, this body's mine." The talons slashed at me again, going for my throat, and only the quickness of angels let me block his arm with mine and block his other arm as it came for my heart.

"Havoc, get down!" Charleston yelled from behind me.

I dropped to my knees, trying to roll away, but the wings were in the way, and Gimble was there. "Down!" Charleston shouted again.

I got to my feet, trying to fill the space of the wings at my back, and pictured them folding around Gimble and me like shields of light that nothing could pierce as I held the smaller man against me, as if I expected the wings to launch us skyward and I was afraid I'd drop him.

The shotgun blast sounded like a small bomb in the hallway, or maybe it was just that close to us. I kept all my concentration on the wing shield around us. I didn't dare use my physical eyes to look at anything. My world had to be the shining wings around us and that phantom sensation of being tall enough to fit the giant arch of them.

The shotgun barked again, and then there was a heavy silence like what happens after explosions and gunfire when your ears stop ringing and you can hear something besides the blood roaring in your ears, except my ears weren't ringing. I could hear perfectly, in fact I could hear better than my human hearing, as if the touch of angel wings had given me more than strength and speed and safety. It wasn't the first time or the hundredth that I'd borrowed the senses of the angelic. I shoved the thought that went with that into the hole in my soul. Eventually I'd fill it up and it would either save me or destroy me forever, but not today.

Charleston said, "Havoc, Gimble, are you in there?"

A man's voice that I wasn't sure of said, "They're right there, Lieutenant."

"They disappeared." And I thought that was the female guard.

It was Bridges who said, "Havoc, stop playing with the light-up feathers and tell us you're in there."

"We're here. Safe," I said, but my voice sounded uncertain enough that even I didn't believe me.

Gimble pushed against me. "Havoc, what the hell, man? I love you, but not that way."

Unlike the flame angel, the wings didn't just vanish when he cursed, they opened as I opened my arms as if I really could control them with my human body.

Gimble stumbled away from me, staring down at the hospital gown and everyone in the hallway. "How did I get here?"

Charleston came up to him with a huge 20-gauge shotgun in his hands. The gun looked exactly right in his hands. He patted the gun like it was a pet and said, "Hoodoo powder and get-the-fuck-away-from-us juice."

"You made that last ingredient up," Lila said, scowling at him.

He just grinned at her.

"Did you kill it?" Kate's voice made me look at her. Nurse Prescott was there with a blanket thrown over Kate. I really did owe her good liquor or something.

"You can't kill a demon, or at least not with anything mortal," Charleston said.

"What the hell is going on?" Gimble demanded.

Bridges said, "Look at Havoc with something besides your eyeballs, Gimble." She pointed at me.

He turned and looked at me. He frowned and it was his frown again. A tightness I didn't know I'd been holding released in my gut, and with the relief the wings began to fade like morning dew as the sun rises, drying the grass and turning the dewdrops to tiny prisms of light and color.

"Rainbow wings, cool," Gimble said, grinning at me. He reached a hand out toward the wings as they faded. Bridges slapped his hand as if he were five and reaching for a cookie before it was cool enough to eat.

"Angel shit is what got you in the hospital, Gimble," she said, voice heavy with disdain.

"Last thing I remember is the crime scene in the off-campus apartment." He frowned, but then looked at the fading rainbow of the wings and smiled. It was a shadow of that beatific one he'd had before. He started to reach out toward them again, but a glance at Bridges and he didn't finish the movement. "Will someone explain what's happening to me? Please?" I think the *please* was aimed at Bridges. She was one of the few women I'd seen be immune to his boyish charm.

The wings vanished to physical sight, but I could still feel them like a heavy curve of feathers as I turned to see half our unit in the hospital hallway. "Which one of you could see Gimble and me standing here?" I asked. Anyone who could see through angel magic had been holding out on us.

CHAPTER SEVENTEEN

started to question Sato, the officer that had seen through the angel wings, but Nurse Prescott came up to me, and after everything she'd done today, I raised a hand and said, "Excuse me for a moment," and turned to her.

"Hello, Nurse Prescott," I said, smiling.

She smiled back. "Hello, Detective Havelock, though after the day we've had I think we could use first names."

"I'm Havoc," I said.

A look of pure cynicism filled her eyes. I realized that her eyes were green, or gray-green. It was an unusual color, but there hadn't been time to notice until now. "Did your parents dislike you, Havoc Havelock?"

I had to smile. "Havoc is what most people call me, but no, it's a nickname."

"So, are you going to share your actual first name or is it even worse than Havoc Havelock?" She looked at me very directly, smile lines curled upward around her eyes and mouth, which let me know she was older than she looked. She was in shape for ten years older than me; if she was older than that I needed to ask what her exercise routine was, because she looked slim and fit.

"Zaniel, my first name is Zaniel."

"I've never heard the name before, but it's lovely, a lot lovelier than mine. I'm Hazel. I've always hated the name. Zaniel would have sounded much better in elementary school, though I guess for a boy it might have been a little too pretty a name."

I didn't try to explain that I hadn't been born Zaniel. "I think Hazel might have been worse for a boy."

She laughed and agreed with me. I was beginning to see where the smile lines came from, and realized she had almost no frown lines, as if she didn't do it often enough for it to leave a mark. I liked that thought a lot.

She let the shared moment of laughter fade, and then said, "Kate wants to see you."

"Is she okay?"

Prescott made a face I couldn't interpret; I just didn't know her that well, it wasn't a happy face. "We're trying to get her to agree to a rape kit, or at least an exam."

"He didn't . . ." I started to say.

"Not full on, but the doctor wants to make sure that one of those claws didn't do more damage than we can see without an exam."

Something must have shown on my face, because she gripped my arm and said, "You did everything you could to save her, Zaniel, everything."

"Not enough."

She frowned at me and got that look that my great-aunt Matilda used to get. The one just before she gave me a talking-to, which made me put Prescott toward the older side of near fifty, just from attitude.

"We won today, Zaniel; don't steal the victory from yourself. There are too many days in our line of work that are losses; you've got to treasure the wins, or you'll burn out and you won't still be saving lives when you're my age."

"I honestly don't know how old you are, but if that comment puts you over what I'd guessed, then tell me your secret to staying young, because I'm going to need it."

She laughed outright then, and it was such a good laugh that it gave me a moment of regret that she was twenty years older than me. "That's the nicest thing a man has said to me in a long time."

"Let me apologize for the rest of my sex, then, because they're idiots." I realized I was flirting, which was weird since I usually had trouble doing it, or at least Reggie told me I was bad at it.

"I have a son about your age," she said, giving me that cynical look again.

"I honestly wouldn't have guessed that." I meant it.

She raised an eyebrow at me, as if she didn't believe me. I gave her the Boy Scout salute. She rolled her eyes. "Well, if anything will remind me that you're too young for me, that did it. I was troop mom one year."

"You brought up your son first, mine's three."

"Congratulations, that's a great age."

I nodded. "It is." And then I heard Kate's voice cutting through all the other noise. She wasn't screaming, but she wasn't happy either. I knew her voice that well already; not a good sign. What the Heaven was wrong with me, flirting with the nurse and already attuned to Kate's voice? It was like I was looking for it. I wasn't. Reggie and I were in couples therapy, though we'd gotten to the point of divorce papers just needing a signature before we decided to try counseling for our son's sake. I'd lived alone so long that she felt like an ex, almost as much as my first wife. We'd been stuck in limbo for over six months. I missed having a woman in my life who didn't make me feel sick to my stomach to be with her. No one does disdain like a beautiful woman, and Reggie was still that. It just wasn't enough to make up for the pain and loneliness anymore. She'd even said I could date while we were separated, but she was throwing every past relationship up in my face; I wasn't going to give her more ammunition, so I was celibate for the first time since I was fifteen. It was like suffocating surrounded by air that I wasn't allowed to breathe.

"What do you want me to tell Kate?" I asked, all laughter and happiness gone from my face, my voice; even my shoulders slumped like something was pushing down on me. It made me straighten up, pull my shoulders back, and I could hear Sergeant Macintosh, my drill, barking, "Don't slump, Havoc, we can see how fucking tall you are, own every damn inch of yourself because it won't help you survive what we're about to do to you, but at least you'll look like a soldier, you'll just never be one." Macintosh had talked like that and worse to all the newbies; it was nothing personal, just his job. His training had kept me alive more than once. I wondered if I'd ever stop hearing him barking in my head. How old did you have to be to stop hearing your drill sergeant in your head?

"Just hold her hand and tell her she's safe, but be careful, Detective, she sees you as her white knight, and she's traumatized enough to want you to take the job up permanently."

"Thanks for the heads-up," I said.

"Just sharing hard-won wisdom. I met my first husband when he was a patient in the ER. I saved his life, too."

"How'd that turn out, if you don't mind me asking?"

"I got my son out of it, but eventually you get tired of saving people off the job when it's your job-job."

"Kate seemed brave and capable," I said.

She gave me that cynical look again, her eyes almost perfectly green now as if the gray had gotten swallowed up. "Maybe she is, but unless you want a damsel in distress on your arm, I'd tone down any white-knight urges you're feeling right now."

I frowned at her, fought to stop, and then sighed heavily. "I'll do my best."

She scowled at my stomach. "You're hurt."

I looked down to see the blood that was finally starting to flow through my shirt. "The angel magic kept it from bleeding," I said, as if everyone knew that.

"Men," she said, rolling her eyes. She grabbed my arm, and it was all nurse or Great-Aunt Matilda, no flirting involved. "Let's get you patched up before you go see your damsel."

Charleston called, "Havoc, I need your opinion in here."

I actually turned toward the broken doorway, but Prescott yelled, "Your detective needs a doctor before he does any more detecting, just like you have to have a doctor look at you before you leave the hospital."

Charleston stuck his head back out. "I told you I'm fine."

"You were unconscious for nearly twenty minutes, so you don't get to leave without a doctor checking you over, or you signing a waiver releasing the hospital of responsibility when you lose consciousness driving home and kill yourself."

"I thought nurses were supposed to be comforting," I said.

She gave me that *been-there-done-it-all* look again. "I keep you alive and help you heal; I leave comfort to the new nurses who haven't lost their youthful optimism."

Lila Bridges snorted from the doorway beside Charleston. "Did you ever have youthful optimism? Because I sure as hell didn't."

Hazel smiled and shook her head. "Come on, white knight, I need to stop the bleeding long enough for you to reassure your damsel so we can treat her."

"Come back as soon as you can, Havoc," Charleston said.

"Roger that, Lieutenant."

"We can't find Mark Cookson's body."

That made me turn back toward him. "The demon should have abandoned the body and left him to die."

"Shoulda, coulda, but didn't," Bridges said.

"That's not how possession works, not even physical possession."

"Nothing about this possession was normal," Charleston said.

Hazel Prescott ushered me down the hall. "Let's see if you need stitches, then you can come back and start figuring out where our patient and your suspect went."

"I'll question the new guy," Lila Bridges said, motioning with her thumb at Sato, who was still waiting in the hallway where I'd left him.

"Thanks, Bridges," I said.

"No problem." She turned back, the brown ponytail bouncing as she moved. She'd made it high up on her head today, which had always been one of my favorite looks on a girl going back to elementary school. I closed my eyes and shook my head. I knew better than to date anyone in our unit; that never ended well.

"I thought you were comforting me," Gimble said to her.

She quirked a smile at him, giving her own cynical look, except her eyes were empty cop eyes that gave nothing away. "You've still got an IV hanging out of your arm."

He looked down at it as if he'd just noticed. "Ow," he said, because like so many things it only hurts when you notice it. Broken hearts are like that, too.

I followed Hazel down the hallway and tried not to notice the way her uniform fit from the back. I tried to think what I'd say to Kate and was happy that I'd been all covered in angel magic when I held her naked in my arms. It meant I would have more objectivity when I saw her again. God, I needed a date.

CHAPTER EIGHTEEN

———■ ■———

P aulson had passed Gonzales the nurse to a surgical team, so he was the one who patched me up. Paulson had me take my shirt off and drop my pants so low I had to hold my gun in place and let everything else slide around. He'd wanted to make sure there were no wounds that I'd missed from the fight. I'd have liked to argue but I knew that sometimes in the heat of battle, or even fighting demons, you don't always feel every wound at first. Paulson inspected my abdomen so long and so closely that I finally asked, "What's wrong, Doc, sad that you don't get to stitch me up?"

Paulson had to raise his face up to see me; he'd been bending that low over my stomach. "You should be hurt enough for stitches. You took more damage from the woman's fingernails than the demon's claws; how, why?"

I debated on what to tell him and finally settled for most of the truth. "It's a side effect of the angelic energy."

"So that healed the demon injuries?"

"Partially?"

"Why didn't it heal it completely?"

"I don't know."

"Why didn't it heal the scratches from the woman?"

"I don't know."

Paulson frowned at me. "Are you holding back information?"

I rose up on my elbows and the scratches where Kate had scored her nails down my skin were a sharp, immediate pain, compared to the dull ache of the abdominal scratches. The ones there felt like the injuries had healed for a few days already, while the scratches on my arm felt fresh. One of the things I'd missed most, other than the friends I'd left behind at the College, had been the healing ability. It had lingered for a few months and then I was just as mortal as anyone else. There'd been moments in the army when I missed the angels for a lot of reasons.

"Angels can heal people if God allows it; people who are angel touched can sometimes heal people, too. Gimble was angel touched, and I . . . knew how to hijack the energy and use it to protect us."

"I've been hearing versions of what you did from staff that witnessed it." He raised a skeptical eyebrow at me. "I didn't believe most of it until I saw how healed the claw marks are on you. After seeing what they did to Gonzales . . ." He stopped talking and just shook his head. "He had you pinned in the hallway for at least five minutes, but you're intact."

"I told you it's a side effect of the angels. If I'd been thinking more clearly, I might have tried to use the energy to heal me completely before the wings faded away."

"Some people saw wings, but others saw . . . other things." He sounded a little grim when he said the last part.

I almost asked what the others had seen, but I wasn't certain I wanted to know. I'd used angel magic in a way I hadn't attempted in over a decade, and it had worked. God hadn't turned his grace from me, and neither had the angels. They could be more judgmental than the Big Guy sometimes.

"I'll bandage up your arm. Will antibiotics work on demon wounds?"

"This demon was more solid and real than any that I've ever touched, so use what you'd use if he was just a monster and not an Infernal. Even if it doesn't help, it won't hurt."

Paulson nodded. "Good to know since we're pumping Gonzales full of them. How about a tetanus shot?"

"Unknown, but again it can't hurt," I said.

He nodded again. "How long has it been since you had a tetanus booster?"

"I'm up-to-date. Got shoved into a pile of scrap metal last year."

I hissed when he put cream on the scratches that Kate had carved into me. I knew that a woman's nails could leave marks, but these seemed deeper, or maybe it had just been so long since I'd had a woman's nails on me, I didn't remember.

"Do they seem deeper than normal?" I asked.

"This is usually what we see if a woman fights back from an attack."

"So I've just never had a woman try to hurt me that much, but it's 'normal'?" I made quote marks in the air with the hand he wasn't bandaging up.

"I can't share patient information with you, but no, this level of damage from human scratches isn't normal." He looked at me as he said it, as if he was trying to tell me something with just the look. Whatever he was trying to say I was missing it. My face must have shown it because he frowned and raised the eyebrow again. "I've said all I can, Detective Havoc."

"Detective Havelock; Havoc is just a nickname," I said.

He half smiled, then shook his head. "Good to know, because Detective Havoc sounds like a comic book hero."

"Dr. Havoc would be worse, that sounds like a comic book villain."

He laughed then. "It really does." He finished patching me up and then he escorted me to Kate.

CHAPTER NINETEEN

—■ ■—

Kate looked younger lying in the new bed in a hospital gown that seemed even larger than the last one, so that her figure was completely hidden. She was only about five foot six standing, so lying down she seemed even smaller. With her brown curls tousled on the pillow and the big brown eyes she looked childlike. It made me wonder if she was Mark Cookson's age. God, had I gotten so needy that I couldn't tell a teenager when I saw one?

"I don't remember the demon hurting your arm," she said, looking at the bandages.

"It didn't," I said.

She turned her face away from me on the pillow so that all those brown curls spilled over her face. I fought the urge to brush the curls away until I could see her better. I couldn't tell if it was a parental gesture because she looked so fragile lying there, or if I just wanted an excuse to touch her, so I kept my hands to myself.

"I'm sorry, Zaniel, I'm so sorry," she said, voice hoarse. I couldn't tell if it was from screaming or emotion.

"You don't have to be sorry, Kate, not for anything. I'm just sorry that I couldn't have gotten you out of the room sooner." It was my turn to look away; I didn't want to see her looking so fragile, knowing that if I'd only gotten her free sooner . . . Heaven help me, Heaven help her, because we were both going to need it after today.

"I was the one who hurt you, so I should be the one who's sorry," she said.

That made me look at her again. She was looking straight at me now, her brown eyes staring up at me through the tangle of her hair. So she looked like a frightened little girl and then her eyes filled up with . . . her, I guess, and suddenly I knew she was no child, no teenager, because you had to be older than that to have a force of personality like that in your eyes. Something eased in my chest and I didn't feel like a dirty thirty-year-old guy who was hitting on teenagers at the mall. Men like that had creeped me out when I was a teenager; my opinion of them had never changed. I didn't always know what kind of man I wanted to be when I grew up, but I knew not that.

"You're stronger than you look," I said, trying to make it light.

"It wasn't human strength that cut your arm."

I looked at her, not sure what to say. I tried for light again. "Is there something I should know?" I even smiled, but she didn't smile back.

"My ancestors are originally from Russia."

"I'm an all-American mongrel, maybe a little extra Irish thrown into the mix," I said, and again I smiled, trying to lighten the mood, but she wasn't going to let me lighten anything.

She stared up at me through that tangle of hair with those big, dark eyes. The strength and fire of her seemed to be burning deep in them, as if brown eyes could be flame. "Do you know any Russian folktales, Zaniel?"

I shook my head.

"Do you know who Baba Yaga was?"

"She was the crone witch, the original wicked witch that lured children to be eaten, right?"

"Some of that's true. Baba Yaga did take bad children away to cook and eat them, or maybe she adopted them and raised them as her own and taught them her magic, or maybe she captured someone's child and a father petitioned her to save his family, or maybe he wanted treasure, or a question answered badly enough to risk the Baba's magic and trickery, because make no mistake if you give her a chance to trick you, she will and if she wins, you die. That part is very, very true."

I didn't know why I was getting the CliffsNotes about the Russian bogeyman—sorry, woman—but I didn't interrupt her. She was too earnest, and her eyes through her hair seemed like the eyes of an animal that you just glimpse through the leaves. I fought the urge to shiver as she continued.

"What we do know is that my great-great-great-grandfather slept with the Baba Yaga and not only survived to tell the tale but had good luck from that time forward. Any business he started prospered, any bet he made he won, it was like all the fates were on his side until the day he died at a hundred and three."

"Good genetics," I said.

She stared up at me with those feral eyes, lost in the wilderness of her own hair, and said, "The Baba would have kept a girl child, but it was a boy and she laid it on his doorstep one night for him to raise. That was my great-great-grandfather who had a son who became my great-grandfather who had a son . . ."

"So, you're saying that your great-great-great-grandmother was *the* Baba Yaga?" I said.

"Yes," she said, and she looked at me as if waiting for me to be angry, or disgusted, or something negative. Her eyes almost dared me to say something bad.

I smiled at her. "Glad you didn't inherit her iron fingernails; you'd have done a lot more damage."

"That's exactly what I inherited," she said.

I frowned at her. "I'd have noticed that, Kate. Your nails may be harder than normal, but they aren't iron."

"They were before I came here to have a magic therapy that one of their specialists created to help make me more human."

"Not just iron fingernails, then?" I asked.

She shook her head so that her hair fell around her face and finally slid to one side like a curtain to show her pale face with those golden freckles across her nose and cheeks. If I'd had to guess her heritage, I'd have thought Irish, or Scottish.

"Do you want to tell me what else the therapy was supposed to change?" I asked, voice soft.

"No," she whispered.

"Then you don't have to tell me."

"If I hadn't had the therapy to change my nails and teeth to something more human, I could have fought the demon off myself. I was stronger than a human woman my size, but I had to give the strength up to lose the nails and teeth. I wanted to be normal. I didn't want to be a monster anymore, but today a monster could have fought that thing off me. I'd have had the strength to help you open that door. It wouldn't have put anything inside me. I could have saved myself, damn it! But I wanted to be like everyone else, to have a normal life."

"There's nothing wrong with wanting that, Kate."

"You see the irony, though, right?" she asked.

"Yeah, I see it," I said.

"I wouldn't have needed you to save me, I could have saved myself, and instead I'm like everyone else, a victim, like everyone else."

She started to cry then, and I tried to find something to say that would help, or make any of it better, but thankfully Hazel came and saved us both.

Hazel mouthed, *Thank you*, and then she showed me the door. There was a new doctor coming through as I left. This one was a woman. I guessed that was better than a male doctor, if anything would have made any of this day better for the Baba Yaga's great-great-great-granddaughter.

CHAPTER TWENTY

was relieved to go back to the hallway and talk about demons and angels or anything but what had happened to Kate and what was about to happen. She wasn't the first victim that I hadn't been in time to save who needed a rape kit, but I always prayed that it would be my last time, that from this point on I would save them all, save everyone. I knew better, knew it was impossible to save everyone, but there was part of me that still agreed with my twenty-something self that we should be able to do it. Younger me might have waited in the hallway as if that helped, but me now . . . I'd have rather wrestled another demon than had to stay in the room and hold her hand during it, even if it would have been appropriate.

The crime scene techs filled the hallway; they were all dressed in full plastic gear. It wasn't hazmat gear with its own oxygen, but it was close. They looked like something out of a science fiction movie and I suddenly felt underdressed.

I looked at Charleston. "Is there something I should know? Why are they all wrapped up like it's contagious?"

"This is the new protocol for all the medical examiner's staff on a case with unknown supernatural elements, according to the techs. The ones who are straight normal had a few issues with magical evidence, so now everyone must wear the gear on supernatural crime scenes regardless of whether they're norm or magic."

"How is this going to save them from a spell?" Lila asked.

"It's supposed to be imbued with a counterspell that protects from most magic or psychic interference."

"It doesn't feel like an enchanted or holy item, I mean I don't feel any power coming off the gear," I said.

"Me either, but it's like most equipment—you won't know until it gets tested in the field."

I looked at the hallway full of the suited evidence techs, police, new hospital staff that I didn't know on sight. "Glad the elevators are working again," I said.

He glanced back at some of the officers in our own unit, frowning. "Yeah, because not everyone made it up the stairs in time for the action. Maybe I should put through mandatory cardio as a prerequisite for being on our unit."

I shrugged without commenting just in case some of my fellow officers were listening. They gave me enough shit about how much I worked out. If it was work out or be home alone in the small apartment without my family . . . the gym was a lot less lonely.

Charleston flashed a grin at me and patted my back like we were on a sports team and I'd scored a point. "You're already doing more cardio than I am, Havoc, so not your problem."

Lila came over and said, "He hangs out with Richardson too much."

"Yeah, Havoc, way to overachieve, having one of the SWAT guys as your workout partner," Detective Carlos Antero said. He damn near waddled over to us with his gut leading the way.

"He wasn't in SWAT when we started working out together," I

said. In my head, I thought Hash, short for Hashim, had wanted a workout partner to help him get in shape to make SWAT, and I was freshly separated. Working out with Hash had saved my sanity and gotten him into SWAT. Now I was working out with him and some of the other SWAT guys. I was in the best shape of my life, better than in the army. I was also depressed and homesick in a way I hadn't been even on deployment in the army.

"You said you were working out with Richardson until he made SWAT," Lila said.

"I like the workout," I said.

"You're making us look bad, Havoc," Carlos said.

"You give us old guys a bad rep, Antero," Charleston said, patting his own flat abs.

Carlos just grinned and rubbed his stomach in a way that was almost sexual. "My Carla knows how to cook for a man, it's one of the reasons I married her."

"I think she's trying to feed you into a heart attack, so she gets your life insurance and then she can marry some young Hispanic stud," Lila said.

"She eats as much as I do, but she's still my *colibrí*."

I knew *colibrí* was Spanish for *hummingbird* because Carlos called his wife that more than her real name. She was still fit and trim and looked twenty years younger than he did. She was also a Pilates and yoga instructor at the gym she co-owned with her twin sister. They both kept trying to fix me up with unmarried nieces and cousins. They considered being separated a prelude to divorce, so why wait? I hadn't told anyone at work that Reggie had said we should both try dating other people; it would have made them work even harder to find me someone.

"Did you find Cookson's body yet?" I asked.

The smiles left everyone's faces, which meant whatever they'd found was bad. It was just a matter of how bad; maybe I'd be rethinking whether I preferred the emotional violence of Kate's pain or the physical violence of the fight scene once I saw what was left of him.

"Yes and no," Charleston said at last.

I just looked at him and then the others. Carlos said, "I'm going to go finish questioning the uni that could see through angel magic."

"I already did that," Lila said.

He shuddered as he turned away.

"I thought you were tougher than this, Carlos," Lila said to his back, which was four times as wide as her slender form.

"I got nothing to prove anymore, Lila. Games like that are for the young guys—sorry, young people. I saw it once, that was enough."

"Scaredy-cat," she said.

"Ball-busting bitch," he said, but kept walking.

She opened her mouth to say more, but Charleston said, "That's enough, Bridges, you don't have kids yet."

She looked up at him. "What does that have to do with anything?"

"The boy was the same age as Carlos's youngest."

"The one who . . ."

He nodded.

"Jeez, I'm sorry, I didn't realize the age thing."

"Like I said, Bridges, you don't have kids yet, and Havoc doesn't have any teenagers. You've got to have grown-ass kids to understand that they never stop being your little boy, and you never stop wanting to protect them just like you did when they were babies."

I swallowed hard. "Connery is only three, I thought it got better as they got older."

"It gets better in some ways, harder in others as they get older, and teenagers through their twenties is a minefield I don't envy any parent."

"I thought eighteen and they were grown-ups," I said.

Charleston laughed.

"I am never having children," Lila said.

CHAPTER TWENTY-ONE

The skin fragments were so thin they were like cloudy plastic that you could see shadows through. "Are you sure that this is human skin?" I asked.

Charleston held the piece delicately between his gloved fingertips. You'd think someone with fingers that thick would be clumsy, but his hands were just as delicate as they had been when he was catching footballs in the NFL.

"There's a piece that they already bagged and tagged that's got what's left of the tattoo from his hip. DNA will tell us for sure that it's Cookson, but the nurses remember the tattoo, and it's distinctive."

"What was it, the tattoo, I mean?"

"The usual devil shit," Lila said.

"What's that mean?" I asked.

Charleston answered, "Upside-down pentagram with a devil-goat-head-looking thing above it. Terrible tattoo, the kind you'll cover up in a few years if you can find someone willing to try."

"At least it was small, that's an easier cover-up than a big one," Lila said.

"I don't think he has to worry about bad ink now," I said, staring at the piece of skin.

"Yeah, I guess not," Lila said, and she looked sad now, as if the cocky, wisecracking mask had slipped.

"Possessed individuals do not turn into full demon form, and they sure as hell don't shed their skins like a damn snake," Charleston said.

"His skin was reddish in the hallway, like whoever's imagination had turned him into the movie demon, so why does the skin left behind look like it was just Cookson's body in this room?" I asked.

"Excellent question," Charleston said.

"Could it have been a really good illusion like most demonic powers?" Lila asked.

"Illusion can make you hurt yourself, or somebody else hurt you, but *it* can't hurt you," Charleston said.

One of the techs came up gloved and covered head to foot in protective gear. "We need that now, Lieutenant."

"Has anyone used the protective suits in a live field exercise with real magic?" I asked.

"They told us everyone wears the suit on all supernatural-related crime scenes until further notice, that's all I know," the tech said.

"That you, Berger?" Bridges asked.

"Yeah, now give me my evidence."

"Our evidence," Bridges said, but Charleston just helped slip it into the container that Berger held up.

"Think what you want to think, Bridges, you always do anyway," Berger said, but his eyes through the face shield were all for the near-translucent sliver of skin until he had it safely contained and closed up nice and safe.

"You're just sore because I wouldn't date you," she said.

"Being attracted to you made me question my masculinity, Bridges; you're just too much man for me."

"That I believe," she said, and smiled, pleased with herself. A lot of female cops tried to be one of the boys, but none of them worked as hard to be better than the men as Lila did.

"I'll take Lila at my back ahead of most of the men I know," I said.

"Me, too," Charleston said.

"Thanks, guys."

"Unless we need someone to reach the top shelf for us," Charleston said.

"Well, there is that," I said, as if it hadn't occurred to me before.

"Screw you guys," she said.

"Lila, I'm shocked, you were at the meeting about sexually appropriate workplace vocabulary," Charleston said, but smiled as he said it.

"Fine," she said, "fuck you guys." She smiled at him and added a middle finger.

"If we did it to her, you'd write us up," Berger said.

"Don't you have evidence to test or something?" she said.

Berger started to reply, but Charleston cut him off. "Go do your job, Berger. Bridges will stay here and do hers."

The tech went off without another comment, but something about the exchange had gone beyond the usual bantering at crime scenes. It made me wonder if Lila had more history with Berger that I didn't know about, but then she didn't know all the details about my personal life either. We were work friends and that was it. I'd worked hard to make sure that the most attractive female officer on our unit was just a friend. The only thing worse than a messy divorce was one that involved someone from work. If I went down in flames with Reggie, I didn't want to burn up my career along with my marriage.

"Are you seriously telling me that skin fragments like that are the most you've found of the . . . Cookson?" I asked.

"So far," Lila said.

I shook my head. "His whole body should be in that room, maybe even still alive, left behind when the demon was forced to flee."

"Yeah, yeah, that's usual for demon possession, but this one, if you hadn't noticed, Havoc, isn't usual anything," Lila said; she sounded disdainful, as if to say *of course*. The tone was close enough to Reggie's that I had to stop myself from rounding my shoulders and hunching from it. If this kept up, I'd have issues with all women, all females. I could be even more broken than I already was.

"Then why is there just skin left?" I asked.

"You tell us, you're the Heaven and Hell expert," she said.

"I'm the expert on the angelic; that doesn't make me an expert on the Infernal."

"The closest thing to an expert in this hallway," she said. That disdainful tone that didn't usually bother me at all dripped from every word, or maybe I just heard it that way. It made it hard to focus on anything but the pain inside me.

Charleston touched my shoulder and I jumped as if it had surprised me. He dropped his hand but said, "Havoc, you all right?"

"Fine, I'm fine." But even to me the words sounded hollow.

"How bad are you hurt?" he asked, looking at the bandages on my arm and the holes in my shirt as if trying to see how many bandages were underneath.

"The demon wounds are almost healed."

"How's that possible?" Lila asked.

"Angelic magic is usually automatically healing once you invoke it," I said.

"So the demon claws are healed, but the scratches from our other victim aren't?" Charleston asked.

I glanced down at the thick dressings on my arm. "The female vic was in here for magical therapy, so there were side effects."

"What kind of side effects?" he asked.

I didn't want to betray Kate's secret. If she'd given up her iron teeth and claws to be normal beautiful, then the fewer people who knew about it the better, because if her new appearance got on social media with her old appearance, then having a normal life was over. If normal was what she wanted, I wanted her to have it.

"Patient confidentiality wouldn't let him tell me much," I finally said, but I'd waited too long to say it. Charleston and Lila both looked at me, waiting for more, because they didn't believe what I'd just told them, and they didn't try to hide the fact.

"Using angelic power the way I did will automatically heal things that are opposed to it like demon injuries, but for other injuries you have to request healing, and it had just been so long since I'd used that kind of power, I forgot." That was true, as far as it went.

Charleston nodded, face softening as if he understood more than I was saying, or something compassionate. "How long has it been since you worked with angel magic like this?"

"Almost ten years," I said.

He studied me like he was trying to read more than I was wanting to show. I gave him my best mild, friendly, blank face. It was my version of trying not to look threatening. It wasn't my cop face exactly, but the face I used to try to ease a stranger's reaction to me being big, physical, and male. When you were my size, or the lieutenant's size, you had to have a softer face that you could put on like a mask, so we'd seem less threatening by just being. He'd know exactly what the look on my face meant, but he'd also know it meant I didn't want him to look deeper. He'd respect that, unless he felt it was negatively impacting my job, and this wasn't.

"The doc cleared you for duty?" he asked.

"Like they cleared you for your getting knocked unconscious," I said, my face mild.

He smiled, his eyes looking down. "Then we'll both ignore doctor's orders about getting some rest and keep doing our jobs."

"Sounds good to me."

"Me, too. Now let's figure out what the hell is going on."

CHAPTER TWENTY-TWO

W e used Gimble's room to decide the game plan. He sat up in the bed, tucking his legs up so that Lila could sit on the end of the bed. Charleston and I took the room's chairs, and Antero stood, because he didn't fit comfortably in the chairs. When Lila offered to stand so he could have the foot of the bed he got offended, so she sat, and he stood.

Charleston had a look on his face like he might not have been kidding about physical fitness requirements for the unit, but out loud he said, "Antero stays here to question the staff. I want him to stay here until the nurse Gonzales is out of surgery and recovery and see if he can get a preliminary statement from him."

"I can help," Gimble said.

Charleston shook his head. "You're going to need a debriefing by Internal Affairs before you can go back on full duty."

"Lieutenant, please, I want to help catch this guy. You weren't at the first scene with Havoc and me. What he did to her . . . I'm fine, let me go with Havoc. He can keep an eye on me in case the angel stuff happens again."

"Havoc got cut up, so I'm going to send him out with Bridges for the rest of the day. I'm going to take Sato, the new uniformed officer that saw through the angelic magic in the hallway. The doctor will be happy I'm not driving with a head bump and I can get a feel for the uniform."

"But you both got hurt in the fight; physically I'm fine."

"You were so blissed out on angel magic you don't remember most of the last few hours, Gimble. Rules are, if any of us are magically incapacitated so that we lose time or are suspected of being possessed, then IA has to clear us for duty."

"It was an angel, not a demon. Angels can't possess anyone," Gimble said. He looked like he was going to pout, which made him look even younger than he was; no wonder he still got carded.

"If I'd been ridden by one of the loa, I wouldn't be allowed back on duty either, and that's not demon possession either, but it's still being too up close and personal with a supernatural power," Charleston said.

"But that's different," Gimble said. "You're a Voodoo Priest; it's part of your religion to call in your Deities and other powers to use your body to speak to your congregation."

"Thanks for making my point," Charleston said.

Gimble frowned at him. "I don't understand."

"If I'm going to call the loa and let them ride me, I have to let IA know ahead of time, because it falls under being magically compromised with or without memory lapses. If I have to deal with IA when I'm a priest and it's part of my faith, then what just happened to you is absolutely something they will want to make a report on."

Gimble sighed and leaned back into his piled-up pillows. "How long do I have to stay here?"

"That's up to Dr. Paulson."

"I'm fine."

"They'll hold you for at least two hours just to make sure it doesn't reoccur," I said.

"Did the doctor tell you that?" Gimble asked.

"No, but you were basically magically drunk by accident. The hospital will want to keep an eye on you to make sure that it's over before they release you."

"Come on, Gimble," Lila said, "you've been here when we brought people in that got power drunk from all sorts of things. You know the drill."

"But this was an angel, they're the good guys."

"You can get power drunk on the good stuff even faster than the bad stuff," Antero said.

We all nodded, except for Gimble. He crossed his arms over his chest. "You're bleeding," Lila said.

He looked at his arm where she pointed. "Damn, they put a bandage on it when they pulled the needle out."

"How big a hole did you put in your arm getting out of bed with the IV needle still in your arm?" Charleston asked.

"Not that bad," he said, but he was lifting his arm up and putting pressure on it.

Lila leaned past him and hit the button to ask for a nurse.

"I can still help Antero question people here."

"No, you were involved in the incident, so you handling the witness statement could potentially compromise them, since you were compromised."

"Lieutenant, please."

There was a soft knock at the door and a younger blond nurse came through the door. "Hi, I'm Bunny, and before you ask, yes, it is my real name." She saw the blood on Gimble and was suddenly all business as she moved toward the bed.

Gimble smiled up at the nurse. "Well, if I have to be under observation for a few hours, I guess that's just the way it is, Lieutenant."

She glanced down at him as she unwrapped the dressing to look at the wound. She got the full weight of his hazel eyes and then he smiled at her. She blinked at him like there was more to the smile than I could see. He was a projective empath, but I'd swear that wasn't what he was doing.

"We'll give you the room," Charleston said, and ushered us out. The nurse came behind us to get supplies she needed to put a fresh dressing on Gimble's arm.

"One of these days he's going to cross the line and end up talking to IA about just how charming he is to the opposite sex," Antero said.

"It's not his empathy," Lila said.

"How can you be so sure?" Antero asked.

"Because I got tired of watching other women fall for him so hard and so fast, so I might have flexed my own power around him while he was flirting."

Antero said, "You can be brought up on charges using your own powers on another officer outside of emergency situations."

"I asked her to double-check what Gimble was doing," Charleston said.

We looked at him. "You saw it just now. It's charisma bordering on magical, so I asked Bridges to flex her null powers around Gimble the next time she saw him wooing a new lady."

Lila was a powerful psychic null; no supernatural powers worked around her or against her. She could keep it tight to her aura only, and then flare it out and even aim it, which made her incredibly useful. If she hadn't been able to control it so well, she'd have still had plenty of job offers in maximum-security facilities that had magically talented prisoners or even psychiatric patients. That was usually the career path for people with her rather rare talent.

"He's not zapping the women. I don't see it myself, but apparently he is just that charming," Lila said.

"I feel slow that it didn't occur to me that Gimble was doing anything wrong until I saw how he was impacting the nurses here," I said.

"You said it was the combo of angelic power and his own talent," Charleston said.

I nodded. "Yes, but I feel naïve that it never occurred to me to wonder if he was cheating with the flirting."

"I'm the boss, it's my job to think about things like that."

I still felt stupid for not thinking of it sooner. Gimble was our newest member, so maybe that was it; but Charleston was right, there was a reason he was the boss, but part of me wondered if I'd have thought about checking Gimble out more closely seven months ago before things went south with Reggie. I pushed the thought away; if I was still thinking it tomorrow, I'd ask Charleston if my job performance was suffering. Tonight, I gave myself the benefit of the doubt. Kate's fingernails were burning on my arm under the bandages. It hadn't even occurred to me to ask the angels to heal the wounds, any of my wounds. I could say that it was because it had been so long that I just didn't think of it, and that was partly true, but the whole truth was I didn't think I deserved to be healed, not after what I had done. Some sins didn't have a shelf life, they stayed fresh and corrupting forever.

"Everyone knows what they're supposed to be doing," Charleston said; "let's go do it."

Lila said, "Before we all high-five and go our separate ways, one question."

Charleston just looked at her; that was all the encouragement he was going to give, and all she needed. "When we visit the parents, is it questioning the family of a suspect who's escaped by magical means, is it looking at him as another potential victim of the demon, or is it a condolence call?"

"Normally if we found just bits of skin it would be a condolence call, but nothing about this has been normal, so we don't know if their son is dead, missing, kidnapped by a demon, or a willing accomplice."

"Mark Cookson is not an unwilling victim here," I said.

"How can you be so sure?" Charleston asked.

"You heard them talking to each other. Cookson is a distinct personality; he's not just somebody who got taken over because he messed with things he didn't understand the consequences of."

"Again, how can you be so sure of that?"

"Because even victims who wanted to deal with demons, once it's inside them, they're afraid. The demon helps them live out their fantasies, but most people don't actually want to do their revenge fantasies. You've seen it before, Lieutenant; the human host is distraught and horrified whenever they can speak to us. Cookson doesn't seem to feel any remorse at all, let alone horror, at what he did to Megan Borowski."

"Just because the kid is enjoying the power trip doesn't mean he's not a victim," Charleston said.

"If he enjoyed doing what he did to her, then he is too dangerous to be out there among other potential victims whether he's sharing a body with a demon or alone in his skin."

"I can't rule anything out, Havoc. We have no way of knowing how much the demon is influencing Cookson. He could be horrified once the demon is out of him."

"Do you really want another of these people to go free and use 'the demon made me do it' as an alibi?"

"No, but the courts have ruled that demon possession is a viable court defense. It's only our job to bag them, Havoc; putting them behind bars is up to the lawyers."

I took a deep breath in and let it out slowly, realizing that my hands were in fists at my sides. I fought to relax my hands as I breathed in and out.

"If you don't feel up to this today, Havoc, you can tap out. You got clawed up by a demon, take the rest of today off."

"No, thank you, Lieutenant, but I want to help get this guy."

He gave me that look that said he wasn't sure he believed me, but he said, "Fine, but if at any point you think you need a break, take it;

Bridges will drop you back at your car, or your apartment, whatever you need."

"I must look worse than I feel for you to baby me like this," I said, smiling to try and make it a joke.

The look he gave back was serious with no hint of a smile. His dark eyes were trying to read past the smiling, pleasant face I was giving him. He knew me too well to believe it, but he finally gave a small nod.

"Tell the parents we're looking for him and you're just there to gather information to help us figure out what is going on."

"Will do, Lieutenant," Bridges said.

"I'll try to keep an open mind about Cookson, sir."

"That's all I ask, Havoc. Now go and find out things. I'll take Sato and head back to the original crime scene and work it from that end."

"Aye-aye, bossman," Bridges said, and headed for the elevators again. This time I followed her without questioning it. I'd try to keep an open mind, but I knew what I'd heard. Mark Cookson wasn't a victim; he was a bad guy.

My watch vibrated against my wrist. One glance was enough to make me groan. I so did not need this right now.

"What's wrong?" Lila asked.

"I'm due at couples therapy with Reggie."

"Oh, Havoc, I'm sorry. Couples therapy sucks," Lila said. She'd gone through her own messy divorce just after I joined the unit. Her ex-wife had come to the precinct once and thrown a box at Lila full of couple gifts. At least my personal issues hadn't gotten that messy, not yet. I tried picturing Reggie throwing stuff at me at work in front of strangers. No, she'd never lose control like that in public. She saved her passion for private, including her anger.

"Thanks, Lila, I appreciate the solidarity."

"Bitches be crazy, and dudes are stupid—I've married one apiece, trust me, it all sucks." I'd met her ex-husband, Rob; he seemed okay and a lot less likely to throw shit at you than her ex-wife, Annie.

Charleston came back to us; apparently he'd overheard. "I've been happily married to my beautiful wife for thirty years. Not all marriages end in divorce."

"You got lucky," Lila said.

"Part of it's luck, finding someone who's willing to work on the marriage and their own personal issues. A couple either grows together or grows apart."

"In the spirit of trying to grow together, I can't miss this appointment, Lieutenant, I'm sorry."

"You don't have to apologize to me, Havoc," he said.

I turned to Lila. "I'm so sorry, I'm leaving you hanging here. You need some magical backup in case the parents are involved somehow, or in case there's been enough black magic done in the house to thin the veil between this reality and Hell."

"I know my job, Havoc," Lila said, giving me a look that made me try to explain.

"I'm not questioning that; you know I'd take you as backup any day. It's just I'm feeling guilty that I won't be there to help you face it, whatever it is."

Her face softened. "You're a good guy, Havoc."

"Thanks, I just hope my wife agrees with you today."

"Well, she won't if you miss the appointment," Charleston said, frowning. "We can get MacGregor to meet Lila at the home."

"Old MacGregor or young?" Lila asked.

Charleston half laughed and half sighed. It was funny, but it was making things more complicated. "They aren't related, Bridges."

"Let me see: a middle-aged or a little older white guy who's nearly six feet tall and hasn't hit a gym in almost as long as Antero, compared to a twenty-something, younger-than-Gimble black man who is as tall as you and Havoc—by God they are twins, or at least long-lost family." She was smiling and overly pleased with herself, but the fact that the newest temporary officer in our unit shared a last name with the detective who had been with us the longest had led to a lot of jokes.

"MacGregor has been in the unit longer than anyone except Ravensong, so he's MacGregor," Charleston said as if he'd just decided it.

"Okay, what do we call MacGregor two, then?" she asked.

"Why not just use his first name?" I asked.

"I tried calling him Goliath," Lila said, "and he gave me this look, said he doesn't go by it."

"I can understand why he doesn't use it, but what does he go by?" I asked.

Charleston said, "I already had this talk with him, and he goes by MacGregor."

"How about Mac?" I suggested.

"His stepdad is Mac," Charleston said.

I glanced at my watch. "I feel like I'm leaving you guys in the lurch, but I have to go if I'm going to make the appointment."

"You sure you feel well enough to drive yourself?" he asked.

"Yeah," Lila said, "I was supposed to be your taxi because you got cut up by a demon."

"I'm good." And in my head I thought, no way was I taking Lila and me off the job for my couples counseling.

They both gave me hard looks, but I managed to just wave and start inching my way toward the elevators. "Just let me know what nickname you decide on for Officer Goliath MacGregor, so I don't get it wrong."

"Oh, don't worry, if you get it wrong Goliath will let you know," Lila said, rolling her eyes.

Charleston grinned. "I told him it could always be worse, try being a boy named Adinka through elementary school and seventh grade."

Lila gave a low whistle. "Everybody thought it was a girl's name, didn't they?"

Charleston nodded.

"Wait," she said, "you said just seventh grade, not junior high, what happened to make it bearable in eighth grade?"

"I hit my growth spurt fast and hard the summer between seventh and eighth grade." He grinned again, but this time it was fiercer, the smile that the sports magazines had touted as his killer smile. I'd seen suspects confess after being offered to be alone with him and that smile. Charleston would never have harmed them, but he gave off raw menace better than almost anyone I knew. He'd tried to teach me how to do it since I had the size to intimidate, but he finally gave up, saying, "I guess you get to be the good cop." I was okay with being the good cop. I wondered if Goliath MacGregor would be able to do bad and good; he was certainly tall enough to intimidate most people.

"Good luck, I'll contact you both when I'm out of the appointment," I said.

"You got this, Havoc," Lila said.

I shook my head. "If I asked you what women want, would you have an answer?"

She smiled, but it was more bitter than funny. Her eyes were bleak as she said, "If I knew the answer to that I'd still be married to my own wife."

CHAPTER TWENTY-THREE

O ur therapist was older than us by at least a decade. There was a
plain silver band on her ring finger. Our first therapist had been
younger than us and the longest she'd managed to live with anyone was less than a year; she'd never been married. How did I know
all that about her? Because I'd asked after a few sessions where I felt
like maybe we knew more than she did about being a couple. It had
been a huge fight with Reggie. She'd almost signed the divorce papers,
so she said later. There was a part of me that would have been relieved
if she'd done it. I didn't want our marriage to end, but I was beginning
to just want it done, yes or no, in or out. Hell might be worse than
Purgatory, but at least you picked a direction and knew your fate.

Dr. Martin sat there looking pleasant, but serious, as if she was
almost smiling, but you could never quite catch her at it. It was a neat
trick, like counselors had their own version of cop face, that mask you
wore when you wanted a suspect or a witness to tell you everything you
needed to know. The best thing she'd accomplished for us so far was
getting Reggie to stop harping on my first marriage to a stripper when

I was a brand-new private in the army. The woman had taken me for everything I had, what little there was of it, and served me papers when I was in a forward area, probably hoping I'd die in combat, so she'd get the most insurance possible. That was the marriage that taught me I didn't have to marry a woman just because I had sex with her once. Did I mention I was raised in what amounted to a religious cult?

"Zaniel, are you even listening to me?" Reggie's voice on the other end of the couch from me.

I hadn't been listening. I didn't even know how long I hadn't been listening; not good. I took a deep breath in and let it out slow as I turned to look at her. Seeing her still hurt like hell. When we'd first started counseling, I'd stared at her as if I wanted to memorize her. The full face, which she thought was too wide, but I thought framed her big, brown eyes perfectly. If her face had been narrower the eyes would have been too big like a Japanese anime character. The strong, high cheekbones that almost overwhelmed her mouth, which was why she wore lip liner and lipstick constantly to give the illusion that her upper lip was closer to the fullness of her bottom lip. I thought she was beautiful without any makeup, but the dark, artful lipstick did help bring her lips out to balance the strength of her face and those huge, dark eyes. The eyes were the third thing I'd noticed about her when we first met. The first was her height. She was five foot nine and had been wearing five-inch stilettos, which made her an inch shorter than me. I'd thought for a second, before I saw the shoes, that she was my height, and I'd loved it. When you're six-three you date shorter women, because it's hard to find taller ones, but I saw those strong shoulders, the fine muscle play in her tanned arms, and I thought, *Athlete*, and I liked that, too.

Her back had been strong and bare with tiny little straps barely there. The pink blossoms and curling green leaves of the tattoo on her right shoulder seemed to cover more than the back of her dress. The tanned skin of her back had been exposed to her waist with just a hint of the swell of her hips as she moved. When I finally got to see her from the front the dress had been solid black, hinting at small, firm breasts, which went along with the amount of slim muscle under all that smooth skin. Most women had to trade curves for that level of fitness, and I was good with the trade. Her hair was a brown so dark I'd thought it was black until I saw it in bright sunlight on our third date. Her hair was thick and wavy, but she straightened it almost as often as she wore the red lipstick that stood out against her tan like a Valentine's Day promise.

She was wearing the lipstick today, along with enough eye makeup to make her eyes huge and romantic, except for the anger in them. She spent most counseling sessions angry. I spent most of them confused. It was like she had the CliffsNotes on how to do couples counseling and hadn't shared them with me.

"Sorry, could you repeat that last part?"

She crossed her arms underneath the fuller breasts that cutting back on the exercise and having a baby had given her. The thin red sweater looked good against her almost year-round tan; she could get lighter if she stayed indoors enough, but she never looked pale. Her grandmother was Colombian and her grandfather Colombian and Mexican, and yes, the distinction is important. So many people just label it all Hispanic or La-tina, but it's so much more multilayered and multicultural than that. Her mother had been the first person in the family to go to college and refused to speak Spanish at home. She was American, damn it. Reggie learned Spanish in college and used it daily as a teacher on the West Coast.

"My eyes are up here, Zaniel," she said, her voice thick with disdain, as if to say, *So like a man to stare at breasts.*

I hadn't been staring at them, not really, but I didn't try to explain that I'd been looking at her breasts and then started thinking about other things but just never changed my eye-line. She wouldn't believe me anyway.

"You look nice today. Why am I in trouble for noticing?"

She covered her face with her hands and said, "What color of eye shadow am I wearing?"

Her nails were a red that matched the sweater and the lipstick. "You wore the extra eyeliner to make your eyes look bigger, and added mascara, which you almost never do, because your eyes are so fabulous you don't need it. You told me once it was overkill for you. Eye shadow is something pink and purplish, with an edge of sparkly red, but it's all blended together so maybe there's a brown in there somewhere."

She lowered her hands and stared at me, with her pink and purple eye shadow; yes, there was some brown in the crease of her eyes, and that sparkle of red like glitter almost. She'd worn makeup either for me or for her own courage, or she had a date later. The thought made my stomach clench tight, which sort of hurt with the demon scratches healing and all.

"I thought you'd stopped looking at me," she said.

"You told me I was staring at you and it made you uncomfortable, so I stopped doing it."

She stared at me as if she didn't know what to say, which was a first in this quiet room with Dr. Martin watching us. She'd expected me to be wrong, to be just another stupid man who stares at women's breasts and doesn't look at their faces. But I'd never been that guy, because the first woman I had ever loved had taught me to notice her, and I'd never stopped noticing women not just sexually, but in all the ways She'd wanted to be noticed. How She made her hair that day, her eyes, her smile; she wanted to be worshipped and I had worshipped her. Women after Her had taught me that they didn't want to be worshipped, or they weren't worthy of it until Reggie. I thought she was The One. It wouldn't be until after our son was born that I realized I was the romantic in our relationship, and Reggie was the practical one. Romance is hard after a baby; practical is easy, practical is necessary, romance not so much. I loved Connery more than I'd ever loved anyone except Reggie and the first woman in my life, but I missed the kind of couple we'd been before he was born. I was beginning to be afraid that we couldn't be a couple and parents at the same time, and it scared me.

"You always noticed the physical stuff, I guess I forgot how much you pay attention. But did you hear what I said, were you listening to me?"

Her body was softer than when we'd met, which meant her hips filled out the skintight jeans really well, and with less muscle on her calves she could fit into a lot more tall boots. She was wearing one of my favorite pairs today. Had she done that on purpose, or had she not even remembered how much I loved to go down on her while she wrapped the boots around my shoulders? If she wore them because she remembered, I liked it; if she'd forgotten I didn't want to know.

"Say something, Zaniel."

I watched the irritation fill her eyes and knew the anger wasn't far behind. "No, I didn't hear what you just said, Reggie."

I had tried to look at her as little as possible during the sessions for a while. If she was never going to be mine again, then I wanted to erase the memory of her body from my mind. I didn't want to remember the strength of her the first few years, or the softer grace of her when she had to quit her job as a fitness instructor to teach high school full-time, because she'd finished her degree. She'd taught women's strength and fitness as her job to help pay for college. Our second date had been working out at her gym. I'd been able to keep up with her, and she'd been able to keep up with me, and some things she was better at, and some things I'd been better at, and that had pleased us both.

I didn't want to remember how the baby weight had made her breasts fuller, and her hips a little wider, so that it was like making love to a third her. I'd loved all of her, whatever weight or size; I looked at her sitting just on the other end of the couch, two feet from me, and for the first time I didn't think just about Reggie. I thought about Kate's face, the feel of her hand on mine, the strength of her, the pain in her. I thought about Hazel Prescott's bravery and competence. Was it unfair to compare their bravery in crisis to Reggie sitting there, arms crossed under the fullness of her breasts, a pout on her face and the anger turning her brown eyes black? I'd thought the pout was cute once. The temper had never been charming.

"What's wrong with you today, Zaniel?"

"You don't want to know."

"I asked, didn't I?" She crossed her legs, one knee beginning to jiggle. It was one of her signs that she was really pissed, and for once I didn't seem to care. I wasn't sure if that was good or bad.

"Fine, I had to leave a crime scene . . ."

"Oh, your job is more important than saving our marriage, is that it?" And just like that we were back to old arguments like the tracks on a roller coaster where the cars can't get off the ride and just keep going round and round.

"You didn't even let me answer the question," I said.

"You answered, you're all about the job."

"Actually, Reggie, you didn't let him answer you. Go ahead, Zaniel, finish your thought," Dr. Martin said.

"It isn't leaving work to come here that's making it hard for me to concentrate, Reggie. It's the kind of crime scene I had to leave to . . . experience. It was sort of awful and people got hurt, and now I'm supposed to sit here and talk about our marriage."

"Because the people who got hurt are more important to you than our marriage," she said, as if I'd made her point for her.

I was suddenly angry, and I let myself be angry at her for once. "I didn't save everyone today, Reggie. A young woman who begged me to save her is getting a rape kit done at the hospital, because I couldn't get to her in time. I couldn't save her from that." The anger in her eyes softened, and it wasn't enough. "Did you notice the bandages on me, or did you just not care that I got hurt today?"

"You could do other jobs, Zaniel."

I shook my head and held my hands up. "So instead of asking me how hurt I am, or what happened, you go straight to the fact that you hate me being a cop, and why can't I go sell insurance for your brother, or maybe go to college, as if that will guarantee me a better job."

"Do you want Reggie to ask about your injuries?" Dr. Martin asked.

"I think I need to know that she cares that I got hurt."

"Do you care about that, Reggie?" the doctor asked, and looked at my wife.

"Of course I do." She sounded more angry than concerned.

"Then ask Zaniel about his day. How he got hurt."

"He didn't ask me about mine."

I stood up and looked down at her. "If you had come in here with your arm wrapped up in a medical dressing, I'd have asked you what happened."

Her eyes narrowed and she looked at my stomach. "Are those more bandages under your shirt?" She reached out toward me; it was the first time she'd reached for me in months. I thought about stepping out of reach, but I thought about it too long and her fingers found the rips in my shirt and the bandages underneath. When she pushed her fingers through the rips and brushed some bare skin between bandages I had to step back or shudder from just that light touch. My body reacted to her being that close, and I hoped she didn't notice. I didn't want her to know that her fingers barely brushing my stomach had that much effect on me. Heaven help me, I still wanted her, but I wasn't sure about being in love anymore, and that helped more than a cold shower.

"I've seen your shirt after a knife went through; that wasn't knives, was it?"

"No," I said.

"Claws, Jesus, Zaniel, what clawed you up like that?"

I shook my head. "Demon."

"Demons aren't that solid."

"It's been a hell of a day," I said.

She looked up at me with fear raw on her face, fear for my safety. She'd started using her anger to mask how scared she was every time I left for work.

"You could die."

"Everyone can die," I said.

She stood up and in the high-heeled boots, which she knew I loved to see her in, she was six feet at least, not that much shorter than me. I'd liked that she was tall and still loved wearing heels, liked that she hadn't tried to hide her height like so many tall women do.

"You'd leave Connery without a father."

"We've had this fight before, Reggie. Now I say that statistically driving a car is more dangerous than my job, or working as an overnight clerk at a 7-Eleven, and you say—"

"The clerk doesn't chase monsters or fight demons every day."

"I go days without chasing anything, and demons are rare even on my job."

"Damn it, Zaniel, stop doing that!"

"Doing what?"

"Missing my point."

"Your point is that you hate my job, because it scares you, because you think I'm more at risk than on most other jobs."

"Yes, yes, that is my point."

"You're a teacher in a public school, Reggie; you've taken knives off of students, and there was a gun scare two months ago."

"There was a rumor two months ago that a student might bring a gun to school, but it was another student trying to get someone in trouble."

"I'm just saying that your job is dangerous, too, but I don't ask you to quit."

"If you asked me to give it up, I would."

"Really? And what would you do?"

"I'd stay home with Connery."

I smiled, and it was a mistake.

"Why is that funny?" She half yelled it.

"You'd be climbing the walls in a month being a stay-at-home mom."

"How do you know that? If you made more money maybe, we could have tried it."

"I'm making pretty good money, especially for a cop."

"Not enough for me to quit my job."

"You don't make enough for me to quit my job and stay at home with Connery either."

"You've never said you wanted to do that before."

"Maybe I do, maybe I would? I'd love to see him every day. I miss dropping him off at preschool. Maybe being a stay-at-home dad would be awesome."

She studied my face, not angry anymore, but thinking, trying to decide if I was serious. She wasn't the only one, but suddenly the thought of tucking my kid in at night and being there when he woke up, taking him to preschool, even cooking meals for all of us while Reggie went to work sounded . . . possible.

"You never said that you wanted to do that before," she said.

"I make more money than you do; if we can't afford to make it on just my salary, there's no way for us to make it on just yours." I shrugged, and then wished I hadn't because it hurt. "If something isn't possible, what good does it do to talk about it?"

"I like knowing that you'd try to be the stay-at-home parent. I love knowing that you'd want to spend all day with our son." She started to touch my bandaged arm and then switched her hand to my other arm. I tried to put my hand over hers, but that hurt the scratched arm too much. I had to stop the movement halfway and take a deep breath not to say *ouch*, or something even less manly.

She slid her hand down my arm and took my hand in hers for the first time in six months, maybe longer. Her hand was like the rest of her, bigger, still slender and feminine, but her hand held mine easily. She had never made me feel like I couldn't shake her hand without overwhelming her.

She held my hand and smiled up at me. My heart did a flip-flop, and just like that I felt hopeful and realized that I still loved her, and that with a little encouragement I could be in love with her again. Part of me was happy and part of me thought I was a damn fool.

CHAPTER TWENTY-FOUR

W e made plans to have dinner together, with Dr. Martin acting like a referee as we negotiated all the details. I'd have called it a date, but Reggie called it just having dinner, so I didn't say the D-word. But the excited, bubbly feeling I had in my stomach and chest felt like more than "just dinner." I felt happy and stupid for feeling that way, but it's how I felt. I tried to enjoy the feelings without thinking too hard about how I'd feel if the dinner was a disaster, or if Reggie backed out on it altogether. I pushed the thought away and tried to hold on to the happy excitement.

I got into my car and texted Charleston and Lila almost the same message: "Done with appointment. Do you need me at the house?" to her, and to him, "Done with appointment. Do you need me at the college?" Then I hesitated because I didn't know where to drive. I'd give them five minutes, then call. Before the separation I'd have been hoping that they didn't need me and I could go home. Now the last thing I wanted to do was go home to the tiny apartment I'd gotten after I moved out of the home that Reggie and I had made together. I'd let her stay in the house with the kiddo because what else could I do? I was supposed to take care of them; making them move out of the house didn't feel like I'd be doing that, so Reggie and Connery stayed in the house and I found a tiny, reasonable apartment in El Segundo where the sound of airplanes going overhead almost never stopped. But there was a pool, and a big sycamore tree outside the window where a mockingbird sang all night. It almost drowned out the airplanes. Connery went back home to Reggie full of the pool and the landlady's pug puppies. He thought sleeping in the big bed with me was an adventure. I'd put him on the couch one weekend, but he'd gotten up in the middle of the night and tried to make popcorn. He'd set off the smoke alarm, so he went in the bedroom and I didn't fit on the couch. I barely fit in the queen-sized bed.

The thought of going back to the apartment drained away the excitement and the last adrenaline from the emergency at the hospital. I wanted to go home, and the apartment would never be that. I wanted to go home with my wife and be there when Connery got home from preschool, but I couldn't have that today. There was a dinner planned, almost a date; we'd take it slow, because Reggie didn't want to take it fast. I took a deep breath and squeezed my hands around the steering wheel until my scratched arm protested as if some of the nail marks had gone into the muscle. I hadn't had stitches because the skin had peeled away underneath her nails; you can't stitch a scrape, just bandage it and wait for it to heal.

I could chase after Reggie like an unwanted dog she'd dropped off at a shelter. I couldn't face the thought of going to the tiny apartment, so what did that leave? Exercise; one of the reasons I was in the best shape of my life was that it was one thing I could do that I could control. I could always lift more weights, or run one more mile, or . . . but I was too hurt to hit the gym, or even run. You use your upper body a lot more than you think when you run. So, what next? What would I do if Charleston told me he didn't need me and to go home, rest, and heal?

I wanted to go home and finish working on one of the dozen projects around the house that had gone on hold when I left. Again, I couldn't do that unless Reggie allowed it, and that hurt more than any wound. I wanted to go home, and I couldn't because it wasn't home anymore. We had a dinner planned, I told myself again, but that pessimistic part of me that had been growing louder over the six-month separation was in my head now, telling me that I should figure out what home meant without Reggie. What would home mean if it was just me and Connery half the time and me alone the rest of the time? The thought made me want to put my head down on the steering wheel and weep. Where could I go? What could I do to keep the dark thoughts from eating up all the good ones? The only answer was work; I could go back to work, I could try to figure out why everything was different with this demon possession, if that was even the correct term for it. I could find the demon that had helped Mark Cookson rape and kill our victim, Megan Borowski. I could find the demon that either had killed Mark Cookson or was using his body to commit crimes, because unlike angels, demons didn't just go back to Hell and get lost in the Infernal fires. They stayed up here until they were forced back to Hell. Angels enjoyed Heaven and being closer to God; no demon I'd met wanted to return to Hell.

A car stopped behind my parked one. It was blocking me in, and it took me a second to realize it was Reggie. She turned the engine off and got out of the car. I had a moment of my heart lifting in pure happiness; maybe she was going to say the date could be tonight, or maybe she wanted me to come home even to do some tool-using chore. I'd take it. I'd be her handyman with no benefits if I could just be in the house when Connery came home from school. Then I saw the tension in her body, the way she held her lips, and knew underneath the big sunglasses her eyes would be black dark with anger.

What in Heaven's name had I done to piss her off now?

CHAPTER TWENTY-FIVE

got out of the car, so I was standing and facing her as she said, "Why are you waiting for me? I agreed to the dinner."

"I'm not waiting for you," I said.

"Were you going to follow me to see if I got a date or something?"

"It never occurred to me to follow you, Reggie."

"You're a cop, it's part of what they teach you, isn't it?"

"I suppose, but I'm just waiting—"

"For what; if you're not waiting to see where I go next, what are you waiting for?" she demanded.

"To know if I join Charleston at the crime scene or go with another detective to get background on a suspect."

That seemed to calm her down a little. "Oh, well, how long does that take to find out?"

My phone rang and saved us both from a conversation that I really didn't understand at all. "Hey, Havoc, wait until you see what we found at the parents' house!"

"Just tell me what it is," I said, smiling because she sounded so excited.

"Who is that?" Reggie asked.

"It's Detective Bridges."

"Lila, you mean." And she raised both her eyebrows up high enough that they showed above the sunglasses.

"Yes, Lila Bridges," I said.

Lila said, "I thought your text said the therapy was over."

"We're in the parking lot," I said.

"Is she asking where we are?" Reggie said.

"Yes," I said.

"What?" Lila asked.

Reggie pantomimed me handing the phone to her, but I was too confused about what was happening, so I put it on speaker. "Lila, you're on speaker, Reggie wanted to talk to you, I think."

"Hi, Reggie," Lila said, her voice neutral friendly.

"Hi, Lila." Reggie's tone was overly friendly and didn't sound right. "Did he text you as soon as our couples therapy was over?"

"Her and Charleston," I said.

"Havoc wanted to know if I was done talking to the parents."

"Parents, what do you mean, parents?" Reggie asked.

"One of the people involved in the crime is a college kid," I said, so that Lila didn't have to figure out how much I'd shared or not shared with my wife.

"Victim or bad guy?" Reggie asked, but her anger seemed to be fading.

"Both," I said.

"You mean this is all college-age kids?" she asked.

"Everyone's young, or as old as they're ever going to get," Lila said, and she couldn't hide the weariness in her voice. She might have been excited about the evidence she'd found, but something about the case was getting to her. It probably meant the parents had been nice. Sometimes it was harder when the family seems like good people, especially if you're trying to tell them their son is suspected in the rape and murder of another college student.

"I didn't know the victim or that everyone else involved was so young. I'm sorry you had to go see the parents." And Reggie sounded more like herself.

"Never my favorite part of the job," Lila said, and she sounded tired.

"I'm sorry I wasn't there to help you with the parents, Lila," I said.

"Hey, I took the new guy, MacGregor 2.0; he didn't suck."

"I'm glad he didn't suck," I said.

"I'm sorry that Zaniel couldn't be there to help, too, Lila," Reggie said.

"It's okay, I just wish my wife had been willing to do counseling with me like you and Havoc are doing."

"Are you saying that Annie refused to go to couples counseling with you?" Reggie asked.

"Yeah, I offered, but she said there was nothing wrong with her, she didn't need therapy, and if I thought I needed it I should go to therapy, but couples therapy without the other half of your couple seemed sort of pointless." Lila sounded about as unhappy as I'd ever heard her.

"That sounds awful," Reggie said, her voice soft. The glasses hid most of her face, but she seemed more affected than I'd expected by Lila sharing.

"It's okay, Reggie, I just want someone else to get the happily-ever-after I keep missing." She sounded genuinely sad, which I knew she was about her divorce, but she was letting Reggie hear it in her voice on purpose. I didn't know why, but I knew it was on purpose, because Lila could control her voice in an interrogation or undercover better than I could.

"Well, I don't think we're ready for happily-ever-after, but the counseling sessions are helpful," Reggie said.

"I thought it was promising," I said, fighting to keep my voice as neutral as hers.

"Promising is good," Lila said on the phone, then added, "I'm taking all the paraphernalia we gathered at the house back to the precinct. I want you to see it before it goes to forensics. Neither I nor the new guy is that versed on this kind of occult."

"I'll meet you there," I said.

"Okay, and good to talk to you, Reggie."

"Good to talk to you, too, Lila."

"See you back at home base, Havoc," Lila said, then hung up.

Reggie looked down at the ground and sighed. I was almost able to ignore how it made the sweater move as she did it. I made sure I was meeting her eyes behind the black lenses when she looked up.

"I'm sorry, Zaniel, I don't know what got into me."

"It's okay, Reggie, but I would never follow you to see what you're doing. I would trust you to tell me if there was something I needed to know."

"Oh, Zaniel," she said, her voice soft and exasperated all at the same time, as if she couldn't decide if she wanted to hug me or get mad at me again.

"What is wrong, Reggie? Why would you block my car in like this, like you're trying to catch me out or something?" That made me ask, "Have you been following me around to see if I'm dating someone?"

"No, of course not," she snapped that time, anger and that disdainful I-wouldn't-stoop-so-low tone in her voice.

I was tired of feeling like I'd done something wrong when I hadn't. "You accused me of doing it, why shouldn't I ask you the same question?"

She opened her mouth to say something sharp and probably hurtful, but she stopped herself. She took a deep breath in and then slowly let it out as if she was counting. She was seriously angry, but I had no idea what about. It was like she was having a hugely different conversation inside her head than the one I was having with her. That wasn't like Reggie; she was emotional, but not usually this confusing.

"You're right, I started this, you have every right to throw it back at me. I am sorry for jumping to stupid conclusions. Too many people giving me bad advice from their divorces, I guess."

"No one at work is telling me anything, except good luck with working it out."

"That's very mature for a bunch of cops." And there was the disdain back in her voice, like she couldn't help it.

"Well, at least the immature cops aren't giving me bad advice that's making me angry at you for things you haven't even done, unlike your mature teacher friends."

I expected her to be angry again, but she surprised me by saying, "You're right, my friends haven't been giving me very good advice."

I didn't know how to react to her just giving up; even if she was in the wrong, she didn't give up on a fight this easily, but then maybe it wasn't a fight—yet.

"I just want to come back home with you and Connery. I'm sorry you hate my job, but I've been a cop the entire time you've known me."

"I know," she said; her voice still sounded defeated, which I didn't hear from her often. I didn't like it, my Regina defeated.

I wanted to touch her face, to make her smile, but I wasn't sure how she'd take the touch, and that made my chest tight like someone had hit me over the heart. Honest, the therapist kept telling us, we needed to be honest.

"May I touch your face?"

"You don't have to ask just to touch my face, Zaniel."

"I'm not sure of the rules, so I've been not touching you or looking at you, because it seemed to piss you off, so I'm asking."

Her lips curled upward just a little. She reached out and took my hand in hers. Even that sped my pulse, and part of me felt stupid for reacting to such a small gesture. She placed my hand against the side of her face and smiled up at me.

I cupped the side of her face in my hand with her hand pressing against mine and it felt so right. "May I kiss you?"

"Yes," she said, and this time I felt her face move as she smiled up at me.

I leaned over her and she turned her face upward to meet me, my hand still cupping the side of her face. My lips touched hers, and the first thought was how soft they were, and then the slight thickness of her lipstick stopped me, because I knew it would smear. She didn't like to have it smeared in public, especially when she was wearing base makeup. Her mouth tasted sweet and alive, but the lipstick was bitter; a lot of the darker lipsticks tasted that way.

I drew back to stare down into her face, which was still raised up toward me like an offering. I couldn't see through the dark glasses to see if her eyes were closed or if she was gazing up at me. It wasn't until I felt her face move slightly against my hand that I realized she'd opened her eyes. For some reason the fact that she'd closed her eyes made me even happier than the kiss alone had.

She moved her head, so I dropped my hand away. "Why did you stop kissing me?" she asked.

"You hate it when I smear your lipstick all over your base."

"I don't hate it," she said.

I almost said, out loud, *You could have fooled me*, but luckily, I was smarter than that and said, "You've told me not to smear your lipstick, especially when you're wearing base."

She leaned her hands against my chest, putting her body weight behind it. I started to put my arms around her automatically but hesitated partway through.

"Hold me, Zaniel," she said.

I wrapped my arms around her, and she leaned into the hug for the first time in longer than I could remember. I finally felt free to smile, but I was still tense holding her, waiting for her to pull away or tell me I'd overstepped my bounds. What had once been so natural and easy between us had become a minefield that I no longer knew how to walk.

"Hold me, Zaniel."

"I am holding you," I said.

"Your arms are around me, but I can feel that you're all tense like you can't relax. What's wrong? Don't you want to hold me?"

"More than anything else in the world."

"Then relax," she said.

I was almost afraid to, but I tried to let go of the tension in my shoulders and arms. It was like I was poised for fight or flight. I realized I was scared, which seemed ridiculous; Reggie wasn't dangerous. And then another part of me whispered that she was more dangerous than any gun or knife. They could only take my life; she was killing parts of me that the hospital couldn't put back together.

"Zaniel," she whispered. She slid her arms around my waist and pressed her body to the front of mine. The feel of it went through me in a wave of need that made me close my eyes so she wouldn't see it, but I couldn't hide my body's reaction to her. She wiggled her hips against me, and I shuddered. God help me, I had better control than this.

I tried to step back, but she held on. I heard a sound that was almost a whimper and realized it was me. "Let me go, please."

"Why?" She made it breathy and sexual, her phone sex operator voice I'd called it when we were dating.

"Because our date isn't until next week." My voice sounded choked and gravelly, that bass growl that usually came only during sex, or a great deal more foreplay than this.

"I love that I can still make you react like this," she said.

I looked at her; she had that teasing, happy look that if we'd been living together would have meant something. Now this was the closest I'd been to any woman in over six months, and I had to go to work, had to look at what they'd found at the Cookson house, had to help find a demon and the sorcerer it was riding. Mark Cookson might not be a real sorcerer with all the power that implied, but he had to have done sorcerous magic that used demons as its fuel and power base or he wouldn't have a demon sharing his body.

"And there it is, you went away into your head and the case, right? It was the case, wasn't it?"

She let me go when I stepped back again. She was back to being angry and I was about to join her. "I want you, but I can't have you now, and I have to go in to work and not be thinking of you, because if I do then I can't do my job."

"You used to like it when I teased you."

"When I knew I was coming home to you and the teasing would be satisfied, yes, very much yes, but not like this, Reggie."

"Like what?"

"Like it's a game, like you do X and I react Y. I love the sense of power it gives you, because it turns you on, and that turns me on. I love that you touched me today, that you let me touch you, hold you, kiss you, but I have to go, and I can't be wound up like this and have to leave, and have to go home alone."

"You really haven't been with anyone else since we separated, have you?"

"No, of course not."

She looked at me like she was trying to memorize my face. "I'm sorry, Zaniel."

"For what?" I asked.

"For a lot of things, but I'm sorry I teased you and then you have to go to work. I'm sorry I'm not ready to have you come home tonight and let me make good on the teasing. You're right, this was mean if I didn't mean to follow through."

"Thank you for the apology, but if you didn't mean it, why did you do it?" It was my turn to study her face. I wished she wasn't wearing the huge sunglasses. They were new since I'd moved out. I didn't like them on her; they hid too much of her face, more like a mask than glasses. Then I thought, *This is Reggie, I know her, stop being a lovestruck teenager and be a grown-up cop.* I didn't need to see her whole face to read her.

"Couldn't I have just wanted to be close to you?" she asked, but the moment she worded it that way I knew that wasn't why she'd done it.

"No," I said, just that, while I forced myself to notice her body language and what parts of her face I could see rather than her body.

"What do you mean, no? I want you, Zaniel. The sex has always been amazing."

I didn't want to have this conversation in the parking lot. It was just us, but there were security cameras; they almost certainly wouldn't be able to hear what we said, but it still seemed too personal to be out in the open. "This doesn't seem like a conversation for the parking lot," I said.

"Why, because you have to rush off to work?" she said, falling back into the irritation bordering on anger that had been her typical with me for a while.

"No, because I don't want to talk about our personal life in a parking lot with security cameras."

She looked up as if she were searching for a bird that had just flown overhead. "I don't see them."

"Try the building entrance and the secondary entrance just two cars past here."

She looked where I directed and saw them. She looked out at the parking lot behind us. "Is that another one attached to a light pole?"

"Yes," I said.

"I wouldn't have looked for them."

"It's my job to notice things like that."

"Okay, you've made your point," she said, still irritated, but calmer. "I want to talk more, Reggie, but just not here."

She licked her lips, which meant she was nervous, especially when she was wearing lipstick. "I don't want to wait a week to finish this talk," she said.

The fact that she wanted to see me sooner than our "date" ran through me like something electric, as if hope could have current to jolt from my fingers to my scalp. Why did that make me feel more hopeful than her rubbing herself up against me? I didn't know, and I didn't care.

"Yes, I mean, I agree I'd like to finish this talk before we meet for dinner."

She smiled then, and even with the sunglasses on I knew that the smile filled her eyes with that light that was warm and mischievous and sexy, and which I'd learned lately was only a few drops away from cruel, but it wasn't cruel today.

"Dinner date," she said, voice low and throaty, her phone sex voice again.

I should have just accepted the win, but it was too confusing, so I said, "Just a few minutes ago you were mad when I called it a date."

"Zaniel, I'm calling it a date now, don't push it." The voice was not sexy when she said it, but she wasn't irritated with me, just impatient.

"Yes, ma'am," I said.

She grinned at me, not sexy, but just her. "You're the only man who ever said that to me, like you're saying 'Yes, sir.'"

I smiled back. "In the army it means the same thing."

"I remember," she said. "Let's do a lunch this weekend where we can talk this out, so when we have the dinner it can be a real date without having to worry about all this."

I wasn't sure what *all this* was, and I really doubted that one lunch conversation would clear up everything that had gone wrong between us, but I didn't push it. "Sounds good," I said.

"Good, I know when you're on a case this serious that you don't know your schedule, but let's try for brunch or lunch tomorrow. My mom will be happy to babysit Connery if she knows we're trying to work things out," she said, and there was that easy confidence in her that I hadn't seen in weeks, maybe longer.

"I won't know my schedule, but I promise that I will do everything I can to see you tomorrow for at least an hour. I want to work things out, Reggie, I really do."

"Me, too, Zaniel," she said.

We had that awkward moment where we weren't sure if we should kiss goodbye. In the end she said, "We better not risk another kiss, or we might get carried away, cameras or no cameras."

I was almost certain she didn't mean it, but I took the upbeat teasing and ran with it. "That would be a shame," I said, putting the heat and eagerness into my words and face that she wanted. If she'd pushed it, I wouldn't have gone through with it, and probably she wouldn't have either. She was a high school teacher; she couldn't afford that kind of scandal. Even with her husband. As a cop, getting caught making out with my wife wouldn't be encouraged, but I wouldn't get in serious trouble.

Reggie laughed then, happy with my response. "I'll move my car so you can go catch the bad guys." She moved past me between my car and the one parked beside us, so that she had to brush lightly against me. It wasn't the body language of earlier, but it still stole my breath for a moment. She trailed her fingers down my arm as she moved past, getting her keys out of her pocket. She always kept a small key ring so if her purse got stolen, they wouldn't have her house keys. A friend in college had gotten mugged and then the guy had cleaned out her apartment with the keys later that week.

I don't know what made me go for broke, but I called after her, "Would it be pushing it if I told you I love you?"

She flashed me that sexy grin over her shoulder as she rounded the back of her car. "No, I love you, too."

Another little jolt of electric hope shot through me. It felt like my hair should be standing on end from it, but I knew it didn't show like that.

She got in her car, started the engine, and drove off, waving at me in the rearview mirror. I waved back until I knew she couldn't see me. I stood there just letting the last few minutes sink in; I wasn't sure how a promising therapy session had turned into a fight, and then into a kiss and two dates, but for once I didn't poke at it. I took the win and got in my car. I'd talk to Charleston. He'd do his best to see that I got to see Reggie tomorrow. No guarantees on a case like this, but he'd do his best. Heck, everyone on the squad would help me see her tomorrow, at least all the regulars that knew Reggie, and the new people wouldn't interfere. We actually had more successfully married couples in our unit than most of the other special squads. Charleston tried to run a family-friendly shop, and Ravensong as his second was seriously into happy wife, happy life. She and Louie had been together twenty-five years and married as soon as it was legal for same-sex couples to marry. Since they couldn't get married any sooner, I counted our unit as having three couples that had passed the twenty-five-year mark and were all still blissful together. For the first time in months, I prayed that Reggie and I would celebrate our seventh anniversary with me back in the house with her and Connery. You can pray for anything, but I try not to pray if I think it will take a miracle unless it's life and death. Being without my family felt like I was dying, but I wasn't; I was miserable, but I wasn't dying. Today I let myself pray that the talk tomorrow would go well, and the date would go better. We had two months until our anniversary; that didn't seem like it needed a miracle, not if Reggie and I both wanted it. I hoped we did. I prayed we did.

CHAPTER TWENTY-SIX

Lila was waiting for me at the head of the stairs inside the door that gave us the privacy of the landing, because almost everyone else but Charleston and me took the elevator. I must have looked surprised, because she said, "I wanted to be sure and talk to you before Adam Thornton found me again."

I frowned at her, confused now instead of surprised. "Why are you hiding from Adam? I know he can be annoying, but he's not that bad."

"He wants the evidence that we took from the parents' house."

"He is the medical examiner's assistant, so she probably sent him."

"I have Dr. Trent's permission to show you the items before they go to her lab."

I widened my eyes at that. "Why would the evidence go to the ME anyway?" I asked.

"Because it's biologicals, and anything that came off a living person or being goes to the ME now."

"Unless it needs special magical protection," I said.

Lila nodded. "Then it goes to the most appropriate authorized body, or organization, or personage that is best capable of dealing with it in a safe and sane manner that does not endanger themselves, the public, or any property or person that might be impacted by said evidence."

"Wow, I'm impressed that you've got that memorized," I said.

"I didn't, but I do after Mr. Adam Thornton has repeated it to me like a hundred times while we waited on you."

"If you have the ME's permission, why is he here?" I asked.

"Because she sent him along to make sure that the evidence goes to her lab after we've investigated it fully," she said, rolling her eyes.

"That means we have time to look at it magically," I said.

"By our definition of 'investigated fully,' yes, but Adam's interpretation is a lot different from ours."

"What do you mean?"

"I am hiding in a stairwell, Havoc, hoping I can sneak you in to look at the evidence without Adam Thornton hanging all over us."

"He's persistent, but he doesn't interfere with us doing our jobs."

"He's persistent with you, but he's always worse with me."

"What do you mean?" I asked.

She shook her head hard enough to make her ponytail bounce. "It doesn't matter right now; what does matter is you getting to see the evidence before Adam pillages it." She crossed her arms, her face far more unhappy than I expected from dealing with any coworker. I felt like I was missing something but didn't know what question to ask. For a second it felt like being back with Reggie, trying to figure out what women want, or what one woman in particular wants, or means. I closed my eyes and took a few deep, even breaths, trying to find my balance, trying to find me after therapy had ripped me open. Okay, after dealing with Reggie had made me deliriously happy, miserable, and confused.

"Sorry, Havoc, was therapy rough?"

I opened my eyes and shook my head. "The parking lot conversation was hard. She accused me of trying to follow her around to see if she was dating anyone else."

Lila sighed and closed her eyes as if I'd said a lot more than that. "Annie accused me of that, too."

"I know I haven't done it, and I'll give you the benefit of the doubt," I said.

"I followed her after she accused me of doing it."

I must have looked surprised, because she added, "I know my wife, my ex-wife, she's crazy, but there's a logic to it. I was pretty sure if she accused me of it, she was worried I would follow her, so I did."

I didn't want to ask, but I wanted to know, and she'd brought it up. "You don't have to answer, but was she?"

"Cheating on me, oh yeah. She'd found this cute brunette working as a barista at one of the coffee shops near her work. If I'd wanted proof, I could have taken plenty of pictures, she wasn't being careful."

"Did she want you to find out?" I asked.

Lila shrugged. "Who knows? I don't think she cheated while we were together, but Annie isn't a woman who likes to be alone. Once we weren't living together, I wasn't surprised she went looking for someone else to sleep over with."

"Reggie is okay alone; her independence was one of the things that I liked about her."

"Annie is not independent; she likes someone to take care of her, but then if you take care of her too much she feels smothered."

"Sounds like a no-win situation," I said.

Lila just nodded.

"I'm sorry," I said.

"And I'm sorry your marriage is going to shit, too."

I smiled before I could stop it and told her about Reggie wanting to clear the air tomorrow before our dinner date. By the time I was finished Lila was grinning at me.

"That's awesome, Havoc, really awesome."

"Thanks, remind me to talk to Charleston about the time off to-morrow."

"Will do, now let's see if we can sneak past Adam and let you see what we found."

"Come on, Lila, give me a hint, what's got you so excited?"

"I guess I could say standing next to a stud like you, but you wouldn't believe me."

I laughed. "No, I wouldn't."

"You'll see it in a few minutes. Charleston told me not to tell you ahead of time in case it's not what we think it is; he doesn't want me to contaminate your expectations or something like that."

"He's the lieutenant," I said.

She reached for the door handle, then said, "Don't talk until we're in the room with the stuff; if Thornton hears your voice, he won't let us see it without him hovering."

"Mum's the word," I said.

She frowned at me. "You use some of the oldest, fuddy-duddy ex-pressions sometimes, Havoc. You'd think you were old enough to be someone's grandpa."

"Where I was raised that's just the way everyone talks," I said.

"Oh, Havoc, I'm sorry, sometimes I forget you were raised in a monastery."

"I was raised at the College of Angels," I said.

"From what I hear, same diff, except it's co-ed."

I didn't know what to say to that, and she must have realized it, so she saved us both from an awkward moment by opening the door, peering through, and then waving me inside. Apparently, the coast was clear.

CHAPTER TWENTY-SEVEN

dam Thornton appeared from around the corner near the break room. He had on latex gloves and was carrying a large, empty paper bag. His gray eyes were very serious behind the round, black frames of his glasses. He was short and slender, and politically incorrect words like *effeminate* came to mind every time I saw him, which was probably why he always kept his brown hair cut short and very traditionally male-presenting.

"Give it up, Havoc," he said, his voice sharp, and if you didn't know him, you'd think he was angry, but he always sounded like that. If he hadn't been brilliant in the lab and at seeing things that everyone else missed, he'd have been fired, but instead he kept getting promoted. The ME just tried to keep him away from people, living people; the dead didn't mind that he had the social skills of a cranky rhinoceros.

"Hey, Adam, it's nice to see you, too."

He scowled at me. "You know I don't do social pleasantries, so we don't have to pretend, just give me my evidence and I'll leave."

"I told you that you can have the evidence after Havoc has seen it," Lila said, peeking out from behind me. I didn't realize that she'd been hidden from Adam's sight line until he jumped like she'd yelled *boo*.

"I-I don't mean the evidence you collected from the house, Li-Lila. I mean the evidence from the hospital."

Him stuttering when he talked to Lila was interesting; maybe there was more than one reason he bugged her more than the rest of us. "You should have all the evidence from the hospital," I told him. If he had a crush on Lila, I wasn't going to mention it.

His scowl deepened until I wanted to use my thumbs to rub his forehead smooth. I knew he was over thirty, older than me, actually, but he looked like he was still in his early twenties, except when he frowned hard enough and then he almost looked his age.

"Don't play games with me, Havoc."

"I'm not playing, Adam, I honestly don't know what you're talking about."

"First, stop calling me by my first name, and second, your shirt. Your shirt became evidence once you were attacked. You should never have left the crime scene with it."

I looked down at my shirt as if it had just appeared on me and realized two things. First, there was no blood on my shirt, but there were claw marks in the cloth—that made no sense; second, that made it even more evidence. "Okay, Thornton, you're right, I should have had it entered into evidence at the hospital."

The frown softened and he looked puzzled. "So, you're just admitting you were wrong?"

"Yes."

He frowned, stopped frowning, and looked at me with those big eyes behind the glasses like he didn't know what to do next. Not for the first time I wondered if he was on the autism spectrum somewhere, but I could never figure out a way to ask, and as long as he did his job it didn't matter anyway.

"Most people get angry when you tell them they're wrong," he said, frowning again.

"I don't get angry when I'm in the wrong. I've got an extra shirt in the locker room; let me change and you can have this one."

He shook the paper bag at me hard enough for it to rattle. "No, you've compromised its value as evidence enough as is, just take it off and put it in the bag."

"Adam," Lila said, "you're being unreasonable again."

"I haven't forgotten that you've kept me from a vital piece of evidence either, Li-Li . . . Detective Bridges. I will be waiting until the rest of the evidence from the home is ready to be transported."

"I thought you were in a hurry to get Havoc's shirt back to the lab," she said, her voice far too sweet for the circumstances. Lila is at her most underhanded when she sounds like that.

The other officers were beginning to stop what they were doing to look at us side-eyed. The buzz of the room was growing quieter as they started trying to listen in on us. Cops are some of the nosiest busybodies on the planet, or we can be.

"You can follow me into the locker room and watch me take it off," I offered.

He shook the bag at me again. "Just give me the shirt and I can get back to processing evidence, I've wasted enough time hunting the shirt down."

Not hunting me down but hunting the shirt down. Adam often talked about objects instead of people. "Just let me change and you can have it."

"Just take it off and give it to me."

"I am not going to strip off here when we can just go back into the locker rooms."

"Oh, come on, Havoc, give us a little show," Detective Athena Ravensong called out from her desk. She was one of the most senior members of the squad, same age as Charleston, but where he hit the gym and watched his nutrition, Ravensong ate cheerfully. She did everything with joyous gusto, so she looked more like someone's slightly overweight grandmother than one of the most powerful witches in the western half of the country.

"Athena, you're being sexist and objectifying Havoc; we had a mandatory class on that," Detective Raymond Stiltskin said as he walked through the squad room with a cup of coffee almost bigger than he was. He looked fat in the boxy suit and jacket, but he wasn't. In fact, he was one of the most serious weight lifters in the department. He was also one of the shortest; combined with the serious weight lifting, getting a suit that fit his shoulders meant that he looked like he was wearing his dad's suits. He had the sleeves and pants hemmed because he had to, but other than that like most cops he couldn't afford professional tailoring, or better yet a tailored designer suit, maybe something from Italy. Nothing short of that was going to make Stiltskin look good in suits.

"He doesn't mind an old lady admiring the view, do you, Havoc?" She waggled her eyebrows behind her wire-rimmed glasses.

I chuckled, because Athena had the ability to say almost anything and make it funny instead of offensive.

"If you take the shirt off here, she can admire the view and I can get back to work," Adam said, holding the bag out to me like a kid at trick-or-treat.

"Athena isn't the only one here; for the consideration of others we need to do this in the locker room," I said.

"As long as I finish this report before I leave today, I don't care who takes off what," Detective MacGregor said. He peered at his computer screen over the half glasses he'd picked up at the nearest Walgreens. They were cheater glasses, but the way MacGregor kept leaning into the screen they weren't helping much. He was MacGregor number one, or Old MacGregor until we found a nickname for the new guy.

"You need new glasses, Mac," Stiltskin said as he went back to his desk with the coffee.

"I'm fine," MacGregor said, moving closer to the screen and then away from it, as if trying to find the perfect distance.

"Come on, Adam, let's hit the locker room, so we can both get back to work," I said. I even started to move that direction, but he moved in front of me, blocking the way.

"Everyone's fine with us doing it here."

I looked down at the smaller man and searched his face, but he truly had taken everyone at face value. They said they were fine with me stripping off in front of them, so as far as Adam was concerned it was okay.

I looked at the larger room to the unit members who hadn't spoken up and said, "Can someone help me explain this to him?"

Athena chimed in with, "Havoc is shy, it would make him uncomfortable to change in public."

"Why?" Adam asked, looking from her to me.

Stiltskin left his coffee at his desk and came to stand near us. He was short enough that he had to look up at Adam; I wondered if he got a crick in his neck when he gave me eye contact. He lowered his voice, so that he wasn't talking to the entire squad room.

"Wouldn't it embarrass you to strip out of your shirt in front of everyone?"

Adam seemed to actually have to give that some thought before he said, "It might, but other people have been making fun of me for being a man of slight build for most of my life. Havoc doesn't have that issue."

"Just because Havoc and I both have more muscles than you do doesn't mean we'd be comfortable taking our shirts off here in the squad room," Stiltskin said.

"But why, if you both look fit and muscular with your shirts off?"

Officer Odette Minis said, "It's not professional to take off your clothes at work." She had her uniform hat under one arm, so her tight cornrows showed in the bun at the back of her neck. Her hair was almost the same pale honey brown as her skin. If she'd had brown eyes, she'd have been monochrome, but her gray eyes looked almost bluish in the dark blue uniform. She was one of the uniforms who had scored so high on the psychic and magical assessment that she was ours as a test run. If her week of being with us in uniform went well, she'd be temporary plainclothes like Officer Goliath MacGregor, but she already had one thing he didn't seem to have. We had plenty of psychics and witches, but common sense, that was rare everywhere.

Adam nodded. "Okay, I understand that." He stepped aside so I could lead the way to the locker room.

I mouthed a *thank you* to Officer Minis as we passed. She nodded and smiled.

"I guess I'll have to actually go to the gym if I'm ever going to see Havoc's six-pack," Athena called after us.

Officer Minis's smile went up a notch. I watched her gray-blue eyes give me the up-and-down look. I fought not to return the look, because I'd noticed the first week that her uniform fit her well. I had done my best not to think too much beyond that. I was happy that I'd gone to couples counseling before I came back in to work, because now I had a dinner date with my wife, and we'd actually kissed. Those facts helped me not to flirt with yet another woman today.

I walked resolutely toward the locker room with Adam and his paper bag trailing behind me. I swore I could feel Minis staring at me. I did not look back to see if she was staring at my ass, because that was on her; if I looked back and smiled at her, then it was on me. I made the locker room without looking back. Point for me.

CHAPTER TWENTY-EIGHT

The locker room was empty except for us. Adam watched me solemnly, not looking away, so I used my body to hide my combination as I spun the lock. It wasn't that I thought he would steal from me, but I'd worked too long as a police officer to trust much of anyone.

It meant my back was to Adam as I took off my jacket and hung it on a hook in the locker. The holes in the jacket were from Kate's nails, not the demon. I undid my belt so I wouldn't have to pull the dress shirt over the stomach wounds. It meant that everything on it slid around a little, but I figured I was safe enough in the locker room. Then Adam started to crowd me.

"I need your jacket, too," Adam said.

"If you're looking for claw marks so you can identify the type of demon, you only need the shirt."

"You've got bandages on your right arm, Havoc, that means I need the jacket to help us line up the cuts in the shirt."

"The arm isn't from the demon," I said.

"Did you have an altercation with something else today?"

I hesitated, because the truth was, yes. I just hated to out Kate. She wanted to be human like everyone else; if I told the truth to Adam, he had no filters. He wouldn't talk about an ongoing case, but he might talk about Kate to the wrong person. If it had been almost anyone else in the ME's office, I'd have told them the truth, and of course they would have just called me to bring my clothes down to them. No one but Adam would have chased me down like this.

"It's hard to explain," I said, and knew it was the wrong thing to have said as soon as I saw his jaw clench.

"I am good at my job, Detective Havelock," he said; his eyes darkened like gray clouds filling up with rain.

"I know you are, Adam, I mean Assistant to the Medical Examiner Thornton." Something on the bandages had caught on the shirtsleeve so I couldn't get it over them.

"I am not stupid, Detective."

"I never said you were." I tried to force the sleeve over, but it actually hurt to press on it. Scratches always hurt worse than deep wounds at first, more nerve endings exposed to the air.

"Then why is it hard to explain to me? Are you afraid I won't understand the attack, the demon, or the magic involved?"

"No, that's not what I meant at all," I said, and tried to think of a way to save the conversation without hurting Kate. She'd been hurt enough for one day.

"I know more magic than you do."

"I don't doubt that," I said, and finally gave up getting the sleeve over the bandages, which meant I turned to the other man with the shirt hanging off my arms like I couldn't dress myself.

"Then why are you insinuating that I won't understand a simple demon attack?" he asked, his gray eyes the color of storm clouds. Apparently, he was one of those people whose eyes just got darker the more pissed they were; if they reached black, I wondered what would happen.

"First, there was nothing simple about the attack," I said, but he wasn't looking at me, or he wasn't looking at my face. He was staring at my stomach.

He reached out to touch my stomach. I jerked back out of reach and that hurt, but I didn't want him touching my bare stomach. Maybe I'd been too fast to say he wasn't bisexual, because he tried to touch my stomach again.

"Stop it, Thornton. We don't know each other that well."

He frowned up at me. "I'm not trying to touch your abs, I'm trying to get a sense of the demon marks. Did anyone get pictures of your wounds or take measurements?"

"Pictures, yes, but no measurements," I said.

"That was careless," he said.

"This isn't like a true physical beast," I said. "The demon's hands can change shape. Measurements don't help with beings like this."

"They do with some demons, Havelock; you have enough background in the Infernal to know that some of the demonic have set shapes."

"This one didn't," I said.

"Let me take measurements now."

"I'd have to remove the bandages for that."

He looked up at me with a so-what? look on his face. "Thornton, you either need to get out of the lab more often, or never leave the lab."

"What is that supposed to mean?" he asked, frowning and ready to take offense.

"It means I am not ripping off a clean medical dressing in a locker room just so you can take measurements that won't matter. The demon changed shape several times while we were fighting it; anything that mutable won't be caught from physical measurements."

Adam leaned closer to my bandages as if he could see through them. I tried to remember what his psychic talent was, but it was something to do with lab work, so why was he bent over like he could see through the bandages?

I finally asked, "What are you looking at, Adam?"

"Your wounds, they're partially healed."

"You can see through the bandages?" I asked.

He nodded and leaned in even closer like his nose was going to bump into me soon. "I can see that which is hidden," he said, as if that explained what he was doing. I knew it was psychic and not magic because I felt nothing. Psychic gifts can be used unseen even around other gifted people, but magic is harder to hide; no one knows why it works that way, it just does.

"Help me get the cuffs unbuttoned and you can have the shirt," I said, hoping to distract him from getting his face any closer to my abdomen.

Adam looked up at me, his gray eyes back to their usual color. He wasn't angry anymore; he was interested. "I've seen bodies cut up by demons; you should be in the hospital, Havoc, not almost healed."

"There was an angel, it helped heal me," I said, and just reached across my own body to start trying to undo the cuff on my injured arm, because Adam didn't seem to want to help. My arm coming across my stomach did move him a little back from me. He even stood up.

"I didn't hear about an angel manifesting at the hospital."

"It wasn't exactly a manifestation," I said. I was not sharing what happened with him, for the same reason I didn't want to share Kate's secret with him; he talked when he shouldn't have about things sometimes. What had happened at the hospital would get around; there'd been too many witnesses for it not to become gossip, but none of it would come from me. They could make up what they wanted, but I wasn't helping the rumors.

"Is that why the wounds are almost closed without scabbing, as if the skin is just closing back up?" he asked.

It was harder to undo the cuff buttons with the shirt inside out, but I finally got them, but realized the bandages still impeded me getting the sleeve off, which meant I needed the other sleeve off first. It's funny that sometimes smaller injuries can surprise you with how inconvenient they can be.

"Yes, if you're healed by Celestial energy it doesn't scar," I said. I started to reach my hands toward each other like normal, but the arm protested. If there was another angel anytime soon, I'd need to remember to ask for extra healing for the arm. I moved the uninjured arm across my body again. Moving my hand on the injured side tugged at the scratches so the pain was sharper. I wasn't sure what fumbling at the buttons moved in my arm that made it hurt so much, but again small movements matter if you're hurt.

"Here, I'll help you," he said, and just reached out to do the same thing I'd asked him to do earlier. It was like he hadn't heard me ask, too lost in peering at my wound through the medical dressing. How had he done that?

"How did you see through the bandages?" I asked, while he focused just as completely on the buttons on my shirt as he had on everything else. When he didn't answer right away, I let him finish the task before I repeated my question.

"I'm sorry," he said, "I didn't think about you being injured and the difficulty of taking the shirt off." He took the shoulder of my shirt down so I could more easily slide my arm out of the sleeve.

"Thanks, okay, I appreciate the help now."

He actually stepped behind me, helping me pull my injured arm out of the other sleeve. He held it up in gloved hands and started letting it fold down into the paper bag. I could have shoved it in the bag, but I couldn't have made it look neat with just one hand like that.

He sealed the bag, then got a marker out of his pocket and wrote on the bag, so it would go with all the rest of the evidence from the hospital. "Please initial here, Detective," he said, holding it out to me and putting his palm underneath the plastic so I had a surface to write on. The shirt was lower than the plastic top, so we weren't pressing on the evidence. It was neatly done.

"How did you see my wound?" I asked again.

"I have a very specialized type of remote viewing, except instead of being able to see something hundreds of miles away I see through things that are directly around me even if they're hidden from my physical sight."

"Like my wounds."

"Yes," he said.

"Or a clue that's hidden under a stain," I said, making a logic leap.

He smiled at me as happy as I'd ever seen him. "Exactly."

"No wonder the ME values you, you're perfect for the job."

He grinned and it transformed his face so that he was . . . pretty. I'd have never said that to his face, but he was just so delicate that *handsome* seemed the wrong word.

"Everyone covered in there? Lieutenant wanted to check what was taking so long," Lila said. She did hesitate, to give us time to yell *stop*. Ravensong would have come on in, assuming she'd warned us enough. It was a co-ed locker room, but we all tried to warn anyone who was shy.

Both Adam and I looked toward the door as she opened it; he still had that great smile on his face. Lila stopped and looked at us as the door swung shut behind her. There was an expression on her face I couldn't quite read.

Adam said, "Are you unhappy with us?"

She shook her head, ponytail bouncing. "No, why do you ask?"

"I'm not always great with reading people's faces, so sometimes I just ask," he said.

"I couldn't decipher her expression either," I said, "and I *am* good at reading people."

Adam looked over his shoulder at me. "Are you making fun of me?"

"No, I'm being honest."

"The expression is me finding two handsome men in the locker room, but I'm at work so I can't be unprofessional," Lila said.

"You're just being polite," Adam said.

"No, I'm not," she said, and I realized what the look had meant at the door now. She'd seen Adam's smile and seen him in a new light just like I had, except it might have meant more to her than it had to me. I wasn't sure, but I was betting she saw him as attractive now. Would it change things between them? Probably not, but then again you never knew with women, or Heaven help us, men either. A small change in perspective can translate to something larger, or it can just sink back into business as usual.

Adam frowned at her. "I know what I look like and I know what Havoc looks like, especially with him shirtless."

"Havoc is my friend and the fact that he looks good out of his clothes isn't something that a friend remarks on," Lila said.

Adam did that frown that made me want to smooth his brow again. "I don't understand the difference when it's just words."

"I know you don't," she said, but she wasn't irritated with him like normal, almost patient especially for Lila. She wasn't incredibly patient with anyone. She wasn't cruel, but she wasn't always kind either.

I turned to open my locker and give them what privacy I could, though Lila wouldn't need privacy from just me if she was intent on moving forward with something, but I thought Adam might be a little shy with me watching. I shouldn't have worried about it.

"I wish I could read your face," Adam said.

"I wish you could, too," she said.

I looked at the clothes folded in my locker; neither of them really matched the dress slacks I was wearing, but I finally chose the black one because I'd bought it most recently. The other one was a tank top that I'd had forever and cut the sleeves off and it was too revealing even with the jacket over it.

"You aren't mad at me, are you?" he asked, and I knew he wasn't asking me.

"No, what made you ask?" Lila said.

"Because I can't always see when people are irritated with me, so I keep pushing and then they get mad."

"You're not being irritating right now, it's a nice change," she said.

He missed the humor and said, "I don't want to irritate you."

"What do you want?" she asked, and I knew that tone in her voice. I'd heard her question suspects with it when she was the good cop, and I'd heard it when she was flirting—for Lila, they were both a type of negotiation.

"I'm really bad at this part," Adam said.

"What part?" she asked.

"If I say the truth, you'll get mad."

"I promise that whatever you say I won't get mad; I may not like it, but I won't get angry."

"I tend to make women upset," he said.

"Just say what you want, because you telling me I'll be upset with you after I've promised not to be is getting on my nerves."

"I told you," he said.

I kept my back to them as I got dressed, and it wasn't for my modesty's sake. The T-shirt didn't hurt going on over my arm, but the suit jacket forced me to go slower. I turned so that I could see myself in the mirror at the end of the locker area. The black looked better than I'd expected, like one of those designer T-shirts instead of the only clean shirt I had that fit me.

"I'm going to give you two a few minutes alone; just tell me what room I need to go to," I said.

"Don't go," Lila said; so that was that, when a female friend asks you to stay around when she's talking to another man, you stay.

Adam glanced at me, then back to her. "I'm sorry I'm being irritating, or weird."

"Do you want a coffee date?" she suggested.

"I'd like a date with you, yes," he said. His affect never changed, and I couldn't tell if he was controlling his emotions so she wouldn't know how much it meant to him, or if it was just the way he processed.

"Let's take it slow, coffee date first, see if we have anything in common," she said, but she was giving that wry smile that meant she was sort of laughing at herself.

"I don't drink coffee; can we make it a tea date?" he asked.

Her smile widened, but she nodded. "Sure, whatever you like to drink. We'll just do it at a coffee shop that serves other things."

"I'd like that," he said.

"Me, too. Let's talk details after we've shown Havoc the evidence. We don't want to keep Lieutenant Charleston waiting any longer than we already have."

"Agreed," he said, and there was none of that bubbling excitement that I would have felt, but that didn't mean he wasn't feeling it.

We all filed out of the locker room with Adam back to his base frown. I held the door and caught Lila's gaze as she went through. She rolled her eyes and gave that smile again. It was enough for me to know that she didn't know if the coffee/tea date was a good idea, but something about that one smile had made her want to try. My personal life wasn't in good enough shape for me to throw stones at anyone else, so I just followed the two of them through, making sure my face was pleasantly blank. If the rumor got out that they were maybe dating, it wouldn't come from me. Though if I had the chance later, I was going to ask Lila what had made Adam go from someone so irritating she hid from him to offering a coffee date. I'd have bet good money that Lila would never have given Adam the time of day; just more proof that I had no idea what any woman would do when it came to romance.

CHAPTER TWENTY-NINE

expected Lila to take us to one of the rooms that were bespelled or warded against supernatural powers, but I was wrong.

"Ravensong and Charleston both wanted you to see the evidence outside a warded room," she said, as if she'd read my mind.

"You must be referring to Havoc," Adam said.

"Yes," she said with a slight upturn of her mouth instead of her usual irritation at his comments. The change in her was almost magical. I didn't think Adam had done something psychic to her, it was more like some memory or feeling had been triggered in her. If the change in attitude continued to be this drastic, I would have to talk to Lila about it just in case some stray bit of magic from some other case had hit her. We'd had it happen before, once with a love potion and once with something murderous. Of the two, infatuation was much preferred.

It was one of the smaller interrogation rooms without an observation window; those were saved for rooms where we put people and things that we wanted to observe, so whatever was in here, no one was expecting it to do anything worth seeing. There'd only be the table and a couple of chairs in the room.

Charleston was standing beside the table, looking at the door. He was frowning, though not at us, more like he was thinking hard and staring into space. Ravensong and Officer MacGregor the Younger were bending over the table like they were looking at something sitting on it. So whatever Lila had collected from Mark Cookson's parents' house was small.

I didn't sense anything evil in the room, in fact I didn't sense much of anything that was wrong. There was always a low hum of energy from Ravensong and Charleston. Their magic was just too much a part of them for me not to notice them at that subliminal level. It was mystical white noise like the heating and cooling in a house; you only notice it when it stops.

Goliath MacGregor unbent and could almost look me in the eye. He was as tall as Charleston, but built leaner like me, except even more willowy—the way I'd looked before the separation had me hitting the gym harder. He and I had only been out together a handful of times and twice people had mistaken him for a famous basketball player. I didn't follow sports, so I didn't know the name, but I looked it up later and I didn't see the resemblance. Goliath was tall, black, and handsome and so was the famous player, but he wasn't as muscled as the athlete and I thought Goliath was more fair of face. First time he got recognized had been by a middle-aged couple, the second by two pretty, star-struck women. He'd told them he wasn't the famous player both times. They'd all been embarrassed at the mistake. He'd gotten the phone numbers of the young women with a line that went something like he could make their fantasy come true. I'd never thought of turning something so awkward into a pickup line, and I'd never asked him if he'd followed up with the "date." I didn't want to know, especially since once they were out of sight, he'd turned to me and said, "We all look alike, I guess." I'd apologized as if somehow it was my fault just by skin association. He'd accepted the apology with a smile, and a "Not your fault, Havoc." I didn't understand how he could think the two women were racist and still want to have sex with them, and not being black I didn't feel like I could ask him to explain it.

Charleston asked, "What do you sense, Havoc?"

I realized I'd been staring at Goliath longer than necessary, but I realized why. I couldn't "hear" the hum of his magic either, but now that I couldn't sense it, I knew that his powers were close to the same level of white noise as Charleston and Ravensong, which made him a lot more powerful than I'd realized.

"Nothing and I mean nothing, Lieutenant. I don't even feel anything coming from you, Ravensong, or MacGregor. It's like all the magic in the room is dampened."

"Hey, it's not me," Lila said.

"I know, because even when you use your powers, I can still feel the hum of Ravensong and Charleston. I haven't been around Mac-Gregor here when you went into full null, so I don't know, but I'm betting it would be the same; right now there's nothing."

"She doesn't aim her powers at us," Charleston said.

"Wait," Goliath MacGregor said, "she's a psychic null, they're like light switches—on, all the magic in the room stops working, off and the magic works again. It's an area-of-effect power, not a point-and-shoot."

Charleston said, "Do you want to explain, Bridges?"

"I can aim my nulling field to the front, leaving my team free to work magic behind me."

"She's being modest," Charleston said. "She can narrow her field of effect down to a few feet, so that the rest of us can move into the room and still work psychic or magical gifts and the criminals can't."

Goliath looked at Lila, and there was nothing but respect on his face. "That's very impressive, I've never heard of any psychic null that was able to narrow their field of effect. It was explained as a sort of psychic version of an electromagnetic pulse."

"Most of them are," Charleston said.

"But I'm not blindsiding Havoc," Lila said.

"We felt it at the house," Goliath said.

"Let me see whatever 'it' is, and we'll go from there," I said.

Ravensong moved aside and I could suddenly see a small bottle. I thought glass, then realized it was crystal set in a delicate lace of gold. It was beautiful like something that you'd see in a museum or in an old black-and-white movie in the hands of a queen. It didn't look like anything that a nineteen-year-old college student like Mark Cookson would have in his possession.

"Before I describe it, tell me if it looks beautiful to anyone else."

"It's pretty," Lila said.

"It's like an old-fashioned perfume bottle that my great-aunt Lottie would have had on her vanity. She wore feather-edged silk robes and nightgowns. When I was ten and my sister was eight Aunt Lottie took us out for high tea at the fanciest hotel restaurant we'd ever seen. She wore a feather boa." Ravensong smiled, her face alight with happy nostalgia.

"It's like an old movie prop," Charleston said.

"Is it an illusion?" Lila asked.

"What do you see?" I asked.

"Crystal and gold, like it's some kind of oversized jewelry," she said.

"I think we all see the same bottle," Charleston said.

"It's a beautiful bottle, what made you gather it as evidence?" I asked.

"First, look at it, does it look like something a nineteen-year-old guy would have in his man cave?" Lila said.

"It did sort of stand out," Goliath said.

"The bottle was sitting in this little alcove hidden behind books like a twelve-year-old girl hides her diary," Lila said.

"His room looked like it belonged to a much younger boy," Goliath said.

"Some parents don't let their kids update their rooms," Charleston said.

"Maybe," Goliath said, "but the room felt like this Mark Cookson just stopped. It was all arrested development."

"According to the techies his browser history was a lot of incel sites, angry-at-women-for-not-fucking-you kind of shit," Lila said.

"That explains the rape and violence," Ravensong said, "but it doesn't explain this."

"It doesn't feel evil, and it seems to dampen magic better than Lila does. What made you look behind the books in the first place?" I asked.

"The choice of books," Lila said.

Goliath nodded. "They were occult, but nothing too unusual except that they were right next to a set of Hardy Boys mysteries."

"Hardy Boys, really?" Ravensong said. "I used to read those when I was in junior high, along with Nancy Drew."

"The whole room was a mix of younger-than-high-school-boy stuff and then the occult," Goliath said.

"Did you say that the bottle was behind the occult books?" Adam asked. It was almost startling that he was still in the room. I'd noticed he could be so quiet that you forgot about him, until he decided to go back to being his usual persistent self.

"Yes," Goliath said.

"So, the occult books marked the spot like an X on a map in a Hardy Boys mystery?" Adam asked.

"I guess," Goliath said.

"It's like it wanted to be found," Adam said.

"You mean Cookson wanted the bottle to be found?" Lila said.

Adam shook his head. "No, the bottle wanted to be found."

"The bottle can't want anything, Thornton, it's an inanimate object," Goliath said.

Adam was shaking his head slowly back and forth, staring at the bottle. "The bottle can't, but what's inside it can."

"How do you know what's inside it?" Goliath said.

"Who told you?" Lila asked.

Adam just kept shaking his head. "I can see it."

"He saw my wounds through my bandages in the locker room," I said.

Adam nodded. "I see what is hidden," he said, his voice distant like he was listening to something we couldn't hear.

"What do you see, Thornton?" Charleston asked.

"Blood," he said.

"He's right about it being blood," Goliath said.

"Human blood?" I asked.

"There was human blood on the outside of the bottle when the techs swiped it," he said.

"Not just human blood," Adam said, still staring at the bottle as if there was a label to read.

"He's right again," Goliath said.

"What's in it, besides human blood?" I asked.

"Demon," Adam said, almost dreamily.

"Now you've spoiled the surprise," Lila said to him.

He did a long, slow blink like he was having to drag himself back from whatever metaphysical music he was listening to in his head.

"You got all that from swabbing the bottle?" I asked.

Ravensong nodded.

"What kind of freak wastes one of the rarest magical ingredients on the planet by spilling it down the bottle?" Goliath asked.

"Mark Cookson," Charleston said.

"What can you sense from it, Havoc?" Ravensong asked.

"Gently," Charleston warned.

I nodded; I could do gentle magically, it's what I'd been doing most of my life once I left the College. I concentrated and just like that I could see the glow at my back that was my Guardian Angel. It wasn't like the cold fire of the angel that had put Gimble in the hospital, but soft, pure white light, steady like a night light to guide you through the darkness. It could grow into something large and powerful to protect us like dawn spreading across the sky until the world was covered in sunlight.

I looked at the bottle again, but this time I asked the angels to help me see more. Angels will do what you ask, because your free will is what makes the choices; you can listen to your better angels when they warn you that something is a bad idea, but if you give them an order, a request, tell them *I need your help*, they will do what you ask, because that's the way free will works—your free will, not theirs, because if everything goes according to God's plan they don't have any.

The spells on the crystal showed like golden lines forming script. It was a mix of Celestial and Infernal as if the bottle had been designed to hold more than just human and demon blood. The metal lacework around it glowed red and orange as if it were being shoved into the forge again.

Adam said, "Don't do it."

"Havoc is just looking at the spell on it," Ravensong said. "I think there's Celestial magic in its creation, not just Infernal."

I nodded, and said softly, "Yes." What I was doing shouldn't have damaged any of the spells. I wasn't putting energy into anything, just reading what was already there, but not everything likes to be read.

The metal glowed orange and yellow now, the red lost as the heat grew. "The metal's glowing."

"The bottle looks the same," Goliath said.

Ravensong moved closer to it. "It's wavering like heat."

"Stop, Havoc, stop what you're doing," Charleston said.

I stopped, pulling back so that I couldn't see the lettering traced on the bottle. The glow at my back had hands now, resting lightly on my shoulders. Guardian Angels don't manifest physically without a reason.

The top of the bottle began to unscrew itself as if some invisible hand were twisting it.

Charleston said, "Lila, disable it."

Lila stepped forward and the rest of us moved back so she had a clear field of "fire." Her hands were loose at her sides, but her stance was solid, stacked, and ready for action. She could do her psychic ability so quietly that the bad guys never saw it coming, but when she didn't have to hide, she looked like she was getting ready for a physical fight instead of a psychic one.

I never felt anything happen when she used her power; it was more like the world got quieter, like floating in silence as if standing in the middle of Lila's power would be the most relaxing thing in the world, but then her power didn't work on Celestial energies, and that was mainly what I did. She just cleared the psychic debris for me.

The stopper on the bottle stopped moving just like it was supposed to, and then it was as if the air in the room took a breath and the stopper began to unscrew itself again.

Lila's voice was controlled as she said, "It's not stopping."

"Ravensong, can you throw up a circle of protection while I get a containment box?" Charleston asked.

"If Havoc plays battery for me, yes," she said.

"Whatever you're going to do, do it fast," Lila said, still standing in front of the bottle, hands in fists now, physical strain showing in her arms and shoulders, feet digging into the floor as if she was standing against some invisible force that she was keeping away from the rest of us.

Charleston yelled, "MacGregor, Thornton, with me." They were running before the door closed behind them. Running not away, but for one of the magical containment boxes that we had in storage on this floor for the rare objects that we couldn't handle any other way.

I went to stand behind Ravensong, who was facing the table behind Lila like a second line of defense. Most witches need words to call the quarters and put up a magical circle; some of them even needed bits of the elements water, rocks, chimes, smoke, a candle. Ravensong spread her arms to the sky, legs wide and firm so she stood like a tree, roots in the earth and hands reaching for the sky. I stood behind her, my legs fixed wide and steadying, and if I'd been a Wiccan priest to her priestess, I would have either mimicked her stance except with my arms pointed in the opposite direction or crossed my arms over my chest; instead I put my left hand on her shoulder and told the angels to help me to help her work this spell. That was enough to drop my psychic shielding and let Ravensong tap into my energy. I was literally acting as a battery to amplify her magic.

"Narrow your field, Bridges," Ravensong said.

The three of us had done this before in the field, never here inside the unit itself, but location didn't matter; magic is everywhere.

"How small?" Lila asked.

"Small as you can make it."

"Got it," Lila said.

I felt the familiar warmth of Ravensong's magic and gave my own power to hers. My Guardian Angel merged with the glow at her back, and then I felt the four quarters spring to life: North like a huge towering oak tree standing phantomlike but so real that I swear I could feel its roots reaching down into the center of the Earth and hear its leaves rustling as it grew skyward; East was wind and birds on the wing and then a towering cyclone whirling and waiting to sweep away all danger if you had the power and nerve to control it; South was fire towering upward as if God's voice should come out of it; West was ocean and rain along the shore gentle and cleansing. It took seconds for it all to happen, but we were already in that time between, so that seconds of real time felt like so much longer for us. Ravensong called Goddess and God, and their power filled the space between with that soft, skin-ruffling power that felt both gentle and powerful. Ravensong's God was not the one I prayed to, and her Goddess was not the mother of my God, but they all blessed this circle because I gave my power to the witch to strengthen her circle and keep us all safe.

Ravensong's voice rang out: "The circle is closed! So mote it be!"

I echoed her: "So mote it be!"

The circle closed with an almost audible pop as if the pressure inside it was denser than the outside world.

"Can't . . . hold," Lila said through gritted teeth.

"Shut down, we've got it," Ravensong said.

Lila didn't argue, just stepped away from the table and let us have a clear view of the enchanted bottle, because that was what it had to be. You didn't find many enchanted items in modern times, things where the magic had been forged into each piece of its making. Most of them were old, the art of their making lost centuries ago, and they were all powerful.

The stopper unscrewed itself, tittering at the mouth of the bottle, balanced to fall. Something dark moved up the side of the crystal bottle. There wasn't time to cross the distance, but we stood within sacred space and there were other ways to move. Ravensong reached toward the bottle with her hand, but it was her totem, a phantom raccoon, that raced across the floor to climb the table and try to grab the stopper. It should have worked, but as the totem reached for the bottle, reality flickered in a way that I'd never seen happen inside a circle before, and when the raccoon reached the bottle, it had moved just out of reach. The stopper fell and the bottle was open. Ravensong yelled, "Bridges, get down!"

Lila dropped to the floor, covering her head as if she was tucking for an explosion. It might help protect her, or it might not. I stayed at Ravensong's back, feeding her energy as she raised her hands and did a spell without a word or a rune, or anything but her faith and the pentagram she always wore, but she had the Goddess and the God like weight and presence inside the circle. Her raccoon had run back to her side, and I saw her other mystical companions begin to manifest around her, and my Guardian Angel began to grow at my back, and then something exploded. Ravensong and I were thrown backward into the wall. I had a choice to save myself or cushion her when we hit; I chose her, she was my priestess in that moment, and as her acting priest one of my jobs was to protect her. My head hit the wall and all the light, all the magic went away, swallowed by the darkness as I lost consciousness. My last thought was *God, please keep them safe.*

CHAPTER THIRTY

Hands on me; I grabbed them, fought them. Someone screamed and it wasn't me. A voice I should have known yelled, "Havoc, they're trying to help you."

"Detective Havelock, stand down! That's an order!" I knew that voice, too. It made me blink and try to look at who I was fighting. There was a paramedic crumpled on the floor beside me. Charleston loomed over both of us standing so that he looked like a giant, as tall as the ceiling. The moment I thought that, I knew something was wrong with me. Was I hurt?

"Do you know who I am?" he asked.

"Yeah," I said, but my voice sounded too low, so I said it again.

"Do you know your name?"

"Havelock, Zaniel Havelock, Havoc."

"Do you know where you are?"

I looked around the room. "Interrogation room."

He almost smiled. "What city are you in?"

I frowned at him. "The City of Angels."

"Do you know who I am?"

"Charleston, you're my lieutenant."

"Yes."

"What happened? Why am I on the floor? What happened to the medic?"

A woman's voice said, "You happened to him."

I looked toward the voice, but I couldn't see her past Charleston. "Who is that?"

She peered around Charleston's side, looking child-sized compared to him. She looked angry. "I'm his partner." She pointed down to the paramedic on the floor.

"What happened to him?"

"I told you, you happened." She knelt beside her fallen partner and she looked even tinier that way. Was she really that petite or was I more out of it than I thought? Charleston was a giant and she was doll-like. It was like everything was all funhouse mirrors.

Her partner groaned and started to push his way up from the floor. She started trying to examine him, but he said, "Look at our patient first, not me."

"Our patient knocked you cold and may have broken your nose," she said, her voice warm with anger.

Her partner turned his head enough for me to see the blood all over the front of his face and shirt. "Did I do that?" I couldn't remember doing it, or maybe I did. I remembered hands on me, and I hadn't wanted them to touch me.

The female paramedic glared at me. "Yes, for the third time, you did this."

"He's hurt, Becki," her partner said, and I realized he was trying to make excuses for me. That seemed really sporting of him since I'd just hit him in the face.

"I'm sorry, I didn't know who was touching me," I said.

"He got attacked by demonic energy, Becki; anyone would fight."

He leaned against the wall and used the dressing she gave him to press against his still-bleeding nose, but that was all he'd let her do for him. He insisted on her looking at me first. I might owe him a drink later if he kept being that nice about it.

Becki grumbled, but she knelt beside me and again she fit between me and the closest chair. I wasn't hallucinating, she was just that tiny.

She looked at my eyes with a flashlight, then told me to use just my eyes to follow her finger as she moved it back and forth. Her frown softened a little. I didn't know if that was good or bad, or just meant she was calming down.

"Neil was trying to put a brace on your neck when you clocked him," she said, and was back to sounding angry, maybe it was just her default.

"Can you wiggle your fingers and toes?" Neil asked, his voice muffled from holding the dressing against his nose.

I looked down my body to try moving everything and noticed there was fresh dressing and medical tape across my stomach. I ignored it for now and tried to move my fingers and toes. "Everything moves," I said.

"Good," he said.

"Why are there fresh bandages on my stomach?"

"The wounds on your stomach started bleeding again," Neil said.

"If they'd put stitches in at the hospital they wouldn't have started bleeding again," Becki said, frowning her disapproval.

"It was already healed closed, so the doctor didn't think it was necessary. Did the wounds reopen?" I asked.

"No, but there was still blood coming through the wounds when we got here," Neil said.

"The attack was just earlier today, though, right?" she asked.

"Yes."

"But angel magic healed it," Neil said, and his voice sounded wetter, as if more blood was going down the back of his throat. That was not a good sound. It meant I'd really done a number on his nose. I might owe him more than just a drink.

"You told them what happened at the hospital," I said, looking up at Charleston.

"I told them what I could, but I'm a Voodoo Priest, not an angel worker, so I could only give them the magic I could sense and what you said was happening."

"Why didn't the angels heal it completely?" Becki asked.

"I didn't ask them to. I asked them to help us save the woman who was in jeopardy."

"Usually that means they will heal you more than you asked, for being selfless," Neil said.

The comment bothered me. "I wasn't being selfless; I'd have done almost anything to save the woman."

"I think they didn't heal it because they couldn't," Becki said.

"And I think they didn't heal it because they knew that there's some magic in there that needs to come out before the skin closes over it," Neil said.

"If I'd thought to ask, or if I'd needed it completely healed, the angelic power would have healed it," I said.

"Well, the claw marks were bleeding when we got here," Becki said.

"Did they tear open?" I asked.

"Not that we could find," she said.

"Then how were they bleeding?" I asked.

"We're not sure."

"It wasn't just blood," Neil said, "there was power mixed in with it. The kind I usually only sense when really bad things have attacked people."

"Like demons," Charleston said.

"Exactly," Neil said, and coughed, wincing visibly enough that I asked Becki to take care of him.

"Not yet," he said, though he was beginning to sound a little less sure. He waved her off and said, "The bandages are holding a magical poultice that will draw out any negative energy that isn't yours."

"Will the dressing need to be changed?" I asked.

"It depends on how much negative shit the demon left behind," Becki said.

"How will I know if it needs to be changed, or if I'm clear again?" I asked.

"I'll help check you. They walked me through it along with one of our newbie witches," Charleston said.

I looked up at him. I was beginning to feel silly lying on the floor. "Thanks."

"We all play to our magical strengths in this unit. You have angels and demons; I have herbalism and folk remedies like poultices that will drain the bad juju out of a wound."

"Can I sit up now?" I asked, not exactly sure whose permission I was asking. If I hadn't felt bad about probably breaking the paramedic's nose, I wouldn't have asked anyone's permission.

"Slowly; if it hurts, lie back down," Becki said. She was back to sounding angry, but I was beginning to think it might be her natural state. She wasn't angry, she was cranky; they sounded the same, but angry usually didn't last, cranky could be a constant.

I sat up using more of my arms to push than I normally did, so that I didn't overtask my abs. There was a pull of the medical tape against my stomach; it didn't hurt more than it had before, but Becki thought my caution was pain and tried to push me back to the floor. I outweighed her by at least a hundred pounds, and most of that was muscle. She wasn't going to be able to push me anywhere.

"It doesn't hurt, I'm just being cautious like you told me to be," I said, looking at her as she kept trying to push her gloved hand against me.

She stopped pushing but didn't move her hand as she looked up at me, because with her kneeling and me sitting she was now shorter than me. "A man who actually listens and does what I ask, that's different." The sarcasm dripped out of the last two words.

"Hey," her partner said, "I am not that guy."

She frowned and looked at him, her small hand still on my shoulder as if she'd forgotten it there. "I didn't mean you, Neil. I meant, you know who I mean, all of them."

"You do need to find better guys to date," he said.

"They see someone this small and think I should be cute and soft, which they think means weak." The one comment probably explained the bad attitude. If she went around with a huge chip on her shoulder, then men might not assume her personality matched her packaging.

"I'm sorry they're jerks," I said.

She looked up at me, then moved her hand as if just realizing she'd left it on my shoulder. "You're over my height limit, sorry."

It took me a second to realize she thought I was flirting. I showed her the wedding band I was wearing. "I was apologizing for other jerky men, not trying to flirt."

She looked embarrassed. "Sorry," she said.

MacGregor the Elder came into the room. "Good to see you conscious, Havoc."

"Good to be conscious," I said.

"The Infernal specialist is here, Lieutenant."

"Infernal specialist? I'm fine."

"It's not for you," Charleston said.

"Wait, what happened to Lila and Ravensong? Where are they?" I heard the panic in my voice and tried to calm down. How had I not asked about them sooner? I felt like a bad friend.

"Lila got the wind knocked out of her."

Charleston hadn't mentioned what happened to Ravensong, just Lila. I felt that tightness inside me that was the body tensing for bad news. "What happened to Ravensong that would need an Infernalist?"

"One of her hands is . . . damaged," Charleston said.

I got to my feet and asked, "Damaged how?"

"Her hand is deformed. It looks like the demon hand from the hospital."

"That's not possible, true transformation magic is not something that demons do. It doesn't work like that."

"Your expertise is angels, Havoc, not demons."

"But we study both sides and demons aren't contagious. They can't turn people into one of them. It does not work like that." I made every word clear and firm because I knew it was true. They had to be wrong.

I turned for the door and Charleston caught my arm. "Havoc, let the specialist look at her. Once they have something to report I'll make sure you're with me when they make it."

I shook my head. "This isn't possible, Lieutenant. I need to see Ravensong."

"Not a good idea," Neil said from where he was still sitting by the wall.

"Why not?" I asked.

"Because whatever is in those wounds is demonic in nature and so is whatever is happening to her hand; until we know what happened, let's keep the two of you separated."

"The doctor at the hospital didn't see anything demonic in my wounds."

"He's a paramedic healer, Havoc; if he advises we keep you away from Ravensong for now, then we do it. Let the specialist from the College of Angels look at Ravensong, then we'll go from there."

That stopped me; I couldn't even think clearly for a second. "Why did you go to the College of Angels for your demon specialist? They aren't who the department normally hires to help with demons."

"You saw that bottle, it's old as hell and has demon blood in it, contained behind spells that keep it fresh and sentient."

"Sentient blood? Even demon blood doesn't think after it leaves the body, Lieutenant."

"Whatever demon ichor is in that bottle opened it and let itself out, Havoc. None of us have ever seen anything like it. We can't even find any precedent in the metaphysical database, so we reached out to the College of Angels. This thing took out some of my best people; if we hadn't had a containment spell box made by one of the best wizards in the country, God knows what harm that damn bottle would have done before help could have arrived," Charleston said.

"Fair point, Lieutenant," I said. I wondered which of my old classmates or teachers was in the building. It didn't really matter; I didn't want to see any of them. "I'm surprised the College sent someone this quickly. Going through channels usually takes days."

"They already knew about the unusual angel activity in the city." Charleston had said it that way on purpose, because he wasn't going to talk in more detail about the angel at the first crime scene today than was needed for my medical care in front of outsiders. It was an ongoing case.

"Who told them that anyway?" MacGregor asked.

"The angels did," I said, without thinking about it.

"They went and tattled on themselves?" he asked.

I shook my head. "Some Angel Speakers become *Angeli Auditor*, Listeners. They might not know all the details, but they'll know it was unusual and they'll flag it."

I could still see that room with its couches and cushions where the Listeners lounged and spent the rest of their lives listening to the singing of angels with human scribes taking notes. It was supposed to be an honor to be offered a place there. Only the purest of angelic channels could even do it. At thirteen I'd been offered a tour, because they thought I might be able to become an *Angelus Auditor*, a listener to angels. I'd had nightmares for weeks after being shown inside that room. Nightmares of being fed through tubes because I'd been consumed by the music of the spheres. One of my classmates, Ambriel, had taken the honor. If she hadn't been driven completely insane, or died, she'd still be there reporting the Celestial news and being cared for like a coma patient. Between twelve and fourteen they divided the Angel Speaker candidates up into specialty studies. A few narrowed down to one specialty and that was that for them, but the rest of us had two to three possibilities for a few more years. I'd begun studies with the higher order of angels and would have eventually become an *Angelus Lucis*—it translated to angel of light, but that could only refer to true angels, so we were just referred to as Lights—if I wasn't consumed mentally or physically by the progressively higher energy levels of the angels I was exposed to. At thirteen I hadn't even been afraid of the possibility, just honored to be singled out. I'd also been sent to train with Master Donel and the Sentinels—*Angeli Extium*, Angels of Destruction. There were rumors that to truly join their ranks you had to fight an angel and win like Jacob in the Old Testament. At fifteen I'd believed the rumor; by nineteen I didn't. It had been the training with Master Donel that had helped me shine during some of Basic and not die in my first battle. Ambriel had trained as a Listener at thirteen, and at fifteen she went into the room of *Angeli Auditor* and never came out again.

"You all right, big guy? You look pale," MacGregor said.

"Sit back down before you fall down," Becki said.

"I'm okay, just . . . worried about my friend."

"Sure, you are," she said, and the cynicism was as thick as her sarcasm had been earlier.

I looked down at her, way down; she had to be barely five feet tall. I felt even taller than I was and awkward around her, like I was fifteen again and not used to my size. "I am worried about Ravensong."

"You better be worried about yourself," she said.

"Once they've seen Ravensong they want to see you, too," Charleston said.

"How do you know they'll want to see me?"

"Because they said so on the phone when they agreed to send someone out. They wanted to see all the police involved in the incident."

"Did they ask for the names of the officers involved?" I asked.

"They did."

I wanted to ask if they'd agreed to send someone out once they
heard my name, but I didn't want to say that in front of anyone but
Charleston, not even MacGregor, let alone two paramedics I'd just
met. Was it arrogant of me to think they'd sent someone because I was
involved? The anxiety that made my pulse and heart rate speed up
didn't feel arrogant. If I hadn't been all grown-up and not a kid, I'd
have said I was afraid.

"I need to go check on Ravensong and the specialist," Charleston
said. "Maybe you should go to the bunk room and lie down until they
want to see you."

What I wanted to do was go home; even my tiny apartment seemed
like a good idea. I wanted to run away, the way I had when I left the
City of Angels and joined the army, but I couldn't leave Ravensong to
them. God knew what they might decide for the betterment of humankind, or to support the latest treaty between Heaven and Hell. I
couldn't leave her with no one here who understood that the betterment of humankind wasn't always better for the single person involved.

"I'm fine, sir."

He looked at me like he didn't believe me, but he let it go. The
paramedics didn't believe me either, but Becki finally started working
on her partner's nose. When he took the dressing off, I knew I owed
him more than just one drink; maybe a case of his favorite liquor
would say *I'm sorry I broke your nose.*

CHAPTER THIRTY-ONE

I couldn't see Ravensong, but I could ask to be introduced to the Infernalist who had come to help us. Once I knew who it was, if it was someone I knew from before, I knew then I had a starting point and maybe I could advocate for Ravensong even if they wouldn't let me in the room with her. I'd have walked out in the bloody T-shirt and slacks, but Charleston caught me in time. I didn't have another pair of slacks to wear, so he suggested I change into the only outfit left in my locker, so I was dressed for the gym when I came out: an oversized tank top that had started as a T-shirt that I'd cut the arms and neck out of, so it was great for lifting weights but left way too much of my upper body exposed for comfort. At least the running pants were the loose ones and not skintight. My dress shoes had been the only things I'd been wearing that didn't have blood on them, but they looked too weird with the exercise gear, so I put on the cross trainers and short exercise socks, and clipped my badge to the drawstring top of the pants. I ended up clipping my backup gun, a Sig Sauer 380, in an appendix carry; both my badge and my gun were completely hidden under the loose tank top. I tried to put my tactical flashlight and folding blade in the pockets, but there wasn't room for them and my wallet. Besides, the pockets were deep, but the material wasn't heavy enough for too much tactical. If I left the building, I'd need to transfer my badge to a lanyard so I could wear it around my neck, or flash my badge and identify myself fast to any other cops if needed. I so did not look like a cop in this outfit unless I was going undercover at a gym.

There were Infernalists at the College who predated me by decades. It could have been one of them, but the moment I saw the woman standing with her back to me I knew it wasn't any of the old guard. She'd cut her hair short since I'd seen her last, so that it was curly and blond like when she was seven. The bright yellow of her hair looked stark and wrong above the black of her robes. Suriel hadn't taken the final loose-fitting robes when I last saw her; she'd still been in street clothes, or what passed for street clothes at the College. Until I left the College, I hadn't realized how outdated the fashions had been; at least they'd let the girls wear pants. Now here she was in black robes like a priest; becoming an Infernalist took longer than almost any other specialty because of the dangers involved. I hadn't realized until this moment that I'd never doubted she would succeed. Suriel never failed unless she decided that she no longer wanted the goal.

She'd been there to see me take the white and even to have the golden sash added, but I hadn't been there to see her finish her studies and take on her mantle of responsibility. She was almost as delicate as the paramedic Becki was. Somehow, I'd forgotten that Suriel was so small. She'd always been the strongest of the three of us, the most determined. She never seemed small; shorter than me, but never small.

She turned and the shock of seeing her after all this time thrilled through me almost like fear. Her eyes were still that pale, bright blue that I remembered, her blond curls like a short startling halo around the triangle of her face. The black robes looked less like a priest from the front: no high, stiff collar, just a rounded neckline more like a regular T-shirt, though I realized for the first time that it was cut more like a woman's T-shirt than a unisex one. There was nothing but the unadorned black, no red sash to mark her as an Infernalist or badge to tell me her rank or if she'd specialized further, though I knew she must have, or she wouldn't have been sent here today. She had to have earned her blue sash for healing, because she was here to help Ravensong, wasn't she?

She smiled and her face looked genuinely happy to see me, though her gaze took in my outfit like it was unexpected. We hadn't been allowed to cut up our clothes at the College, so exercise was always white T-shirts with black shorts or pants; sweatshirts were allowed when it was cold. There had been a uniform for everything we did at the College of Angels.

There were smile lines around her mouth and the edges of her eyes now, but I thought it added to her beauty. I knew that my face had new lines for her to see. I was so happy to see her that it was all I could do not to hug her. I forgot about Ravensong being hurt, or that there was a major relic in a magical containment box on the floor, or that I'd bled through wounds that two medical professionals had said were too healed to bleed. All I could think of was here was my friend, the first girl I'd had a crush on, the person who had helped me study for Celestial mathematics or I'd have failed. She'd simply been Surrie, back when Jamie was still Levanael, Lev, and I had been Z, until we got older and then she didn't like her nickname anymore.

Suriel extended both hands to me in the greeting that we all did at the College, like a double handshake.

"Zaniel, it is so good to see you."

"It is good to see you, too, Suriel," I said, taking her hands in mine. I did remember her hands being small in mine once I'd hit my growth spurt, but somehow that never made me think the rest of her was small, too. She was just one of those people who took up more space than her physical body did, like she was concentrated awesomeness.

The handshake wasn't enough. "May I hug you, or is that not permitted since I'm an outsider?"

She smiled, but looked down and then said, "It isn't allowed, but you know that as well as I do, Zaniel."

"You're right, I know the rules," I said, squeezing her hands and letting them go. I started to step back, but Suriel stepped into me and wrapped her arms around my waist. I didn't hesitate, just bent over her and hugged her back. The size difference might have made it awkward, but I'd spent a lot of years dating smaller women, because I didn't have much choice. I knew how to fold myself down and around her. I buried my face in her hair and the smell was like coming home. She still smelled like herself, and like the College. It was both comforting and frightening that it wasn't just the scent of Suriel's hair that was comforting but the familiarity of the place I was raised. Be it ever so traumatic, it was still the only home I had ever known.

"Hey, Havoc, I didn't know that the two of you knew each other that well," Lila said; her voice had that teasing drawl to it.

I uncurled from the hug and looked at Lila with Suriel still hugging me around the waist. "We grew up together at the College."

"I don't hug the boys I grew up with," Lila said, raising one eyebrow at me.

"We haven't seen each other in twelve years," I said.

Suriel stepped back from me and there was a stiffness to her that hadn't been there a second before. "Zaniel and I were fast friends once."

"Losing our friendship was the only regret I had when I left the College," I said.

"The only regret?" Suriel said, and she looked me in the eyes in that way I remembered—so direct, her blue eyes to my brown, like she was weighing and measuring me. She'd been able to do that since she was about twelve.

"How many cuties did you leave behind at the College of Angels, Havoc?" Lila asked, giving me a knowing smile.

"What did you call Zaniel?"

"Havoc," Lila said.

"It's a nickname I picked up in the army," I said, "Havoc Havelock."

"You were in the army?" Suriel said.

"Yes."

"When?" she asked.

"Just after I left the College of Angels."

She stared at me again. "Your hair used to be almost black, it's much lighter now."

"Too much sun," I said.

"It suits you."

"Thanks, you cut yours," I said.

She touched the curling edge of her hair almost self-consciously. "It's easier to take care of."

I smoothed my hands through my own short hair. "That it is."

"Was he this much of a stud muffin when you were in school together?" Lila asked.

Suriel looked at me and this time she didn't look at my face. "He did not have so many muscles back then," she said in a voice that was utterly serious, as if Lila wasn't teasing her, or she didn't realize it was teasing.

"Yeah, if he keeps wearing shirts that show off his chest like that, I'm going to want to give him a hug," Lila said, again still teasing, but she was watching Suriel with a look that was more serious than her tone of voice.

"I thought you liked girls, Bridges," Goliath said as he walked up to us.

"Even a fish lover can admire this much beef," she said, flashing him a shit-eating grin, one of her I'm-just-one-of-the-boys looks, which she only used on men who were giving her a hard time being a woman in a man's profession—or, combined with the fish comment, she didn't want MacGregor the Younger to know she was bisexual and not a lesbian.

Which probably meant either he had hit on her or she was afraid he would if he thought he had a shot; either way I wasn't going to out her, but I would ask her in private why she felt the need to pretend to be a lesbian in front of the new guy. Lila could handle herself, so if she was having issues with Goliath this quickly then we needed to know that before he got an offer to become a permanent member of the unit.

"I have interviewed Detective Bridges and Detective Ravensong; is it true that you were acting as a priest to Detective Ravensong's priestess in a pagan ritual when the metaphysical incident happened?"

"Yes," I said.

She studied my face again like she was searching my face for answers. I was remembering now that some of the other students had found her eye contact unsettling. It had never bothered me.

"Have you left the fold and joined the wolves?" Suriel asked.

It was my turn to search her face to see if she understood how rude what she'd just said had been. Her big blue eyes looked back at me, peaceful and uncomprehending. I'd almost forgotten the utter certainty that God and the angels were the only path and anything else was wrong, or even evil.

"If you think there are no wolves at the College of Angels, Suriel, then you are blind."

"I've angered you," she said.

"You've offended me on behalf of my friend and colleague."

"So, you are no longer Christian," she said.

"I am still a follower of Christ."

"How is that different from being Christian?" she asked.

"I find organized religion difficult to deal with."

"What does that mean, Zaniel?"

"What does my religion have to do with you helping Ravensong and advising us on the object that harmed her?"

"I want your help to heal her, Zaniel, but if the angels no longer speak to you, then you cannot aid me."

"The angels still speak to me, Suriel."

"Even though you take part in pagan rituals?" she said.

"Angels aren't Christian, Suriel, you know that."

She nodded. "We share the same angels with all the religions of the Book."

"The book?" Goliath asked.

"The Bible," Lila said.

"The Qur'an, and the Torah," I added.

"Oh, you mean Judaism, Christianity, and Islam," Goliath said.

"Yes," I said.

Goliath nodded. "Okay, but what does that have to do with what happened to Detective Ravensong or the two of you getting knocked out?"

"Nothing," I said.

"Zaniel, you know that's not true; our faith protects us from the powers of evil better than any other."

"I know that is what you believe, because I believed it once, too, but I have seen too much of the world outside the College of Angels, Suriel. I have seen Ravensong back down a demon by invoking the Goddess more than once; all good faiths shine a light into the darkness."

She shook her head. "That is not what I believe, and it is not what you believed once."

"Once upon a time I believed many things, Suriel, but that time is not now."

"When I knew you were involved, I did not request a second to accompany me, for there is no one better at my side for the work ahead, but now I am unsure that you are up to the work."

"You've had over ten years more training than I have, Suriel."

"Why did you not call upon the angels to deal with the relic, Zaniel?"

"Because we needed a magic circle up as quickly as possible so we could keep the rest of the unit safe; Ravensong is faster at that than anyone else I know."

"The witch says you gave her your power to tap into for her spell."

I didn't like the inflection on the word *witch* when she said it, but it was Lila who said it out loud. "You say *witch* like it's a bad thing."

"I was taught that all ways of power are lesser than the way I was taught. I mean no offense, but it is what I believe."

"Do you think that witches are all evil?" Lila asked.

"Don't ask her that, Lila, you won't like the answer," I said.

"If you think witches are evil, then why are you willing to help us?" Goliath asked.

"Yes," Charleston said from behind us all, "if you think we are all evil pagans, why are you helping us?"

"I did not say you were evil, just misled."

"Misled?" He said the one word in that tone he used sometimes when you knew that you were in trouble. Either Suriel didn't understand the tone or she wasn't worried about the consequences. She was still comfortable and secure in the College of Angels and everything they taught us there. No, not taught, indoctrinated. How do you know you're in a cult? You usually don't until something happens that is so terrible you can't ignore it, or pretend it didn't happen, and then you start questioning everything.

Suriel's face was peaceful; she hadn't had her moment yet, and maybe she never would. Maybe she'd be one of those people who go through life without anything forcing her to question everything; part of me envied her that, but the rest of me was sorry for her.

"It is my duty to help those afflicted by forces of the Enemy."

"She means Lucifer," I said.

"I know who she means," Charleston said, still with that purr of threat in his voice.

She was looking around at all of us. "I have offended you again. I did not mean to be offensive."

"When is the last time you were outside the College, Suriel?"

"I am not cloistered away, Zaniel."

"How often are you allowed outside the walls?" I asked.

"It is not a prison, Zaniel."

"You're right, the day I left no one tried to stop me."

"I did not mean to offend anyone, but I do find it difficult to deal with people outside."

"You don't get out much, do you?" Lila said, not sounding exactly friendly.

"No," Suriel said as if she hadn't heard the sarcasm, or just hadn't understood it.

"What color of sash is in your bag besides red?" I asked. I'd finally noticed her small black bag like an old-fashioned doctor's bag from a movie. When I'd left there'd been talk of going to a backpack, but apparently they'd decided it was too modern.

She looked up at me, startled at last, as if she hadn't expected the question. She should have known I'd ask, even if it had only been for old times' sake.

"What sash?" Goliath asked.

"We all come in to be trained as Angel Speakers, but there are different specialties. We differentiate by sashes worn over the robes," I said.

"You should not be telling secrets to strangers," Suriel said.

"Honey, all of us that watched *Where Do Our Children Go?*, that documentary on Netflix, knew about your little sashes and a lot more," Lila said.

"I do not know what you are talking about," Suriel said.

"It was a documentary about parents trying to get their children back from the College of Angels," I said. I hadn't been able to watch all of it; it had been too hard to watch the kids going into the big double gates with their parents. That would be the last time they saw their families unless they failed the training.

"I did not know there was such a documentary," she said.

"Are there still no televisions at the College?" I asked.

"There is one for playing DVDs of movies and educational programming in the teachers' lounge now," she said.

"Well, at least that's some progress," I said.

"You say the angels still speak to you, Zaniel."

"They do."

"I need your skills with the angels in order to help your coworker."

"You have studied a decade longer than I have, Suriel; I can give you nothing that you do not already have in your arsenal."

She smiled, but this was a sad smile. "You always underestimate your worth, Zaniel."

I shook my head. "I did, and then I thought too much of myself, and the price of that was too high, so let me be humble, Suriel. I'm too dangerous any other way."

"Oh, Zaniel, that is not what happened."

"I was there, Suriel, I know what happened."

She shook her head hard enough that her blond curls bounced the way they had when they were longer, and we were younger. "I will not argue old wounds with you here and now, Zaniel."

"Good."

"Whatever wounds we have, Zaniel, I need your help."

"What help can I possibly be?"

"Have you seen what happened to your friend Ravensong?"

"The lieutenant described it to me, but I haven't seen it."

Suriel's face was serious again. "It is something that should not be."

"What do you mean?" I asked.

"I mean that demon flesh can do this, but not mortal human flesh."

"I'm not sure I understand."

"Lieutenant Charleston, can you please show him a picture of the hand?"

Charleston stepped forward, using his smartphone to bring up an image. We took a lot of pictures with our phones because phenomena didn't always last long enough to wait for forensics to arrive with better cameras. Some of it couldn't even be captured by technology, but apparently this could.

The first image was Ravensong sitting in a chair with something on the end of her arm. It wasn't a bad picture, but I think my eyes just didn't want to make sense of it. The next one had an arm resting on a table with a Halloween glove on it; that's what I thought, that it couldn't be real. It was so outsized, compared to the pale wrist that it was attached to, that it looked like something people wore on Halloween with black claws. My pulse started beating a little faster as I looked at those claws, because I remembered them slashing at me, pressing into my stomach while I fought not to let them gut me.

"Are you unwell, Zaniel?"

I swallowed before I answered, because my mouth was dry. "I'm fine."

"You are sweating, and it is not warm in here," she said.

I touched my forehead and realized she was right. Staring at the claws that had almost . . . No, I didn't let myself finish the thought. The monster had tried to kill me; it failed, I lived, I won, it lost, time to get dinner, or lunch, or a drink. That was the way you thought about it in the military and on the job.

Charleston took the phone out of my hand. He was studying my face. I tried to give him my best blank cop face, but I couldn't fix the sick, cold sweat on my forehead except by wiping it off. I took even, deep breaths and that helped slow my pulse and heart. I was probably pale, and that didn't have a quick fix.

"I did tell you the hand looks like the demon from the hospital," Charleston said.

I nodded and let my breath out slow. "You did. I didn't think it would bother me."

"I'm sorry, I do not understand," Suriel said.

"The claws," I said, swallowed hard, "the claws are the same ones that tried to kill me in the hospital hallway."

"You're saying that this hand is an exact match for the demon you all fought at the hospital?" she asked.

"Looks to be," I said.

"But it shouldn't be identical," she said.

"No, it shouldn't be, and it's not possible that it's done that to Ravensong. You're right, mortal flesh does not do this."

"It changed the kid in the hospital into its image," Charleston said.

"No, it changed him into a half-human version of a demon. Real ones don't look like that except in the movies, and that's mostly because they're being played by human beings, so they need the makeup or suit to fit the actor," I said.

"They can change into what your lieutenant described to me, but only if mortal thought has impacted immortal flesh," Suriel said.

"But that only happens if many humans think an immortal being should look a certain way; one person can't permanently change the immortal's shape."

"They can if they are the sorcerer that works with the immortal spirit most often," she said. "Frequency of contact with one mortal can add up over time so that one person's vision can change the spiritual being, in the same way that hundreds viewing it at once can change its appearance."

"You mean that one person dealing with the same demon over and over can impact it like being viewed on television did to the Archangel Michael a few years back?" Charleston asked.

"Yes, he was chosen because it was felt that he could withstand so many mortals around the world seeing him physically manifest and be interviewed on television, but even he was unable to withstand so much mortal energy shaping him into their ideal."

"There were riots in the streets because he ended up being dark-haired and darker-skinned," Lila said.

"Black or brown hair with darker skin tone is the most common in the world, and most people prefer to see the angelic in their own form. It shouldn't have been a surprise," Goliath said.

"Some of the rioting was from the dark-skinned folks like you and me," Charleston said, "because they thought God should look all shiny and blond like you." He nodded toward Suriel.

"Not God," Suriel and I said together. She smiled at me and I couldn't help smiling back. I motioned for her to continue.

"Not God, but the Archangel Michael, the right hand of God, but he is not God," she said.

"Either way, people wanted him to look like all those old Renaissance paintings of angels, not like a Hispanic, Middle Eastern stud muffin," Lila said.

"People always envision angels as beautiful," Suriel said.

"They *are* beautiful," I said, and I had a moment of seeing that golden white light, not the paltry fire of the angel at the first crime scene, but the power of the higher orders. I could almost see her face, the face and body that I had created from the ages of fifteen to nineteen until she became real and could no longer change to another form. That was when she had known something was wrong, and when I had believed her lies as if they were my only truth.

Suriel said, "Yes, but not in the way that the masses think of beauty."

I did my best to focus on Suriel's face, her smile, her humanity, and push the ideal beauty of angels out of the front of my head. I wasn't sure that I would ever be able to get that beauty out of the back of my head. It isn't just ugliness that has the power to haunt; beauty has its own ghosts.

"No, angels don't look like we think they will," I said, finally, but I must have not taken all those memories out of my voice, because she looked at me more closely. Or maybe it was just that Suriel knew; she knew because she had been one of the people I went to for advice. She'd taken me to the masters of the school so they could decide how badly I had fucked up. Suriel had just been in training then, like me.

Her with a black badge on her polo shirt, and me with a white one on mine, showing what specialties we'd chosen to study. Later my white badge had been given a gold stripe down it to show that I dealt with the higher orders. Had I stayed at the College my black robes would have been crossed by a white-and-gold sash. I'd been one of only two in our class to be chosen to try to earn the gold sash. The other one had been Jamie, who was now homeless and a diagnosed schizophrenic. The angels had broken Jamie's mind; they'd only broken my heart, so I'd gotten the better deal. It was why I'd let him crash on my couch when he wasn't too crazy and I didn't have Connery. It could have been me instead of him, maybe even should have been me. Jamie didn't do anything wrong; I'd been the one who had sinned, and yet I was okay, and he was broken.

"Havoc, you okay?" Charleston asked.

I looked at him and wanted to say the truth, that no, I wasn't okay, and I hadn't been okay since I left the College of Angels twelve years ago. Out loud I said, "It's been a hell of a day, but I'm okay."

He narrowed his eyes at me.

"I will be okay," I said, and meant it this time. I would be okay, because I had to be okay, there wasn't another option.

"Good, because I need your help to change the form of the hand," Suriel said.

I looked at her. "You're the Infernal specialist, not me."

"But this is not about demons, Zaniel, it is about changing the appearance of immortal flesh, and you are better at that than I am."

"Ravensong isn't immortal flesh," I said.

"No, but I hope that the hand will be."

"If it's her hand, then it's her hand. Human will alone cannot re-shape mortal forms," I said.

"Nor can a woman who has no taint of the Infernal about her soul suddenly have a demonic hand. That is a punishment or a payment between someone using Infernal magic."

"I thought you said this isn't possible under any circumstances," Charleston said.

"I said that under these circumstances it was impossible, but I have seen long-term users of demonic magic with their bodies misshapen. It was never this—I don't know what word to use—complete, or . . . the hand isn't deformed, it's transformed, and that is incredibly rare."

"I don't see the difference between what's happened to my detective and what happened to the college kid in the hospital," Charleston said.

"We found books and occult paraphernalia at Mark Cookson's house. He's been studying dark shit since he was about midteens if the parents are accurate and I think they are," Lila said.

"The library book that he stole dates from about that time, coinciding with the personality changes and trouble at school," Goliath said.

"A lot of online Satanists that recruit teenagers ask them to steal to prove that they're serious," Charleston said.

"If the library book date is accurate, Mark Cookson had been experimenting with demons and maybe even trying to summon devils for at least five years," Lila said.

"What name did you say?" Suriel asked.

I repeated it for her.

Her smile faded. "I know that name."

"How?" Charleston asked.

"He came to the College. He wanted permission to use the library, and you're correct, Zaniel, he was researching the Infernal powers."

"You're an Infernalist, you had other duties, why would you know the name of someone who came to use the library?" I asked.

"It was one of our exorcists who was originally alerted to the list of books and manuscripts he requested. They did see him in person, but he was not possessed by an evil spirit at that time, and that is all an exorcist cares about. They cannot cleanse a human soul that has chosen the wrong path, for that is free will and not to be tampered with by any of us."

"The list of books he wanted to see must have been important enough for the exorcist to show it to you," I said.

She nodded, still not smiling. "It wasn't what Mark Cookson requested; it was the fact that he knew we had certain manuscripts within our library. No human living today could know that we had . . . certain things within our walls for safekeeping."

"Like what?" Lila said.

"Like the bottle that Lieutenant Charleston showed me on his phone."

"Charleston said it just appeared outside the room after we were knocked out, hovered in the air while he threw the containment box around it. He says it tried to dodge like it was aware, alive," Lila said.

"It is not a relic easily faced down by any human magic. That your lieutenant was able to make it hesitate for a moment is very impressive," Suriel said.

"Are you saying this bottle is one of the relics that were stored at the College?" I asked.

"It looks like the twin of one that we have at the College," she said.

"Are you in charge of the forbidden objects at the College?" I asked.

She shook her head. "No, and it cannot be the one in our archives, but that there is another like it anywhere is something the masters at the College need to know. It was supposed to be a singular artifact." She looked worried for a moment, maybe more.

"Which would be worse news, that this bottle is the one from the College, or that there are two of them?" Charleston asked.

"For the world, two would be worse, but for the College both would be terrible . . ." She shook her head, then forced herself to smile, and said, "but in answer to your question, Zaniel, my sash is red, blue, and black with a silver-and-gold badge."

I was glad she had blue for Ravensong's sake, and black meant she dealt with the worst of the demonic. "You're third in line for the head of your specialty, congratulations," I said, but I knew my face wasn't neutral. I don't know why it was a shock that Suriel had done so well in her chosen path; she always did well at anything she set her mind to, but somehow knowing that she was that far up in the hierarchy of the College bothered me. It shouldn't have, but it did, and I had no idea why.

"You knew this guy was trying to work black magic and you didn't think to alert the police to the danger?" Charleston said.

Suriel gave him a weak version of her smile, but it left her eyes colder, the steel underneath the baby blues showing through for a second. "If we wished everyone in the human world to know we had certain things, we would advertise it. There are many who would pay well to see into the mystical archives, but some things are better left alone, and far too dangerous for mortal humans to read, or to be in human hands. You've all seen the evil that can come of it."

"How long ago did Mark Cookson come to you?" I asked.

She thought about it. "A year, or a little more."

"And you remembered his name all this time after reading it once?" Lila said, laying the cynicism and sarcasm on equally thick.

I almost came to Suriel's defense, but I should have remembered that glimpse of steel; she didn't need me to ride to her rescue, she never had. "I read his name over a dozen times, because that is how many pieces he wished to read in our library."

"You make them sign out a request per book?" Goliath asked.

"They do the same at reference libraries," I said.

"Sorry, I was never much of a bookworm," he said.

"Me either," Lila said, "but I'm glad to know that people have to sign their names if they're trying to borrow something as dangerous as that damn bottle."

"We would never have let that out of our vaults," she said.

"What about the books?" Charleston asked.

"He could have read them in the library under supervision, but he would never have been allowed to remove them from our holy wards."

"And you're saying the entire list of books was all things he shouldn't have known were in the library?" I asked.

"Known that they once existed, perhaps, but that they all are still intact and in our library, no. No mortal human would know that."

"Was it just books that he wanted to see or were there objects on the list?" I asked.

"He knew we had things, Zaniel, things that no mortal human could have known about."

"You keep saying *mortal human* like there's another option," Lila said.

"There are always other options, but a boy so young had not the decades of life to research and find out half of what he seemed to know," Suriel said.

"Did anyone from the College follow up with the Cookson kid and try to find out how he knew all this?" Charleston asked.

"We took steps to find out more about him."

"What kind of steps?" I asked.

"Steps that should have worked, unless he was being championed by someone or something that was far more powerful than we antici-pated." She looked at me as she said it, as if trying to tell me more than her words meant.

"If you want to tell Havoc something in private, say so and we'll give you some space," Lila said.

"Thank you, that would be most appreciated," Suriel said.

"She was being sarcastic," I said.

"Was she?"

"I was," Lila said.

"What did the College do to find Mark Cookson?" Charleston asked.

"We petitioned the angels to aid us in the search," she said, as if it was an everyday occurrence to ask angels to help you find someone.

"And they couldn't find Cookson?" I asked.

She shook her head. "They could not."

"That's not possible; if the angels are given someone to find they do not miss their prey," I said.

"Prey, what do you mean, *prey*?" Lila asked.

I glanced at her and then looked at Suriel. We met each other's eyes and then she made a small up gesture with her hands, as if it was more my choice what to share.

"If God tells his angels to find you, they will find you; you cannot hide from them," I said.

Suriel gave me a look as if waiting for me to add more; when I didn't, she just looked away, but Lila and Charleston had both caught it. I saw them look at me and then at each other, but I was done on the topic of angels and their prey. There were truths that I had learned at too high a cost to ever share unless forced.

"So how did they miss the Cookson kid?" Charleston asked.

"Because something was protecting him," I said.

"That was our thinking," Suriel said.

"So, you had a college student running around our city asking about dark tomes of power and you didn't think to give us a heads-up?" Lila asked.

"He had not broken any of your laws. What were we supposed to tell you, that we didn't like his reading habits? That we thought he might be under the protection of a major demon, or worse? We cannot approach the human authorities every time we think someone is tainted; if we did, you would be chasing down our fears constantly."

"There can't be that many," Goliath said.

She gave him a look that was more like Reggie, full of scorn, as if he was being naïve beyond words. He frowned at her, as if he wasn't used to being on the receiving end of that look very often.

"People travel to the College of Angels from all over the world," I said.

"We do not bother the human police unless we feel the person is a danger to themselves or others. We knew he could not find what he sought anywhere else, and we would not agree to him reading any of the things he listed, so without the knowledge he was harmless. We treated him as such."

I knew she was leaving out things. I knew that if they suspected there was a human in the city, or the world, who was that well protected by the Infernal forces, they would make it their job to find out the how, why, and who involved. That over a year had passed without any resolution meant that something had gone wrong. I would ask Suriel in private and hope she told me. I knew better than to ask in front of others outside the College. I'd be lucky if she confided in me.

"Well, the demon exploded out of him and killed him, so he's harmless now," Lila said.

"Lieutenant Charleston explained the bits of skin at the scene. I am not sure what to make of that and I will consult with others at the College, but at this moment we need to save Detective Ravensong's hand."

"There is no *we*, Suriel," I said.

"Would you let the doctors amputate her hand, when you could help me save it?"

I looked at Charleston. "Is that true, are they really talking about amputating her hand?"

He nodded. "It's true."

"Zaniel," she said, "your power is a gift from God. It is your gift to him that you use that power to serve others. Would you deny that aid to your own friend and coworker?"

"I haven't done anything like what you are asking since I walked out the gates of the College," I said.

"Thirteen years or thirteen minutes is all the same to the angels," she said.

"I'm not an angel," I said.

"Nor am I a demon, we just work with them."

That made me smile. She took my hand in hers, not as the formal greeting, but the way she used to when we were seven. It felt right to have her hand in mine again, as if I'd been missing her far more than I'd allowed myself to realize. I fell back into that old habit of letting her lead, as if I didn't outweigh her by over a hundred pounds now. I could have tucked her under one arm, but it isn't always about size. She'd always been the bravest of the three of us, our leader without any vote taking place, or any questions asked. Once that had been enough, and I prayed that it would be again.

She led me to the door to one of our specially warded interrogation rooms. The entire floor had more wards on it than the rest of the building, but these rooms were self-contained, magically warded, and isolated from the rest of the building. The rooms also had steel-reinforced doors just in case supernatural strength came with supernatural magic.

"Why is Ravensong in here?" I asked.

"The hand was transforming when I found her. It kept changing as I watched, getting more . . . I decided to bring her in here to see if it would slow down what was happening to her," Charleston said.

"Did it slow it down?" I asked.

"It stopped at her wrist. I've been trying to remember if it stopped as soon as we crossed the industrial-strength wards, but honestly I'm not sure if it would have stopped outside the interrogation room just the same."

"You think that the transformation would have kept going past her hand?"

"I was afraid it would, so I brought her here to try to slow it down."

"Why aren't I in one of these?"

"You're not turning into a demon," Charleston said.

"We don't know what happened when the bottle did whatever it did," I said, pulling free of Suriel's hand.

"We do not have time for your self-doubt, Zaniel."

I realized it wasn't self-doubt, it was fear. I'd reacted to just a picture of Ravensong's hand; I wasn't sure I was up to seeing those claws in person again this soon.

I said, "Whoever helped the Archangel Michael get back to his true form is better at this than I am. Send to the school for them."

"It wasn't just one person who aided the Archangel, Zaniel, and besides there is no time to send for anyone. The longer your friend looks at the hand, the more her mind accepts that it is real and solid. We must act now."

"If it's immortal flesh, then mortal will can change it, there is no time limit on that," I said.

"It is immortal flesh attached to mortal flesh; the mortal part will solidify things quickly. We must act now or leave it to the human doctors, and they will have only one solution, Zaniel."

"You know why I stopped doing this kind of angel magic, Suriel."

"I do, but is your fear and shame worth your friend losing her hand?"

"No, of course not."

"Then help me save her hand."

"It's not that simple."

"It *is* that simple, but your fear and self-doubt cripple you; will you allow them to cripple your friend, too?"

Charleston said, "I don't know what you're planning to do, but if you can help Ravensong keep her hand, then do it."

Seeing Suriel had brought up great memories and awful ones. I was still afraid to use some of my magic, but if anything I had ever learned could help Ravensong, I would do it. Suriel was here, and together we could do it. I had to believe that. I did believe that. "Yes, sir. Suriel and I can help Ravensong."

"Then go do it," he said.

CHAPTER THIRTY-TWO

Ravensong had propped the hand on the table because it was too heavy to hang at her side. I'd thought the hand would be sized to her, but it wasn't. It was sized for the nearly ten-foot-tall demon from the hospital hallway, which made it almost cartoonishly large for her. Even my wrist wouldn't have been thick enough for it, but hers . . . She wasn't a small woman, but she was still a woman, with everything done a little more delicately. It was like her wrist had swollen to match the hand, but even then, the dark, scaled skin had to be pinched down to set on the pale wrist.

I expected to be traumatized seeing the claws in person, but the pain and fear on Ravensong's face that she tried so hard to hide from me overrode my own issues.

"Does it hurt?" I asked.

"Everyone keeps asking me that, and the answer is no."

"Can you move it?" I asked.

She wiggled the fingers for me. "And before you ask, I can lift it, but it's just heavier than my hand should be, it's like having to carry one of those stupid kettlebells from the gym forever on the end of your wrist."

I had to smile at the description, it was so her. The wrist was half hers, but the rest was not. It just didn't belong. I could see it, everyone could see it, but . . . I turned to Suriel.

"You see it, where they don't match," I said.

"We all see it," Charleston said.

"Not like Zaniel sees it," she said.

"May I have your permission to do energy work on you, Athena?" I asked.

For once she didn't tell me to use her last name at work; she just looked up at me, frowned a little, then studied my face, eyes narrowing. "Zaniel, if you can really help fix this, then you have my permission to do anything you need to do."

I smiled at her, and I felt the first pulse of peace. Sometimes I didn't know why I denied myself so many of my gifts, and then other times I knew it was guilt, survivor's guilt, sinner's guilt, but I wanted to help Ravensong more than I wanted to beat myself up for past sins.

There are always angels around us; they wait to help, to heal, to share God's grace with us, but they can't help us unless we ask them to, give them permission to—so do it with me now, say, "Angels around me, I give you permission to help me and help those around me." There are more formal words, but simple ones will do. Angels only need to be freed to help us; Guardian Angels hover near everyone, and some people have more than one, but they are trapped watching us screw our lives up, unless we allow them to help us. When Suriel, Jamie, and I were about ten we came up with our own shorthand to help the angels to help us.

"Angels up," I whispered, and just like that I could feel the warmth of them around me. I could see the shine of them front and back because I'd been born with two Guardian Angels. If I'd looked behind me, I would have seen the two that Suriel had with her, but I looked at

Ravensong and saw her angel, but I also saw other spirits around her. The raccoon was at her right side, one minute almost solid like everyone in the room should see it, the next ghostly. It chittered at me, washing its hands in the air the way they did when they dipped them in water. It wanted me to help her, to give them back their hands. There was a tall blond woman at her back. Her hair was in thick braids, and she wore armor, one hand resting on the pommel of her sword. She had a helmet, and the moment I thought *Valkyrie*, she had wings on the sides of her helmet, and then they vanished to leave it unadorned and ready for battle. I had a moment of hearing/feeling in my mind that she didn't need feathers on her helmet to have wings. There was a moment when I could have known a name, a Goddess, but it wasn't my magic, my secret, my power. I was blessed with the ability to see Ravensong's guardian spirits and I thanked them all for showing themselves to me, for there were other figures standing shadowlike around her. But I didn't need to see them all; the ones that were most important for this moment would be clearest. I was given the gift of seeing her magic, her guides and guardians; I had learned not to abuse the privilege by pushing for more information than needed, and to trust that I would be shown what I needed to see.

Her angel was formed of light, not fire like the one at the first crime scene, but light, soft and pale yellow and white, with a brush of white feathered wings around the edges. I could have focused on that trailing edge of wings and the angel would have become more solid, but it wasn't necessary. When I'd first started working with the angels, I had needed them to look "human" or at least solid, but I'd learned to accept them as they were and rejoice in not needing the surety of fixed form.

The shining figure bowed a glowing "head" in acknowledgment of the thought. That let me know that I was getting lost in the power; it could be intoxicating, and new angel workers had to be watched for signs of addiction.

I had to reach through the edge of the angel's "wing" to touch her arm. The brush of those invisible wings, less solid than the ones at the hospital that had shielded me, pushed a warm, homelike energy through me, as if it was all hearth and home, tea and fresh-baked cookies. It wasn't what I'd expected from Ravensong's angel, but I did not judge that breath of power, but just kept reaching toward her arm and let the deeper sense of her Guardian Angel drift to the back of my senses.

My own angel was present, but did not let their power hamper my vision or tamper with the things I was sensing from everything else. One of the hardest things for an energy worker of any kind to learn was not allowing their own energy to interfere with the interpretation and insight from and of their patients and their patients' spiritual guides.

As I moved closer to Ravensong, the large shining figure on her left side turned into a ghostly bear that reached across the front of her body and sniffed her arm as I looked at it. The bear looked at me, as if to say *Well, go ahead*. The raccoon chittered near her arm where it had started and still "stood" on its hind legs, its hands clutched together like a person wringing their hands with anxiety.

"It's all right," I said to the figure. It looked up at me and made a different sound, more a chirp.

"I'm not all right yet," Ravensong said.

Suriel said, "He wasn't talking to you."

"You see them, too?" I said to her.

"Yes."

Ravensong looked at us and then she looked around her. "Oh," she said, "do what you need to do, Havoc."

"Zaniel," Suriel said.

Ravensong nodded. "Zaniel; names have power, and magical names have more."

"Precisely," Suriel said.

This time I didn't argue, because they were right; I'd been Corey and then at seven I'd been chosen by the angels and I became Zaniel. I left the angels and went straight into the army, where I was Havoc, and now I was Detective Havelock. Corey, Zaniel, Havoc—different people, different *mes*. I could see the point in her arm where the corrupting magic started. I didn't just see the demon's hand on her arm, but I saw the dark smoke—no, thicker than that, black water swirling not over her skin but under it. The heavier wards in this room were acting with her own magic to stop the corruption from spreading, because that was what it wanted to do. It was like water, meant to flow, to fill the vessel of the body it touched.

I knew what I had to do. I heard my voice almost from a distance; the magic had almost taken me too far into the vision to be attached that much to the physical world. "Everyone out but Suriel and Ravensong, now." I didn't look around to see if Charleston and the other officers obeyed me, not because I assumed they'd just do it, but because I couldn't divide my attention. The world narrowed down to the black "water" under her skin. I reached toward it, my angels pulsed, and I had a moment of seeing an army of angels connected to my guardian in a shining endless line of holy fire and power. I blinked and I was back in the room seeing the corruption in her skin. Her raccoon laid its paw on my arm and there was another flare of power; the bear laid its great head against my shoulder, the Valkyrie at her back touched me with a shining hand against my forehead, and the power built. Suriel was at my back and her power joined mine, feeding into all of us so that we were a circuit of power and magic. It was a group effort when I let my fingers finally touch her skin.

CHAPTER THIRTY-THREE

began to strip the darkness off her skin. It swirled in the air, half smoke, half liquid, raising part of itself like the head of a snake searching for its next victim, and in the moment I thought that it was a black cobra rearing up to strike. I blanked my mind, took back the power I had given the energy, and it flowed back to just curling liquid smoke. I kept my mind even, empty, peaceful, and gave no strength to the blackness between my hands, but it was seeking someone else to corrupt. It wasn't always this active, but clearing the room of anyone but the patient was standard practice for a reason. Some types of dark energy sought new vessels to enter even as you pulled them out of the first, contagious like a flu virus.

Suriel came up to "catch" it as it spilled out. I could see the pale yellow glow of the angelic script and other symbols between her hands as she captured the darkness. She would take it back to the College for study, before it was released to return to Hell. I had to blink to unsee the glowing symbols and concentrate back on the dark energy that I was still cleaning out of the arm. I trusted Suriel to do her part, and she trusted me to do my part. It was as if no time had passed and we were back in the College of Angels curing the corruption of the world together.

The blackness filled the cage that Suriel had built, but the last bit of dark energy clung to the arm like a root that had to be dug up. I didn't want to dig into Ravensong's arm; I wanted to change the arm and take the roots away with it.

"Why are you hesitating?" Suriel said. "Just strip it off like a glove and let me cage it."

I tried, but this wasn't an illusion or the impermanence of immortal substance; this was mortal flesh and though we drained the negative darkness out of it, the shape of the flesh did not change instantly back to match the pale skin of the rest of the arm.

"It is no longer immortal substance painted over mortal flesh; it is somehow merged together."

"Impossible," she said.

"But still true," I said.

"If you've done all you can, I understand," Ravensong said.

I did not look up at her but kept my gaze on the arm and the darkness that was still rooted in it. I had one hand on her arm, which was as it should be, but the other hand rested on the demon part, which should not have been real. At best it should have been a temporary spell, but under no magic that I knew should the monstrous hand have been as solid as the arm.

A small black paw came to rest on my arm. I could feel the weight of it against my arm. It made me turn and look at her spirit animal. The raccoon looked up at me with large, dark brown eyes. Real-life raccoons could give you looks that made you anthropomorphize them and believe they think just like us, but totem animals are both the original animal and a piece of the human they walk beside. Which meant it wasn't just me projecting human emotions into those inhuman eyes.

I almost asked out loud, *What is it, little fellow?* But I didn't have to speak, I just had to listen.

Out of the corner of my eye the raccoon had looked solid, but looking directly at it made it less physically substantial, except for the eyes. They were big and dark and lustrous and very alive. It raised a paw and wiggled its clawed fingers and then touched its other hand to it, showing that the hands were the same size, placing fingertip to fingertip so that they mirrored each other.

"The hand just has to match," I said softly.

The phantom face smiled at me as much as the shape of the face allowed. It wasn't a human smile, but that didn't make it any less happy.

I put both my hands on the heavy scaled hand. It still felt wrong, like a jarring when someone in a band doesn't hit the right note, but this was a tactile jarring; my fingers were feeling something that shouldn't have been.

I began to smooth the heavy, mismatched flesh like wet clay, except that I wasn't just shaping the clay, I was getting rid of excess, and as I whittled down the heavy skin and flesh it turned into more of the dark liquid smoke. Suriel was there to siphon it off into the magical cage.

I kept working the flesh until it was much smaller, and then finally small enough that it matched the width of the wrist it was attached to, and still I kept working my hands over the skin, smoothing the rough scales down smaller and finer until they were almost as smooth as the skin of the arm. The nails had become smaller to match the rest. I drew my fingers over them to lessen the razor sharpness of them, so she'd be able to touch another person without slicing their skin. The nails were still more claw than human fingernail, but having an extra weapon wasn't always a bad thing. I remembered Kate and her mourning for the claws she'd had before the magical therapy that made her more human. What was so great about being only human?

I was almost too far gone in the magic, but part of me that wasn't Zaniel but still Detective Havelock swam to the surface of all the power. I was able to look up at Ravensong, though I saw her face through the shine of her angel, and then I realized that the Goddess behind her had placed a ghostly shield in front of Ravensong's head

and chest as if the hand were a bomb I was defusing and she was protecting her charge from possible shrapnel. The bear had somehow
merged with the shield as if the bear had given its strength to it, or
perhaps the bear wasn't a personal totem, but a part of the Goddess's
power. I didn't need to know, so I stopped thinking about it and
searched for Ravensong's face through all the layers of power.

It was like trying to see her through gauze, or misty glass. I found my
voice, but it was thicker, so resonant with power that it sounded strange to
my ears, like it was my mouth but someone else's voice. I knew I could
have simply thought what I wanted to know and planted it in the woman's
mind, but that was an intrusion, rude at best, and potentially illegal,
though I knew that Ravensong wouldn't worry about it; but it isn't about
whether you will be blamed for something, it's about is it right, or is it
wrong, will it cause harm? I hadn't used this much power in this many
layers in so long; if there was even a small chance that my control was less
perfect than it had been, I couldn't risk telepathy with anyone right now,
especially someone who wasn't initiated into the same mysteries. Ravensong wouldn't want me helping her conjure at full moon, because I didn't
know how her magic worked; the same worked in reverse here.

"I can't understand, Havoc," she said.

"He's speaking in the language of the spheres," Suriel said.

I tried to remember how to speak in a language that she would
understand, embarrassed that I'd lost so much so quickly to the power.
I threw my willpower into speaking English to Ravensong and still
holding on to all the power I needed to finish this. It was like holding
on to a string that was being pulled out of my hands while I was looking in the wrong direction.

"You okay with claws—little ones?" I managed to say out loud.

"Can you make them human fingernails?" she asked.

Which meant she wasn't okay with it, but I'd taken my attention
away from it too long, the power was unraveling. The small paw
touched my hands this time and I could feel every texture of the rac-

coon's hand, rough and smooth, the tiny prick of the claws at the end of the dexterous fingers, and that was my answer. This was her totem, a piece of her spirit; there was nothing wrong with delicate claws at the end of clever fingers.

I had a moment of cradling the small hand between my larger ones. It was a pretty hand, a feminine hand, but it was still covered in red scales like a snake and had black fingernails that ended in points that made her raccoon chitter excitedly.

The power flowed away from me, all the many pieces of spirit sliding back to where they normally existed. I had a moment of wanting to see spirit all the time, all the totems and guardians and Deities that surrounded us until the world was made glorious and haunted by it. I knew there was even a chance I might keep that double and triple vision, but I also knew that it would drive me mad, because that was part of what happened to Jamie. It hadn't even been a choice for him; the angels had awakened his deeper vision and then he hadn't been able to shut it off. The College had seen his inability to control his psychic gifts as a failure. He wasn't strong enough to be an Angel Speaker, so they'd expelled him as if he'd flunked a final or failed to turn in his last research paper. Jamie had excelled at any paper test or essay, but you could fail all of those in the College of Angels if you were gifted enough in other areas. If you could survive the power, stay sane and functional, they would find a place for you, but madness that failed to be useful? That was unforgivable. Angels are about order, and any angel that preferred chaos was cast out. If Heaven would cast out the angels themselves, how could they do less to a human being who had proven too frail a vessel?

Thinking about Jamie shut down the flow of power. I clanged my shields into place as fast as I could. I wanted out of the room, away from Ravensong's thanks and Suriel's questions of "Zaniel, what is wrong?"

I could still see the glow of her cage and the swirl of darkness trapped inside. The cage floated by her shoulder like a well-trained dog. The flare of angel wings glittered around us all, filling the room with white-yellow light and I could not bear it.

I went to the door, pounded on it. "I need out!" I knew they were watching on the cameras. I knew they heard me, saw me. A small hand touched my leg and I looked down to see the raccoon with too much knowledge in its dark eyes. I needed out, not because I wanted to see it, all of it. I wanted to wrap myself in the glow of angelic power like a blanket that I'd missed, like I was a child and needed my comfort object, but it wasn't that. It wasn't a comfort; it was an addiction. The brush of one angel's wing is much like another's and there was one set of wings that I had loved, been in love with their owner, and been loved in turn, but though an angel may love humanity, they are not allowed to be in love with one person. They are not allowed to put the well-being of one human being above all others. Angels are meant to serve God and humanity and creation, not necessarily in that order. Once, I had had the sole attention of an angel of one of the highest orders aimed at just me. She had loved me above all others, and I had felt the same, and that had been when everything went to hell.

I pounded on the door again, but the white-yellow light of all the angels was filling the room until I couldn't breathe; no, that was a lie, until I wanted to breathe them in, wrap them around me like I had with the energy at the hospital, but this was more, so much more, and it was offered, it was there. They wanted me back. I was an Angel Speaker and there were so few of us.

I pressed my palms against the door and yelled to be let out, to be away from the temptation. The raccoon chattered at me and I realized as I looked into its eyes that it helped ground me, helped chase back some of the glowing energy.

I whispered, "Thank you."

Then Suriel touched my bare arm and her angel echoed her so that the power whispered over my skin like a sea of kisses that I could swim in, or sink in, or . . . I screamed and slammed my hands against the door. I had to get out!

The white-yellow light filled my vision and there was nothing but the light, and in the light were strands of gold and silver and copper and colors that humans have no words for; symbols and angelic script and scripts that humans are not meant to read trailed around the threads of the universe like music made visible. For one shining moment I heard the music of the spheres and I knew if I reached out far enough I could travel those shining lines on a river of words and sound that had driven Jamie out of his mind, but that I had loved.

I let myself relax into the beauty of it, and then I heard a voice down those shining strings. A female voice said, "Zaniel, is that you?"

I pushed myself out of that glorious view, arms flailing wildly as if I could touch music and sound, as if there was anything solid enough to push against in that place. I fell backward, landing on my ass on the floor, hard enough to jar up my spine and into my head so that I felt stunned as if I'd fallen much farther than just from my feet to the floor.

A woman's voice said, "Zaniel, are you all right?"

For a moment that voice merged with the one in the vision and I cried out. If I hadn't been too manly for it, I'd have said I screamed.

Suriel's voice came again, because of course it was Suriel and not that other voice at all. "Zaniel, are you well? Please answer me."

"You okay there, Havoc?" Ravensong asked. Her voice sounded hoarse, almost like the croak of her namesake. Human voices would sound rough for a few minutes until my hearing adjusted. The singing of angels could spoil you if you listened too long.

Suriel knelt beside me but did not try to touch me. She knew better. Ravensong didn't. Her hand rested on my bare arm. If she had been just human it would have been okay, but she was a witch and magic calls to magic.

CHAPTER THIRTY-FOUR

was thrown back into that place of song and color, where angels traveled on golden threads like spider silk that ran throughout the universe, holding everything together. I realized that the spider analogy wasn't me. I heard Ravensong think *Grandmother Spider*, and there was movement along the threads like something huge and monstrous. I thought *NO*, and the movement was gone, and we were back in the crystal, silver, and gold space where angels in pure form raced back and forth along the singing notes of creation.

One of the angels paused and looked in our direction. It was like looking into fire, except the fire could look back at you. Would her mind survive this? I felt tiny hands on my arm and somehow I knew there was another one touching her, and then I felt pressure, metal slicing through reality, pulling her back from the brink of staring too long into the abyss, even if it was a space that went up instead of down, or maybe went everywhere at once, but even filled with fire and warmth it was still an abyss that would look back at you.

I was back on the floor of the interrogation room with Ravensong gasping beside me as if she'd run a long distance as fast as she could. I could see the Valkyrie standing over her with pale braids and metal helm, her shield held in front of Ravensong, a sword that burned with a light of its own in her other hand. The eyes that glared at me from the helmet were a storm-cloud gray and angry.

I wanted to say *It's not my fault, she touched me*, but you do not argue with gods, or demigods, or the messengers of Deities unless you have no choice. Short of that, let it go, because divine beings do not take well to mortals that argue back, or most of them don't. I'd been told that the Norse pantheon and some other more warlike pantheons liked for their followers to have a fighting spirit that extended even to fighting the gods, but that was all theoretical for me. The Big Guy that I followed wasn't big on defiance.

The raccoon chittered up at me, patting my arm. I wasn't sure if it was reassuring me or scolding me for endangering Ravensong. I just didn't speak enough raccoon to be certain, and then I looked into those shining dark eyes and I knew it wasn't chastising me. It was more a pat on the arm to say *It's okay*.

I smiled at him, and then Ravensong said, "That was intense."

"That's one way of saying it," I said, and looked at her. We stared at each other for a second, her blue eyes to my brown, and then she smiled at me. It was a little lopsided as if she couldn't quite find her usual smile, but it made me smile back, because she'd just survived so much more than Gimble had, and it had put him in the hospital. Looking into her older, wiser face, I knew she wasn't going to need a doctor for the glimpse of the infinite. They'd want to look at her hand, but her mind was intact. She was good.

The Valkyrie was back to standing at her back again rather than covering her with a shield and having a bare sword in her hand. The danger was over but the glare in those storm-cloud eyes didn't like me much. It was a silent warning to knock that shit off, or we would have words.

"It wasn't his fault," Ravensong said, looking up at the towering figure. The Valkyrie glared at me one more time, then faded from sight, though the huge bear appeared and roared at me before they both faded.

"Sorry about that, I know it wasn't your fault; you'd think after this"—she held up her hand—"I'd know to keep my hands to myself."

The raccoon petted me again with its strangely human-looking paw and then moved to Ravensong, cuddling against her like it was a cat. She reached out to it as if she could touch it as solidly as it touched her. I watched its gray ombre of hair move under her hand, reacting to her touch. Was that just an illusion my mind was filling in, or was she able to pet her totem for real?

She smiled at me. "It's as real as the sword and shield that saved me in your shining palace," she said.

"Did you read my mind?"

She shook her head. "I read your face."

"I thought I did better cop face than that."

"You do, or Detective Havelock does, but this Zaniel of the Angels, his face shows every thought."

I didn't like that doing angel magic made me easier to read, but it made me more vulnerable in all sorts of ways, so I shouldn't have been surprised. Me losing my poker face was the least of it.

"Your friend seems no worse for seeing . . . the shining palace," Suriel said, using Ravensong's phrase rather than the words we had learned for it.

"Her guides and Goddess saved her," I said.

"Her magic saved her," Suriel said.

"That, too," Ravensong said.

I stood up and offered Ravensong a hand.

"What, you think the old lady can't do it on her own?"

"Aren't you ladies always complaining that chivalry is dead?" I asked, smiling at her.

She grinned and took my hand, using her right hand without thinking about it. I didn't think about it either until I felt the difference in skin texture. I pulled her to her feet using the new hand. The scales felt cool and smooth, but I could still feel them so though I thought *smooth*, it wasn't the same kind of smooth as human skin. The skin was red with darker highlights like an antique ruby that sat in the crown of some long-ago king. The delicate black claws pressed into my skin, dimpling it. I realized her hand looked more like the raccoon's paw than the demon's hand from the hospital.

Once she was standing, we let go of each other. A pinprick of blood popped out on my skin where one of her nails had dimpled the flesh.

She didn't notice, but Suriel did. "You might want to be careful until you adjust to your new hand."

"It will take some getting used to," Ravensong said, holding it up and wiggling the fingers in front of her face.

"The nails seem quite sharp," Suriel said, looking at my arm.

Ravensong saw it, her eyes going wide. "Oh shit, Havoc, I'm sorry."

"It's nothing," I said, and wiped the blood away, but the bead of red welled up again. Apparently, I was going to need to hold pressure on it before I put a bandage on it.

"How deep is it?" she asked, looking worried. The Goddess may have vanished from my sight at least, but the raccoon was still there at her side, on its hind legs now looking worriedly between us.

"Not bad, I just need to hold pressure on it and then put a Band-Aid on it. I cut myself worse shaving."

"But you will have to practice with the hand to find out how much pressure human skin can take from the nails," Suriel said.

"Yeah, I'll have to be careful with the little woman when I get home tonight."

"Little woman?" Suriel asked.

"My wife."

"Ah," Suriel said, and the one sound held disapproval.

Ravensong heard it, too, because she frowned at her.

I decided to try to lighten the moment. "It took me a while to figure out that the woman who teased me the most at work didn't even like men."

Ravensong grinned at me. "A woman can admire the view without wanting to marry it."

"So your wife explained to me at the Christmas party."

She smiled and a look came into her eyes that showed just thinking about her wife was a good thing. I hoped to get back to that with Reggie. What Louie, short for Louanne, had told me at the party was that when Ravensong joined the force, being lesbian wasn't a good thing, so she'd been more flirtatious with the men to cover it and never lost the habit. It had helped that she could talk about Louie instead of Louanne. They'd been together twenty-five years and were still stupid happy together; they were what I hoped to have with someone someday. It startled me that I had thought *someone someday*, not *Reggie* and *now*. We would have lunch tomorrow and then a date after that. We'd kissed today, held each other and it had felt so good, but it had been six months between kisses. It still scared me that I hadn't put her name in that thought, but it would be okay, we would work things out.

"What's wrong, Havoc?"

I shook my head. "Nothing, just remembering when you met Reggie at the first holiday party."

Ravensong grinned at me. "Well, your wife is quite the looker."

"Zaniel, do you have a wife?" Suriel asked.

"I do," I said, smiling before I could stop myself.

"How could you do that, Zaniel? You are an Angel Speaker; it is forbidden for us to marry."

"I stopped being an Angel Speaker when I left the College."

"You were not cast out, Zaniel. You are an Angel Speaker in the good graces of both the College of Angels and God. You took a vow to serve him above all others. We cannot do that and divide ourselves between him and a spouse."

"When I left the College, Suriel, I left it in every way."

"What do you mean by that, Zaniel?"

"I told you I joined the army just after I left the College."

"The army, as clergy?"

I shook my head. "I joined as a regular soldier."

"Why would you do that?" She stared at me as if I'd said something obscene.

"Because being raised at the College of Angels didn't prepare me for any job in the real world. I didn't know how to fill out a job application, or use a computer, but I was big and strong, and an army recruiter saw me walk past. I didn't know what else to do."

"You could have come back to us," she said.

"No, I couldn't."

"It wasn't your fault, Zaniel."

I glanced at Ravensong.

"How about you send Charleston in here, so he can decide if I need to see a magical healer before I step outside here?"

"You will be fine," Suriel said.

"That has to be the lieutenant's call, he's the boss," I said.

"Havoc's right," Ravensong said.

"Then we will wait until your lieutenant comes, but perhaps we could visit and talk of old times before I have to go back," Suriel said.

"I'd like that," I said, and I meant it.

CHAPTER THIRTY-FIVE

I got us both hot teas from the break room and then we sat down across a table in one of the empty interrogation rooms. She took a sip out of one of the few plain mugs I was able to find. She held the mug with her hands curled around it, fingers through the handle as if it wasn't there.

She lowered the mug and smiled. "You remembered how I liked my tea."

I smiled back. "Of course I did, I could probably order food for you at almost any restaurant, unless your taste buds have changed completely in the last twelve years."

"You were always good when it came time for kitchen rotation," she said.

"You weren't bad at it either."

"You were the better cook," she said.

"I was; do you remember the time that Levanael set the kitchen on fire? They wouldn't let him cook after that." I laughed, but she didn't.

"That is not his name," she said.

I suddenly didn't feel like laughing either. "I know they stripped him of his angel name when they cast him out. He goes by his birth name of Jamie now."

"It is forbidden to speak to anyone who was cast out," she said.

"I am no longer of the College; I don't have to abide by their rules."

"So you see the exiles?"

"Exiles, no, not exiles, just Jamie. How many other exiles are there?" I asked.

She looked down into her mug. "Enough."

I would have pushed about that one-word answer, but there were other things I wanted to know more, and I knew that her time here was limited. She would have to be back inside the walls before dark unless she had special permission.

"Why are you here, Suriel?"

"To help you and your coworkers," she said, and she raised her bright blue eyes to me; her delicate face was unreadable, and that let me know she was lying or at least not telling the whole truth.

"You have a silver badge that marks you as third in line of all the Infernalists at the College, Suriel. Someone that senior would not have been sent out alone like this for anything. They would have sent at least one of the College Sentinels to be your bodyguard."

"I have enough authority to come out alone, and enough power to protect myself, but I am expected back soon."

"How soon?" I said.

"They do not like us out much after dark," she said.

"Why did you use your authority to come here alone?"

"I heard that it was a police matter, and then I heard your name, Zaniel, and I had to come and see if . . ." She took another drink of tea, as if the sentence was done.

"If what?" I asked.

"If the angels still spoke to you, if they still answered your call, and they do."

"I did not fail my training, Suriel."

"When you left the College, Zaniel, we all thought you would be back. We all believed you would find the outer world corrupt and come back to us. When you did not return, the elder teachers told us that you must have been flawed all along and that the angels no longer spoke to you for fear your flaw would spread to them."

I stared into my tea mug but didn't want it anymore. "I was flawed, am flawed, and I didn't use my magical gifts until other lives would have been lost; only then did I risk reaching out to the angels again."

"And when you called, they answered just as they always had," she said, her voice soft.

"Yes," I said, and looked up to meet her eyes. They were staring at me like two blue diamonds of righteous intensity. Suriel never looked away, never flinched, but there was a tiredness in her eyes now that might have been more. Was that doubt in her clear blue gaze for once? Of course, she doubted me, how could she not, how could I not?

"What happened at the College was not your fault, Zaniel," she said.

"You thought it was at the time; in fact, you were shocked and disappointed in me, you said so."

"I didn't know the full details then," she said, but she looked down as she said it, which wasn't like her, or hadn't been like her years ago. Did I really know her now, or she me? How much had the years changed us? She felt so familiar to me, but in a way we were strangers; just thinking that made my chest ache as if there was more than one way to have a broken heart.

Charleston came into the room looking larger than normal with Suriel in the foreground. "Havoc, there's an escort here from the College of Angels."

I had one wild second of thinking they'd come for me, but the next thought was they had no power over me anymore, and I knew why they were here before Suriel said, "They've come to escort me home."

"That's what they said, but they look a lot more"—and Charleston seemed to search a long time for the right word before saying—"athletic than the normal Angel Speaker."

"They are Sentinels; they do not travel openly outside the College often," she said, and then she stood.

"What do you mean, openly?" I asked.

She shook her head as if she didn't want to have the conversation in front of Charleston. I stood up and asked, "Can you give us a few more minutes alone, please, Lieutenant?"

He nodded. "I'll keep them busy as long as I can, but talk fast, they don't seem very patient."

"Give me five minutes," I said.

He just nodded and left us, but he looked back once, and I knew he'd ask me later. He was my boss; he had the right.

"We're alone, now what did you mean about the Sentinels not going openly into the outside world?"

She came to stand beside me and lowered her voice to a near whisper. "I have seen Sentinels dressed like outsiders leaving the College. I am told they are checking on some of the failed Angel Speakers, but when I asked why that would be necessary, the answers I was given were not satisfactory."

"How long have the Sentinels been going outside like that?"

"Not long, or not long that I have seen."

"Why do you think they're going out?"

She shook her head. "I am not certain. I have suspicions, but only that."

"Tell me."

"It is my home, Zaniel, the only one I remember. I will not betray it to someone whose loyalties lie elsewhere. I saw the look between you and your lieutenant; I know you will be duty bound to report what I say, so I will say very little."

"I wish I could tell you that your secrets are safe with me, but the

Sentinels are dangerous, Suriel; they should not be roaming outside, they are meant to protect what is inside."

"That is why I am telling you this much, because you are a policeman, and it is your job to keep safe what is out here from anyone that would cause harm—*anyone*, Zaniel." She grabbed my arm tight, as if she was trying to tell me more with the touch than just her words. I stared into her eyes, trying to understand, and then I realized she was afraid. Suriel had been fearless once, but she wasn't now.

"Suriel," I said, and I was going to ask what was wrong, but I heard Charleston's raised voice outside say, "We are not holding Master Suriel against her will, she came out to help us with a demon problem."

I heard that deep purring voice and knew who it was: Harshiel, of course it would be him. "Show her to us and we will believe you."

"We don't hold innocent people against their will," Charleston said.

"We understand that, Lieutenant Charleston," said a second, much less aggressive male voice. Turmiel was here to soothe and balance Harshiel's usual belligerence. His nickname at the College was Harsh, and he'd never outgrown it.

"I demand to see Suriel," Harshiel said; his deep voice sounded like a musical growl. He sang bass in the choir at the College, as Jamie and I had sung tenor, though none of us had been true *Angeli Cantor*, Angel Singers. That was one of the rarest gifts of voice among us; no one from our year had been so blessed.

"You don't get to demand anything here," Charleston said, and if his voice wasn't as deep or as musical as Harshiel's it had the ring of authority that the Sentinel's lacked.

"Standing in my way would be a mistake, Lieutenant."

"Are you threatening me?"

Turmiel's voice. "No, we would never do anything so disrespectful and so against the orders we were given." There was a note of warning in the last words, and it wasn't aimed at Charleston.

Suriel let go of my arm and started to walk toward the doorway, but I caught her arm, turning her back to look at me. She let me draw her back toward me so I could whisper, "What are you afraid of, Surrie?"

She smiled at the nickname, I think. "That what I have devoted my life to has been corrupted."

"What does that mean, Surrie?" I whispered.

Turmiel yelled, "Harshiel, no!"

We were moving toward the doorway together; Suriel called out, "Harshiel, don't you dare do anything rash. I am coming." She sounded like a scolding teacher to a pupil. The Harshiel I knew wouldn't take that from her, or anyone that he didn't see as superior to him, which meant almost no one. I felt magic breathe along my skin and prepared to fight.

CHAPTER THIRTY-SIX

t was Suriel's hand on my arm that helped me think and realize that it wasn't angelic magic that was breathing through the room. Charleston stood between the doorway and the two Sentinels, but both MacGregors were behind them as well. Officer Odette Minis was standing to one side, so she had a clear line of sight to the Sentinels that didn't cross any of us. Her hand rested on her sidearm; the holster was unsnapped. Apparently she wasn't going to try magic if it came to a fight. I was okay with that; sometimes bringing a gun to a magic fight is exactly what you need to win.

The two Sentinels stood in the center of my fellow police officers. Both were dressed in leather vests with hard leather bracers on their lower arms and loose pants like an ancient version of exercise pants. Turmiel tall and tan with his empty hands out to his sides. Harshiel taller with skin that was the closest to true black that I'd ever seen on a human being. Turmiel was handsome, but Harshiel was devastating in his beauty. I'd lived in the City of Angels long enough to know that movie stars would have paid a fortune for cheekbones like his, and there were women who injected their lips to get the fullness that Harshiel had naturally. He'd been one of Suriel's first crushes besides me. We were allowed childish crushes at the College, just nothing more.

"You have taken our weapons so that we could be allowed up onto this floor, and we mean no harm here," Turmiel said.

"The powers of the enemy cannot win against us," Harshiel said. "Even without our weapons the angels will protect us from such deviltry."

"Is he calling us Satanists?" Young MacGregor asked.

"Yep," Old MacGregor said.

"There will be no need to test our magic here today," Suriel said, and her voice had the ring of authority, as if she just expected everyone to obey her. Either she was bluffing or she'd been in her current exalted position longer than I'd thought.

"It would be a certainty, not a test," Harshiel growled in that thrummingly deep voice that I'd heard so often in choir.

"Well, there will be no certainty today," Suriel said in that no-nonsense teacher voice. It was a tone of voice that we'd grown up obeying from them, our teachers and masters at the College.

"As you say, so shall it be," Turmiel said, bowing with a hand to his chest like the Sentinels would to any master at the College. It shocked me to see him do it for Suriel, even though I knew it was her due now.

Harshiel didn't bow; he glared at her and then at me. I looked into his dark brown eyes and saw something I hadn't expected to see: hatred. We'd never been good friends, but I didn't know he thought we were enemies.

"There's no evil here unless they brought it with them," Goliath said.

"There is no evil among the angels," Turmiel said, as if it was just fact.

"The Fallen are still angels," I said, before I could think that it might have been better to keep my mouth shut.

Turmiel looked at me startled, as if I'd said something he didn't know, but we were all warned in our training to never forget that the Fallen were not stripped of their angelic powers, or at least not all of them.

"You would know all about the Fallen, wouldn't you, Zaniel," Harshiel said, his voice thick with the emotion I'd seen in his eyes.

"She is not fallen," I said, but my voice wasn't certain.

He went after that sign of weakness just like he had on the practice mat when we were learning to fight. "Your flesh was weak, Zaniel, or were you just not good enough to complete the seduction?"

"What did you just say?" I asked.

"Did he just say you were bad in bed, Havoc? All those fantasies down the drain," Lila asked, coming to join the outer limits of the loose circle that the squad had formed around the Sentinels.

"Do you spread corruption among all the females you meet?" Harshiel yelled.

"Harshiel, enough!" Suriel said.

"Why do you defend him?"

"I am not defending him, I am stopping you from speaking out of school," she said.

"Oh, Havoc isn't just the star in the fantasies among us females," Lila said, her voice full of sarcasm that Harshiel probably wouldn't understand, "he's the favorite in a lot of the male fantasies, too."

"Don't help me, Lila," I said.

Harshiel turned on me. "Have you fallen so low as that, you who once were almost our brother in arms?"

There'd been a time in my life when I would have defended my honor against that kind of suggestion, but that time had passed; love was too precious to deny, even if it wasn't my kind of love.

"I have been on real battlefields, held soldiers in my arms while they bled and I fought to save them, killed enemies that were trying to kill me. I have been a real solider, a real policeman fighting to keep

Heaven and Hell from destroying the Earth, not a hyped-up security guard training for a battle that will never come."

"How dare you!" he said, taking a step toward me.

I went into a soft fighting stance, hoping that he wouldn't notice, but I should have known better. We'd both begun our lives with the same training.

Harshiel went into a much more obvious stance, knees soft, hands loose as he raised them to protect his upper body, but not fists, too easy to break your hand that way, elbows and knees were better.

I fell into a stance that almost mirrored his, bouncing a little on the balls of my feet, rotating my neck and shoulders. I realized that I wanted to fight him. I had spent thirteen years using our training in the real world against people who were trying to hurt or kill me. No matter how good your training is—and Master Donel was the best—it's still not the same as real combat. Training to fight for your life is still not the same thing as actually fighting for it. A few minutes of real violence will teach you things that a lifetime of practice can't.

"Harshiel, stand down," Suriel ordered.

"We are here to protect Master Suriel, not to serve some private grievance," Turmiel said. He started to reach out to grab Harshiel's arm but seemed to think better of it, letting his hand fall to his side. He looked at Suriel and then at me.

I kept my eyes on Harshiel. He had beaten me regularly as a child. Not as a bully, but just because Harshiel was the best at hand-to-hand. No one but Donel or one of the adult Sentinels could beat him when I was at the College.

I didn't think of myself as that competitive in that stupid male way that caused so much trouble for every police officer, but suddenly I realized that for the right person, for Harshiel at least, I was that guy. Part of me didn't like that I had this in me, and another part thought, *About damn time.*

"As much as I hate to say it, Havoc, stand down," Charleston said.

"If I said *please*, Lieutenant?"

"I agree with Havoc; I think tall, dark, and handsome here deserves to get his ass kicked," Lila said.

"You just met him, Bridges, how do you know he deserves an ass-whooping?" MacGregor the Elder asked.

"A woman knows these things," she said.

"Zaniel could never beat me before, I doubt that has changed," Harshiel said. He settled more solidly into his stance.

"That was when we were boys, Harshiel; we're all grown-up now," I said.

"You have to take off your shirt when you say things like that," Lila said.

Officer Minis chuckled and lowered her gun, holstering it. "Yeah, like in the movies."

Lila nodded. "Yeah, you know, Havoc says 'all grown-up' and then he tears off that little bit of a tank top and shows us that six-pack he's been working on."

I laughed and relaxed my fighting stance. It was too ridiculous.

Charleston said, "Bridges, stop being a corrupting influence on the new guy."

"The only corrupting influence here is Zaniel," Harshiel said, and was totally serious.

"New girl," Lila corrected. "As a bisexual woman I can tell the difference between girls and guys."

"*Girl* is a sexist term; don't you ever read the gender sensitivity emails?" Charleston said, smiling.

"Nope," she said.

"I do, and *guy* is fine, but thanks for the heads-up, no sharing the shower with you," Minis said, but she was grinning.

"You are making fun of me," Harshiel said, but stayed in his stance as if Donel was going to come walking by and criticize him.

"Well, handsome, if you take your shirt off, I'll stop teasing and just admire the view," Lila said.

"Bridges, enough," Charleston said, but he was fighting not to smile.

"I do not take my clothes off for strange women."

"Pity," Minis said, softly.

"So, do you take them off for strange men?" Lila asked.

"Are you talking to me?" Harshiel asked.

"I am," she said, but this time she wasn't smiling. She gave him a look as straight and unflinching as Suriel usually did.

"Stop picking on our guests," Charleston said.

"Sorry, Lieutenant," she said, still giving Harshiel serious eye contact. She wasn't smiling now, as if the teasing was over and she was on to something more solemn, but what? If she had had her own magic and not been a null, I might have worried that she was going to use a spell on him; if she'd been better at hand-to-hand, I'd have accused her of trying to make him fight her instead of me, but as it was, I had no idea what she was thinking.

Apparently Charleston didn't know what she was up to either, because he said, "Bridges, back away from the Sentinels. They're going to escort Havoc's friend Suriel here back to the College, and we're going to let them do that unless she says she doesn't want to go."

"Master Suriel is expected back at the College," Turmiel said.

"I am expected," Suriel said, folding her hands in front of her.

"She must come back with us now," Harshiel said, and he was finally standing up straight and tall again, and not like he was about to participate in training.

"I am a master, you are not, Harshiel; you do not dictate to me," Suriel said.

"Of course, we do not dictate to you," Turmiel said.

"Are you refusing to return to the College?" Harshiel demanded.

"No, but I will return because I wish to and because it is my home, not because you drag me back like some runaway child. I did healing work on someone who had been demon touched, which is my job as one of the Chief Infernalists of the College of Angels."

"It is customary for such work to be done in pairs even for the Chief Infernalist himself," Turmiel said.

"How could you risk yourself by doing such dangerous work on your own, Suriel?" Harshiel said.

"She wasn't alone," I said.

"The angels do not speak through you anymore, seducer," Harshiel said.

"The angels do still speak to Zaniel, and do not call him that again," Suriel said.

"He is corrupt and separated from the grace of God," Harshiel said.

"God still hears my prayers, and the angels still know me," I said.

"The enemy tricks you into believing that, but it is not angels that sing to you, but demons," Harshiel said.

"I swear by the angels themselves that they know Zaniel as they always did," Suriel said.

"You know that cannot be true," he said.

"I came to test the truth of it for myself, as is my right as a master teacher at the College," she said.

"Why would you risk yourself, Master Suriel?" Turmiel asked.

"Yes, Suriel, why would you risk yourself for someone that you haven't seen in so very long?" Harshiel asked. He studied her face as if he was trying to read past the passive expression on it now.

"If you would use the gifts that God gave you instead of letting your prejudices blind you, Harshiel, you would know that it was not a risk to work angel magic with Zaniel." She looked past him to the other Sentinel.

"Turmiel, look at Zaniel with something other than your physical eyes," she said.

"Why should he do that? Why should Turmiel care about Zaniel's powers or lack thereof; why should you?" Harshiel asked.

"Turmiel," she said again, ignoring Harshiel.

I felt a warm wind against my skin like the perfect breath of spring. I looked at Turmiel—he was still the tallest Filipino I'd ever met in all my years on the outside. He towered over Master Donel. When I was at the College, I hadn't questioned that Turmiel would specialize as a Sentinel like his uncle, but over the years I had rethought a lot of things about those years, and with Turmiel's magic blessedly gentle I realized I had been right in one thought: He should have specialized in something else. He was no warrior, no bringer of death. He should have been a healer, a bringer of joy, but like most of us he hadn't argued with the path the College chose for him.

"It's considered rude to peek at someone's magic without asking permission first," Lila said.

Turmiel's magic began to fade like a wind dying away. "It's all right," I said, "let him look." I smiled at him. "It's all right, Turmiel, do what Suriel says."

Turmiel smiled and it was as gentle as the springlike wind that danced over my skin. It brought my Guardian Angel shining at my back like an all-body halo in a medieval painting of a saint.

"Wow," said Young MacGregor, "do you feel that?"

"Feel it, no, but I see it," Minis said.

"He always did shine pretty like that," Turmiel said, his voice almost dreamy with the power.

"No," Harshiel said, "no, it cannot be."

"He partnered me in healing the injured police officer as of old," Suriel said.

"There is nothing wrong with Zaniel's angel," Turmiel said, his voice still dreamy. "He feels sadder like he has seen and done things that hurt him, but he has done nothing to make the angels turn from him. In fact, when I think that, they hover closer and want to offer comfort." As if his words made it so, I felt the brush of wings, and if I hadn't known it was angel wings, I'd have said birds, because they felt smaller than the angels that came when I called, but there were no birds to see and the touch was more wind and thought than physical feathers. The touch of them opened something inside me and began to heal it. I didn't even know what it was, only that it hurt and if I and my angels allowed it, Turmiel's angels would make it better.

I heard Harshiel yell, "No!" and then I felt the wind around my body disturbed as if something was moving close to me. I opened my eyes to see Harshiel's elbow coming for my face. I had time to block it with my forearm but missed the knee he drove into my stomach. I was able to turn a little, so he didn't hit my solar plexus solidly, but it was enough that he doubled me over. I put my arms to either side of my head to protect myself as best I could as I fought to breathe. I couldn't make myself stand upright, so I stopped trying and threw myself into Harshiel. He wasn't expecting it and was in the middle of trying to elbow me in the back of my head, so I could sweep his arm past me and came up under his arm with my left and hit him in the ribs like I was driving into a heavy bag in the gym. Elbows were better, but sometimes fists are all you have to make it work. The blow caused him to stumble, which let me come at his back and hit him in the kidney once, twice. Then there were hands on both of us pulling us apart while Suriel and Turmiel yelled for him to stop fighting and Charleston yelled at me.

Harshiel collapsed to his knees even with the hands trying to hold him up. I had a moment of satisfaction and then I saw the blood on my tank top. The demon wounds were bleeding again; suddenly I didn't feel so satisfied.

CHAPTER THIRTY-SEVEN

W e had to call the paramedics again, twice in one day. It was a record, one that Charleston made it clear he did not want to repeat. "I cannot believe that you had a fistfight in the squad room, Havoc. You're usually one of my most levelheaded people."

I was sitting in the squad room in the chair at my own desk. The paramedics Roger and Sam bagged up the bloody bandages and shirt to be processed by the ME, just like the ones earlier. We wouldn't make Adam hunt me down this time. This paramedic pair were both middle-aged men with that world-weary air that said they'd seen it all, patched up all the survivors, and were tired of stupid people hurting themselves for no good reason, or maybe I was projecting on that last part. I was now out of clean shirts to wear until I went home for one, so I was sitting shirtless in my exercise pants and shoes with fresh bandages across my stomach and totally agreeing with Charleston.

"I called Patterson," Roger, the brown-haired white paramedic said. "She described your wounds earlier and they look about the same to me."

"Patterson?" I asked.

"Becki Patterson," he said.

I nodded. "I remember her."

"Most guys do."

"Her partner used her first name, but not her last," I said, and I knew I sounded defensive, though I wasn't sure why.

"Sure, but I bet you don't remember his first name," Roger said, giving me a look that was so weary and cynical I wanted to ask him how hard his shift had been. I didn't for the same reason he wouldn't ask me. First responders barely admit weakness to their friends, let alone to strangers.

I had to admit he was right, I only remembered Becki's name and I owed her partner for the bloody nose. I suddenly felt shallow and sexist.

His partner looked Pakistani maybe, but certainly some members of his family had come from a part of the world that was near Pakistan at some point. At the College of Angels, you could just ask someone's ethnic background and they'd tell you even if your guess was wrong. They appreciated being asked and you trying; in the outside world some people appreciated the curiosity, and some people didn't, so I'd learned to not ask unless the conversation gave me an opening.

The second paramedic that might or might not be part Pakistani spoke with absolutely no accent other than East Coast American with emphasis on Manhattan, New York. "The other guy won't let us take him to the hospital for tests. He's got bruising over his kidney and it's painful when I palpate it. If either of you can talk some sense into him, I'd really like a doctor to look at him. You never know with a kidney shot that's this tender."

"Suriel, the blond woman with him, is his superior. She might be able to order him to see a doctor," I said.

The paramedic shook his head. "She tried pulling rank and the patient wasn't having any of it. He's her bodyguard according to him, so he's supposed to keep her safe and he can't do that from the hospital."

"How hurt is he?" I asked.

He shrugged. "Hard to say without a doctor and maybe more tests."

"I didn't mean to hurt him seriously," I said.

"Then maybe you shouldn't have hit him in the kidney with your fist, twice," the paramedic said.

"We're trained to fight angels, not mortals; that means you go for the kill."

The look on his face let me know that I'd overshared. Charleston said, "It's a metaphor; the kid was raised in the College of Angels before he wised up."

"Oh, that cult, glad you escaped, that documentary about the divorced parents fighting for their kids was a heartbreaker. My wife and me, if someone tried to take our kids when they were just little bitty kids like that . . ." He just shook his head at the thought of what they'd be willing to do to save their kids from the "cult."

I took a breath to say something but felt Charleston's hand squeeze my shoulder. I knew what he meant. I shut my mouth. He was the boss and he'd just saved me from the fact that I'd told a stranger one of the deepest and most esoteric secrets that the College of Angels had.

"Can you give us some privacy, then we'll be over to try to talk Harshiel into seeing a doctor," Charleston said.

"Is that how you pronounce the name?" the paramedic asked.

"Yes," I said, "Har-SHAY-el."

"Okay, the other guy didn't correct me," the paramedic said.

"Then he's in even more pain than he's showing," I said.

"I sympathize on the name thing; I just go by Sam now. I'll give you some privacy and then help me get the other guy to a hospital."

"My first name is Adinka," Charleston said.

Sam grinned. "I'd fist-bump you if I wasn't wearing gloves."

They had a chuckle together and then we were alone, in a room with other people in it, but if we spoke low, we had privacy. "First, tell me the truth: Have you ever fought an angel?"

I shook my head. "We're trained with the idea that we would be able to stand our ground, or even win like Moses and Jacob in the Old Testament."

"But you don't train with angels?" he asked.

"I never did, and most don't. Centuries ago, it was the final test for becoming a Sentinel."

"What, winning a wrestling match with an angel?"

"No, just surviving was enough. Winning meant you were destined to lead and train others. The head of all the Sentinels was the last one to fight an angel to earn his right to guard the College. Something happened during that fight that he has never spoken of that I know of, but it was enough for them to stop the tradition."

"It can't be that long ago if he's still teaching and training."

"He's over ninety and you'd never know it."

"Over ninety, that's impressive."

"He is very impressive." What I didn't say out loud was that all of us aged slower and lived longer than people in the outside world. We were told it was God's grace so that we could serve him better, but I believed it was being surrounded by so much angelic magic. Angels didn't age, and being so close to them some of that rubbed off on us, but whatever the reason we were told not to speak of it to outsiders.

"Why didn't you stay with the Sentinel training?"

I shook my head. "The Sentinels work very closely and more physically with the angelic than any other specialty, and one day in the middle of training we discovered that I had one of the rarer gifts among the Angel Speakers."

"Which was?"

"I can speak with the higher forms of Celestial beings without dying or going mad. It's a rare gift even among Angel Speakers. Having it meant I was moved to even more specialized training. I kept up with the Sentinel training for a time, but eventually I had to leave it to concentrate on my own studies with my Celestial tutors."

"I didn't think any of the teachers at the College were actual angels."

"They aren't."

"But you said . . ."

"I said tutors, not teachers. A tutor is one-on-one instruction in private. The Celestial don't teach in the public classes." I did my best to blank my mind and not think about what those few sentences meant for me as a teenager. I'd been thirteen when in the middle of Sentinel training the angels and Master Donel had discovered my true gifts. I'd split my time between my tutors and Donel's training for two years; at fifteen I left the Sentinel training except for one-on-one instruction with Donel and a few of his best and brightest, which had included Harshiel. Donel had not wanted my gifts in his specialty to be lost through lack of training.

"You look a million miles away, Havoc," Charleston said.

"Not miles, years, though not a million." I managed a smile, but I didn't feel it and doubted it touched my eyes.

"Is there a personal beef between you and Harshiel?"

"Yes."

He stared down at me. "'Yes,' that's all you're going to say?"

"You asked, I answered."

"If your friend over there wasn't a tough motherfucker you could have killed him. You know better than to go for the kidneys unless lives are in danger."

"I did know better, Lieutenant, but it was like I was back in the College, Harshiel and me fighting each other for the top spot. He was the only person who ever made me feel competitive like that. I think I wouldn't have fought to stay in the training as long as I did if I hadn't wanted to be better than him, or at least not worse."

"He's your frenemy."

I nodded. "We were friends once, and then he couldn't take that I might be as good at some things and better at others. He hates to lose." In my head I thought, *I just hate to lose to him.*

"The two of you made each other train better and harder because of it?"

"Very much so," I said.

"Can you talk him into going to the hospital?"

"If Suriel can't, then he won't listen to me."

"Try."

"I saw his eyes, Lieutenant, he hates me. I didn't know he hated me."

"You're frenemies, Havoc, it's a love-hate kind of thing. He's probably missed you being there to push him to greater heights."

"I doubt very much that he missed me, Lieutenant."

"Talk to him, maybe I can persuade both of you to go to the hospital for more tests."

I looked up at him, startled. "I'm okay now, the bleeding stopped."

"You were attacked by a demon, Havoc, and the wounds keep bleeding even though all the medical personnel tell us the wounds are too healed to bleed. You need a healing specialist to look at you, Havoc."

"You want me to try to make it a sort of dare for Harshiel—if you go to the hospital, so will I?"

"Now you're getting the idea."

"He hit me in the wounds and opened them back up, simple as that," I said.

"The wounds are healed, Havoc, they shouldn't be able to bleed."

"The first paramedics are testing the blood to see if it's mine. You know how demons borrow body fluids from other places to use," I said.

"That's when they borrow shit or money from somewhere else to smear all over the place, or to trick some fool into letting the demon make them rich as a price for their soul. One case they tested the bodily substances at a possession and found out it belonged to half a dozen different people, none of them related to the possession," Charleston said.

"That's my point, sir, I think it's not my blood."

"Why would the demon keep wasting something as precious to them as fresh human blood to keep smearing it on you, and why aren't you sensing the demonic activity that's doing it?"

"I don't know."

"Thanks for making my point, Havoc, now go talk your friend into the hospital and agree to sign up for more testing yourself."

I wanted Harshiel to see a doctor, because what if I had damaged his kidneys, but I didn't want to go back to the hospital for a lot of reasons. "I'm afraid if I go back for tests they'll keep me overnight, and I have tentative plans to see Reggie for lunch tomorrow to talk over some stuff. I don't want to have to cancel on her for something that can wait until we get the blood work on my clothes and bandages."

"I take it this lunch is a positive sign, not just a hash-the-details-of-our-separation-out?"

I smiled. "Yes, very positive."

He grinned at me and clapped me on the shoulder. "I am glad to hear that, Havoc. Okay, we'll wait until some of the older blood work comes back, as long as you promise that if you start bleeding again for any reason you'll head to an ER, or call me, and if the blood is all yours, you'll agree to go in for tests after your lunch date."

I finally nodded. "That all sounds reasonable, Lieutenant."

"Good, then let's try to talk sense into Harshiel and you can go home and get some rest at least."

"I'm fine."

"That's bullshit, I should have sent you home sooner."

"I'm . . ."

"Don't say *fine*."

"I'm okay."

He rolled his eyes at me, then motioned me up to walk across the room to try to reason with Harshiel. I didn't think anything I could say would make any difference, but if Charleston thought it would, I'd try. I trusted his judgment about people, even when I thought I knew everyone involved better than he did. The hate in Harshiel's eyes had shocked me; maybe it wasn't just women that I didn't understand, maybe it was everybody.

CHAPTER THIRTY-EIGHT

They had stripped Harshiel out of his shirt so they could see his back, but the very darkness of his skin made it harder for them to see if it was bruising badly, blood rushing to the surface. His usual upright posture in the chair was strained. I could see the tension in his shoulders and his hands gripping the arms of the chair as he tried to not hunch over the pain. I'd hurt him and hadn't meant to, or had I? Charleston was right; if I hadn't meant to hurt him, I wouldn't have punched him like I had, so why had I done it? I honestly had no idea which made me feel worse somehow.

I started to say I was sorry, but he spoke first. "I did not know you were injured, Zaniel. It is not honorable to strike an opponent in an injury that I did not give them."

"It's all right, Harshiel, you could not have known."

"Is it true that it was a demon that clawed you?"

"It is true," I said, falling back into the rhythm of the language I'd grown up with instead of just saying yes.

"You fought a demon hand-to-hand and kept him from killing you?"

"I did, or I would not be here to speak with you."

"And I used the wound against you in a fight; I am ashamed of taking advantage of such a thing."

I started to touch his shoulder, then stopped, because I wasn't sure how he'd take it. "There is no shame because you could not have known I was injured. I am the one who should be ashamed; I should not have hit you the way I did, such a blow should be saved for life-or-death battles only."

"I thought you would be slower, less able because you left Master Donel's training, but you were fierce and fought well."

I bowed my head, putting my right hand over my chest, fingertips lightly touching my opposite shoulder. Falling back into the old gesture without thinking. "I am honored that you found me a worthy opponent."

He tried to bow his head in return, but stopped the gesture halfway, frozen in pain. "Most worthy."

"As a worthy opponent may I ask you to see a doctor, so that I will know that I have not injured you too badly?"

He raised his dark face toward me but had to finish the gesture with just his eyes, as if even that small movement hurt. I touched his shoulder then and fought not to touch the side of his face. When we were children, I had loved how dark his skin was compared to mine, but especially compared to Cosmiel; she'd been a natural redhead with the palest of skin to offset her green eyes. At seven, I had marveled at all the colors we came in, and it had been one of the hardest things to learn in the outside world that it was considered racist to remark on skin color. I had been raised to believe that our differences made us beautiful, and no matter how wrong some things at the College had been, it hadn't all been bad; in fact some of it I wanted to teach to my son.

Harshiel was studying my face as if he was trying to read my thoughts, and then I realized he could read my mind. I'd touched him enough for him to be able to know what I was thinking. It was one of his gifts, but only with close contact. He couldn't read someone across a room or across the world like others at the College. It was one of the reasons he'd been trained to fight, because if he could touch you, he had a chance of literally picking your brain.

"Zaniel," he said, and reached up to put his hand over mine where I touched his shoulder. "If you missed us so much, why did you stay away?"

"Because I could not have all of you and leave the College," I said. His palm and fingers were rougher than they had been the last time I'd felt his hand on mine. We'd both lifted more weapons, more weights, touched more of life. I felt the loss of not having been there for each other, but then I stopped my thoughts, let myself sink into that stillness that we'd been taught. If you didn't want someone reading your mind or emotions you could prevent it by simply not thinking, not feeling. It was like the empty mind of meditation but reached in an instant. When you deal with angels, blanking yourself for a fellow human is so much easier.

He pulled back first and then we let each other go, but the eye contact stayed. Frenemies, Charleston had called us, but that wasn't exactly it, more brokenhearted friends.

Suriel said softly, "I am not the only one who missed you, Zaniel."

"I did not miss him," Harshiel said, looking away, but the lie was too obvious, or too late.

"The angels hear you," Turmiel said, which was something we said at the College if you thought someone was lying.

"And the angels will heal me if I am worthy of it, I have no need of human doctors." He started to stand but had to grab the edge of the nearest desk. I caught his arm and steadied him. He let me help him for a moment and then glared that hatred back at me, but now I was even more puzzled by it. He tried to jerk away from me, but the movement hurt enough that if I hadn't been there, he'd have fallen.

"Please, Harshiel, let them do more tests; I could not bear it if something happens to you because I had been too zealous."

"You were not zealous, you fought to win, as we are taught." He looked around. "Turmiel, help me."

The other man came but his dark eyes had widened; evidently

Harshiel still didn't ask for help very often. Turmiel came to take my place at his side, so he could keep standing.

"You are obviously too hurt to do your duty as Sentinel," Suriel said.

"I have failed you," he said.

She shook her head. "You have not failed me, not yet, but if you cannot move without Turmiel's aid, then I am without either of you at my side."

"Tell him to go to the hospital," I said.

"We must all be back inside the walls before dark," Harshiel said. The wording was odd, not *back to the College*, but *inside the walls*.

I looked from one to the other of them, trying to figure out what I was missing.

"If you collapse for need of a healer before we get to the College, that could keep us all out after dark," Suriel said.

"If I am too weak to serve the angels as Sentinel, then I will take whatever fate awaits me."

She touched his bare arm. "No, Harshiel, no."

He looked where she touched him as if her pale hand against his muscled dark meant far more than just the hand of a friend. For the first time I wondered if there was more than friendship between them, or if he wished there was more—did Suriel feel the same? I had a moment of thinking what it would be like to be near to someone you wanted, loved, and be forever denied. I had proven that I was not that strong long ago. Had they been stronger?

She dropped her hand away from him. "We will need a car to take us home, you can't walk far like this."

"Maybe we can give you an escort to make up for the poor hospitality?" Charleston said.

"We would gladly accept," Suriel said.

"Zaniel cannot be part of that escort," Harshiel said; his voice had fallen back into the growling warning again.

"On this we agree," I said.

He frowned at me, still leaning on Turmiel. He could not stand unaided—that wasn't good. How badly had I hurt him? I was angry and disappointed in myself for the loss of control. I knew better.

"Are you really going to refuse medical treatment?" paramedic Roger asked.

"I will return to my home," Harshiel said.

"Fine, if you start peeing blood then your kidneys are ruptured. If the pain gets really severe, maybe same thing."

"Are you trying to frighten me into going to your doctor?"

"Wouldn't dream of ruining your chance to martyr yourself on some kind of macho power kick," Roger said.

"I don't know what you mean."

Paramedic Sam said, "Maybe you don't, but I hope your healers at this College of yours are better than our hospitals."

"They are far superior," Harshiel said. He took in a deep breath and stood a little straighter. His grip on Turmiel loosened, but he leaned against the desk almost like he'd sit on the edge of it.

"I'll help escort them," Lila said, as she came to stand beside Harshiel, as if ready to catch him if he fell again. She was looking somewhere around his abs, which were a little compressed as he sat. I suddenly saw him from Lila's perspective as a very in-shape, athletic man and she was single. I tried to remember if I'd ever mentioned that Angel Speakers were celibate. It probably hadn't come up in conversation.

I had a moment of debating on letting her pursue him, or saving them both the trouble. If he hadn't been hurt I'd have been tempted to let Lila try, but he was hurt and . . . I moved toward her, planning to say something, but the paramedics moved in again with more warnings and notes for the healers, and Turmiel caught my attention.

I let him lead me to the side of everything. "Master Donel requests a favor if you are willing."

"For Master Donel, anything."

"His sister is alone in the city now; everyone has moved away, or passed away. He would like someone to check on her. If she is in need, could you leave a message at the College?"

I was startled because we gave up all birth family when we became an Angel Speaker, but Turmiel was part of Donel's family of birth so maybe that changed things, but in the end it didn't matter. I said the only thing I could say. "Of course, what is her name, and do you have an address?"

"Only her name," he said.

I wrote down the name, both the Americanized version she'd been using when Turmiel had come to the College of Angels at age seven and her original first name when she and Donel arrived from the Philippines as children. Turmiel only knew the last address of his own mother and siblings, not his aunt, but he'd been seven; you memorize your home address, not everyone else's. I put the information in my phone and had barely gotten it when Harshiel almost yelled, "Turmiel, we are leaving."

I reached out and clasped Turmiel's arm above the leather bracers on his wrists, so that we gave the greeting of Sentinel brothers-in-arms. It was strange how quickly I was falling back into old habits. "Give my best to Master Donel."

He clasped my arm and said, "I will."

"And please tell me how Harshiel is. If I've truly injured him I'll never forgive myself. It was careless."

"I will find a way to let you know, I promise.

I wanted to hug Suriel goodbye, but there was no chance to say any other goodbyes; they were ready to go and that was that. Harshiel was determined to be gone and Suriel couldn't seem to find an excuse to delay. Lila and Old MacGregor drove them back to the College. I realized after they left that I hadn't warned Lila that Harshiel was celibate. I hoped she didn't flirt too hard with him on the drive.

CHAPTER THIRTY-NINE

I went home, glad about it for once. Whatever they'd given me at the hospital when they bandaged my arm and stomach was wearing off, or maybe my body was finally letting me feel it. The nail marks in my arm hurt the worst, as if every scratch suddenly decided to be a sharp pain every time I used it, and since I'm right-handed, I used it a lot. The stomach was a little tender, I mean I wouldn't want to do sit-ups, but it didn't hurt like I'd been stabbed by a demon, though it did hurt like I'd taken a good shot to the gut. I was grateful that it didn't hurt worse and said a little prayer of gratitude, but it was still unsettling that the wounds kept bleeding when a doctor, a nurse, and four paramedics had all assured me it was impossible for wounds this closed to bleed, at all.

My apartment building was in El Segundo, close to the airport, not too close to the runways, but sometimes, depending on the wind or other air traffic, the main flight path shifted and the planes went directly overhead. Those nights the sounds of planes turned into the sound of bombs and mortars and I really regretted signing a yearlong lease instead of renting month to month, but the places that would let me rent by the month weren't good enough to bring Connery or Reggie to. The idea was that she would come over to the apartment and visit in a more neutral place than the house we'd made together. It hadn't worked out that way; she'd been in the apartment just once to make sure she was comfortable with Connery staying overnight.

I pulled into the street in front of the building. I had to go around to get into the covered parking area. A parking area that was covered and not visible from the street was one of the reasons I'd taken the apartment. There was a man sitting on the steps in front of the gated front entrance as I drove around for parking. He was clean-cut, shortish brown hair, Caucasian or pale Hispanic, checked flannel shirt, jeans, running shoes that had seen better days. It was too hot for the flannel and the clothes didn't fit right; if he hadn't been clean, I'd have thought maybe homeless. I pulled into the parking area and was starting to park the car when I slammed on the brakes because my head finally realized I knew the face. I hadn't seen it without a beard and long hair in ten years, but it was Jamie.

I managed not to hit the wall in the parking garage, but it took effort. I had to control my breathing like I'd seen a ghost. I so did not need this today after seeing Suriel, Harshiel, Turmiel, but especially Suriel, but I couldn't leave Jamie sitting on the steps; part of me wanted to just pretend I didn't recognize him with the new haircut, but I couldn't be that shitty to him. I owed him more than that. I owed myself more than that.

I went up the stairs from the parking area to the main floor, though it was narrow enough I had to be careful that my shoulders didn't scrape on the walls. It was also dimmer and cooler like a narrow bit of cave; I used to take my sunglasses off in the tunnel, but I knew better now. Full sunshine dazzled the eyes at the top of the stairs, bouncing off the blue water of the pool, so that without sunglasses you were blinded until your eyes adjusted.

The pool was at the center of an open courtyard with first-floor apartments on the pool level, and stairs leading up to the second-floor apartments. I started to make the turn up the stairs to my apartment but stopped with my foot on the first step. I looked across the pool toward the far entrance. I could glimpse the black iron gate that stayed locked to keep anyone out who didn't have the code. There was a short corridor that led from the pool area to the gate, and it was just enough distance that standing outside the gate you couldn't see into the main courtyard except for a glimpse of the pool. The privacy from casual passersby was one of the main selling points of the place, that and a pool for Connery. Our house didn't have a pool, and I'd wanted something for him to do when he visited. I'd heard too many parents on the job who divorced and then couldn't get the kids to visit them, or spent too much money on amusement parks, or other things like it was a contest. Who could be more interesting? Who would buy them more stuff? Reggie and I had agreed we wouldn't let that happen; so far, we'd managed it. It helped that Connery was only three.

I started walking around the pool toward the gate. Maybe Jamie was back on his meds, or they'd found better ones for him? I prayed as I walked and hoped someone heard me that cared. Seeing so many old friends from the College had shaken me, and now Jamie, it seemed like an awfully big coincidence. I didn't mean Surrie or Jamie planned it, I meant higher up. God doesn't usually interfere directly, but some of his angels can. One dose of full-blown angel magic and I was suddenly paranoid, but that didn't mean I was wrong.

My neighbor and apartment manager, Doris, opened the door of her apartment, which sat like a homey guard shack at the entrance to the corridor and its locked gate. She came out into the bright sunshine shielding her eyes with her hand above her cat's-eye glasses, not the new ones that everyone seemed to be wearing this year regardless of age, but the original old-lady design, because Doris admitted to being over sixty, and I was betting over seventy was more honest, but Reggie had taught me not to question a woman's age whether she's turning thirty for the third time or staying in her sixties for the next twenty years.

"The man says he's your friend, but I didn't recognize him. He says he shaved his beard and cut his hair, and maybe he did, but you know I don't buzz anyone in that I don't know."

"You did exactly right, Doris. It is my friend, but even I didn't recognize him for a second."

"Who knew there was such a handsome young man under all that hair," she said, smiling up at me. Doris was short enough that looking up at me always looked like it hurt her neck. I usually tried to sit down if we had to talk for any length of time.

"I'll just go see what he wants," I said, and tried to move past her, but it wasn't always easy to get out of conversation with Doris. She trailed after me in her slippers. She almost never put on real shoes unless she left the apartment building. She seemed to live in oversized shirts and long shorts or those pants that almost reach your ankles but don't. Reggie didn't wear them so I didn't know what they were called, but they always puzzled me as if the person couldn't decide if they wanted to wear shorts or pants.

I didn't want to be rude, and I also didn't want an audience for talking to Jamie through the gate, but I was going to start with the gate between us. I didn't want to invite him into the building if he wasn't safe to be around the other tenants. That wouldn't be fair.

There was a bark from behind us and then her two pug puppies came racing out. They capered around her ankles and made it impossible for her to follow me until she'd calmed them down. Her elderly pug, Fred, had fooled me into thinking pugs were couch potatoes, but apparently that was just an elderly-pug thing, because the two tiny puppies were bundles of energy with tiny curly tails that wagged constantly. She leaned down, talking to them in that high-pitched pet voice. "What are you two doing out here? Did Fred knock the baby gate over for you again?"

Watching the two puppies bark, pant, and circle around her like furry little mushed-face potatoes on speed, I was pretty sure they'd escaped all on their own. Either way I was free to walk to the locked gate and talk to Jamie.

He got up off the steps and walked toward me, as if he'd heard me coming. He was older than the last time I'd seen his face bare and though I'd seen him regularly for years, it reminded me of the changes in Suriel's face. It was them, just more grown-up. The look in his eyes was calm, happy, peaceful. It was his eyes before the angels broke him. I had to swallow past a lump in my throat. For the first time I felt like it was Jamie and not this other person that his mental illness had transformed him into. He had become his illness, so broken, eyes frantic, startling at things that I couldn't see or feel, as if he were always surrounded by an evil, taller version of the pug puppies leaping and demanding attention.

I walked toward those familiar gentle eyes and was afraid to speak first, as if it were a dream and words would shatter it, but Doris had seen him, too. I wasn't hallucinating, or seeing a vision, but still I stood there and didn't know what to say first. So much I wanted to say while he looked like he could hear me and understand. I wanted to tell him so much before his illness took him away again. Jamie had helped teach me that death wasn't the only way to lose someone.

"Say something, Havoc."

I startled and realized I'd half expected him to call me Zaniel. "Something," I said.

He laughed, and it was a real laugh, his old laugh, which I'd grown to love when we were kids. I hadn't realized how much I'd missed the sound of it.

"You were always the serious one, but then you'd say something like that and be funny as Heaven." His voice was rougher than of old, but then he'd spent nearly thirteen years screaming his madness at anyone that would listen or couldn't get away fast enough. He'd been cast out of the College two years before I left voluntarily.

I hit the buzzer on the gate so I could swing it open and step through. I needed to be sure before I let him inside. I could hear Doris talking baby talk to the puppies. We had other families here with kids.

His smile wilted a little around the edges, and his eyes showed the first pain. "I'm so sorry for anything I did before." His face started to crumple and suddenly lines were in his face that the beard had hidden. The years on the streets had carved their way onto that boyishly handsome face, but now he looked like an older, more tired version of himself and not some bearded stranger. I couldn't bear to see unhappiness in this new old face.

I took the steps that let me put a hand on either side of his face and leaned down so I could touch my forehead to his. Then we were hugging, and the body was still that stranger's body, too thin and frail from never enough food, never enough care and attention to it. I held him tight, the old and the new, and thanked God and the angels for this moment of clarity. If it never came again, I'd seen his brown eyes filled up again, his smile on the face I remembered, and for that I was truly thankful, but because I was human, I asked for more. I asked for him to stay sane and whole and be my family again, and I asked forgiveness for wanting more when I'd just been given so much.

I found my voice first, and asked, "Jamie, how?" Because it's also human to question miracles.

He pulled back enough to look up at me. There were tears on his face, too. "That is not my name and hasn't been my name since I walked through the gates of the College of Angels and they christened us with our angel names."

I wiped at my face with the back of my hands as we both stepped back out of the hug. I wanted to take his hand in mine and keep holding on, because only that would make it real.

"Levanael," I said.

He shook his head. "No, that name is still forbidden."

"Then what do I call you?"

"Levi, call me Levi."

"Levi," I said, trying the new name out; it felt okay. I reached out and took his hand like I was shaking it, but I just needed to keep touching him, as if he'd change back into crazy Jamie if I didn't hold on to him.

He squeezed my hand and didn't let go, as if he understood some of what was happening inside me. He'd been my best friend, closer to me than my actual brother, closer to me even than Suriel, or maybe his loss had driven us apart, I couldn't remember anymore; all I knew was that I didn't want to let him go, and part of me wanted to call Surrie and say, *Look, look, he's back, our other third, the person who helped make the three of us whole.*

"How? How did you . . . get cleaned up?" It sounded like I was asking him about drug rehab instead of recovering his sanity, but I didn't know how to ask the other.

"I'll tell you everything I remember."

"Are you hungry?" I asked.

He grinned at me, and it hurt my heart to see that old expression in his face. "Aren't I always?"

The truth was that Jamie wasn't. He never ate enough even when I tried to give him food. Levanael had eaten like the teenage boy he'd been.

"Come on up, I'll fix you something."

"I remember you learned to cook for just you, or you and Connery, or you and me. When you first left the College, you could only cook for big groups."

"That's right," I said, squeezing his hand and starting to lead him inside the gate by the hand like he was Connery. "We never cooked for just ourselves in the College, it was always a group activity."

"We didn't have to do a lot of things for ourselves," he said, and sounded sad.

I pulled on his hand so I could get him to look at me. He still looked sane, but sad and tired. "I'll feed you and then maybe you can catch some sleep."

He shook his head. "Food, then I tell you what I remember. I'm afraid to sleep. I've spent so many years not knowing which is real and which is dream and which is . . . other."

I wanted to ask what he meant by other, but I didn't. I'd ask after he'd eaten, or maybe I wouldn't. I didn't have to know all the details of the miracle all at once.

CHAPTER FORTY

W e helped Doris catch the puppies, which were doing laps around the pool. Jamie laughed as he held a squirming puppy. It struggled not to get down, but to lick his face. He'd been afraid of dogs, of most animals, for years, and now he acted like an armful of puppy was the best thing in the world. It made my heart ache to see him so happy about anything, but especially one of the many things he'd seemed terrified of for over ten years. I would not cry in front of him while he was laughing, but I wanted to; luckily the puppy in my hands gave a serious squirm and I had to concentrate not to drop it. The thought that I might drop the tiny dog instead of saving it was enough to dry up any thoughts of tears.

"You really need to get them life jackets, Doris," I said as I handed the puppy to her.

"I got them, they have little handles on them and everything. They're supposed to be napping, not out by the pool, and thank you for getting Charlie out of the pool when he fell in last week."

"I'm happy to help, and thank you for letting Connery play with them."

"Pugs love kids, and he helped tire these little maniacs out," she said, laughing as Donald tried to lick her face.

Jamie offered her the other puppy, and she tucked one under each arm. "Thank you both for catching the little hooligans."

"Our pleasure," Jamie said, and seemed to mean it.

One puppy started barking. "Charlie, stop that." He didn't stop and now it was a duo of puppy barks. "Don't you start, Donald."

"I'm going to take Jam . . . Levi upstairs for some food. We'll see you later."

"Have him make you some of that veggie pasta with the white sauce, it's delicious," she said as she turned with the wriggling puppies.

"I don't have the ingredients for that right now, Doris, maybe next time he visits."

"Invite me next time you make it," she called back as she used her foot to close the door, and the sound of excited barking grew a little dimmer.

"That was great," Jamie said.

I almost said, *But you're scared of dogs*, but I didn't, because his face was shining with joy, almost like the way Connery's did after he'd played with the dogs. It was like Jamie was reborn, childlike and happy, like the last thirteen years had been washed away. I said another quick prayer of gratitude and led him toward the only stairs leading up. My apartment was at the top of the stairs; just turn slightly to the right.

It was the smallest apartment in the building, tucked away on the top floor, but there was a picture window that went from almost ceiling to floor so the living room got a lot of light, and a second smaller window on the other side of the door made the two-seater kitchen table cheerful. The sunlight hit the pool below and bounced even more light up to us, so that it was almost never dark or gloomy. As a cop, I wasn't happy with the big window right by the front door, but as a person who'd just been kicked out of his home, I'd needed the light. The other apartments I could afford had been like dark holes. Neither my depression or my son would have done well there. Connery liked sitting at the table eating breakfast and watching the water shadows bounce along the roof overhang just outside the kitchen window. There were days when his happiness was everything to me.

"You always could do that," Jamie said.

I turned from the table and realized that I'd totally lost track of things for a second. Jamie seemed okay, better than okay, but bringing a potentially unstable person into my apartment and then zoning out was not a good idea.

"Do what?" I asked, and tried not to frown or act upset. Jamie could be sensitive to moods.

"Smile and have it look happy and sad at the same time."

"So, I've always been a gloomy overthinker, even at seven?" I asked with a smile.

He grinned. "Maybe not gloomy, but you've always been serious and an overthinker."

"Hey, I kept us out of trouble more than once, because I thought things through." I took off my suit jacket and put it on the back of the kitchen chair.

"I didn't think you followed sports, Havoc."

"What do you mean?" I asked.

He motioned at the shirt.

I looked down and realized I was wearing a Broncos shirt I'd borrowed from Charleston after my last clean shirt had been cut off me.

"I forgot I borrowed a shirt from my lieutenant."

"Why'd you need the shirt?"

"It's long story and I'd rather hear your story while I fix us dinner."

"What are we having?"

"Paninis."

"What kind of hot sandwiches?" he asked.

"Roast beef, three kinds of cheese, and a choice of dill or sweet bread-and-butter pickles. I've got mayonnaise, dijonnaise, and stone-ground mustard."

"What's dijonnaise?" he asked.

"A mix of mayonnaise and mustard in one bottle."

He made a face. "No, I don't want that."

"Hey, my kid loves the stuff."

"What toddler doesn't like mayonnaise and ketchup?"

"He's three, so don't call him a toddler to his face. He's a big boy now."

Jamie smiled. "I still can't believe you have a child, that any of us have a child."

I knew he meant Surrie, him, and me. "Yeah, Suriel was surprised, too."

"You've seen Surrie? Where? When?"

I mentally cursed myself for just blurting it out. "Tell me how you got better, and I'll tell you how I ran into Surrie."

His face crumpled and I watched an echo of the crazy Jamie in his eyes. "Suriel came to give us her expertise on a demon-related case today, that's all." It wasn't all, but I wanted to chase away that shadow in his eyes. I'd fill in the blanks after I got him talking about something else.

"So she stayed an Infernalist," he said, face serious and sad, and his eyes still not good.

"Yes."

"How was she?"

"She's third in line of all the Infernalists."

"I knew she'd do well at whatever she chose." It was almost an echo of what I'd thought, but he didn't look happy about it. He looked sad, worse.

I thought about telling him that I'd see Harshiel and Turmiel, too, but he'd never been friends with them, and his eyes still didn't look right. I wanted him well more than I wanted to talk about anyone at the College. I got the cheese out of the fridge, slicing some samples off the three kinds of cheese I had. I handed him a taste of muenster. He took it without thinking about it and ate it the same way. The moment he tasted it his eyes cleared. I'd noticed over the years that sometimes food could bring him back out of whatever trap his mind had become. It never brought him back completely; Gordon Ramsay couldn't have fixed a meal that would have cured him, but food helped, especially if he hadn't been eating enough.

"That's good, muenster, right."

"Yeah," I said and handed him a piece of the Old Croc cheddar, though it wouldn't melt well enough for a panini.

"Okay, that's amazing, what is it?"

"Old Croc cheddar, it doesn't melt well, but I can cut some with crackers for us to snack on while I cook the sandwiches."

"Yes, please," he said, and he looked happy again. His eyes were clearing of that shadow. He was better, so much better, but the broken bits were still inside him. I guess we never really get rid of the broken pieces; we heal, but the scar tissue stays to remind us of what happened.

I put the cheese and crackers on a small plate. They were supposed to be salad plates, but I'd never seen anyone serve salads on them; desserts yes, salads no. Reggie had explained to me that the tiniest plates in our wedding china were supposed to be the dessert plates.

"You look sad, what's wrong?" he asked.

"Did you know this is supposed to be a salad plate?" I said.

He looked down at the cheese and crackers, which were half gone. I almost told him that he was going to ruin his dinner as if he were Connery. Instead I reached for a cracker and a chunk of cheese, before he finished them all. If we shared, then neither of us would ruin our dinners.

"I thought it was for desserts."

"Me, too, but according to my wife they're salad plates and the really tiny plates are the dessert plates."

"You thought about Regina, that's why you looked sad," Jamie said. His dark eyes studied my face as if they could see inside my head to every thought, which had been true once, before he lost the gift along with his mind. He'd tested so high on the Methodius scale that teachers had compared him to Bachiel, who stayed in his high tower and listened to thoughts of the human world. It was a rare gift to be able to see angels and read human thoughts.

"Did you hear me thinking?" I asked.

"No, I am thankfully alone inside my head. It is so quiet, so peaceful inside me right now. Blessedly so." He closed his eyes and let out a deep sigh of contentment.

"I'm glad," I said, and meant it, but I had so many more questions that I wanted answered; I was just afraid that too many questions would undo the peace inside him.

"Is that supposed to be smoking?" he asked, pointing back at the stove.

"Crap!" I grabbed the pan off the heat and flipped the sandwich over. The bread wasn't black, but it wasn't the light golden brown I'd been aiming at either.

"I guess this one is mine," I said.

"Why?" he asked.

"Because I'm the cook and I burned it."

"I'm not sure I follow your reasoning, but okay." He took another piece of cheddar, broke it in half and put it on a cracker.

I put a second sandwich together and lowered the heat before I put it back on the flame. I watched this one more carefully, turning it over when the bread was a golden brown and not burned. By the time I had it finished, the Old Croc cheddar was gone, the plate empty except for two lonely crackers. I'd have offered him more cheese, but the sand-

wich was done. I plated it and set it down in front of him, trying not
to grin as he said, "Smells great, Z."

I did grin then, because it had been his nickname for me since we
were small. Suriel had never liked it, said it wasn't dignified. She'd always cared more about stuff like that even at eleven.

"Thanks, Lev," I said, using his old nickname.

He shook his head. "Levi is short enough, Z, maybe someday I'll
earn the other name back, but let's not jump the gun."

"Okay . . . Levi."

He gave me a truly dazzling smile as if I'd done something a lot more
special than use his new name. His teeth flashed white and I realized he'd
cleaned up everything. It wasn't that he was dirty exactly, but there just
weren't a lot of places to do a lot of personal hygiene when you were homeless. Especially when you wouldn't stay in a shelter for long. He had said
that the voices in his head were louder indoors, or he was closer to God
outside. Either way, I'd stopped trying to help him get a bed in some of the
better shelters, and halfway houses were out because he wouldn't stay on
the meds that the newest doctor had prescribed. I wanted to ask if he was
on meds now, but it wasn't a safe question. If he was on meds that worked,
I didn't want to do anything to make him question them.

I put my sandwich on another plate and sat down at the table with
him. Sunlight spilled a warm yellow rectangle across the table as we
ate. We didn't talk, but it wasn't awkward, it felt peaceful. We ate in
companionable silence. I normally liked the sandwich, but today it
could have been almost anything, and I still would have enjoyed it,
because Jamie was there, really there. Not just the shell of his body, but
his eyes were lit up, alive and full of humor and joy, and he was enjoying the food in front of him.

I was hungering for the sight of him sitting happily beside me more
than any food. How did I ask the questions I wanted to ask without
risking raising the shadows inside him?

"I'd forgotten that food could taste like this."

"Thanks, but it's just a hot sandwich."

"It's not the sandwich, though that was good. It's like I can taste food again. I can see color and light. It's like I was trapped in the valley of death and everything was gray and dark. Now I'm out and it's so much better."

"How did you get out?" I asked; because he'd brought it up, it seemed safer.

His smile wilted a little around the edges, and the shadows in his brown eyes were there for a second like a flinching, but then he took a deep breath and shook himself like a dog coming out of water.

"Can I have some tea, while I try to explain it all?"

"What kind of tea?" I asked.

"Hot, sweet, like I liked it before."

I got up smiling and went to the cabinet in the narrow galley kitchen. I got to turn around with a box of Bigelow's Chinese Fortune Oolong. I'd kept a box of it and made sure it was a fresh box, just in case. I'd kept it the way you'd keep your friend's favorite whiskey waiting for that one last drink together. We hadn't been allowed strong drink in the College, though we'd both made up for it once we left. I'd never stayed drunk the way that Jamie had, and I'd never done drugs, but I'd tried most of the things the College of Angels had forbidden us. Teenage rebellion, just done a decade late.

"Real cream, sugar in the raw, right?"

He gave me a big smile. "You remembered."

"You don't forget how your best friend likes his tea."

"I've spent so many years drinking and popping and injecting anything, everything, but I could never drink coffee. Even as lost as I was, that still tasted bitter to me."

"But tea didn't taste good?"

He shook his head. "Nothing tasted good, but things could taste bad." Again, there was that shadow across his face.

I put on hot water in a rapid-boil kettle that I'd gotten so I could do tea before I went to work. "I drink coffee at work mostly."

"Yuck," he said.

"Yuck? I've seen you drink liquor, cheap shit that I wouldn't clean my gun with, and coffee is yuck."

"Weird, huh?"

"Yeah, a little. So how did you get back to this, to you, to here?" I asked.

He looked down at his hands spread flat on the table in the sunlight. His hands were clean, but they were also the most tanned part of him, because he'd never worn gloves on the street, but he had covered most of the rest of him. I'd come to hate the old trench coat he'd worn over everything else. Not just because it was stained and smelled bad, but because he huddled in it like a security blanket, and because it reminded me of the wings of angels the way it would flap and billow around him when he was walking fast down the street. It was like a double slap in the face, the loss of him and the loss of being with the angels. Wings weren't necessary for an angel to translocate; nothing was, they could vanish in the blink of an eye. They could travel back to God, or wherever he wanted to send them, instantly. Yet most angels appeared as human forms with large, sweeping wings big enough to carry a human body upward like an eagle, because humans expected them to have wings. We expected them to be beautiful and to have wings. Only two things weren't humans projecting onto the angelic: halos of light, where the true forms of angels licked out around the edges, and height. Angels were tall; six feet was short for them. It was as if you couldn't shrink all that power down enough to be short. There were exceptions, there are always exceptions, but most angels couldn't squash themselves down enough to look truly human.

"You always were good at that," Jamie said.

I blinked and looked at him, realizing that I had been thinking more about angels than about the man sitting in my kitchen. "Good at what?" I asked.

"Silence, you could always be quiet and wait for me to talk."

I wondered how many times in the past my "silence" had been me lost in thoughts like now. I pushed the thought away to look at it later and tried to really be present for my friend. I needed to be here and now.

The timer on the microwave sounded. "Tea's ready," I said, and got up to get it.

He smiled, but he was staring at his hands on the tabletop, so I wasn't sure if he was smiling at that or at his own inner thoughts. One of the things that had made us friends was that he was almost as introspective as I was. Surrie was cautious, but even she told us, "You think too much, sometimes you just have to do things."

"Whatcha thinking about?" I asked, using the phrase that we'd used when the three of us were younger, before everything went wrong.

"It feels like Suriel should be here to say that, and get us talking instead of just brooding," he said. His smile somehow was sad now.

I put the tea bags on the spoon rest and said, "She stopped saying it by the time we were fifteen or sixteen."

"When we all finalized our specialties," he said. He was staring at his hands now, smile gone.

I added sugar to both teas and real cream to his, and set it down in front of him. "Tea just the way you like it," I said, smiling, hoping for one in return.

He warmed his hands over the steam like it was a fire and the day had turned cold. The sunlight was still warm; it was Southern California, it wasn't cold.

"Talk to me, Jamie, please." I sat down at the table not across from him, but in the chair facing the window so I could be closer. We weren't eating now, so elbow room wasn't an issue.

"Levi, my name is Levi now."

"Okay, Levi, sorry but it's going to take me a little bit to get used to the new name."

"Like it took for you to finally call me Jamie."

"You had been Levanael since we were seven. I didn't even remember your birth name by the time we were nineteen."

"Nor I yours."

He was somber again, almost sad.

"You look great, Jam . . . Levi," I said, trying to sound cheerful and chase the shadows away.

"I look a lot better than I did two weeks ago." He took his first sip of tea and closed his eyes as if he was letting it melt on his tongue like it was his favorite candy.

"What happened two weeks ago?" I asked, my voice soft, tone neutral like I'd learned in interrogations when the victim was potentially fragile.

He opened his big brown eyes and looked directly at me with that burn of intelligence and insight fully behind them. It sent a thrill through me that was somewhere between sexual and scary. I'd wanted this for so long, but I didn't trust the change to last, and I didn't know if I had another crushing disappointment in me. I wasn't sure I could take it if he reverted. I prayed, prayed that this would last, that he was cured, well.

"I woke up," he said.

"I don't understand."

"I'm not sure I do either, but did you ever have a dream where you think you woke up, but it's just another kind of nightmare, so that you keep dreaming you get out of bed, but you're actually still trapped in the dream?"

"Yes, I guess everyone has them sometimes."

"Maybe, but everyone else wakes up. I've been trapped in a nightmare for over thirteen years."

"Do you think the last fifteen years have been just dreams and nightmares?" I tried to study his face, to see his answer there, but he was looking down at the tea so I saw mostly the top of his thick brown hair and a rim of face. His hands looked so much darker as he lifted his cup to drink more tea. They were tanned and weathered more than his face, as if the beard and wild hair had protected him like fur, but his poor hands . . . they looked like they belonged to someone older. Someone who'd worked outdoors their whole life maybe, but not the soft, smiling boy I remembered. He'd been the best of us all, the gentlest soul, the kindest heart, and the highest scorer on all the tests for psychic ability, as long as it was pure power being tested and not control of that power.

He sipped the tea and looked at me over the rim of the cup. His eyes looked very dark for a moment, almost black, the way they'd get the few times he got truly angry.

"Maybe I just want to think of it as a nightmare so I don't have to think too hard about everything I did while I was sick." The voice was deeper, not a hint of laughter in it; this was how he'd sounded on good days over the last decade.

"I can understand that." I finally sipped my tea and it was good, but I'd let it start to get cool. I didn't want tea, I wanted Levanael, I wanted to undo the shadow in his eyes and the tone in his voice.

"I can feel your questions hanging like something heavy around you."

"You can't hear them?" I asked, and took another sip of tea.

His eyes held that bitterness I'd come to dread, but it was better than the rage, or the terror. That was the worst. "Not right now. I told you my head is quiet, quieter than it's been since I hit puberty. You know the theory that God doesn't let our full powers hit while we're too little to cope with them?"

"Of course, that's why they recruit so early for the College. They want to train us to control our powers before they are fully fledged. Untrained psychics and witches who suddenly grow into their power as teenagers are dangerous to everyone, including themselves."

"I don't remember when I couldn't hear other people's thoughts," he said, and upended his teacup like you'd finish off liquor, or maybe his was getting cold, too.

"I remember that your parents brought you into the College to see if the angels could help you."

He flashed me a smile and asked, "Could I have another cup?"

"I'll make us a pot if you want."

"Do you have a real teapot?"

I grinned and went to the cabinet over the microwave. I got down a carefully covered bundle and set it on the cabinet by the stove.

"Is that a tea cozy on it?" he asked, and sounded happy again like I hadn't heard him in so long. I didn't want the serious sad coming back; it made me feel like the positive change was only temporary. I wanted it to last.

"Yes, though I like thinking of them as tea sleeping bags," I said, and lifted off the deep blue tea cozy.

He laughed again, head back and just so happy. "I'd forgotten that we used to call them tea sleeping bags when we were little, and how did you get a nice heavy teapot like Master Sarphiel had?"

"I sent away to England for it when we bought our house." I pushed the thought away that Reggie had packed it up in a box with some other things she thought I'd need in the apartment, as if I wouldn't need a big teapot at the house anymore.

"What did Master Sarphiel here call it, a Brown Betty?"

"Yes, though since this one is a deep blue is it still a Brown Betty, or is it a Blue Betty?"

He chuckled. "I don't know, and I don't care. It takes me back to those endless pots of tea when we were all still together before we had to choose specialties."

I nodded. "I've told Connery it's a tea cozy, but when he asked what that meant, I told him it was a sleeping bag for the teapot to keep it warm."

"Does he call it a tea sleeping bag?"

"He says, 'Don't forget the sleeping bag, Daddy. The tea needs to be warm.'"

"That's great, I'm sorry I scared him the last time. I didn't mean to."

"I know you didn't mean to."

The sadness started to slip back over his face as I put enough water in the teakettle to fill the big pot. "You can feel my questions, so I'll just ask, how did your head get so quiet? How did you clean up and get . . . better?"

He smiled, chasing back the shadow in his eyes. "I was sleeping in an alley, I'm not even sure where I was exactly, but I woke up and there were people standing over me. I thought I was going to get robbed or beaten up again."

I fought to keep my face neutral at the *again*. I'd taken him to the emergency room at least five times myself. I'd hated that he wouldn't stay in the shelters where he was safer, not safe, I knew better, but safer than that.

"But they didn't hurt you?"

"They were prophets," he said, his face sliding into that seriousness again.

"Oh," was all I said, because street prophets could be just another name for crazy homeless person, except that they thought they had the ear of God, or the angels, or a saint, or even occasionally the devil. A lot of schizophrenics thought they heard the voice of God; how did you tell delusion from true prophecy?

"I know what you're thinking, Z. They were the real deal."

"I thought you couldn't read my thoughts."

"I don't need to; that little *oh* and the way you go all stiff through the shoulders, that was enough."

"Sorry, I didn't mean to insult the prophets."

"I know some of them are crazy like I was, but in between the crazy some of us truly do hear the angels, or spirits and powers of one kind or another." He was getting sullen again. I had a glimpse of what his face must have looked like behind the beard and hair all these years. There was a sourness to it that looked wrong on his shaved face, as if the old crazy Jamie was getting mixed up with the original Jamie, which I guess was exactly what was happening. Even if he stayed sane from this day on, the years on the street had to have left their mark.

I sat back down across from him this time, because I wanted to see his expression full on. "What did the prophets tell you?"

"That I needed to go to a shop and talk to a woman who worked there."

"What shop?"

He gave me a sly smile that had always been edged with beard before this; I didn't like the smile still being in him. It was an unpleasant smile, the one that meant he was usually about to say something crazy, or mean, or both. I prayed that whatever he said next wouldn't be either.

He looked confused. "Part of me wants to say *I bet you'd like to know*, or *It's none of your business*, but it's like habit. It's not what I want to say to you."

"What do you want to say to me?" I asked, trying to keep my voice and face neutral so I didn't trigger any negative urges in him.

"I want to tell you about the shop and that Emma works there. She does reiki and reads tarot. The prophets told me a woman wearing a rose would help me close my shields so I could be alone inside my head." The confusion moved to something else, something that didn't quite believe in going to look for a woman with a rose.

"Why did you do what they said?" I asked.

"Is it that obvious that I didn't believe them?" he asked.

"To me, it is," I said.

He smiled then. "I guess expressions and body language don't change that much with time."

"I don't know about that, but we can still read each other."

He offered me a fist bump and I touched his fist with mine just as the rapid-boil kettle beeped to let me know the water was hot.

"Make the tea, Z. I'll talk while you do it."

"Sounds good," I said, and got up to pour hot water into the big blue teapot. I swirled a splash of hot water around to warm the pot. Master Sarphiel had always been very firm on that. The tea steeped better in a warm pot than in a cold one.

"I can't tell you everything, because I don't remember all of it, or understand what I do remember."

"That's okay, Jam . . . Levi, just tell me what you can."

"I honestly don't remember what alley I was sleeping in when they woke me up. I just stared up at this group of shapes. I had a few seconds of wondering if they were real, or I was seeing spirits, or hallucinating, or having someone else's nightmare, or maybe my own? I thought I was flashing back to the last bad beating I got."

"The hospital called me on that one." I was glad I had finished pouring the hot water into the pot, because my hands shook. I lost one of the tea bags, but with the others I got their strings tight underneath the lid of the teapot. I slid the tea cozy over the pot to make sure it stayed hot while the tea steeped, then set the timer for ten minutes.

"You're still my emergency contact," he said.

"But you said they were prophets, not thugs."

"Yes, when I was sure I wasn't still dreaming, they gave me their message about going to the shop and talking to a woman with a rose."

I leaned against the edge of the cabinet and watched him instead of sitting back down. "But you didn't believe them?"

"No, I thought they were just crazy like me, so I laid back down and told them to leave me alone."

"And did they, leave you alone?"

He gave a little chuckle. "No, because at least two of them were prophets, the real thing. They grabbed my arms and pulled me to my feet. I started to try and fight them, but they were a lot stronger than they seemed. I wondered if they were angels in disguise for a second, because of how strong their hands were on my arms."

"Angels don't do that much anymore," I said.

"No, but they had the strength of God in their hands. I felt that and knew they were real." He was quiet so long I prompted him and asked what happened next.

"I started walking in the direction of the shop. It wasn't close to where I was, and I didn't have money for any other way to travel. I was lucky that I didn't get arrested for walking in the middle of the road, because I did that some, I remember getting honked at and then realizing I was in the middle of the damn road."

It startled me that he cursed. We had all been taught that curses should be saved for when you meant them. Jamie didn't mean the road to be damned, or a road to Hell. I wanted to remind him why he shouldn't use it so casually, but I kept my mouth shut and listened.

"I made it to the street where the shop is, but then I heard or saw someone's thoughts. This man just walked by and he was thinking so hard that I just started following him. I probably would have followed him for miles, or until his thoughts calmed down, but a woman walked by us wearing a T-shirt with roses on it. It made me stop, literally stop on the sidewalk. I was able to let the man's thoughts go. I could hear them getting farther away, but I turned and started following her."

I wondered how the woman had felt about being followed by Jamie before he'd cleaned himself up. The tea timer sounded and saved me from letting my body language tell him what I was thinking. I was too busy lifting the tea cozy off, taking the tea bags out, and fishing with the tongs for the one that I'd lost in the tea.

"I followed her through the door into her shop. I mean I was right behind her. I'm lucky she didn't call the cops."

"Were you able to tell her why you were there?" I asked, getting our mugs off the table so I could put sugar in them.

He gave a laugh that was more bitter than funny. "Tell her that a bunch of wandering prophets told me to look for a woman with roses. The truth didn't sound very sane."

"Did she believe you?" I asked, as I poured tea into the mugs, adding cream to both.

"She did, and I know whatever I said to her wasn't as clear as what I'm saying now. She should have called the cops, or told me to leave her shop, but she had this gentle energy. It reminded me of how I used to feel when I prayed, and God liked the prayer."

I set his tea in front of him and sat down across the table from him, because I wanted to see as much of his face as I could. Profile wasn't enough for me to read him.

He looked at me with those big brown eyes. They'd always dominated his face so that you saw his eyes and then the rest of him. *Compelling* was what one of the other female Angel Speakers had said once: "Levanael's eyes are so compelling." She'd been right.

"What happened next?" I asked.

"Emma, that's her name, said that she dreamed about me coming to the shop."

"Wow," I said, and felt like we were ten again and had just seen some bit of angel magic we'd only read about before.

"I know, it was extraordinary. Not just that she had the dream but that she was willing to trust it enough to take me back to one of the small rooms where they do reiki and tarot. You know what I looked like before, Heaven help me, smelled like before, but Emma just took me in the room as if I was normal." He smiled and sipped his tea before adding, "The owner of the shop was there and wouldn't let Emma close the door. In fact, she stayed at the door watching over us. I can't blame her. In fact, I'm glad she was looking out for Emma. She's this amazing gentle energy that just feels good to be near."

"Like the right kind of angel," I said.

He nodded. "That's sort of how she feels, but it's like when we were around the priests that felt right. The energy of faith, true faith."

"That's really rare," I said, drinking my own tea. It was good and I really needed to drink it before it got cold this time.

"It is."

"What did she do to"—I made a vague motion at him—"for you?"

He took another sip of tea, sighing happily. "I'm so glad I can taste things again."

"Me, too," I said, and meant it.

"The healing started with Emma's energy, and then she did actual energy work on me. Part of it was reiki, that's what she's got certificates in, but part of it was just intuitive energy work, that's what she called it."

I drank my tea and didn't say that I'd never seen just energy work make a miracle like this. It could help, but this kind of change took more than one miracle cure.

"It was crystals and herbs and her guides talking to my guides."

"You mean your Guardian Angels?"

"Not just the angels, but the other spiritual beings that are supposed to help protect me."

I thought about Ravensong's raccoon, the great bear and the blond Goddess or Valkyrie at her back. "Spirit guides and totems, you mean?"

"Yes," he said.

I wondered if I lowered my shields and opened my senses, would I see some new power around him? I didn't do it because it was too risky. I'd seen what was around Ravensong, and then I'd been in that place beyond where music was visible and angels moved along the humming strings of the universe. I couldn't risk having Jamie follow me into that place, because it was traveling to it that had driven him mad.

"Did Emma help you get cleaned up, too?"

"She helped me get some clothes from Goodwill and she let me use her bathroom to get cleaned up. Her boss made sure that Emma's roommates were home while I was there."

"I take it that the owner of the New Age shop doesn't have the same energy as Emma."

He stirred his tea, smiled, frowned, smiled again, and said, "No, her energy feels very pointy like a porcupine, so that nothing gets in her shields."

"Anyone sensitive to energy wouldn't want to be around that."

"True, maybe she only was pointy at me, keeping my energy off outside her shields," he said, sitting back down with his tea. He wrapped his hands around the mug as if it didn't have a handle. He didn't drink from it right away, as if he was more warming his hands on the mug.

"You look great," I said.

He shook his head. "I look better, but great, I'll get there."

I reached across the table and put my hand on his arm. "You look great to me, Lev-I, Levi."

He put his hand over mine. "Thanks, Z. I'm sorry for everything I put you through."

"You don't have to apologize, you were sick."

"I do need to apologize, but thank you for saying that."

"Does Emma know what caused everything to go . . . off?"

"You mean why I went crazy at the very end of training to be an Angel Speaker?"

"Yes, but if it's hard to talk about we can wait. It's just that no one at the College understood what happened."

"We're not a hundred percent certain, but we think it's my telepathy."

"There are other telepaths at the College," I said.

"But no one as powerful as I am, Z."

"No one but Master Bachiel," I said.

"Emma thinks that he, or some of the teachers, should have protected me more. She says I had almost no ability to shield my gift."

"They did teach us how to shield ourselves," I said.

"I never got good at personal shielding, remember?"

I thought about it. "That's right, it was your weakest skill set."

"Inside the College it didn't matter; the wards around it are so solid and well constructed that they protected me."

"They protected us all," I said.

He nodded. "But when we started working directly with the realm of angels, there was nothing to shield me from them."

"Shield you from the angels?" I asked.

He shook his head. "No, not from them, from the thoughts of all the people praying to the angels and to God."

"I don't understand."

"Can't you hear prayers?"

"Sometimes, if I'm not shielding tight enough, or if the prayer has a lot of need or emotion behind it."

"How did you filter out the prayers inside the angelic realm?"

"I don't hear prayers unless I'm listening for them there."

"What do you hear?"

"Music," I said.

"Music, just music?"

"Beautiful, amazing music like the universe is created out of music and light."

He stared at me as if I'd said something terrible. "Music and light, just music and light?"

"I see angels and I see the light and lines of creation."

"You didn't hear the voices of all the people praying, asking for God's help?"

"No," I said.

The blood drained from his face so suddenly that I got up to put a hand on his shoulder in case he fainted. "Jamie, Levi, are you okay?"

"I heard voices, millions and millions of thoughts, prayers, screams of pain, people screaming in agony and begging God to help them."

I knelt by him so I could look into his face. "You heard people screaming for help, while the rest of us saw music and lights?"

He nodded, his face so pale his lips looked bloodless. "I couldn't shut it out. Even when the teachers brought me back from the heart of creation, I could still hear them."

"You could still hear prayers all the time?"

"No, I could shut out prayers, you know, unless they were strong like you said, but it was the people screaming and crying for God to help them that I couldn't shut out. So many people calling for help and no one answering."

"God answers prayers, but sometimes the answer is no," I said.

His eyes looked black in the white of his face like burned holes. "These weren't prayers, Z, they were people crying out in torment, begging God, or someone, to help them, and no one ever came. I didn't hear the people that were being helped, all I heard were the ones that didn't get a visit from an angel, or anything good."

"And you've heard that in your head for fifteen years?"

"Yes." I didn't know what to say. What could I say to make up for him being trapped like that for so long? Nothing. I said the only thing possible.

"I am so sorry, Jamie."

"Levi, I am Levi now, a name of my choice. Not my parents or the College, but my choice."

"Levi, I am so sorry that happened to you and that no one at the College understood what was happening to you."

"Emma found some other psychics to help me. One of them is a telepath almost as powerful as I am. He says that if Master Bachiel had a similar gift he should have known I couldn't shield well enough, and he should have been able to hear the voices I was hearing."

"I was there when he came to look at you. He said that no one at the College of Angels could help you."

"Is that exactly what he said?" Jamie asked.

"Yes, I made him repeat it, because I didn't want to believe it."

"He didn't say *wouldn't*, but that they couldn't, you're sure?"

"I'm sure, because I kept going over and over everything that happened, looking for something else I could have done to help you, to keep them from kicking you out. I should have gone with you."

"No, Z, we were both kids. I was too crazy in the head for you to take care of me. Your place was there."

"How did Emma teach you to shield when the masters at the College couldn't?"

"She gave me objects, magical objects to help me shield while I learned. She brought in other witches to do a spell to help me quiet the voices while I got stronger."

"They prayed over you at the College."

"But they didn't do any active magic to help me."

"Prayer and the angels are the only magic we need."

"Well, I needed something else. Did they even consult a witch, or anyone outside the College?"

"They don't deal with witches, you know that."

"They deal with psychics, that's God's gift being used. Did they ask any psychics to help diagnose me?"

"They brought in healers and doctors to see you."

"And none of them could figure it out, really?"

"No," I said.

"Bachiel should have known, or at least suspected, that's what Emma says anyway. That if he was as powerful a telepath as he's supposed to be, he should have heard the voices in my head."

"If that's what was wrong, then yes, he should have heard the voices when he examined you."

"What do you mean, if that's what was wrong?"

"I just can't believe that Bachiel, Master Bachiel, would have let you suffer if he could have helped you."

"Maybe he couldn't have helped heal me, but he should have known what was wrong."

"I don't know what to say. How did Emma do what the entire College of Angels couldn't?"

"It's a medi-spell, an experimental medi-spell that's part medicine and part magic. It's designed to help teenagers who are just getting their full powers to shield and control them. Emma's brother is a doctor, that's how she got me into the medical trials."

"Then Bachiel was right, no one back then could have helped you."

Jamie pushed the chair back and stood up. "Why are you defending him? If he is as strong a telepath as he claims, he knew what I was hearing, knew what drove me insane. If he'd just told the doctors that it was telepathy stuck on and too loud, maybe they could have helped me?"

I stood up, too. "They tried, but the only thing that helped was to drug you out of your mind. Your eyes were open, but it was like you weren't there. They couldn't keep you on the dosage that made everything quiet, because it made all of you quiet. You stared at the wall, or at nothing, for hours. I'd never felt so helpless in my life."

"I don't remember any of that," he said.

"The drugs wouldn't let you remember. They wouldn't let you do anything."

He shook his head. "Someone should have been powerful enough to figure this out sooner, Z."

"I don't know why they couldn't help you more, Jamie."

He screamed, "That is not my name!" His hands were in fists at his sides. He was so angry he was shaking.

"Levi," I said, my voice as calm as I could make it, "Levi, I don't know why the College failed you."

"I'm sorry, Z, I shouldn't have yelled at you." His voice was calmer, but he was still shaking.

"It's okay, Levi."

"I should go."

"Let me drive you," I said.

"You mean you want to see if I'm lying, or hallucinating Emma and the shop. You want to see if I'm still homeless." A look slid through his eyes that I didn't like at all; it was that sly, almost evil look. It always seemed like it was someone else looking out of Jamie's eyes. It was there for a moment and then he was back, blinking gentle brown eyes at me. "I don't know why I said that, Z."

"I believe you about Emma and the rest, because I can see the change in you."

"I know you believe me, Z."

"I'd like to meet the person who helped you and see the shop. I'd really like to talk to them about how they helped you in more detail, because if the masters at the College messed up with you this badly, then are there others that we could find and help?"

Jamie looked up at me. "I hadn't thought about that. I've just been so happy that I was back to myself that I never thought about others. It's like I've been trapped in their prayers and pain so long, I just want to concentrate on me." He got that look on his face that he'd had from the moment I knew him at seven, so sincere, so worried. "Is that bad of me, Z?"

"No, no, if you don't take care of yourself, you can't take care of anyone else."

"Are you sure?"

"I'm sure," I said, but I hugged him so he couldn't see my face, because I worried about the same kind of thing. I was a detective. One of the things that Reggie had hated was that sometimes I couldn't get a case out of my head. I'd tried to explain that people could die, or murderers could get away, or victims might never be found, or Heaven and Hell could go to war again and destroy the world and everything and everyone on it. When I'd said that last, she'd gotten the angriest of all, because she said, "So I'm a selfish bitch to want my husband's full attention, because it could cause the apocalypse? No pressure there."

I hugged Jamie a little harder, because he and Suriel were the first people that I thought would always be there for me. They'd been my family until I found Reggie and we had Connery.

Jamie pulled back from the hug to study my face. "What did you just think about, Z?"

I shook my head and stepped back, but he grabbed my arm. "Talk to me, Z, please. I've been missing for years, let me be here, really be here for you and for me again."

My eyes felt hot, damn it I was not going to let him see me cry, but my throat was too tight with grief to speak. God help me, God help us both.

"Z, please, talk to me."

The first hard tear trailed down my face. I pulled away and went to the kitchen with my back to him. "Let's do more tea and then you can call Emma or let me drive you." My voice was neutral, but the first tear had been joined by more. I'd learned to cry without letting it show in my voice or face years ago. Men didn't cry, especially in the military, or on the force. Hell, soldiers and cops of either sex weren't supposed to cry. We were supposed to be strong, and tears weren't strong, but more than that I didn't want to explain the tears to Jamie. I was afraid that it would trigger something in him that would undo all the progress that he'd made. It was a miracle that he was standing here with me. I didn't want to spoil it by being weak and human.

I knew he was behind me before he wrapped his arms around my waist and hugged me from behind. I startled, stiffening in the embrace, because I'd been too long in the outside world where men didn't do this. I'd almost forgotten that there had been a time in my life when I hadn't thought anything about it. The College of Angels taught that male and female didn't matter, that we were all one, and affection was innocent like small children. I'd believed that until I was about fifteen. Suriel had already started to pull away from casual physical affection, but Jamie never had. He'd come to us for cuddling like we were all still seven years old huddling in little homesick puppy piles.

"I'm here, Z, just like when we were kids. You can tell me anything."

I patted his hands where they held me and told him part of the truth. "I was thinking about Reggie and Connery, and you and Suriel. Everyone I've ever loved." I almost choked on that last part because it was too much truth.

Jamie held me tighter and only the height difference kept it from being more intimate than it could be. "Is that all you have ever loved, truly, Zaniel?" The cadence of the words wasn't Jamie.

My skin ran cold with terror because I knew that voice. The tears were gone, dried up along with the inside of my mouth.

Jamie's arms were less tight, but he leaned against me in a way that wasn't just friends and was . . . softer, something, as if it wasn't just the cadence of Her speech that he was channeling, but Her body movements, too.

"Zaniel, why did you leave the College?"

"Jamie, let go of me."

"Why did you leave, Zaniel?"

"Let go of me, now."

"I felt your touch for the first time in so long when you came into the light."

I finally used his angel name. "Levanael, let me go, please." If Jamie could hear me, then I had a choice of using violence to stop him from touching me or let her get a stronger hold on me. Clothes helped; bare skin was always . . . harder with her.

Jamie let go of my waist with one arm, as if he'd finally heard me, and then his hand touched the skin of my arm, as if she'd heard my thoughts about bare skin.

I saw her in my head like a daydream, hair spun of light so that you could never call it blond, but yellow, or even gold didn't describe the color of her hair, not really. Her skin was a shade of paler light as if I needed other words that meant white and energy, and fire, and ice, and elemental things that did not exist for humans. Her body was perfect, because she'd created it for me, the fantasies of a teenage boy and her own preferences from human media, thoughts and wishes. She would always be my fantasy made almost flesh, except she could never get it quite right, because short of incarnating she couldn't be human, but then human was overrated, I thought as I stared into her eyes like blue sky, but a sky that never ended and never touched the Earth. It was like looking into eternity, beautiful eternity.

She reached one shining hand out toward me, and I knew that all I had to do was reach back and I could travel the music of the spheres and the light of God to find her.

I tore myself away from Jamie, screaming, "NO!"

Jamie stumbled back against the table as if I'd shoved him. He had to grab the edge of it to steady himself or I would have knocked him to the ground. "I didn't know she was still there waiting for you."

"She's eternal, she can wait forever," I said.

"I'm sorry, Z, I didn't mean to channel her."

"You were the clearest, purest channeler in our year at the College. It's not your fault; when the higher angelic orders want to speak through you, it's not like you can say no."

"You said no."

"She isn't trying to use me as a channel to speak through, Levanael."

"No, she wants you the way a woman wants a man. I didn't know that she had fallen, I'm so sorry, Zaniel."

"Is she completely fallen now? Did I damn us both?"

"You're not damned, Z, and neither is she."

The tears were back, why was I crying? "Are you sure?"

"She hasn't joined the enemy, so she's not damned, and not completely fallen, just sort of . . . crisped around the edges."

"She didn't look burned to me."

"I don't mean literal fire, Zaniel, you should know that."

I nodded and wiped at the stupid, traitorous tears.

"I'd forgotten how good it felt to channel the higher levels of the angelic." He raised his hand up in front of his face. "I feel like my skin should glow with all the power."

I didn't know what to say, because I was so scared, I could taste iron on my tongue. I'd felt her twice today. The first time was my fault, getting too caught up in my old abilities, but this time, I hadn't done anything to call her to me this time, which meant she'd sought me out.

"I can't imagine what it was like to touch her for real like you did, Z. If it felt better than this, I couldn't have told her no."

"One of us had to be strong enough to stop, or she would have fallen. I couldn't let that happen. I couldn't be responsible for that, for her being . . . lost."

"You were what nineteen, twenty?"

"Yeah, somewhere in there."

"How did you have the strength to question it at only twenty?"

"I prayed for guidance and strength and God gave it to me."

"When I prayed for God to help quiet my mind, nothing came." The happiness in his face began to fade. The confidence and power that he'd gained from channeling an angel began to seep away like a cup with a crack in it. It hurt my heart to see it happening in front of me.

I wanted to hug him again, but I was afraid to touch him too much, afraid that She would come back through the clear channel of Jamie's talent. I put my hand on his shoulder where the shirt protected us both from skin-to-skin contact. I prayed that it would be enough to protect us from her attention. The touch on his shoulder made him look at me. "Some prayers take longer to answer than others, Levanael."

His eyes held sorrow like rain to drown all the sunshine in the world. His eyes had always been like that; *expressive* didn't quite cover Jamie's eyes. How could I help him? Then the thought came, and I thought, *Oh, yeah*, and felt slow for not thinking of it sooner.

"Let's pray," I said.

His eyes focused on me instead of on the dark thoughts in his head. "I remember you used to ask me that when you found me on the streets. We even tried it a few times and it didn't help."

"'Prayer isn't a grocery list for miracles, it's a tool for talking to God.'"

Jamie smiled and his eyes filled with it. "Master Sarphiel said that all the time in every class we had with him."

"'Prayer is just one way to bring yourself into alignment with the divine,'" I said, repeating another common refrain from Master Sarphiel.

"'Any person on the planet can pray, Levanael, you must do better than that.'" He even got the inflection of the voice right.

It made me laugh. "Inside the College with all the wards and magical shielding, yes, but outside in the world let's just pray, okay?"

Jamie's smile wilted around the edges. His serious eyes studied my face. "You're afraid she'll come back through me again, aren't you?"

I took a breath trying to think how to word it, then finally nodded.

"It felt good to channel her. It felt good to be an Angel Speaker again," Jamie said.

"Angels speak to me, but they speak through you."

"Only because I'm not strong enough to meet them in person like you are, like Suriel was."

"Neither of us was a clear enough channel for God's grace and light to shine through us."

"Master Bachiel said I was too empty, and the two of you were too full of yourselves, to be a clear channel for the divine."

"You mean we were too arrogant in our power to let anyone speak through us, even God."

"No, you both had strong enough personalities that there wasn't room for anyone else. I was always less sure of myself than either of you. Master Bachiel said I didn't fill up all the room inside myself, that's why I channeled so easily and why I could hear prayers. I was closer to the angels that sat nearer to God, reflecting his glory and praise."

"I don't remember him saying that to you."

"It was in one of our private sessions. He was training me to be his successor at one point, remember?"

I nodded. "I remember." I had thought it was a bad idea at the time. Surrie and I had both thought that Jamie was too gentle and felt too deeply to match the sternness of Bachiel. I'd been amazed when the College said that Jamie was the first student in decades that rivaled Master Bachiel's abilities, and that he should train him. Their gifts from God might have matched, but nothing else did.

"What are you thinking, Zaniel?"

I was startled too far into my own memories, so I told him the truth. "I always thought that Bachiel wasn't a good mentor for you; just because your gifts matched didn't mean that he was the right teacher for you."

"You and Surrie said so at the time, but the College and Bachiel insisted, and everyone else told me it was an honor to be groomed to take Bachiel's duties on. Why didn't he help me shut out the pain of all the unanswered prayers, Z?"

"I don't know, but I'd like to contact the College and find out."

He grabbed my arm and I startled, half expecting her to take him over again, but it was just his hand on my skin, just him and me. Something tight and scared in my gut eased.

"Don't go back, Z, if you do she'll find you."

I nodded. "After I told the College what had happened between us, She was put in a place between."

"You mean they imprisoned her?"

"No, She agreed to enter because there's really no way to lock up one of the seraphim, not really. She agreed to meditate on her transgression to decide if she saw it as an actual sin. She thought I would stay at the College and finish my training if she exiled herself, and she was half right."

"You finished your training. I remember you coming and finding me to tell me you'd become an Angel Speaker. I was proud and happy for you, but I was ashamed that I had failed so utterly."

"I'm sorry, Levanael, I just wanted to share it with you, but I was selfish and didn't think how you'd take it."

"That was the first time you took me to a hospital and got me locked up."

"You were trying to hurt yourself."

"I don't remember everything, but I know it was bad. You were trying to keep me alive; some of the voices told me that you'd help me stay alive. It's probably why I kept coming to find you sometimes."

"I'm sorry I couldn't let you stay with me all the time."

"I scared your little boy the last time. I remember that much. I'm so sorry, Z. I hope he won't be scared of me forever. I hope he'll forgive me."

"I think he will," I said, but thought that I wouldn't put the two of them in the same room until Jamie had proven the recovery was permanent. Connery would get over one scare, but multiple ones . . . I didn't want to push it. If I got my best friend back, I wanted my son to love him like I did.

"I'm too nervous to pray to God right now, Z. Emma introduced me to the Goddess and she's, they're both, it's like the energy I've been missing. I'm not sure what God will think about that."

"I work with a lot of people that follow the Goddess. They're good people, and I don't think God is as jealous a God as the Old Testament makes him out to be."

"I think you're right, but I'd still rather wait to test the theory."

"You had an angel, a seraph, speak through you, Levanael. If that doesn't speak to your purity of heart and soul, I don't know what does."

He smiled then. "I hadn't thought about it like that. If you'd tried to get me to agree to channel an angel, especially one of the higher orders, then I'd have been too scared, felt unworthy, but it just happened and it worked. It means I'm not damned after all."

"Why would you be damned, Levanael?"

"God judged me and found me wanting, and then he cast me out. The original idea of Hell is to be cut off from contact with God, and I have been that for ten years."

"I'm so sorry, Levanael."

"I've been letting you call me that since She spoke through me, but they stripped the name from me when they cast me out of the College."

"You know how rare the ability to channel the more powerful angels is even among the trained Angel Speakers," I said.

He nodded. "But they took my name and forced me to be Jamie again. I hadn't been that name in so long that it didn't feel like me. I was Levanael and they made me Jamie again. He was a child; I was five when I gave up that name."

"Sometimes I forget that you were chosen two years earlier than either Suriel or me."

"Yeah, we were all seven, but I'd been at the College longer than anyone in my year. They brought me inside at five because I was already hearing voices; my parents brought me to get me some miracle from the angels, and as soon as I went inside the walls and all the wards and mystical shielding, it was better. It was a miracle, but it only worked inside the College, and then it stopped working even inside. When they threw me out . . . it was so much worse than before."

His eyes went haunted again, and I didn't know what to say, because I'd let him go. I'd protested and appealed to everyone inside the College who would talk to me, but in the end that was all I'd done, talk to people. I'd gone back to my own training, because She had been waiting for me, all gold and light and power and . . . she'd been my whole world, and that she consumed me enough to make me forget about what had happened to Jamie was the beginning of me questioning it, questioning her.

"I'm sorry, Levanael, sorry that I didn't do more to help you when it happened."

"It's okay, Z, you were the only one from the College who ever came to find me. Even Surrie never came looking, I really thought she would."

I debated again on telling him more about her visit, but wasn't sure if it would help or hurt. A phone rang and saved me the debate, because it was the smartphone in his pocket, not mine.

"Emma!" The way he said her name was enough for me to know that he had a crush on her, if not more. They talked back and forth for a few minutes. Jamie's face was more animated than I'd seen it in years. I prayed that Emma was enjoying her end of the conversation as much as Jamie was.

Jamie's face sobered a little around the edges and then he held the phone out to me. "Emma says she needs to speak to you."

I might have questioned it, but I wanted to talk to the person who had helped Jamie so much, so I just took the phone and said, "Hello."

"Hello, Zaniel, if I can call you that. Levi says that you don't always like people using your full name."

"Of course you may."

She gave this laugh that made me smile without meaning to, and said, "Then call me Emma."

"Okay, Emma, you wanted to speak to me."

"Yes, my guides said that you and Levi had experienced a major channeling event."

I was quiet on my end of the phone.

"What's wrong, Z?" Jamie asked, watching my face.

I repeated what she'd said.

He smiled. "Oh yeah, Emma is way hooked up magically. Her guides are good."

I was so startled that I said the truth out loud. "I'm not sure anyone on my unit is this good."

She gave that infectious laugh again, but I managed to fight off the smile this time. "Flattery like that will turn a witch's head clean around." I almost asked the mundane question of whether she meant that for real before another peal of laughter made me realize she'd made a joke. She was a witch, not a supernatural; her physicality and physics still worked like normal. I knew that, but for just a second, I wondered, and I knew better. I had to meet this woman. If she was this good, then even as a consultant for the unit she'd be valuable. There was a moment where I got that little psychic slap of *That's not what you're supposed to be thinking*. I took a breath and tried to center myself, quiet myself and hear the voice of God, or the angels, or I guess Emma would say my guides. I tried to be still and listen, instead of rushing ahead and thinking I understood everything.

I was rewarded with a faint warmth, that pulse of yes. I asked, quietly in my head, "What am I supposed to be thinking? What am I supposed to do here and now?"

Emma said, "There's a great coffee and tea shop just down the street from where I work. If you and Levi can meet me there, we'd have enough time to talk before my first client."

"Client?" I made the word a question with the inflection at the end.

"Reiki," she said, fully expecting that I'd know it was a type of healing energy work.

"If Levanael is okay with it, that sounds great."

"He doesn't like being called that name," she said, her voice more serious.

"He's okay with it since the . . . major channeling event."

"Really, that's fascinating. I can't wait to meet you and find out all the details."

"What's the name of the coffee shop?" I asked.

"The Cozy Cauldron. Can you please put Levi back on the phone and then I'll see you both soon."

Again, I found myself smiling without meaning to, as if she exuded joy. Was it a spell? I got that psychic poke saying *Stop being so damn cynical.* I handed the phone to Jamie and tried to be less cynical, but after this many years of being a cop it wasn't easy to switch gears from cynicism to whatever the opposite of that was, and then I realized that I honestly didn't know the antonym for *cynical.* I watched Jamie's face light up again as he spoke to Emma and fought not to think it was too good to be true. I realized that what I'd lost somewhere along the way was belief in the basic goodness of things, that somewhere in all the everyday mess God still had a plan. Combat had made me question it, being a police officer had made me question it more, but it was losing Reggie and Connery that had finally broken something in me. Something I needed to keep trusting that the loss of Jamie to his illness, the loss of the first person who made me fall in love with Her, the loss of Surrie when I left the College, through all of it I had still believed, still had hope. I stood there watching Jamie's face, the happy lilt in his voice like a small song of praise to the possibility of love with Emma, and I didn't believe it was possible. They could fall in love, but the love that is supposed to be the purest reflection of God's love for us, the love of a man for his wife and children, that was what I'd lost faith in, because I'd believed with all my heart and soul that Reggie was *the* one, and when Connery came along the love had just expanded until I thought my heart would explode with it. Instead, I had a dinner date with Reggie, and I'd been hopeful until I saw Jamie talking on the phone to a woman he was falling for, and I suddenly didn't believe that Reggie and I would ever get back to that. We might get back to something, but it wouldn't be this pure, unstained, shining adoration, and for a second, I hated them both, and then I was afraid for Jamie. Afraid of how hurt he could be if he followed his heart and Emma decided one day that he wasn't the man she thought she married, and the man he really was, the reality of him, wasn't what she wanted. How in the name of Heaven did a man cope with that?

I stood there and prayed that I wouldn't let my broken heart harm Jamie and whatever was happening with Emma. I prayed for the grace not to be jealous or angry about it, and not to share out loud or by psychic leaks how I really felt.

He got off the phone and smiled up at me. "Emma says she can't wait to meet you."

I nodded, not trusting my voice, and finally said, "Gotta get a fresh shirt, then we'll go."

"Why did you need to borrow a shirt from your boss?" he asked.

"Got messy at work, you know how it is," I said, and kept heading for the far door and the bedroom and away from his questions.

"I hugged you that last time, my hands touched something." He started walking after me, saying, "Z, are you hurt? Is that why you have the day off?"

"It's not that bad and it means I get to spend more time with you." I didn't turn around or slow down. I didn't want to answer questions about the injury, especially not to Jamie, because I still wasn't sure how fragile he was, or wasn't. Talk about demons being corporeal enough to claw a person up would spook anyone.

"Why don't you want to tell me about it?" His voice sounded plaintive behind me.

I stopped with the door to the bedroom partially open. "Because bad things happened today, and people got hurt a lot worse than me. People that I was supposed to protect."

"You don't have to talk about it if you don't want to, Z, but just promise me you really aren't hurt that badly. If you need to rest, then we can do this another day."

I was suddenly tired, as if it had all caught up with me at once, but I shook my head. Jamie was here; he was Levanael again, or sounded like him. I didn't want to lose a minute of the miracle of it. I'd stay with him as long as I could, or until the miracle started to unravel. In my head, not a voice exactly, but maybe my own self was talking back to me, chiding me, because miracles don't unravel.

"I wouldn't miss the chance of spending time with you, Levanael, and I meant what I said about asking Emma if what she did for you might help others." I started to put on a plain dark blue polo shirt that Reggie had grown to hate, she said it was my I'm-not-a-cop cop shirt but it was loose on me now that I'd leaned down so the bandages wouldn't show. I looked down at myself and realized the polo shirt looked like it was going to a casual Friday office and the bottom half screamed gym. If I just changed shirts then I'd be done, so I settled for another oversized tank top that was cut around the shoulders and neck but left enough material to hide both the bandages on my stomach, my badge, and my gun. I almost changed so I could have my full-sized duty weapon, but I didn't want to keep Jamie waiting longer than necessary. When you've got a miracle sitting in your living room you don't leave it waiting so you can pack more firepower, or that's what I told myself as I opened the bedroom door to step out. Reggie told me I didn't know how to stop being a cop. Was the thought that she'd be pleased that I hadn't changed everything to carry a bigger gun influencing my choice? I'd have liked to say no, but I try not to lie to myself. Lunch with her wasn't until tomorrow, but I made the choice as if she was the one waiting in the living room and not Jamie.

CHAPTER FORTY-ONE

The Cozy Cauldron's sign was a teacup the size of an old-fashioned witch's cauldron being stirred by a smiling woman wearing a black pointy hat and a frilly apron, as if the artist hadn't been sure if they were drawing a witch or a French maid pinup. It made me smile because it was just so fun. If Reggie had been here, she would have thought it was sexist at the minimum. When we met, she'd enjoyed dressing up for what she called Slut-o-ween, but now that Connery was old enough to trick-or-treat, she hated all the women's costumes. "Don't you want him to grow up respecting women?"

I'd been honest before I thought it through. "You used to dress up like that and other people's little boys saw you."

It devolved into a serious fight in which I wasn't even sure what I was fighting about, but Reggie was certain, and I didn't know how to get out of the circular arguments.

Jamie touched my arm, jerking me back to the here and now. "You okay, Z?"

I shook my head and said, "I'm fine."

"No, you're not." Jamie said it with such conviction that there was no doubt; I'd forgotten he used to do that before he . . . went away. He'd been able to see through my emotions, no matter how I tried to hide them.

"I like the sign and I thought that Reggie wouldn't like it."

"Why?"

I told him.

He frowned. "I don't know if that makes sense, but she isn't here right now, so you can smile at the sign. Emma giggles every time she sees it." He smiled as if even the thought made him happy.

Lots of things made me think about Reggie, but they didn't make me smile. I followed him through the door; it rang a little bell above the door instead of the usual electronic sensor.

"Bells to keep the bad things out," Jamie said over his shoulder to me as he looked around the crowded restaurant.

"Bells don't keep out everything," I said, scanning the full tables for a woman sitting alone. The extra height helped me spot two tables, each with a woman sitting alone. A dark-haired woman wearing glasses was sitting against the far wall close to the bathroom sign, and a blonde was sitting almost catty-corner from her. The brunette looked younger, but maybe it was the fact that she wasn't wearing any makeup. Thanks to living with Reggie, I knew the blonde was wearing a lot more than most men would notice. She looked good, beautiful even, but Reggie had taught me that good makeup could turn a five into a ten, or higher. I'd thought Reggie was a twenty without makeup, but she didn't, and it was her opinion that counted.

"What does Emma look like?" I asked.

"Long, curly hair and the cutest freckles . . ."

"Glasses and dark hair?" I asked.

"Yes."

"Then she's sitting against the far wall close to the bathrooms."

He started through the line waiting for coffee, which had snaked through the tables. He didn't even apologize as he pushed through. The old Jamie would have hesitated or apologized, but not this one. I wondered what else would stay changed if he stayed . . . okay?

I apologized coming up behind him, but then like all tall men, if I didn't try to be nicer people saw it as aggressive. I'd learned to smile more than I wanted to, because without it some people were afraid of a man over six feet tall. We didn't have to do anything to threaten them, it just seemed to be a size thing. Of course, if I smiled too much some people thought I was flirting. Two women and one man in line smiled back wide enough that I knew I needed to tone it down. Reggie used to think it was funny that I didn't know how to modify the smile, until she got jealous of any woman who flirted with me. The men who flirted back never bothered her.

The man in line who smiled back had his boyfriend jerk his arm to let him know to stop it. The man turned back to his boyfriend with a smile and a kiss to let him know I wasn't important, just eye candy. I'd seen the interaction too often not to recognize it regardless of the gender involved. The two women were alone in line, so I just stopped making eye contact and hurried after Jamie. I'd been noticing too many women lately; I had to stop before something happened that completely ruined my chances of getting back with Reggie.

Jamie was already at the table, the woman with the glasses up and hugging him. It had to be Emma. I finally won free of the crowd without offending anyone. The blonde at the table nearest to Emma was looking at me, that appraising look that made me realize she was tall, or at least long-waisted because of how much of her was sitting above the table. Her hair was a rich honey blond that was rare enough in humans that it was probably not her natural color, but that didn't make it any less eye-catching as it framed her face and complemented a pair of big blue eyes and the almost neutral lipstick she was wearing, so that even though she was wearing a lot of makeup, it was all understated, so it didn't take away from the eyes and the hair. I wanted to compliment her on it, but she'd think I was flirting. I'd already stared, too long, and her smile was a little surer of itself, her eyes filling up with that weighing and measuring look like she was trying to decide if she wanted to take me off the rack and try me on.

I looked away a little too fast, making it awkward enough that she laughed, the kind of laugh that a certain kind of beautiful woman seems to practice: throaty, sensual, as if the sound should only be heard in high-end bars and bedrooms. It was a sound that would make men and some women turn to look for its source. I looked before I could catch myself. Her blue eyes were solid on mine, the look on her face a challenge, or an invitation. I still couldn't always tell the difference, and sometimes there was no difference, because some women see dating like a game with winners and losers, and them as both the prize and the contestant. I didn't know how to date women like this, but sometimes they hunted me even when I ignored them, something again about being tall and in shape, or so Reggie had tried to explain to me.

I was blushing by the time I offered my hand to Emma, not the way I wanted to introduce myself to her.

She laughed, but her laugh was just laughter, not practiced, not throaty, but it made me smile automatically, but what she said next cured my smile.

"You look like one of the men Shelby would date, but you aren't, are you?"

I frowned at her as I let go of her hand, not sure what to say, except, "Who's Shelby?"

"The blonde."

I glanced back and found the blonde in question still looking at me. I turned away and felt the blush start to flare up again. For the love of Heaven, you'd think after being married with a kid I wouldn't react to certain things like I was still fifteen and didn't know that girls liked me.

Emma used one arm to hug Jamie to her. "You didn't tell me he was so cute."

Jamie pulled a little away, studying her face and frowning. I realized he was jealous. She noticed it, too, because she took his hand and said, "I meant he's charmingly awkward, I thought police detectives were all worldly and sophisticated."

Jamie relaxed, then looked from her to me, and then finally to the woman behind us. "Oh, she's checking Zaniel out."

She bumped her head against his shoulder, smiling. He was five-eight, so that made her about five-six because she was wearing jogging shoes, so no heel to cheat.

"I love how oblivious you are, Levi," she said, pulling him down beside her on her side of the table. I slid into my side of the booth so that I could put my back pretty much to the wall and keep a view of the rest of the restaurant. It was a cop thing that Reggie hated, but she knew that if she wanted me to eat out in a restaurant in peace, I had to sit where I could see around me and feel as secure as possible in a crowded restaurant.

The blonde, Shelby, was still looking at me, as if she thought I'd sat like this to keep a better view of her and not everything else. I raised my left hand up to touch my face, so my wedding band showed more clearly. Her smile just curled up a little more at the edges. Either she didn't care that I was married, or she liked that I'd felt I had to flash my ring at her. I did the one thing that beautiful women who are very sure of themselves hate most of all: I ignored her and turned to give all my attention to Jamie and Emma.

They hadn't noticed the little exchange between me and the blonde because they were smiling at each other, their shoulders touching. I was betting they were holding hands under the table. It made me smile just to see Jamie like that with someone. We hadn't been allowed to date each other at the College, and when he'd been cast out, he'd been too sick to worry about it. I realized in all the years I'd seen him on the street I'd never seen him with anyone romantically. I'd seen other homeless people that managed relationships, but Jamie had never been one of them. Was this the first relationship for him? I'd have asked, but I didn't want to point out anything unhappy as I looked at them together. The shy happiness of them together, the obvious newness of their attraction, made something tight and sad inside me lighten up. I wasn't jealous of it, or afraid for Jamie getting his heart broken anymore, because she was as gone on him as he was on her. They felt good together, like there was a hum of energy between them that was better for both of them. I was relieved to feel it, because part of me had been afraid she was like some of the empathic healers I'd met lately that gave their energy away but didn't seem to know how to keep energy for themselves. It meant that Emma was already better trained than a lot of the civilian energy workers I'd met.

"I ordered tea for all of us, I hope you don't mind," Emma said. She smiled, her large, gray eyes framed by the even larger dark frames of her glasses dominating her face the same way that Jamie's brown dominated his; if they had children the babies would look like those big-eyed doll paintings, but cuter. I had to shake my head and rotate my neck to help clear the thought away, because it wasn't all mine. One of them was projecting, and since Jamie had never been projective but just receptive psychically, it was probably Emma.

I answered her while I thought about that. "It depends on what you ordered." But I ended with a smile to answer hers. It seemed to be her natural facial expression, like the opposite of resting bitch face— resting happy face, maybe?

"Earl Grey latte, extra sweet, it's Levi's favorite and he said you both like your tea the same."

I kept myself from making a face at the idea of an Earl Grey latte, but I managed to ask, "Just tell me it's not got coffee mixed in with it and we're fine."

"No coffee in it, I promise. That sounds awful." She laughed, and it was almost a giggle, which usually wasn't my favorite from a grown-up woman, but it worked for her somehow. It was like she couldn't do anything that irritated me, which made me instantly suspicious. Was she using magic on me?

"My guides say to look with something besides your eyes, Zaniel," Emma said, staring at me with those big gray eyes that were somewhere between the color of rain clouds and gray kitten fur. Everything about her was . . . cute, from the curly shoulder-length hair, the light sprinkling of freckles, the big glasses, the small, upturned nose, the oval face, the lips that gleamed with the barest touch of lip gloss. She screamed *harmless* to a point that made me want to doubt it.

But now she'd given me permission to use my own gifts on her, or at her. It was considered rude to peek at people with active power unless they hit your radar so hard you couldn't not see them. I didn't have to lower my psychic shields, I just needed to focus to try to see more than just the physical. She was surrounded by white light; angels fluttered around her like a white, glowing outline. Most people had one, two at most Guardian Angels that hovered near them, around them, but the sense of wings and light around Emma was like a flock, a sense of energy and light that I hadn't seen around anyone since I left the College of Angels.

I tried to concentrate just on Emma, just on the human in front of me, but the white light spilled out so bright and full of the movement of angels that Jamie was lost in the shine of it, as if his light merged with hers. I tried not to see anyone else, but it was like the power once opened couldn't stop with one; it showed me the white flares around the room of other angels, usually just one, but sometimes two, all around the rooms. There were a few people who didn't glow with angelic possibilities, and I almost broadened my power to see why, or what else was near them spiritually, but I stopped myself in time. It wasn't my job, and if they were gifted enough to sense me, they'd see it as an intrusion.

Some of the angels "asked" for help. *Give me permission to help my person*, because you have to give your angel permission to help you. Free will protects us from many things, but it can also keep out energies that would help us. If you go to church, or temple, or mosque, or a coven, and are a true believer, then the angels have a conduit to you; they can help and protect you daily, but with so many people not having a regular spiritual practice the angels are trapped to watch the horrible choices people make without being able to help or stop it.

I was trained to give permission and free the angels to help their charges. I gave it without thinking, and the spurt of joy from the angelic as they were free to help was like flashes of relief throughout the room.

"The angels like you," Emma said.

"Sometimes a little too much," I said, and the moment I thought something that negative, the energy conduit to the angels began to close. Flesh can impact spirit, and the angels didn't need my negativity on top of what they were getting from the people they were attached to; the angels had enough mortal interference without me being gloomy at them.

"I could almost hear the angels singing and then something shut the energy down," Emma said.

I looked at her and now that I'd seen it once, I had trouble not seeing the shining outline of angels around her. If she had guides that weren't angelic like Ravensong did, I hadn't noticed them, but then we weren't in sacred or warded space; maybe that mattered?

"Do you hear the angels singing?" I asked.

She smiled a little more, because the smile was almost always there. "Sometimes, like the edge of music in a room you can't find, or birdsong seems to have more to it."

I nodded. "Some Angel Speakers talk to the birds a lot, or through them. It's not one of my gifts so I don't understand all of it. How did you not get recruited to the College of Angels as a child?"

She shook her head hard enough for her curls to bounce around her shoulders. The smile went away. Her eyes stopped looking kind. "Recruited, you make it sound like high school kids being scouted for sports teams, or college for professional sports, but it's little kids between five and seven years old. They can't give consent to go anywhere for anything."

"Our parents give the consent just like for boarding school for other children," I said.

She did that curl-bouncing head shake again. "You can get your kid out of a boarding school. Once a child is inside the College of Angels the families can't get them out, you knew that, right?"

I blinked at her because I hadn't thought about it that way.

"You didn't know either," Jamie said.

I looked at him and shook my head.

"There have been three cases of divorced parents losing a child to the College, because the main custodial parent gave permission. One father fought for ten years before he could even have a visit with his son."

"What happened?" I asked.

"The boy was a teenager by then and happy where he was, or brainwashed into staying," she said, and her face was all unhappy suspicion. It didn't look right on her face, as if she wasn't meant for doubts and cynicism.

"I didn't know about any of this," I said.

"Well, my parents knew and a lot of others in the pagan community know, so when the College came to get me my parents refused." She said it with such pride and respect in her parents. It was rare for a person in their twenties to still sound that certain about them.

"The angels found you anyway," I said.

She smiled then and it was like clouds parting and letting the sunshine spill around me. I had to smile back; it was a type of magic, or glamor, almost like some of the fey and other supernatural beings could do.

"If the angels want to find someone they can; time and place mean nothing to them, because they are not trapped in time as we are, and that means they can be many places all at the same time. How can anyone ever be hidden from beings that can do all that?"

"They can't." And then I realized what I'd said, and spoke without thinking. "Then how did she not find me sooner?"

"You said she was in prison, a place between," Jamie said.

Emma said, "Who is she?"

I looked across the table at Jamie and he just shook his head. He hadn't told her.

"I've never told anyone, unless I raved about it when I was out of my head," he said.

I reached across the table and squeezed his arm. "Thanks."

He gave a gentle smile that left his eyes sad. "I would never betray your trust, not on purpose, Z."

"Same," I said.

"If you don't want to tell me, you don't have to," Emma said; her eyes were still soft, but more serious, and the smile was barely there, as if her lips just naturally fell that way, no matter what she was actually feeling.

Jamie patted my hand where it still lay on his arm. "She's good people, Z."

I took my hand back, nodding. "I can feel that, Levanael."

"Have you taken your angel name back?" Emma asked.

"Z told me that if I could channel one of the higher angels, then that meant I was pure and not weak like the College told me when they cast me out. If they're wrong about that, then they can't take my name away either."

She leaned her shoulder in against his and did that fall-into hug that couples do when sitting on a bench together. "I'm so happy you finally see that."

I had to fight not to beam at seeing Jamie so happy in such a normal way. It was miraculous and I said another prayer of thanks for it.

That little flash of warmth came in reply, which made me grin like an idiot and enjoy all the happiness of the moment. One thing we'd been taught at the College of Angels was if God gave you good things, to enjoy it, be grateful for it, and give your happiness like an offering to God and the angels. I didn't always remember that lesson, but it was good to be reminded of it.

"So, tell me, Levanael"—she seemed to savor being able to say the name—"what or who did you channel to make you feel so good? Your energy is even better than normal."

Jamie looked at me. "This is more your story than mine, Zaniel. What are you okay with me sharing?"

I was debating what to say, or how to start, when the waitress came with our drinks. She was wearing a scoop-necked T-shirt with the sign logo on it. I smiled at seeing it, then realized she might think I was staring at her chest. Heaven help me, it was like I didn't know how to interact with women anymore.

I was dubious when I saw the foam on top of the "tea." It looked more like fancy coffee, but it smelled like Earl Grey. In fact, it smelled rich and thick with the herby, citrus scent of real bergamot.

I raised the glass slowly, enjoying the aroma, then blew on it and finally took the first small sip. It was as good as the scent promised. A weaker tea would have been overwhelmed with what they'd done to make it a latte, but the bergamot was strong enough that it comple-mented it instead of being lost.

"Levanael drank his first latte here the same way," Emma said.

It was like her voice had intruded on the moment and I had to fight not to spill the full cup. I looked at her, putting the cup of hot liquid safely down on the table first. "What do you mean?"

"Savoring it, enjoying the moment."

"I told you, Emma, Master Sarphiel taught us mindfulness."

"He taught us to take pleasure in small things, which I guess is what they call mindfulness these days," I added.

"Do you always drink tea so reverently?" she asked.

I shook my head. "No, but if something smells this good, or tastes amazing, then we were taught to honor it with our attention. It's like a compliment to the Creator for all the wonderful ingredients that came together to make something."

"And the barista who made it?" she asked.

"Of course, it's a compliment to the cook, or barista."

"But if it's just okay food and drink, you don't do it?" she asked.

I shook my head. "I don't do it at work because people would remark on it just like you did. I learned in the army that looking like you were praying over things made the other people give you a hard time."

"I want to know how you went from the College of Angels to the military, I can't imagine the culture shock, but first tell me why Levanael's psychic experience is your story more than his." Her eyes didn't look like soft kitten fur now, more steel gray. There was strength and determination underneath all the smiles and angelic energy.

I tried to think how to explain it, and how much I wanted to share. "Levanael channeled one of the higher orders of angels."

"How high?" she asked.

"Do you channel? Is it one of your gifts?" I asked.

"I can hear them sometimes, like I can hear people, like I heard Levi, I mean Levanael."

"She doesn't hear everyone like I do," Jamie said, "just certain people for specific reasons."

"I dreamed of Levanael and my guides told me to be on the lookout for him, but I don't channel like he does. In fact, my boss says she's only met one other person who has the ability to channel so easily and so completely as Levanael."

I nodded. "Even at the College he was one of the purest channels they'd seen in years."

"You make it sound like it was more common at the College of Angels."

"Not common, but there are always a few in any new group of students," I said.

"Really," she said, and looked at Jamie as if for confirmation. He nodded, and she turned back to me. "As clear a channel as Levi, Levanael?"

"Almost." I didn't tell her about the room where the gifted lay fed through tubes while they spoke from the highest angels and the students with the gift to interpret it wrote it down. It was recorded now, but the gift of interpretation worked best in person. Speaking in tongues was only half a gift; you needed someone with the talent to interpret it, or it was just gibberish. You had people who spouted in tongues, and those like me who could deal directly with the higher order of angels, and those like Jamie who could let other people's prayers come out of their mouths—all of them were given a chance to be in the room where once you went in, you never left. I'd refused my chance, and so had Jamie.

"Bast, my boss, has been active in the pagan community for over forty years and she says Levanael is like a glass that just fills up with spirit. She says it's a really rare gift."

"Maybe it's more common among the angel-touched," I said.

"Maybe," Emma said, but she didn't look convinced.

"Or they cherry-pick the ones who can do it and lock them away or break them so that no other spiritual power can use them." Jamie sounded bitter, like a throwback to some of his saner moments on the street. Saner had not meant happier.

"What do you mean?" Emma asked.

He looked across the table at me. I wanted to look away from the anger in his eyes, but I didn't. I tried to give him calm energy back to cool his anger. I prayed that this wasn't the beginning of him falling back into the abyss.

"Don't you remember when they stripped away all your other guides and totems, everything but the angels?"

I shook my head. "All I had was my Guardian Angel."

"I bet you had more. You just don't remember."

Emma reached out to touch his hand where it was clenched on the table, then hesitated. "May I touch you, Levanael?"

He gave a small nod, so she finished the gesture, laying her hand over his. "I thought you meant something else besides what you told me about your personal guides being stripped from you. I'm sorry, I didn't think what it might mean for channeling."

For the first time since I'd seen them together, he didn't touch her back, just glared at me across the table. His shoulders had hunched forward like he was collapsing on himself. It was the way he'd held himself on the street sometimes, like he had something heavy sitting on his shoulders. Just seeing that made me afraid for him. He said, "I had an imaginary friend when I came to the College of Angels. She was a little girl with long curls and ribbons in her hair. I know now that her clothes meant she was from the 1930s or '40s. Emma and Bast and others at the shop have helped me get a clearer picture of her, and the others."

"What others?" I asked.

He shook his head. "I don't want to talk about all of it."

If it had been almost anyone else, I would have reminded him that he brought it up, but I wouldn't push Jamie today, not if I could help it.

"You've regained your totem," Emma said, squeezing his hand as if she were trying to press some of her positivity into him.

His expression softened and some of the awful tension went out of his shoulders. He let out a long sigh as if he'd been holding his breath. "Yeah, he helps me."

"Who helps you?" I asked.

"My totem, my animal guide." He glanced at Emma and turned his hand so he could hold her hand back. He looked at me, but this time he was smiling. "Your totem is like a spirit guide, but it's an animal guide. We have one from birth or even before, just like a Guardian Angel."

"I've seen totems and animal guides with other spirit workers," I said.

"There are also animal messengers that come and go in our lives as we need them," Emma said.

"But we have one main totem that will help us be the best version of ourselves," Jamie said.

"It sounds like a Guardian Angel," I said.

"Angels are forced to ask permission to help their human charge; totems can be more active even if the person is unwilling to make the right choice," Emma said.

"Spirit guides don't have to wait for permission either," Jamie said. "But the person has to actually listen to them."

"I've heard some of this before from coworkers and others, but never had them equate it so closely with Guardian Angels."

"They probably thought you'd be insulted," she said.

"Insulted how?"

"When people from the College of Angels come to the store they are very insulted when we equate animal totems and spirit guides with angels of any kind. They are even insulted when we try talking about guides that are usually human ancestors or relationships from other reincarnations."

I laughed. "Oh, don't talk reincarnation to anyone at the College." Jamie laughed, too.

She looked at both of us. "What did I miss?"

"Suriel, our friend, she got memories in meditation from what she thought might be a past life, but when she tried to tell our meditation teacher that, well, he used it as a chance to tell all of us that there was no such thing as reincarnation. We had one lifetime to make our place in Heaven and if we screwed it up, we went to Hell forever."

"Wow, that's harsh," she said.

"It's the truth," Jamie said.

"No," she said, "no, it's not true, or at least it's not to my faith. You and I have known each other in past lives, Levanael. You felt the connection from the moment we met."

He nodded. Then looked at her with eyes as full of sadness as they'd held anger earlier. "I know we've known each other before, Emma, but I still believe in Heaven and Hell and all the awful things they terrified me with as a child."

"Before Dante wrote his fictional Hell, it was just separation from God, that's it," she said.

I nodded. "She's right; I found people who read the original languages that the Bible is written in, and that's all Hell was: separation from God. It's like the Fallen can no longer hear the voice of God."

"You don't believe I'm going to burn in Hell for all the shit I did on the street?"

I reached across the table and put my hand over his other hand while she held the other one. "No, Jamie, Levanael, no, I don't believe you are going to Hell. A seraph spoke through you today and you felt energized and better. If you were impure and damaged, you would have been destroyed by it."

That smile lit his face almost as if he were glowing from inside. I blinked and called that second sight, and he was shining with white light and there was an angel behind him towering up to the ceiling and beyond like a winged shadow at his back. I hadn't seen his angel looking this good in years. I started to tear up and looked down to hide it. I wasn't ashamed to cry in front of them, but I didn't want Jamie to think he was making me sad. I didn't want to upset him or take that glow from him.

"Did you say a seraph, as in one of the seraphim?" Emma said.

Jamie and I looked at each other. I finally answered, "Yes."

"Wow, they are like the closest to the throne of God, right?"

We both nodded.

"I didn't think it was possible for anyone to channel one of them."

"It's rare even at the College of Angels," I said.

"I've never done it before. The highest before was a cherub," he said.

"One of the cherubim? That is impressive, too; you do understand that the higher orders of angels almost never interact directly with human beings, right?"

He looked at me again, and I nodded. "I've been crazy for ten years; I don't know what normal is outside of the College. Inside, a handful of us were able to work with the higher orders of angels, but it wasn't long after I channeled a cherub that I went insane." He looked very seriously across the table at me. "So how did I do a seraph today without going crazy again? We weren't in a warded area, no special magical protection except what I was carrying with me."

"I had the apartment blessed when I moved in," I offered.

"Maybe that was it," he said, then frowned. "No, Z, a blessed apartment isn't as much protection as everything that surrounds the College of Angels."

"You have your totem protecting you now," Emma said.

I wanted to ask what his totem was, but I knew from working with Ravensong that it was considered a very personal question. I tried not to remember her raccoon too vividly, because I knew that if you thought too much about something mystically it was like trying not to think of the color blue; when people tell you to think of anything but blue, it's all you can think of. I saw a white bird on Emma's right shoulder. There was a dove cuddled up against her cheek. It was so real that for a second, I thought a real bird had flown in here somehow to perch on her, and then I realized it wasn't a flesh-and-blood dove.

I glanced at Jamie and found myself staring not at him, but at the round face and dark orange hair of an orangutan. A huge male orangutan. It looked at me with gold-brown eyes that were not even close to the darker brown of Jamie's eyes, but the look in the eyes seemed alike somehow, both gentle and waiting, but waiting for what? I tried to turn away, because I knew it was looking without permission, but of all the spirit animals that Jamie could have had . . . why an orangutan? And yet the longer I looked at Jamie with the great ape beside him, the rightness of it settled over me. They matched in a way that Guardian Angels never worried about. Babies were given an angel like the color of their eyes, just part of the equipment of being human, but somehow I felt that totem animals didn't work that way.

I finally looked away as if I'd been caught staring at something too personal, and found Emma watching me. "What do you see, Zaniel?"

"I'm sorry, I didn't mean to . . ."

"I didn't ask you to apologize, I asked you to tell me what you see."

"There's a dove on your shoulder, and there's an orangutan sitting beside Levanael."

Jamie smiled. "I didn't know you could see totems."

"I can see the totems of people I work with when we're doing magic together, though I'd thought my coworker had a bear as one of her totems, but today I realized that the bear felt different from a totem, more and less, more power, but less personal."

"Bear is the symbol for several Deities, so it could be the representative of one of the Gods or Goddesses that your friend works with in her magical practice or her path of faith," Emma said.

"I think Goddess, it felt like that kind of energy," I said.

Emma nodded and smiled, though her eyes were darker gray and more serious than the smile. She seemed to be studying me, or maybe she was looking at me with more than just her physical eyes, too. I'd started it, so I guess I couldn't complain.

"Can you see anyone else's totem?" she asked finally.

I turned and looked at the rest of the customers. They were sipping their tea and coffee. Some of them were eating scones and muffins, a few sandwiches, and drinking bottled waters, but it was just people enjoying themselves at a café. There wasn't another animal in sight, real or metaphysical.

"What do you see, Zaniel?" Emma asked.

"Nothing, I expected to see everyone's totems the way I see angels once I concentrate." I turned back to her and the dove was still cuddled close to her cheek as if it liked being there. The orangutan was still looking at me with that peaceful, gentle expression that mirrored Jamie's to the point that when Jamie raised his tea, the orangutan raised its own phantom cup and drank.

"Jamie's orangutan is drinking tea, is that typical?" I asked.

"You mean for the totem to mimic what we're doing?" she asked.

"Yeah," I said, fighting the urge to blink rapidly so I wouldn't see the ape echoing Jamie's movements. I don't know why, but that bothered me.

"Sometimes; sometimes it works the other way. If we are in danger we can borrow or be filled with the fierceness of our animal, or we can imitate how they survive in their environment and it will keep us safe. They can also help us study or find our best way to live our lives in so many ways. Embracing the characteristics of our co-walker can teach us so much about ourselves and how we fit into the world around us."

"Did you say *co-walker*?"

"Yes."

"I've never heard that term."

"Out totems, especially our major totems, walk beside us on our path of faith, our journey through life. They are always with us, just most people can't see them."

"Like Guardian Angels."

"Yes and no; angels need permission to help us once we stop being children and start making our own choices. Totems can interfere without permission, but they can't force us to make the right decisions, and they can't stop us if we're determined to do something that all our instincts are telling us not to do."

"How is that different from angels?" I asked.

"Totems can show up and make themselves known in more obvious ways than most Guardian Angels. Totems can be pushier and fight for your attention more than angels. You have to be quiet and listen to hear the brush of angel wings."

"You have to be quiet and listen for your totems, too," Jamie said.

Emma smiled at him and leaned her head against his, but now her hair went through the dove on her shoulder; but unlike a flesh-and-blood bird it didn't get squished, it was more like it was suddenly more misty and less solid, but it rubbed its head between their heads as if the bird liked them touching, or liked them both.

"I guess so; I've seen my dove since I was a little girl, so for me she's always been with me."

"I had no idea I had a totem at all," Jamie said, "let alone what it was." He glanced at the orangutan as if he could see it, too, and I realized of course he could. He could see angels just like I could, so of course he could see other spiritual guides.

"When did you realize you had a totem?" I asked.

"A few weeks after I met Emma. I thought I was hallucinating again like I was being chased by this big orange monkey"—the orangutan gave him a look—"sorry, big orange ape." The orangutan settled back satisfied and drank more from its phantom cup.

"Did the orangutan just get upset that you called it a monkey and not an ape?" I asked.

"Yes," Jamie said, "and that's part of what's different about them, Z. Angels don't have preferences about what you call them, they're like shiny bits of God that are attached to you, but they don't have personalities."

"Most Guardian Angels don't have what most people consider personalities," I said.

"True, but most totems have more energy of the animal they represent, and animals have strong preferences just like we do."

"Really?" I asked.

"They can," Emma said, "but most totems are quieter. They're more guiding spirits than interfering spirits."

"When I first saw mine, I thought I was backsliding and going crazy again."

"He called me in a panic," Emma said.

"I bet."

"Do you have any other questions about totems, Zaniel?" Emma asked, and then sipped her tea while she seemed to wait for me to think.

I drank some more tea, which was getting colder faster because it had so much milk in it, I think. It was still good, even cold; usually I reheated tea or made fresh, but this was like milky, sweet Earl Grey. It might even be good iced, and I usually hated iced coffee or tea drinks.

"You think that the orang . . . totem is what helped Levanael channel a seraph without any negative side effects?"

"He keeps me safe and helps me stay calm and just more even," Jamie said.

"Then I am very grateful to him." I frowned and turned to Emma. "Guardian Angels aren't usually any gender, but you both have referred to your totems by gender; is that typical?"

"Some totems are very certain what gender they are, some don't care about gender at all. Your totem is leopard with all the lessons that can teach you, but it's not about being a male or female leopard, just a leopard. Other totems come to us to teach us specific lessons that need gender, like how to mother our inner child and heal from abuse from a mother figure, and your totem may need to be female to help you heal."

"Or for me the orangutan is male because I've never been very good at being the typical male, so my orangutan is helping me learn to be comfortable with being sort of unconventional as a man."

Emma leaned her head against him again, smiling and obviously perfectly happy with the type of man Jamie was. "Some totems switch genders back and forth depending on different lessons or protection or nurturing that their person needs. One of the witches I know is all about lion, but it's male and female, in fact sometimes he's surrounded by an entire pride of lions. That's rare, but a lot of people have more than one totem, though most people have one main animal that's their co-walker, or co-creator."

"That's fascinating, but do they all see their totems this clearly? I know many people can't see their Guardian Angels, but they still believe in them and they still work with them and ask them for help," I said.

"Most people can't see their totems just like most people can't see angels," Emma said, "but they still collect images, figurines, anything and everything with their totem on it. Sometimes they don't know why they do it, and other times they know that's their animal, but they don't understand what it means. They just know they're incredibly drawn to wolf, or rabbit, or swallow and it makes them happy."

"Do real animals show up?" I asked.

"They can; doves show up a lot around me. Sometimes a real animal will show up to warn you of danger, or give you a message by being somewhere you wouldn't expect them, or by doing something that's weird for the animal," she said.

"Once Emma explained what was happening, I realized I'd been seeing orangutans on a poster for the zoo, in TV commercials, and there's this one special about them that was playing every time anyone turned on a TV around me. There'd even been a little girl at the bus stop who had a stuffed toy, and a little boy who was coloring a picture of one on the bus on another day."

"Totems aren't nearly as circumspect as angels," Emma said.

"You sure you don't see any other totems in the room, Z?"

I glanced back at the people at the tables, looked harder at the new ones in line, and then at the staff behind the coffee bar. The blonde at the next table wasted another come-hither smile on me, which I did my best to ignore. I was looking for spirit animals, not blondes. "Could the bar hide a smaller totem from me, just like they were a real animal?" I asked.

"If you're meant to see them, you'll see them," Emma said.

I turned back to her and Jamie and caught movement out of the corner of my eye. I looked for someone and then realized there was a wall there, so it couldn't be a person, but there was something there. I looked down and there was a raccoon under the table. I startled as if it had been real, and then looked into the little masked face. I remembered Ravensong's raccoon. It looked the same to me.

"Can someone share their totem with you?"

"You mean send it to give you a message?"

"Maybe," I said, looking at the little animal where it stood on its hind legs looking up at me. It had one paw on the seat beside me and I had a serious urge to try to touch the clawed fingers; that reminded me of how I'd left Ravensong with a hand that was no longer human.

The raccoon reached its paw up toward me and trilled at me, that was the only word I had for it. I reached my finger out toward that small, raised hand and felt calmer. My finger touched its palm and the finger wrapped around the tip of my finger. It wasn't solid-solid, not real for lack of a better term, but for a second, I swear I felt something. It startled me, made me take my hand back. I didn't know if I wanted to wipe my hand on napkins to get the sensation off my skin, or if I wanted to touch it and see if I could feel its fur like a phantom touch.

"What in Heaven is that?" I asked.

"What does it look like?" Emma asked.

I leaned over the table toward them as if it was a secret, so I could say, "A raccoon."

"Do you know someone with one as a totem?" Emma asked.

"Yes, could she have sent it to me?"

"Does she know that you could see it?"

I nodded.

"Is she a witch, or shaman?"

"Witch," I said.

"She could send her totem to give you a message or even watch over you if she thought you were in danger, but that's usually a real version of the animal, and it's usually only done if they are very close to you. Have you ever been in a relationship with this friend?"

"No."

"Some witches will send their totems to look in on loved ones, children, lovers, but not usually just friends."

I looked under the table, but the raccoon was gone, and I was relieved; when I looked up at the others their totems were gone, too.

"I've seen you stand up to demons, Z; why did this spook you?" Jamie asked.

"It didn't," I lied, and then the look in his face made me say, "I don't know, but *spooked* is a good word for it. I'm not afraid, but it did bother me."

"Please tell me it's not some guy thing where you don't think a raccoon is a manly enough totem for you?" Emma said. She quirked an eyebrow at me.

I smiled and laughed, trying to think my way through it before I answered. "I don't think so, but it's just it looks identical to the raccoon of my friend, but I'm new to this so maybe I just don't know the animal well enough to see differences."

"It could be an animal messenger instead of a totem," she said.

"What's the difference?" I asked.

"A messenger comes to deliver a message or a life lesson, but it's not your co-walker, and it's usually only a temporary companion."

"Do you think doing magic with my friend's totem activated it for me?"

"It could," she said, but not like she believed it.

"Tell me what you're thinking," I said.

She smiled. "Was it that obvious?"

"Yes," Jamie and I said at the same time, which made us all laugh.

"When you worked magic with your friend, you said you saw a bear and a raccoon; which was the clearest to you or which did you interact with the most?"

"The raccoon; the bear and other spirit guides were much less . . . real to me."

"Then either this is your main totem, or it's a messenger for a life lesson, or even a temporary animal guide."

"What's the difference between the three?"

"Main totems are with you for years or even for your entire life. They are the animal that most represents you, or teaches you, either the closest to your own personality, or the animal that has characteristics that you don't have and need the most."

"That makes sense," I said.

"A messenger totem can just come in for a moment, or even be a real bird, animal, or insect that interacts with you in an unusual way for just one message, like you shouldn't go down that alley because you'll get hurt, so a rat comes and stands in your way, or a flock of sparrows attracts your attention and saves you from walking out into the street so a speeding car misses you, that kind of thing."

"Okay, I get that."

"An animal guide can be with you on and off for a lifetime, coming back when you need to relearn a lesson, or you need its strength or skill again. It can stay with you for months or even years, but usually days to months."

"If a raccoon has come into my life to be a guide, what is it guiding me for, or to?"

"If you were pagan I'd say go into a sacred space and meditate on *raccoon* until you figure out what it means to you."

"But since I'm not pagan?" I asked.

"We have some books at the shop on totems and working with animal guides. I'd say start there."

"Okay," I said.

We finished our tea, talking about the halfway house that Jamie was staying in, and that Emma's professor had helped her get him a place in it. That he was working one afternoon a week at Harm None, and it had gone well enough that there was talk of more hours. Emma wanted to do traditional counseling at Harm None after she finished her degree, but not everyone at the shop was excited at the idea. They were happy doing reiki, tarot, and other metaphysical healing and guidance work, and many of them were strangely dubious of traditional therapy without magic.

"I might even work here at the Cauldron if one of the staff calls in sick," Jamie said.

"The people who own Harm None also own part of the Cozy Cauldron," Emma explained.

"Maybe you could get one of the shop fronts that's for rent here to be your counseling place. Then you could do regular counseling and send patients to Harm None for magical therapy if needed, and they could do it in reverse," I suggested.

She gave me a smile so happy that it was like sunshine on my face. I didn't have to concentrate to hear wings as she said, "That's a good idea, Zaniel. That way, Harm None can stay what it is, which is a great shop, and we can offer more services at a different, but close location. It's a perfect solution." I realized that I didn't know if the wings were angels or doves, just that I could "hear" them around her.

"I told you, Z was the smart one," Jamie said.

"You are smart," she said, at the same time I said, "I did some seriously stupid things that you wouldn't have done, or I wouldn't have done if you'd been with me to tell me better."

"Really?" Jamie asked, and he looked serious again.

"Absolutely, you were always more cautious than me, or Suriel. You kept us out of trouble."

"I tried, but sometimes Suriel came up with the best ideas."

We laughed together, remembering what it had been like before everything went wrong. I looked across the table at Jamie and realized that things were going right again. I was so grateful as I watched him smile across the table at me. I saw the phantom edge of an exceptionally long red furred arm across his shoulders as if his totem was hugging him, and I was grateful for that, too. If having a spirit animal guide helped Jamie heal, I was all for it. Something brushed against my leg, not quite as solid as a real animal, but enough to make me look under the table and meet the glittering gaze of the raccoon again.

"Let's go look at those books on totems," I said.

CHAPTER FORTY-TWO

was relieved that when we got up from the table, I couldn't see any of the totems. I'd grown up seeing angels and later demons and things that I couldn't have imagined when I entered the College of Angels at seven, so why did seeing a phantom raccoon at my side weird me out? I had no idea, but I was glad that the three of us walked down the sidewalk to Harm None without the animal escort.

Emma and Jamie led the way inside. I noticed they didn't hold hands in the store. I didn't know if that was a rule for employees in the workplace, or if they were keeping the relationship on the down low. I just noticed that they weren't as cozy here and let it go. We weren't encouraged to date at work either.

There was a counter with the cash register to the right and floor-to-ceiling windows to the left with glass shelves covered in crystals and stones of all kinds and colors. The stones circled around to the back wall, but without windows so the crystals that would fade in direct sunlight could still be displayed.

There was a woman behind the counter who was almost as tall as

I was, and since she was wearing no makeup and had salt-and-pepper hair that looked natural, I was betting she wasn't wearing heels. She was checking out a couple of women, handing them a sack with a smile that didn't hold nearly the warmth of Emma's.

"Sorry I couldn't talk you out of it, but may the best possible outcome be yours," she said as she handed the sack to the taller of the two women.

"Thank you so much, Bast, I know he loves me." Her face was glowing with happiness. She went past us with her friend, giggling together like they were twelve though they had to be older than Emma and maybe older than me. I wasn't good at ages, especially women's ages.

When the door closed behind them, the woman behind the counter made an exasperated sound. "Goddess help me, the next customer that comes in here asking for a love spell, I'm just going to tell them there's no such thing and send them packing."

Emma went around the counter and gave the bigger woman a hug. Bast tried to keep frowning but then smiled and hugged her back. "Thank you, sweetie, you make even dealing with stupid customers better."

Emma laughed and backed away enough to look up into the other woman's face. "If you're calling them stupid, the store must be empty except for us."

The other woman threw back her head and gave a huge laugh that was almost a bray. It was a laugh that went with the rest of her, larger than life, but it made me smile.

"Good to see you again, Levi, and who is the friend you brought with you?"

He didn't correct her with his angel name, but just motioned me forward and introduced me by my nickname. "This is Havoc; Havoc, this is Bast."

Bast raised eyebrows that were more solid black than her hair, like an echo to what the rest had been before time changed it. "Really, did you pick the name when you were younger, because you don't seem like someone who would want to invite that kind of energy into your life."

"It's a nickname that other people chose for me," I said.

Her eyes narrowed a little and I knew without having to be told that she was "looking" at me the same way that I could look at people's angels or totems. I didn't feel her putting any energy into or on me, so it was a natural ability like my vision. You could do some natural gifts without any energy exchange. Any magic you had to learn to use was almost always intrusive, and you needed to ask permission even to help someone, because to do otherwise is treating them like they have no agency or will of their own. You can do protective magic on your own family, especially children, without permission, but for the rest keep your magic to yourself.

"Havoc has just started working with totems, so I suggested he look at some books," Emma said.

"I'm not sure it's his totem that's following him around. Have you done energy or spell work on someone else recently?" Bast asked.

I just nodded.

"I'd call them up and see if they're missing a raccoon."

I caught my breath for a second, then said, "I did not do anything to damage her connection to her spirit guides."

"Totems aren't exactly the same as spirit guides," she said.

"Her raccoon faded from view just like the rest of her . . . guides."

"Is she a civilian?" Bast asked.

"No, she's a police detective."

"I don't mean civilian like that; I mean is she a mystical practitioner or a mundane?"

"She's a witch."

"Wiccan, or do you mean something else?"

"Wiccan," I said.

"Then contact her and see if she's missing her totem. If she's not, then you need to either ask her why she sent it with you, or keep your mouth shut and come back here so we can help you find out."

"Are you always this abrupt?" I asked.

"No, but my guides are yelling at me that there's something wrong with you and you need to fix it before your phone rings."

I looked at Jamie and Emma. "What's going on?"

"I don't know," Jamie said.

Emma said, "Bast almost never pushes like this unless it's important, like really important."

"You only have a few minutes, Havoc; even your name feels wrong."

"Zaniel," I said, "I'm Zaniel."

She smiled and it was like some tension slipped away from her. "That works. Okay, Zaniel, call the woman you worked on magically today and ask her about her totem." She seemed to be listening to voices I couldn't hear, and then her eyes went back to looking very directly at me. "Call the person who helped you work on her. Whoever that is tampered with the totem, or tried to; your energy offset the ill intent of the other mystic that helped you, and the client being a witch probably made it harder for the person to strip her of her magical aid."

"No other ethical light worker would try to steal someone's totem," Emma said.

"Why did it attach to me and not just stay with my friend?" I asked.

"Your energy hid it from whoever tried to strip it away from your client," Bast said.

"No one who worked with your unit would try to steal away someone's spiritual protection like that," Jamie said. He looked at me with those big brown eyes of his, and just like before they looked all the way through me as if we were seven, and I couldn't lie to him.

"It was Suriel, wasn't it?" he asked.

"Yes," I said.

His face crumpled as if he was going to cry.

Emma reached out to touch his arm, but then stopped in mid-motion.

"You told me earlier that Suriel helped you with a case," Jamie said, his voice tight with unshed tears, or just too many emotions.

"I hadn't seen her until today. We had a demon problem."

"She took the red sash, then?" he asked.

I nodded, and wasn't sure he saw, so I added, "Yes."

"You swear to me that you hadn't seen her until today?"

"My hand to God that I hadn't seen Suriel until today."

Tears glittered in his eyes as he said, "She tried to steal a witch's totem. She tried to strip away everything but the angels. Suriel had no right to do that. The College had no right to do that to all of us."

I reached a hand out to touch his shoulder, but I stopped just like Emma had. I was afraid if I touched him it would get worse, as if offering comfort would break him.

"I didn't know what Suriel was doing."

"How could you not know?" Jamie sounded accusatory.

"It was an emergency and there was a lot happening. We were trying to save . . ." I stopped and tried to think; was it a life, or just Ravensong from being deformed? What would have happened if we hadn't been able to reverse the damage? Would she have died, or would it have consumed her and made her into something else? Demons weren't contagious; what had happened earlier today was impossible.

"She helped me save my friend from . . . a demon." I had to be careful what I said, because they weren't police or anyone who should know what was happening with an ongoing investigation. A witch was supposed to keep anything said to them sacred like a priest in the confessional, but there were a lot of different kinds of witches and mystics, so the pointy-hat rule didn't automatically apply.

"But she couldn't leave it at that, she's just like all the rest of them up at the College. She had to meddle and take more than she was supposed to." He wrapped his arms around himself as if he was trying to hold himself together.

I went to him and said, "Levanael, without Suriel there today, something terrible would have happened."

"She was always gifted," he said, crying and starting to rock himself. I couldn't stand to see him starting to break without touching him. I wrapped my arms around him and he didn't fight me. I hugged him tight and prayed that he would be all right.

Emma laid her hand on his shoulder and then her other hand on my arm, and it jolted through me like a circuit had been completed. We were surrounded by white wings and the singing of angels and between the feathers was the golden light and I knew if the wings unfolded we'd be standing in the light of God.

Jamie screamed a sound of such hopelessness that it broke my heart and the light was gone, the angels fled. Jamie pushed and fought against me. I let him go and he stumbled into Emma, almost knocking her down. She grabbed his arm to steady them both and he tore away from her.

"No! No! I won't let them destroy you the way they destroyed me!" He turned back to me. "Get out, Zaniel, get out, stay away from Emma. I won't let you take her to that place where the angels sing. I won't let you break her the way it broke me."

Emma tried to reassure him. "You channeled a seraph today, Jamie. You're not broken."

He pointed a finger at her and shook his head over and over. "You don't know what they do to you. You don't know what it's like to be alone in the light and then to have the light taken away, too, so that you're alone in the darkness."

"Levanael," she said, crying.

"No, Levi, just Levi, I can't be the other, not if it will hurt you, Emma. I won't feed you to them, the way my family fed me."

He turned to me then, and said, "The way your family fed you to them, Zaniel."

"Fed us to who, Jamie?"

"Yes, I'm Jamie, just Jamie alone in the dark."

"Fed us to who, Levi," I said.

He shook his head. "You know who, Z."

"The College of Angels," I said.

He nodded, tears streaming down his face.

"They can't force me to go to the College of Angels," Emma said.

"Why do you think they send people from the College here to the store, Emma? They're looking for more angel-touched that they missed, and they missed you."

"They didn't miss me, Levi. I told you my parents refused to let them take me."

"Levi." Bast's voice soothed over all of us; I smelled lavender, but not incense. I found her with a spritz bottle in her hand, spraying lavender-scented water in the air, but it was more than that; her voice seemed to calm us, too. It was her store; she had a right to use magic to calm us down. She was speaking and I couldn't remember the words, as if they weren't meant for me, or maybe I wasn't supposed to remember them.

Bast hugged Jamie and he let her hold him, but I realized there was movement on the other side of him as if there was something there I couldn't quite see. I concentrated and it was his totem. The orangutan wrapped its overly long arms around Jamie. Emma was crying on the other side of them, her dove like an echo of angel feathers around her head with a glowing almost-halo to make it even more confusing. I saw movement out of the corner of my eye again and it was the raccoon standing there on two feet beside my left leg. It looked up at me as I looked down at it. It—no, he—looked at me with those big, dark eyes and seemed to be trying to tell me something, but I didn't know how to hear the message. Did I say, *What's wrong, Lassie, is Timmy down the well*, or would it be like a Disney movie where he started talking like a person?

"I don't know what you want, boy," I said, as if he were a real pet.

"He wants you to call your friend and see if she's missed him," Bast said. She was taking Jamie back to one of their rooms where they usually read tarot or did reiki. Emma tried to follow, but Bast made her stay out.

"You're on the register. I can't keep all our customers from wanting to come inside forever." The moment she said it, the door to the store opened and a group of people came inside.

Bast called back over her shoulder, "We've got this, Zaniel. Call your friend before your phone rings for work." The door shut behind them.

I glanced down at the raccoon. He didn't look solid in the way that a real animal would, but it was more solid than some Guardian Angels, but then it wouldn't blast a human's mind to look at a raccoon, and even a Guardian Angel in its pure form could be too much for some people.

I hadn't known that the College took people's totems and non-angelic spirit guides away from them. I didn't remember it happening to me as a child, but I trusted Jamie's pain on this. The College had told us all that only angels were worthy guardians and guides and that all the rest were if not evil at least unworthy. We were taught to counsel people to only listen to their Celestial guides. I concentrated in a way that was more familiar, and my own Guardian Angel was still at my back like a halo of light and white feathers. The raccoon was still there at my side, and either they ignored each other or the two energies were so different it didn't matter to them. A tightness in my shoulders loosened. Had I really believed that just because I had a totem, my angel would leave me as unworthy? Maybe, okay, probably. I'd never taken anyone's spirit anything away from them, but I'd been taught that anything short of angelic was lesser, and that the angelic didn't like being around lower spirits, and everything was less than angels.

I blinked and let go of both types of seeing. I was just standing in the store watching Emma answer questions from the small crowd of customers. She glanced my way, then mouthed the words *Call your friend*. She turned back to the couple who were asking her questions with a smile.

I walked to the side of the room near the crystals and the outer door and away from the customers. It was the best I could do for privacy without leaving the store, and I wasn't ready to leave without seeing Jamie again.

"Hi, Havoc, aren't you supposed to be resting, too?" Ravensong sounded so ordinary and like her usual self that it made me smile.

"I wanted to check on you, see how you're doing."

"I'm okay and the hand works."

"I'm sorry that I couldn't give you back . . . more," I said, which was a totally inadequate word for not being able to give her back her hand, complete and whole.

"The doctors would have cut my hand off, Havoc, you and I both know that, so stop beating yourself up about cosmetic issues. Besides, all the other witches will be jealous they don't have their own dainty demonic hand." She tried to make a joke of it, and it made me feel worse.

I caught movement out of the corner of my eye and focused on the raccoon gazing up at me with big eyes; it looked like it was trying to talk to me, but there was no sound.

"Are you missing anything since we healed you earlier?" I asked.

"Missing something? The extra flesh of that monstrous hand, but other than that, I'm fine. I mean, if you could have shaved a few pounds off other places so I didn't have to keep hitting the gym that would have been great, but I forgot to ask if there's an angelic weight loss program." Another joke; her trying to make me feel better when she was the one who was permanently changed was making me feel worse.

The raccoon waved its paws at me almost like it was asking me to give it the phone, but I knew it wasn't solid enough for that. "I've got . . . somebody here who wants to talk to you."

"Put them on the phone."

"I don't know how," I said.

"No more riddles, Havoc, it's been a long day." Her voice held tiredness and the edge of exasperation. If I pushed hard enough, she'd get angry with me and part of me thought I deserved it. Surrie had been my friend and she was the reason Ravensong was missing one of her totems now.

Some teenagers were peering into the case of crystals near me. I lowered my voice and asked, "Are you missing one of your totems, or spirit guides?"

She was quiet for a second and then said, "Son of a bitch. Where is the little bugger?"

"I think he's with me."

"Why would my totem be with you?"

"It's complicated and I'm in public."

"It's not impossible to damage a witch's ties to their totems and guides, but it's not an easy type of magic and it will come back and bite you on your karmic ass so hard that you'll wish you hadn't done it." She sounded angry now, and now I felt I didn't deserve it, not for this, this hadn't been my fault.

"I didn't do anything to cause this," I said.

"Then how did it happen?"

I glanced at the teenagers, who were close enough that I had to move to let them see something in the cases. I looked for Emma, but she was out of sight in the store, still helping other customers. The door to the room where Bast had taken Jamie was still closed.

"Talk to me, Havoc," Ravensong said.

"Let me get someplace quieter," I said, having to move so that the teenagers could get a better look at stones in the case behind me. I looked around the store and finally spotted Emma walking with an older woman, but their backs were to me as they looked at books. God help me, I didn't want to leave Jamie upset. I didn't want him to think that I'd abandoned him again.

"Havoc, talk to me," Ravensong said; her patience was starting to wear thin, and I couldn't blame her.

"I'm here, Athena, just give me a second." I pushed through the doors to the sidewalk. It was a lot less crowded than the store. I stood where I could glance in the windows in case I saw Jamie, but I owed Ravensong my attention.

"You almost never call me by my first name unless you're at the house socializing with the missus and me," she said, her voice wary now instead of angry.

"I just learned that some of the people at the College of Angels may be stripping people of their totems and guides, all except their Guardian Angels."

"I'd heard the rumor," she said.

"I hadn't," I said.

"You don't hang out with enough pagans to hear the rumors."

"I've talked to someone who has regained his totem after the College stripped it away from him as a child."

"Are you saying that your little friend from the College, the Infernalist, took my raccoon?" Her voice rose, the anger back and hotter than before.

"No, she may have tried, but somehow it's with me."

"What do you mean, it's with you?" She sounded surprised, maybe even shocked.

"When I was able to see my friend's totem and his girlfriend's totem, then I could see the raccoon with me. It looked like the same one that I saw with you in the interrogation room, but I'm not an expert on raccoons so the friend told me to call and check with you."

"I can't guarantee it's mine, but I'm missing my little guy and it would be a hell of a coincidence if it was someone else's raccoon that you absconded with."

"I didn't abscond with anyone. The friend thinks that when the Infernalist tried to strip it away from you, it hid using my energy so she couldn't damage its tie to you."

"That raccoon has been my co-walker through life for over thirty years, so I'd call that damaged."

"But he's not gone, in fact he's looking at me like he wants me to hand him the phone again, but he's not that solid." Then I realized that I didn't know much about totems yet, so I added, "Is he? I mean, can a totem be solid enough to hold a phone?"

"Not really, or not usually, but then you're not supposed to be able to take someone's totem away from them. Trauma or abuse can change your totem, either its nature from nice to more protective, or even switch one animal for another that will help you survive what you're going through, but it's not possible to steal someone's totem."

"I thought you said that magic could do exactly that?"

"It's possible to damage someone's totem, or their connection to it, or sometimes in rare cases totems can even take some of the mental or emotional damage so the human they're with doesn't suffer the full brunt of it, but no magic can steal it from you."

"Guardian Angels do that, take some of the mental and emotional and spiritual damage for the people they guard, especially children," I said.

"One day we'll sit down and have a long discussion on the differences between totems, angels, spirit guides, the works, but right now I need you to come for a visit, so I can get back with my little buddy there."

"Let me say goodbye to my friend and I'll head your way, and I'm sorry, Ravensong, sorry about all of it."

"You didn't do anything wrong, Havoc, you backed me up magically like you've done a dozen times before. I'm too upset to meditate about it yet, but I think my raccoon even tried to warn me off, he was certainly waving at me just before everything went sideways. If a witch ignores her own guides, then it's her own damn fault."

"I'm still sorry that your hand isn't completely back to normal, and that Suriel seems to have tried to strip you of your totem."

"Okay, you can be sorry since it was your friend that did the second part, but I'll tell you this: All my other totems and guides are exactly where they're supposed to be, so your little friend wasn't able to do what she tried to do."

"I don't agree with the College stripping children of their totems, but I can see their reasoning, but for Suriel to try to strip you of your totem, that's . . . an outrage and an insult to a witch of your strength and talent."

"The Infernalists are the ones most likely to come out of the College to help with demon shit; this makes me wonder if we need to double-check anyone they've helped and double-check that their totems and spirit guides are intact," she said.

"God help us, I hadn't even thought that far yet."

"Seeing someone from your past can be hard, especially if you were close once; it messes with all of us, Havoc."

"Thanks for understanding, Athena."

"There you go again using my first name, keep that up and I'll think you're sweet on me."

Her tone made me smile. "You're my favorite witch, you know that."

"Well, then it's lucky we'll have a chaperone; Louie came home early from work to take care of me, so you'll have to fantasize about sexy witches on your own time." She laughed then, her I'm-a-dirty-old-lady laugh, which she wasn't supposed to use at work anymore. It made me feel better that she could laugh, and I knew she didn't mean it. She never meant it.

"Your wife is a good enough witch to keep us both in line," I said.

She laughed again. "Get your fabulous body over here so we can figure out what's going on, Havoc."

I heard a voice in the background and Ravensong said, "Louie reminded me that I'm supposed to practice politically correct speech even when I'm not at work, so I don't get written up again."

I almost pointed out that she'd been saying things that sexual at work to me earlier today but stopped myself in time. I was not going to tattle to her wife about work stuff. "I did not report you for sexual harassment," I finally said.

"I know you didn't, Havoc, but someone did, and so I've got to behave myself a little better." She had to be thinking she'd already misbehaved today, but we were both going to pretend in case her wife could hear my end of the conversation.

"I'll help you behave at work, if that's what you want?"

She sighed. "Not what I want, but . . ." She took the phone away from her mouth and then came back on. "Louie says she'll have tea waiting for you when you get here."

"Tell her thanks."

"You can tell her yourself once you get here."

I glimpsed Emma in the shop between customers. "I've got to say goodbye to my friends, then I'll be heading your way."

"See you soon, Havoc."

"Same, Ravensong." We both hung up and I went into the shop to at least leave a message for Jamie with Emma. I was waiting while Emma finished checking out some customers when my phone rang again. It was Charleston.

"Hello, Lieutenant, is everything okay?"

"No, if you are fit for duty, I need you."

"I'm out with friends, I'm good, what's wrong?"

"I'm looking at what's left of another college student and her boyfriend."

"What do you mean, what's left?" I asked, and started walking away from the happy customers and Emma, because whatever he was about to say was nothing they needed to hear.

"I mean that it's worse than the last victim, but it's another woman that Cookson was stalking."

"He's dead, we found his body exploded into bits at the hospital," I said.

"We found skin, just skin."

"Are you saying he's alive and that he did this?"

"I don't know, Havoc. I've already got a request in for the ME to give me a piece of the skin so I can ask the loa which side of the veil Cookson is on. Give me a piece of him and I'll find him on Earth or in Hell."

"Give me the address and I'll—"

"No, I don't need you here. I assumed that the demon inside Cookson had betrayed and killed him like they usually do, but either Cookson is still alive or the demon is doing it as part of the bargain, so either way the women are in danger."

"Agreed, what do you want me to do, Lieutenant?"

"We have three more women to protect. I've got uniforms en route to them, but they're going to need magic."

"Just tell me where and I'll meet them."

"Tell me where you are, Havoc, and I'll send you to the nearest potential victim. You may be the closest to the university campus and to the two women we have a bead on."

"Where's the third?"

"She's meeting her boyfriend somewhere, no one seems to know where."

"Okay, send me pictures so I can recognize them all, and I'll head to the university to back up the uniforms. Are you sure you don't need me at the crime scene?"

"We got plenty of hands at the crime scene. What I don't have is enough people covering these girls."

"Yes, sir."

I sent a quick text to Ravensong, apologizing for canceling our meet-up and promising to reschedule as soon as I could. I'd pressed SEND when the first pictures came through. They all had long, straight, dark hair and looked eerily like our first victim. Cookson really did have a type. Then a fourth picture came through that was a blonde and it wasn't a school photo, but something more candid.

"Are we looking for three or four other potential victims?" I asked.

"Three, but the last girl dyed her hair blond recently, so I'm sending you her school shot and one her roommate took this week."

I stared at the last two photos. "Can you send me a better full face of the blonde, sir?"

"I'll check, what's up?"

"I think I know where she is, but I want to be sure I'm guarding the right person. I don't want to divide our resources on the wrong blonde."

"I'll check with the roommate, hold on." Then I was listening to silence on hold.

I went to Emma, who was between customers. "I have to go to work, please hug Jamie for me."

"The hugging is easy." Then her eyes were less full of smiles and more serious. "But whatever is at work is bad, isn't it?"

"Don't try to read me on this one, Emma, because you don't want these images in your head."

She nodded, almost briskly, sending her thick hair bobbing. "It's more your emotions that I'm reading, but I'll shield harder."

"Thanks, and thanks for all you've done for Jamie."

She was all smiles again. "You don't have to thank me for that."

I realized I didn't have to wait for a picture. "The blonde in the café, what was her name again?"

Emma looked less happy. "I thought you had better taste than that, Zaniel."

"I do, but there's been another incident on campus and we're trying to locate a girl who dyed her hair blond recently and that wasn't her natural hair color, so just checking before I run off to the university to look."

"Oh," Emma said, "it's Shelby Jackson and she dyed her hair a week ago, or less. Is that the name?"

"I'm waiting to see a second picture to make sure of the face, but now I'll just check the name."

"Havoc, sending you another photo," Charleston said in my ear.

"What's the name of the blonde?"

"Shelby Jackson."

"She's next door to my location, sir."

"Where?"

"The Cozy Cauldron, it's a tea and coffee shop just off campus two doors down from the metaphysical shop I'm at."

"You're at Harm None?"

"Yes, sir."

"Good shop, now get eyes on Shelby Jackson."

"Moving that way now, sir, can I tell her she's in danger?"

"We don't know that she is in danger, so just keep an eye on her. We're not supposed to start a panic if it can be avoided. If any demons show up, then the panic will start without us."

"Let's hope it doesn't come to that, sir, the coffee shop is packed with customers." I waved at Emma and went for the door.

"I'll send uniforms your way ASAP, Havoc."

"I'll keep an eye out for them."

"Havoc, be careful; the demon or whatever it is just tore the latest victim's boyfriend into pieces."

"You mentioned it, Lieutenant."

"I wanted to mention it a little more forcefully since you're on your own."

"Thanks, I understand what's at stake."

"Good, uniforms are en route to you."

"I'm going in." I reached for the door.

"Keep your phone to your ear and pretend to be having a normal conversation while you order your coffee."

"Can do," I said, voice already heartier and guy-guy than my normal. I was dressed like I was headed to the gym in a tank top cut to expose more of my muscles than normal; the usual guy who went with that had a certain attitude. I fell into that attitude and undercover between one step and the next. I was now playing the part of a guy who had been with friends and come back to check out someone that he didn't want his friends to see him with, or maybe tell his wife/girlfriend/husband/boyfriend.

"I'm just getting another cup of coffee. I'll meet you after. What's with all the questions, honey bunny?" I said.

Charleston said on the phone, "You always did do good undercover."

"You say the nicest things, baby."

Charleston chuckled.

I chuckled back like he'd said something sexy. I made it the guy equivalent of that laugh that turns heads in bars. People in the line glanced my way, but the only person I cared about was still sitting in her booth across the restaurant. She was too far away to hear the laugh and she'd been joined by a man who was as tall and blond as she was; Reggie called couples like that Barbie and Ken couples. It had taken me years to figure out that there was a certain amount of envy in the teasing. We'd even talked in therapy about her desire to be blond and blue-eyed as a little girl instead of the Hispanic beauty she was; since I preferred dark hair to blond I hadn't had much to add to the conversation.

I also knew that Barbie had been a brunette less than a week ago, which would have amused Reggie. It made me want her with me to share the joke. I stopped being the confident dudebro who was trying to cheat and started to sink back into myself. I didn't want to cheat, I wanted to go home to Reggie so bad it literally hurt.

"Whoever is making you so unhappy on the phone should lighten up," a woman standing behind me said. She had short brown hair styled to follow the curve of her oval face. The makeup was understated except for the lipstick, which was a red so bright it made her lips the first thing I saw. They looked small and full and kissable, but she needed darker eye shadow to balance it, because I had to fight to make myself notice that her eyes were gray, or maybe I just preferred that shade of lipstick on my wife.

"What's going on, Havoc?" Charleston asked in my ear.

I felt that sexy, untrustworthy smile that I had literally practiced in the mirror before one undercover operation. I'd been so good at playing the part that Charleston had loaned me out a couple of times.

"Nothing's wrong, I'm just waiting in line, honey."

The woman beside me smiled with those crimson lips. Her gray eyes matched the color of her skirt suit, and the fact that she was wearing that with sensible black heels made me think maybe she wasn't a college student, maybe grad school?

I widened my smile and debated how old she thought I was.

Charleston said, "Do you see the subject?"

"Of course, honey, just tell me what you want, and I'll bring it home for you."

The woman mouthed, *You*, with her red lips.

I looked past her to the table with Shelby Jackson and her boyfriend. The woman in front of me noticed me looking and frowned. "Sorry, honey, what did you say? I think I see some of our friends at a table here."

The woman in the red lipstick glanced behind her, but she was only about five-eight in the heels so she couldn't see through the crowd.

The barista called out, "Miranda, coffee for Miranda."

The woman looked up and started to move forward, then glanced at me. She mouthed, *Wait here.*

I gave her a smile I hoped meant I was willing to wait, then realized that I might have been too successful at the flirting. That was my downfall when I did undercover; sometimes I was too good at it. Not just the flirting douchebag, but I'd scared myself a couple of times playing the threatening muscle. I'd asked Charleston to not have me do that one again.

I stayed in line while Miranda went for her coffee. It gave me time to check the room for threats and to make sure that Shelby and her date were still settled in at their table.

"Are you being too successful at flirting again?" Charleston asked.

"Yes," I said.

"Let me know if you need an out and I'll call you a cheating bastard. I'll make sure to use the deep, ghetto voice like the one I did when you pretended to be my leg breaker."

The thought of Miranda's face when she heard Charleston play my ghetto boyfriend made me laugh out loud, not the sexy chuckle, but just a real laugh.

Charleston's deep chuckle on the other end made two of the men in line look at me, which made me laugh more; if only my real love life was as good as my pretend one.

I saw Shelby's boyfriend stand up. I told Charleston, "Keep sounding like that and I might have to leave before I get the coffee."

Charleston's voice was serious now. "Is subject moving location?"

I grinned like he'd said something flirty. "Maybe." The boyfriend went toward the bathroom; Shelby stayed sitting at the booth.

"I really would like that coffee, sweetheart. Sure, I can bring you something, what do you want?"

"I take it the subject isn't moving after all," Charleston said.

"That's right, baby."

Miranda came back through the crowd with her coffee in hand. She stood close enough to brush the back of her hand along my biceps. I did what she expected and flexed for her. Reggie would have laughed at me or rolled her eyes; Miranda smiled like she'd enjoyed it. Maybe she had, or maybe she'd tolerate it until after she got what she wanted from me, which was at least a coffee date.

"What's your major?" Miranda asked.

"Who's that?" Charleston asked.

"Someone I met in line, I told you it was long, we're reduced to making small talk with each other."

"Gotta take a call," Charleston said, and hung up. His voice sounded urgent, but I knew better than to try to keep him on the phone when he sounded like that.

I put my phone in the pocket of my exercise pants and said, "Pre-law."

Miranda smiled up at me; her red lips looked somewhere between sexy and predatory. Even if I'd been free to take her up on the invitation, I wasn't sure about that smile.

She looked me up and down like she was thinking about buying more than just the coffee. "You know my name," she said, motioning with the coffee, "but I don't know yours yet."

I looked over her head to the table where Shelby was still sitting. Her boyfriend was coming back from the bathroom. "I'm Havoc."

"Friends of yours?" she asked.

"Not my friends." I put too much emphasis on the *my*, but I also raised my hand so she could see the wedding ring.

She moved the coffee cup so I could see the wedding set on her own hand. "Everyone needs friends of their own, Havoc." Then she giggled and that was a better sound, a real sound that she'd probably been making long before she started wearing scarlet lipstick. I liked the sound and fought to stay in character and not give her my real smile, which didn't match the act.

"Agreed," I said, then looked back over the crowd like I was worried that my spouse's friends would see us together.

"I'll make it quick, how old are you? The truth."

"Thirty-two," I said.

"Liar," she said.

I wasn't lying, but I gave her that fake roguish smile and said, "Thirty-two."

She looked me up and down again and sighed. "With your friends here, I won't make you show me ID."

"I swear I'm legal," I said.

"Sorry, but I'm too old to believe you without proof."

"You're not that old," I said, and meant it. I caught movement out of the corner of my eye. Shelby and the boyfriend were getting up. "Her friends are coming this way," I said, voice lower.

"Nice to meet you, Havoc, if that's really your name."

"Nice to meet you, Miranda, and yes, it's really my name."

"No one is really named Havoc."

"I am," I said, and looked past her to Shelby coming closer through the crowd.

"Good luck, Havoc, or whatever your name is," Miranda said, and went for the door.

I didn't argue with her this time, just let her go and realized I was almost up to the coffee counter, but Shelby and her boyfriend were headed for the door. I looked at my watch like I had run out of time, just in case Shelby recognized me from earlier. She was so wrapped around the arm of her boyfriend, I don't think she noticed anything else. Her face had been perfect and almost harsh when I'd seen her earlier, but now she was soft and happy, and the makeup and hair now seemed to match the boyfriend's natural coloring. I wondered if she'd done it on purpose, or if it had been subconscious. Either way she looked like a woman in love as she went out the door arm in arm with her Ken.

My phone rang as I put my sunglasses on and followed them out. Charleston said, "The crime scene at the dorm wasn't the first, it was the second. Three of the five women Cookson was stalking are dead."

I strolled down the sidewalk, trying to look like I was enjoying the conversation and not following anyone. I smiled while I lowered my voice and said, "Is it definitely Cookson?"

"The ME is messengering over the skin to me."

"Doesn't this prove he's on this side of the veil?" I asked. Shelby and her boyfriend slowed to look in the window of a shop just ahead, so I turned to the shop near me.

"Yeah, this proves Cookson is here. I'm going to ask the loa to help me locate his ass." Shelby and her boyfriend were still looking at the shop window as if it was fascinating, so I turned to my shop window, trying to seem as interested. It was a florist; staring at the flowers and plants made me wonder if sending flowers to Reggie would be too much; yes, it would be too much, but I filed it away for later. If tomorrow went well, and the date night went well, then maybe flowers.

"Did you hear me?" Charleston asked.

"I'm sorry, sir, no." I felt incredibly careless.

"The uniforms should be driving by any minute. Bridges and Antero, and the MacGregors are en route to you."

"The subject is window-shopping with the boyfriend just ahead of me. Street is clear." I saw movement in the window behind the flowers and realized that Miranda was in the shop. Dear God, she was going to think I was following her. I tried to move away, but the look on her face let me know she'd spotted me.

I couldn't think of what to say as she came out with a wrapped bouquet of cut flowers. She knew exactly what to say. "Do I need a policeman to stop you from following me, or a hotel room so we can cure this sexual tension?"

I said loudly on the phone, "Honey, of course I remembered it was the anniversary of our first date. I wanted it to be a surprise, but that's why I'm running late."

"The skin is here, make sure your angels guard your ass until your backup arrives," Charleston said.

"Of course I remember what your favorite flower is," I said, but Charleston had already hung up. He had a voodoo ceremony to perform that would hopefully help us locate Cookson.

"Are you off the phone?" Miranda whispered.

I put the phone in my pocket and nodded.

"Wow, almost cheated on your anniversary, you would have been in hot water."

"She reminded me in time," I said.

"Do you really remember her favorite flowers?"

"Sunflowers, and if they're out of season, gerbera daisies in as many colors as I can find them." I smiled saying it, because they were Reggie's favorites. I glanced down the street and saw Shelby and her boyfriend still cuddling in front of the window two shops down.

I looked at the mixed bouquet of flowers in Miranda's arms. "Who are you buying them for?"

"Me," she said.

I raised eyebrows at that, using the dark glasses to hopefully hide the fact that I was looking at the couple down the street. They'd started to kiss, which was good for me since it kept them stationary.

"Shouldn't the person who put a ring on your finger be buying them for you?"

"I could say that's sexist."

"You could, and if you prefer to buy your own flowers I apologize."

She smiled, but it left her eyes dull. "No, I don't prefer to buy my own, but I got tired of hinting years ago, and outright asking got to be humiliating, so now I buy my own."

"I would say shame on him, but it would sound hypocritical."

"That you noticed that puts you ahead of most men."

"Then I'm sorry on behalf of all of us. You deserve better."

"Doesn't your wife deserve better?"

"She wanted a separation, not me."

"You cheated on her?"

"No, she wanted us to date other people."

"And now she's calling about anniversaries and wanting you to come back? Looks like dating didn't go like she thought it would."

"What do you mean?" I asked, and I was genuinely interested now. There was no threat to Shelby and her guy, and me talking to another woman made it less suspicious when I would have to keep following them on a nearly empty sidewalk.

Miranda gave me a look that made me feel younger, or maybe just naïve. "Your wife either thought you would be bad at dating and come crawling home, or she had someone in mind to date and it hasn't worked out."

I frowned and couldn't keep up the undercover persona, because what she was saying made sense and I didn't want it to make sense. I couldn't tell her that Reggie wanted the separation because of my job, because I was a pre-law student who didn't have a job yet. "That's not why she wanted the separation."

"If you say so, and that look on your face says there is no way you're thirty."

Shelby and her boyfriend wrapped themselves around each other and started kissing even more passionately; maybe that's why she was wearing the neutral lipstick? Miranda looked at them, too; maybe she'd noticed me looking even through the sunglasses. "We all start out that way, and then it changes," she said.

"They seem like they're in love," I said.

"They're standing in front of a jewelry store that's known for helping college students get nice wedding sets at discount prices, so they think they are," she said.

The boyfriend got the door of the shop and escorted Shelby inside. They were still holding hands. I didn't like that I couldn't see them anymore, but I didn't expect her to dive out the back to escape me either. In fact, it was going to get awkward fast if I didn't have more people helping me tail them.

Of course, right now I had the perfect reason to follow them. "Maybe I should try for some jewelry instead of flowers, then," I said.

"Or maybe she should be buying you apology gifts," Miranda said.

"I don't believe she owes me anything."

"Is the flirting the act, or is the vulnerability the lure when the confident flirt fails?"

"You're lovely, Miranda, and if you were my wife, I'd remember to buy you flowers, but I think I'm going to go with jewelry before I actually do something that I need to apologize for to my own wife."

"You're big and boyish and yummy, Havoc."

I smiled. "And you're beautiful and insightful, and it would be a pleasure to take you to bed, but . . ."

"But you're going to go buy jewelry for your wife?"

"I am."

"If you want to go back to her, then stop flirting so damn well, before someone takes you up on it," she said, and went up on her tiptoes to touch the side of my face. I wanted to rub my face into it like a cat scent-marking. The urge was so strong that I put my hand over hers, trapping it against my skin, so that I wouldn't follow through on what felt too intimate to do with a stranger. Miranda took the hand over hers pressing her against my face as the more intimate gesture, which I guess outside my head it was; she was right, I should really stop flirting before something happened that I couldn't take back.

Miranda let herself collapse against me still on her tiptoes, so that I put my arm around her waist to keep her steady. The flowers were pressed between us, her other arm around my neck. The flowers saved us from being pressed completely together, and I was grateful for the space because my body reacted instantly to her in my arms. I couldn't control the reaction, but I could keep her from feeling it and my gun if I was careful.

She leaned her face upward for a kiss. I couldn't blame her for expecting one. I wasn't going to do it, but then I felt the warmth at my back; my Guardian Angel was trying to get my attention. There was a brush of invisible wings on my right side, up the sidewalk from where we'd come. I looked in that direction and saw an early-twenties-aged white male over six feet tall, but shorter than me so under six-three. Short dark hair, cut and styled in a way that Reggie called *movie star leading man trying too hard*, paired with dark eyes, probably brown. All his clothes looked brand-new: solid red T-shirt made out of something satiny or silky, tight blue jeans distressed from the store, very expensive high-top jogging shoes artfully unlaced, so that they were useless for actually running. He had a watch on his right wrist that looked like Cartier and if it was, then it cost more than everything else he was wearing plus a car.

The man looked at me looking at him and there was a jolt of recognition, as if I not only knew him but I'd seen him in a bad place as a bad guy. I needed to figure out where I'd seen him before he figured out the reverse on me, so I bent over Miranda and met her offered kiss. If he'd seen me as a cop, I'd have probably been in a suit surrounded by other cops, not like this with a woman and flowers. People see what they expect to see most of the time, so I'd be a guy in gym clothes giving his girlfriend flowers and getting a kiss in return.

Miranda melted into the kiss, her arm encircling my waist so only the pressure of our bodies kept the flowers pinned. Her hand slid inside my tank top, tracing along the bare skin of my back. The feel of her fingertips tracing along my spine made me shudder in her arms. Which made her dig her nails lightly into my back. My knees almost buckled, sending me falling into her arms so that she had to brace before I caught myself.

The man passed behind us, and the angel at his back screamed for help. The psychic push of it stabbed through me like a spear. I pulled away from Miranda, but my arms were still on her arms; the flowers fell to the sidewalk as I turned to watch the man walking away from us.

My angel flared halo-bright at my back and I could see Miranda's glow white and pale yellow in the sun, but the angel on the man's back . . . It should have been all light, or a tall humanlike figure at his back with outspread wings and hands on his shoulders or spread above his head, but the white figure was covered in blackness like tar or ink had been poured over it, and the arm I could see was white and free of the blackness but was bent at horrible angles as if it had been broken in multiple places and let heal that way. It turned its head like the blackness was a hood over it, like the kind a kidnapper would use except this darkness wasn't cloth but something liquid and heavy that clung. The angel opened its mouth like a hole in the darkness and screamed again. The sound stabbed through me, but I braced for it this time. I'd heard the cries of the damned before, and this was a shadow of it, except that angels couldn't be tortured like this; they could choose to take some of the damage that their human suffered. I'd seen guardians that were damaged from that, but that was part of them helping their human in this lifetime. What I was seeing now wasn't that. The man looked and felt fine; if his angel had taken damage for him it would have shown more on the human. He would not have been able to stride past us confident and whole.

"What's wrong?" Miranda asked.

"Where's your car?"

She smiled, but her eyes were still worried. "That way." And she nodded in the same direction the man was walking. "Go back inside the florist, no, go back to the Cozy Cauldron and stay inside until it's safe."

"What are you talking about?"

I moved my oversized shirt enough for her to glimpse the badge at my waistband. I picked up the dropped flowers and put them in her hands. "Please, Miranda, I have to go, but I want you safe."

She nodded. "I'll go save us a table," she said, trying for normal.

"Get under the table when it starts."

"When what starts?" she asked.

I glanced back and saw the man reaching for the door of the jewelry store just like I'd known he would. I didn't know how, but I knew that was Mark Cookson if he'd hit the gym and put muscle on his thin frame, with better clothes, a better haircut. It was like a demonic make-over. I prayed that he would try to seduce Shelby away from her boy-friend, because that would give me more time to think of something.

"I have to go."

She handed me a Kleenex. "Clean off the lipstick or the other cops will make fun of you."

I had to smile. I realized that her face was smeared with it too. We both started cleaning our faces.

I started hurrying toward the jewelry store, just another guy look-ing for an engagement ring for the woman he'd just seen me kissing. I prayed that Mark Cookson would pretend to be normal while I pre-tended to look for rings.

Mark Cookson paused and looked at the window just like Shelby and her boyfriend had done. I hit Charleston on speed dial as I walked toward Cookson. "Subject is inside Newton's Jewelry Store, ninety per-cent certain our suspect is about to walk inside and confront her and the boyfriend."

"Uniforms should be on the street five minutes, ten tops. We have security footage that shows a man that matches Cookson's height and general coloring coming out of crime scene covered in blood."

"New clothes and haircut," I whispered, and then was too close to the man, so I switched to a normal voice and said, "Looking for a ring to pop the question."

"Does he recognize you?"

"No, Dad, I don't need you to help me get the ring."

"Be careful, Havoc."

"Of course," I said, smiling and happy, doing my best to show only that as I paused at the door and asked, "Are you about to go in? Don't want to cut in line."

The man turned and looked at me; the moment I saw his eyes I knew it was Cookson. Once I was sure, I could see that the bone structure of the face was the same; the demon had just given him the body he'd have had if he took better care of it. Like all demons, it could only give the person what they could have accomplished on their own with hard work or steal it from somewhere else.

His lip curled up in an expression I'd seen at the hospital, and I held my breath thinking he'd recognized me. "No, Chad, you go ahead, I'm still deciding."

"Um, I'm not Chad, my name's Hank," I said, because I couldn't remember if Miranda had called me Havoc within his hearing, and *Hank* was the closest soundalike I could think of in the moment. I couldn't risk him hearing *Havoc* and remembering who I really was.

The disdain on his face took the handsome face and curled it back into the ugly one he'd had at the hospital. "Hank, Chad, you're all the same."

I frowned at him as if I didn't understand what he meant, because he'd basically called me a dudebro jock. "Sorry, I don't know what you mean."

"Don't think too hard about it, Hank."

"Okay," I said, being puzzled and being Hank. I opened the door, keeping my attention half on him as I went through, but as a confused college-age Hank, not as police officer Havoc who didn't want to turn his back on the bad guy.

A sound like an electronic doorbell sounded as the door opened and then closed behind me. The air conditioning was on so high that all my exposed skin ran in goose bumps.

I spotted Shelby Jackson and her boyfriend at the far end of the room in front of a glass-covered jewelry display that ran around the room in a U shape. There was an elderly man helping them look at rings. The glass display at the back of the room was only partially filled and next to what looked like an area with equipment where maybe you could watch the jeweler actually create some of the sparkly things in the displays. There was one door beside the work area that was closed and marked *Private*. It probably led to the offices and private restrooms, maybe a break area. There was an entrance near the door that let you walk back behind the display area so the salespeople could go back and forth and another larger opening in front of the far door and the workstation.

The older man looked up at me and said in a soothing voice with just a trace of accent, "We will be right with you, please feel free to look around and see if anything catches your fancy."

I thanked him and pretended to look at the jewelry, but I was really keeping an eye on Mark Cookson, who was still standing there, staring through the window. He wasn't looking at the jewelry in the window display either. He was staring at Shelby and her boyfriend. He didn't look angry, or even upset, he looked thoughtful. Was he going to wait until they were somewhere less public? I would have. He looked so completely different from in the hospital and in all his pictures that he could start a new life somewhere else. He could have a true do-over if he was patient and willing to wait on taking Shelby. The fact that he was hesitating this much let me know that he didn't realize there was security film of him coming out of one of today's crime scenes in this new body.

I wanted him to wait until I had more backup, but I didn't want him to disappear. We needed to catch him before he hurt anyone else.

A younger woman came out of the door in the back of the shop. She had long dark hair and glasses. She moved past the older man and walked toward me on the other side of the display cases.

"How can we help you today?" she said with a smile that was pleasant and professional.

"I'm wanting to buy an engagement ring."

She glanced down and I realized too late I was still wearing my wedding band. I'd been too worried about Cookson to think my cover story through.

I smiled at her and put everything I had into the smile, so that she put her hand to her throat and her breathing changed. *Okay, tone down the smile*, I thought, *we aren't flirting, we're just undercover while we guard Shelby*.

"I couldn't afford to give her an engagement ring when we married, but for our anniversary I want to surprise her with one."

The saleswoman liked the story, because her smile filled her eyes, as she said, "What a great idea, I'm sure your wife will be thrilled."

I smiled back. "I think she will be."

"What were you thinking about spending?"

I hadn't thought that far, so I said, "I'm not sure, I know the kind of ring I want. Can we go backward from there?"

She smiled. "Of course," she said, though her eyes were a little less sure than her smile. She probably had a lot of people come in here without a budget in mind and then freak out about the prices.

"Promise I won't freak out about the prices, but since my wife waited so long for an engagement ring, I want it to be special."

Her eyes matched her smile again. "I'm sure we'll be able to find the perfect ring for you."

I nodded as if I believed that, and half watched Cookson at the window as the saleswoman started to point out different styles of engagement rings.

Someone's cell phone rang, and it turned out to be the boyfriend's. "We're looking at rings, don't you dare answer that," Shelby said. Her tone was serious; if Reggie had used that voice with me, I would have ignored my phone.

"It's my coach, babe, there are scouts coming to the next game. He was supposed to learn what pro teams are coming and then call all of us that have a chance in hell of getting drafted."

"Fine, take the call," she said, with an eye roll that I saw from across the room. The boyfriend took the call, getting up from the seat to stand in the middle of the room as if he couldn't take the news sitting down.

Shelby saw me then or recognized me. "Didn't I see you at the Cozy Cauldron earlier today?"

"You did," I said, smiling at her.

Her boyfriend had walked across the shop like he wanted privacy for the call.

"You were sitting with what's her name, Elizabeth?" Shelby said to me.

"Emma," I said.

"That's right, her and her new boyfriend."

I nodded, still smiling. "That's right."

She glanced behind at the boyfriend, who was standing with his back to us. It was an important call for him; his whole future was on the line, and if they married, Shelby's future, too.

The saleslady hesitated with a tray of rings in her hands. They were princess cuts, and I shook my head. "They'll stick out too much at work, she'll hate that. Do you have anything that is more flush to the ring mounting?"

"What's her job?" the saleslady asked.

"She's a teacher," I said.

"Was she the lady I saw you with at the coffee shop?" Shelby asked. I hadn't even known she'd noticed me with Miranda. I'd thought Shelby was totally into her boyfriend as she left the café. It meant she was a far better actor than I thought and that she noticed men even when she was on the arm of her soon-to-be fiancé. It was none of my business, but if I had been dating her it would have given me pause; lucky for all of us I was just there to keep her from getting killed by her stalker.

The boyfriend came back pumped and over the moon, listing

teams that would be scouting him tomorrow. He actually did a little bounce on his toes like he was a little boy, too excited to hide it. I liked him better for it, but Shelby got that disdainful crook to her upper lip, and the eyes said clearly that he was behaving like a child and she did not approve. Reggie had a similar look; so had my first wife. Most women had it.

Boyfriend didn't notice; he was too busy bouncing. Shelby saw me notice. She gave me the full force of that disdain and then her mouth softened into a smile, but her eyes didn't go softer. No, the look in her eyes was hard and sharp as if her eyes were blue glass with edges hard enough to cut yourself on, but it just might be worth it. She was too harsh for me, reminded me too much of my first wife, and she had been a woman who used men until either she used them up or they wised up and moved on to someone safer to love.

The saleslady said, "How about these rings?"

I turned to look at the new tray of rings and took the chance to look at the window. Mark Cookson was still there but he wasn't looking at Shelby, he was looking at the boyfriend and me. The boyfriend I understood; hadn't Charleston said that one of the boyfriends had been killed along with the woman? I wasn't sure why he was noticing me, but in case he was about to make a connection to me from the hospital I looked back at the rings as if I was serious about them. Before Cookson or the demon inside him recognized me as a cop, I needed backup.

The rings were pretty enough, but none of them were right, because the right one was on Reggie's finger along with the wedding band that matched mine. I was suddenly homesick for her, for us. I shook my head at the rings.

Mark Cookson reached for the door. The homesickness vanished in a spurt of adrenaline.

"I want that one," Shelby said.

"Babe, that's got to be one of the most expensive rings in the store, I can't afford that."

Cookson walked into the store smiling and looking normal. If I hadn't known what his angel looked like, or remembered his eyes from the hospital, I wouldn't have given him a second look, but Shelby did. Maybe she was just one of those women who notice men?

"You have excellent taste in jewelry. This ring is one of my best," the older salesperson said.

"Don't I deserve the best?" she asked, gazing up at her boyfriend.

"Of course you do, and in a few years maybe we can do what this guy's doing and buy you the biggest, most perfect diamond, but I can't do it right now, babe, I'm sorry."

"I can," Mark Cookson said.

"You can what?" the boyfriend asked.

"I can buy her the ring she wants."

"Why would you buy her a ring?"

"Because a woman as beautiful as Shelby deserves a ring like that."

"How did you know my name?" Shelby asked.

"You went to school with my brother Mark, I'm Sam Cookson."

"You mean Mark Cookson? I didn't even know he had a brother."

"We only became close recently," he said with a smile that managed to be both charming and unsettling. Though that might have been me projecting.

"I can see the family resemblance, but you're definitely the cute brother," Shelby said with a smile that she shouldn't have been flashing at other men, especially in front of her almost-fiancé.

"I don't care who you are, offering to buy Shelby a ring is inappropriate," her boyfriend said.

"Inappropriate . . . well, I lost my bet," Mark, alias Sam, Cookson said.

"What bet?" the boyfriend asked.

"That you'd know any five-syllable words and how to use them appropriately."

It took Boyfriend a second or two to catch on and then his face flushed. "Are you making fun of me?"

"Would I do that?"

Boyfriend frowned at him.

Cookson ignored him and turned to Shelby. "Let me buy you the ring or anything else you desire."

"Back off," the boyfriend said.

Cookson kept staring at Shelby, as if the boyfriend hadn't said anything. "Anything that money can buy, name it, and it will be yours."

"Anything?" she asked.

"Shelby!" her boyfriend said.

She smiled up at him. "Come on, sweetheart, you know I'm your girl. I'm just curious what he means when he says *anything*."

"I mean anything, Shelby. Pick any piece of jewelry in the shop and it's yours."

She looked around the store like she was thinking about it.

Boyfriend grabbed her shoulder and moved her to look at him. He stood between her and Cookson, blocking their view of each other and giving the other man his back. That let me know that her boyfriend was an athlete but not a fighter, or maybe he'd just been bigger and stronger all his life, so he felt secure. I knew size and strength weren't everything in a fight, but then I'd fought it for real.

"I thought you wanted me to buy you an engagement ring today," he asked her.

"I do," she said.

"Then stop screwing around and let's pick out a ring."

"The lady deserves the best, and you can't give her that," Cookson said, his voice calm and very certain.

The boyfriend whirled and yelled, "I can give her plenty!"

Cookson laughed, and he was definitely laughing at the boyfriend.

Apparently that open mocking laugh crossed a line for Shelby, because she stood up, wrapping her arms around the boyfriend's waist from behind. "Don't get mad, honey, it's you I want to spend the rest of my life with, not him, no matter how cute he is."

Boyfriend smiled and turned in her arms so they could kiss. "I love you, babe."

"I love you, too," she said, and seemed to mean it.

"Are you sure that's your choice?" Cookson asked.

I almost wished I could have told Shelby to lie and choose Cookson until my backup arrived, but I couldn't think of a way to tell her, or to keep her boyfriend from losing his temper if she did.

At least the uniforms should have been here by now. I prayed for help to save everyone in the shop and to make sure that demon or human, Cookson never hurt anyone else again. Warmth breathed through me and voices like an unfelt wind whispered, *"Angelus Lucis."*

I almost said yes out loud, then realized the angels weren't calling me by my title, they were reminding me what I was, and what that could mean, if I would allow myself to embrace my truth instead of hiding from it.

Cookson sniffed the air like a dog on a scent. "Better get busy before the other side gets their wings under them." He didn't know it was me that smelled of angels, he just thought the angels were coming for him. Good.

The saleswoman said, "What's happening?"

I focused and I could see everyone's Guardian Angels at their backs. They were all soft shining light except for Cookson's. It hurt me to see his angel tortured and dimmed at his back. I'd never seen a Guardian Angel that needed its own rescue more than it needed to rescue its person.

For the first time in years, I broke the rule that the *Angeli Lucis* are forbidden to break: I didn't just give the Guardians permission to help their people—I told the elder salesman's angel to take him and the saleswoman to the back room. We weren't allowed to dictate to people's angels, because that interfered with the human's free will. Most, even among the *Angeli Lucis*, couldn't command an angel to do anything, but I could.

"Come, daughter, let us give them room to decide these things." I was betting if anyone had asked the elderly jeweler what things they were leaving their customers to decide, he wouldn't have been able to answer the question, but I didn't care, I just wanted them safe.

He held out his hand and his daughter went to him, looking at us as if she knew something was wrong, but she wasn't sure what.

"Angels, angels, why do you care about the jeweler and his daughter?" Cookson asked, watching them go toward the back door. He still wasn't talking to me, but to the air, to the listening angels.

"Let's go, babe, we can pick the ring another day," the boyfriend said, trying to lead her toward the front door.

"Oh no, boyfriend, you don't get to take Shelby away from me."

"What do you mean, take her away from you?" He looked at Shelby. "You didn't fuck him, please tell me you didn't."

"No, I promised you I wouldn't sleep around, and I haven't. I don't even know this guy," Shelby said.

"Get the hell out of our way," the boyfriend said.

"No," Cookson said. The angel trapped at his back opened its misshapen mouth and wailed soundlessly to the other people in the room, but the sound stabbed through me like a spear to my heart. I put a hand out and caught myself on the glass display cabinets. If Cookson's human body died, the angel would be free to go back to the light of God. He would cleanse it and make it whole again, but first Cookson had to die.

"I won't leave you," I said to the angel. I didn't realize I'd said it out loud until Cookson spoke.

"Shelby, you must be even more special than Mark told me for a stranger to stay and risk his life for you."

"I wasn't talking to Shelby," I said, and drew my gun underneath the oversized tank top.

CHAPTER FORTY-THREE

olice, don't move," I said, and I sounded like Detective Zaniel
Havelock—Hank and his flirting and ring searching were gone.
But for the first time since I'd become a cop, I was also Zaniel the
Angelus Dictum, and *Angelus Lucis*. I was a light against the darkness,
but this time I had a gun.

"Wait, we know that voice," Cookson said. He started to look back.

"Hands on your head, lace your fingers together."

"I don't think so."

"I will shoot you in the head if you move. You won't survive that."

The demon laughed, the sound of it echoing so that the hair on my
arms rose in goose bumps from the sound. "I won't die."

"Mark Cookson's body will, and that sends you back to Hell," I
said.

The demon laughed again. "You still don't understand what we are,
do you?"

"I know you're a demon and he's a college student who thought
you'd give him his heart's desire for the use of his body."

"Well, you aren't wrong as far as that goes," Cookson said.

"Demon, what do you mean, demon? What are you talking about?" the boyfriend asked.

Shelby was pulling him farther away from Cookson. She looked frightened. I don't know what Cookson's face looked like because all I could see was the back of his head, but she was seeing something that made her want them both out of his reach. I approved, one less thing to worry about. Where was my backup?

"Lace your fingers on top of your head, now," I said.

"And if I don't, are you really going to shoot me in the head for just standing here with my hands raised? Will you honestly shoot me, kill me, just because I won't follow every order to the letter? You're a good man, Detective. Good men don't shoot unarmed civilians in the head when their arms are raised in the air."

"I will not let you hurt anyone else," I said, holding the Sig Sauer P238 in a steady one-handed grip aimed at the back of his head. The gun was so small in my hand that a standard two-handed grip was awkward.

"A bad cop that doesn't want to spend the rest of his life in jail doesn't shoot unarmed civilians, even murderers, when he's on security camera," Cookson said.

I glanced up and there it was: a camera angled exactly right to see me shoot someone that looked human. If I shot him before he did something threatening, and he died, losing my career was the least of my worries.

"I can smell your hesitation, Detective—Havoc, wasn't that what they called you at the hospital?"

I ignored him and said, "Shelby, take your boyfriend and stay as far across the room from us as you can; do not let him grab you, but go out the front door. There should be uniformed cops out there in a marked car."

"I won't let them leave," Cookson said with his hands raised at the elbow as if he were doing the minimum to look cooperative. Most security cameras didn't have sound, or not good sound, so his hands up were clearly visible; me yelling for him to lace his fingers might not be clear in the video. It would look like I shot him after he gave up. Heaven help me, but I needed him to look dangerous on the security tape before I fired.

"I won't let you hurt them," I said. I nodded at Shelby and she took her boyfriend as far from us as the glass jewelry cases on the other side would allow.

"Unless you have a major holy relic on you, Detective Havoc, you can't stop me."

"A holy object will be enough," I said, still staring at the back of his well-cut hair. My gun was still pointed, one-handed and steady.

Shelby and her beau were moving slowly along the far display cases toward the door.

"I'm not a vampire, Detective; you can't chase me away with crosses."

"Not that kind of holy object," I said.

"Ankh, pentagram, Star of David, throw the Qur'an at me, it's all the same and all just as useless against me now."

I thought about what he'd said, against him now. What did he mean by that?

"Don't lose your nerve, Shelby," Cookson said.

My gaze flicked to them but didn't actually look away from the man I was aiming at, so it was hard for me to judge what he was talking to her about.

"If you run for the door, I will stop you," Cookson said.

"Just move slow," I said, "don't run. Demons are like big cats, you run, and they will chase you."

"He doesn't look like a demon," she said, but her voice was strained thin. Cookson was right, her nerve was failing; she was going to make a break for the door soon unless she regained control of herself.

"He's possessed Mark Cookson's body," I said.

"It was a fixer-upper," Cookson said, "but I've done wonders with it, don't you think, Shelby?"

"Ye . . . yes," she almost stuttered.

"What's your boyfriend's name?" I asked.

"Jeff, my name's Jeff."

"Keep her calm, Jeff, go slow for the door."

"I won't let them leave, Detective, you know that."

"How are you going to stop us?" Jeff asked.

"I'm going to kill you, Jeff. I'm going to kill you both."

"I won't let that happen," I said.

"How will you protect them from me after you're dead?"

"You won't kill me," I said.

"Oh, I think I will."

"I know you won't," I said.

"Cocky, I like that in a victim. It's always the confident ones that beg the most at the end."

I was fighting so my hand didn't start to shake with the gun held out and aimed. I was either going to have to lower it, change hands, or change to a two-handed grip. I'd wanted to keep one hand free just in case, because I'd shot him in the hospital and hadn't killed him; of course I hadn't tried shooting him in the head point-blank, but guns were never the first choice for demon fighting.

Cookson looked completely human now; I was hoping that meant his body was more bullet friendly, but I'd have to shoot him to find out.

"They are too close to the door, Detective. I will not allow them to leave."

"Are you sure that Mark Cookson's head is bulletproof?"

"Yes," he said.

"A hundred percent bulletproof, you're absolutely sure of that?"

"Yes." But he sounded a little less certain.

"Because if he dies then you go back to Hell."

"He'll go with me."

"He'll probably go to Hell, but he won't be in the same section as a demon that disobeyed the laws of Hell," I said.

"I have acted within the parameters of the clauses in the treaty that pertain to my kind."

"You mean the treaty between Heaven and Hell?" I asked.

"What other treaty is there for my kind?"

I couldn't argue that, so I said, "A little angel told me that you've been doing things that aren't allowed."

"Heaven is always pissy, but no one in Hell is upset with me, and since that is where I will eventually be cast back into, that is all that matters to me. Heaven can go fuck itself, for I will never see inside its pearly gates."

I couldn't argue that with him, so I didn't try.

"Shelby, don't!" Jeff yelled.

The demon turned in a blur of speed that no human could match. I pulled the trigger and he'd been so busy turning, he hadn't tried to dodge the bullet. The bullet hit his shoulder, turning him; he reacted like a human being that had never been shot before, hesitating to act, so that I had time to aim at the back of his head and pull the trigger again. He collapsed face forward to the floor. He didn't try to catch himself. He just fell. I kept the gun pointed at the body just in case he hopped up and went *Just fooling!* But as the seconds ticked by, I began to breathe again. Maybe Cookson and his demon weren't faster than a speeding bullet after all.

Shelby was screaming, and there were men shouting that I could barely hear through the ringing in my ears from shooting the gun without ear protection inside. I moved so my back was to the display cases and I could see the body on the ground and the uniformed officers coming through the door. My backup was here, not exactly in the nick of time, but I'd take it. I raised my shirt to flash my badge and I identified myself as the detective they were supposed to be backing up.

CHAPTER FORTY-FOUR

Cookson's body lay facedown, one arm caught underneath it, the other flung to the side, the legs at odd angles that no actor ever manages on TV. A dead body just falls differently even from an unconscious one, and yet I didn't believe it. The demon had taken a lot more bullets than this at the hospital and it had barely fazed it. There was blood around the head and shoulder, but not enough. At close range the nine-millimeter bullet should have blown out the other side of the head. There just wasn't enough damage, but . . . the body lay like it was dead, and then I realized I had a way to be certain without getting close enough to check for a pulse. I tried to see the angel at his back, and it was still there, trapped and screaming for help like someone half trapped in quicksand. Cookson was still alive, or his angel would have been free to escape back to Heaven.

One uniform wanted to check the body, but I said, "He's alive." I might have yelled it accidentally as my ears stopped ringing.

"Ambulance is on its way, but shouldn't we stop the bleeding or something?" Officer Stevens asked.

"Demonic possession, stay clear until we have a priest or a witch to check it for us."

He went a little paler than his natural skin color, which was damn near pasty. You didn't meet that many people out here on the West Coast who looked like they'd spent the nonexistent winter indoors. He was probably from back east somewhere. Once I was sure that Mark Cookson wouldn't get up and kill everyone, including us, I'd ask Stevens about his background and see if my guess was right.

He moved up beside me and aimed his gun at the body, which meant this probably wasn't his first demonic rodeo. His partner, whose name I didn't catch, took Shelby and Jeff out the front of the shop and to the sunny day that was still outside waiting.

I'd switched to a two-handed grip at last; I could hold that for a lot longer than the one-handed grip I'd had earlier. I kept my gun aimed at Cookson and waited. His angel screamed and writhed, trying to get away. I let myself lean against the glass cases as the sound of its pain stabbed through me.

"I will save you," I whispered. The angel quieted as it lay trapped on Cookson. Killing him would free the angel once and for all, but if bullets wouldn't do it, what would?

The "body" twitched, then groaned, and the ringing in my ears had died down enough that I heard it. The uniformed officer jumped and said, "Jesus, I hate supernatural cases, you never know what's going on."

"You get used to it," I said.

The body groaned again, and moved more like it was waking up than injured. The voice was thick and sounded wrong, but the words were clear enough. "That hurt more than expected, but as I said bullets cannot kill Mark now."

Stevens hit his shoulder microphone and was calling for more backup. ". . . and we need a priest, we've got a full-on possession."

Cookson laughed, but it sounded like he was having trouble clearing some of the blood out of somewhere. "I am beyond priests." He started to get to his knees.

"Stay on your knees," I said.

"Hands behind your head," the uniform said.

"Or what, you'll shoot me again?"

"You said it hurt, we could just keep shooting you until the priest arrives."

"I also said that a priest can't get rid of me, and that was the truth, too, Detective."

"You're just a demon using a human body; exorcism is designed to fix that," I said. I was fishing, trying to figure out what was different about this demon and Mark Cookson.

"You think you've saved Shelby, but you haven't. She can't hide from me, Detective."

"You could have had a new life in this body if you had just left Shelby alone," I said.

"Mark wanted sex with those five women. We did try for willing and seduction, but like dear Shelby they chose force. Willing sex would have saved their lives, but if not that, then he wanted their deaths. Until we finish that part of the bargain, we are not free to have another life," he said from his knees. He didn't seem in a hurry to stand up; maybe he was still feeling weak from being shot twice?

"A woman doesn't force a man to rape her," I said. "A man refuses to take no for an answer, then forces himself on a woman, that's the definition of rape."

"Look at this body, we could have made passionate love to them, but they would not have us. That's not our fault, that's their fault."

My finger caressed the trigger, not pulling it, but God help me, I wanted to. "A woman is allowed to say no to anyone that she doesn't want to have sex with."

"It doesn't work that way in Hell," he said.

"Enjoy it when you get back there," I said.

"I won't be going back."

"Tell that to your exorcist."

"I'd rather tell it to you, Havoc. What a lovely name, Havoc. It suits you somehow."

"You know my name, what's yours?"

He looked over his shoulder, smiling. "Now, Havoc, that wouldn't be any fun. If you want to know my name, you'll have to guess."

"I won't play twenty questions with you," I said.

Cookson sniffed the air like he had earlier. "Shelby is nearby, still within my reach."

"No, she's not," I said.

A shudder ran through Cookson.

"What was that?" Stevens asked.

Another shudder ran through Cookson. "There are a few downsides to this new form," he said in a voice that almost sounded like he was in pain.

"You feel pain," I said.

"Demons feel pain, Detective, or what would be the point of torturing us in Hell?"

"But you don't feel the pain of the human body you possess," I said.

"Not normally," the demon said, and shuddered so hard that he fell forward onto all fours.

"Don't move!" Stevens shouted.

"Sorry," said Cookson, "a side effect."

"Are you sick or something?" Stevens asked.

"Or something," Cookson said, and fell to the floor writhing.

"He's having a seizure," Stevens said.

"You said the ambulance was on the way, right?" I said.

"Yeah, but we have to do what we can to keep him from busting his head open." Stevens holstered his gun and started toward Cookson.

"Stevens, don't."

Cookson's body shuddered and writhed on the carpet. It looked enough like someone having a grand mal seizure that even an emergency room might have been fooled, but it wasn't right. Seizures of any kind were flagged in possible possession cases, because they'd been mistaken for demonic interference for centuries along with so many things.

"We can't let him hurt himself like this," Stevens said.

"He's a demon wearing a human suit, that's not a seizure," I said.

"You can't know that," he said, and was careful to kneel without spoiling my aim.

There was fresh blood. I had a second of wondering if Stevens was right. Had Cookson melding with the demon caused seizures? Then I realized the blood was coming from Cookson's hand—there was no reason for that to bleed.

"Stevens, get away from him!"

Stevens froze in midmotion as he reached out to try to help. I thought he was going to do what I'd told him to do and back away, and then his shoulders hunched forward, and claw tips sprouted out of the back of his body armor. I pulled the trigger, aiming at the center of Cookson's back, but he rolled in a blur of speed so that I shot into the back of Stevens's body armor.

"God!" I yelled it and pulled my gun to the side, aiming at the floor so I didn't shoot Stevens again. I tried to move around so I could shoot Cookson, but he rolled and took Stevens with him, turning the other cop into a shield. The claws through his chest and out his back held him in place. A second set of claws curled around Stevens's shoulder, pinning him in place so I had no shot. I moved to the side, trying to circle around them and shoot Cookson. There was blood on Stevens's face, spilling out of his mouth. God help him!

It was a bad idea, but I walked up on them, trying to find a way to hurt Cookson enough for him to let Stevens go. If he was going to be saved, I had to get him away from the demon now, not later. I prayed that I'd live through crowding the demon, but I had to try to save the other cop.

I had to almost stand on top of them to catch a glimpse of a yellow eye peering over the cop's shoulder, but the demon jerked back so that the head and all the rest of the main part of the body was lost between Stevens and his body armor, and then I realized the policeman was shorter than the demon. I had a clear shot at the legs, so I took it.

"Damn you!" Cookson yelled, and then he was pushing Stevens into me like a battering ram. I stumbled, fighting to keep my feet, and that was enough time for Cookson to get to his feet, still holding the other cop's body like a shield. I tried to shoot the demon again, but he rushed forward, stronger and faster than humanly possible. Cookson shoved me into the glass case, and it exploded under us in a thousand biting shards.

I ended up on the bottom with Stevens between us, the demon pinning us to the broken glass. I still had my gun but it was trapped underneath the body and the demon's weight. I fought to work it free to aim—and realized that the officer's Guardian Angel wasn't glowing anymore; he was dead, and his angel was free to return to God. Only my glow and the twisted thing at the demon's back remained.

Cookson's face was humanoid, but the mouth was full of black fangs to match the curved black claws. His skin had turned red like the scales he'd worn at the hospital. The fangs snapped at my face, and I thought, *You don't have fangs, toothless*, but nothing changed. The demon snarled, "I'm half human, and we have our own imagination, Havoc. You can't fuck with our form now, too late for that!"

I got my gun free and aimed at its face. The demon grinned and opened its mouth wide to engulf the gun and half my hand, and bit down as I pulled the trigger. I screamed and the bullet went out the back of the demon's head while it laughed. It bit down and I screamed again.

The angel trapped at its back shrieked with me. I balled my hand into a fist and kept firing the bullets into the demon. I couldn't kill it, but maybe I could keep it from biting my hand off. It finally reared back and spat a bullet at my face.

"That still hurts, damn, but pain is worth free will."

His Guardian Angel screamed again as the demon's claws scrambled for my face. If I died, the angel was trapped in torment. I prayed that if I died, I'd be able to set the angel free first.

There was the sound of wings like birds, and a voice breathed through me, "Zaniel, come to me."

I didn't think I could be any more scared, but I was wrong. I didn't want to see Her again, ever, because I was afraid of what would happen. If it had been just my death on the line I might have hesitated, but I couldn't leave the Guardian Angel to be tortured.

"I will destroy that handsome face and body, Havoc, and then I will hunt down the last women and be free to roam the Earth. No priest will exorcise me to Hell, because I will be half human."

"That's not possible," I said through gritted teeth as I fought to keep his claws from my face.

"No, but it's still true," the demon said.

My gun clicked empty, and I couldn't reach the extra magazine in my pocket. He raised black claws upward like five daggers. I was still trapped under the weight of two bodies, ground into the glass and diamonds. I was out of time to decide, so I did the only thing I could be certain would free the angel. I opened the space between here and where the angels dance on golden threads and sing the universe into continuous creation.

Our blood spilled out like rubies shining and bouncing in round globes because there was no gravity here. Golden lines of power sang and gleamed around us, and the angels sang the universe into being, creating and re-creating over and over. Matter is neither created nor destroyed, it simply is. The perfection of it filled me and I wasn't even afraid as I watched the rubies sparkle against the gold and silver and . . . colors that had no words to describe them surrounded us.

Stevens didn't care, because the dead feel nothing, but Mark Cookson cared. He began to scream. The human part of him wasn't ready to go among the angels. The demon part of him got control and growled at me, "You cannot destroy us that easily."

The angel on his back screamed for help and now there were many others that could hear its cry. The angels came glowing and burning and I heard a familiar voice. "Zaniel, what have they done to you?"

I said, "Save the angel, set it free."

"And what of you, Zaniel?"

"I want to go home."

"You are home," she said, and I could almost see her golden hair, almost see her eyes, and then she was too far inside my head and she saw what I thought home meant, and it wasn't Her. We floated in the middle of holy fire; the seraphim had come, and neither Mark Cookson nor the demon sharing his body was pure enough of heart to survive their six-winged embrace.

CHAPTER FORTY-FIVE

woke up in the hospital with Dr. Paulson looking down at me. "Good to see you awake," he said, smiling.

"Good to be awake," I said; my voice sounded rough as if I'd been out longer than I realized.

I don't know if he saw it on my face, but he answered my question. "You've been unconscious for almost two days."

"How bad?" I asked, and looked down at myself. I had expected my hand to be in bandages, but it wasn't. I remembered the fangs biting into me; that shouldn't have healed in two days.

"The officers who came to try to rescue you and the other policeman said you were on fire, but it gave off no heat and cast no shadows. I'd love to know how you conjured fire to kill the demon without setting the building and yourself ablaze."

"It was holy fire, and I've walked through it before, so I knew I would be fine."

"Mark Cookson's body wasn't fine; the other police saw it burn, but there was nothing left of it."

"The Infernal can't survive the touch of holy flame," I said.

"The dead police officer's body was intact and unharmed, though the witnesses aren't sure why it didn't burn."

"Stevens was dead; he couldn't be afraid of the holy flame and its messengers, and he must have been a good person when he was alive," I said.

"From all accounts he was," Paulson said. He then proceeded to check me top to bottom to see if there were any lingering effects from what had happened. At the end he said, "You are remarkably well for someone who was attacked by a demon and burned with holy fire."

"Thank you."

"I don't think it's me you should be thanking."

"You're right," I said, and sent a prayer of gratitude to God and the angels, though I was careful not to think too hard about the latter. I did not need another visitation.

"Your lieutenant is outside waiting for me to give him permission to see you. Are you up to answering questions about what happened?"

"Yes," I said.

He shook his head. "I knew you would say that, but talk fast, because you need to rest."

"I thought I wasn't hurt?"

"You don't seem to be, but you were unconscious for almost forty-eight hours, that makes me cautious."

"I feel fine."

"All your wounds are healed, even the arm and stomach," he said.

"Why don't you look happier about that?" I asked.

"Raise up your hospital gown and look at your right arm," he said.

It was an odd request, but I did what he asked, because it was simple, and he had that look that you never want to see on your doctor's face. The one just before they told you something you didn't want to hear about your health or someone else's.

I pushed up the sleeve and there was what looked like a tattoo in a band that encircled my arm just below the shoulder. It was pale blue and looked tribal. I touched my skin and it felt like it always felt. I closed my eyes and ran my fingertips over my skin, and there it was, the slightest of texture differences. I opened my eyes and stared at it.

"You didn't have a tattoo there when I treated you for the demon attack at the hospital," Dr. Paulson said.

"I don't have any tattoos," I said.

He motioned toward my arm. "You do now."

I stared at it, and he handed me his phone with pictures of the outside of my arm. "I figured you'd want to see them and I'd rather you not rush to the bathroom mirror just yet."

I stared at the pictures.

"It looks like a stylized tribal monster," he said.

"It's a demon," I said.

"You sound certain, tribal isn't usually that realistic."

"I've seen it before," I said.

"Where?"

"One of the instructors at the College of Angels had one exactly like it. He said it was supposed to represent a successful fight and slaying of a demon. I thought it was more metaphorical."

"I thought what all you Angel Speakers did was carry messages for God. I didn't think you got on the front lines of the battle between good and evil."

"It's not that simple," I said, still staring at the pictures of my arm—my arm. Master Donel had a shoulder cap above this tattoo and more bands decorating down his arm. They were supposed to represent the path of the Seven Archangels. There was the Archangels pattern in Kali, which was one of the styles that Master Donel taught, part of his Filipino heritage, but staring at the pictures I realized that maybe what I had taken for metaphor in studying the Archangels had been far more real.

Had Donel known this was coming? Is that why he asked Turmiel to reach out to me about finding his sister? I would find her and that would give me an opening to speak with Donel, or at least with Turmiel. I couldn't go back to the College of Angels, especially not now. The seraphim had come to my aid with Her at their head. She was awake and active after years of being locked in meditation with God, that was how they had put it. She had been meditating and trying to decide if She would repent or fall. Had what happened two days ago already changed Her decision or forced Her to choose? God, I hoped not.

"You look shaken," Paulson said.

"I'm okay."

"If it had been a real tattoo it would still be healing and sore," he said.

"I've seen other people heal from them, but never done it myself." Reggie had tattoos when I met her, and I remembered that the seraphim—no, one seraph in particular—had asked me to come home, and home had been Reggie and Connery. Did I remember Her being sad that I loved someone else, that I had a child? Or had I dreamed that part?

"I'll go tell your lieutenant that physically you're fine. He's been wanting to ask you some questions about what happened."

I handed him back his phone. "Thank you, Doctor."

"Are you up to questions, Detective?"

I nodded, but I wasn't looking at him or even seeing the room. I was trying to remember something that had happened, but it was like the harder I tried to remember all the details once I had taken us into angelic space, the fuzzier it all got. The mind protects us from trauma; if I was meant to remember I would, but if not I needed to believe that it was for the best. No, I didn't believe it was for the best; I felt like something was being hidden from me.

"I'll go tell Charleston you're up for questions if you're sure?"

I blinked up at him, rubbing my arm, though it didn't hurt at all. "Yes, I'm sure."

Paulson looked like he didn't believe me, but he went to get Charleston.

I answered questions from Charleston and later from Internal Affairs, because there was one dead uniformed officer. Mark Cookson's body didn't come back with me. It had burned up in the holy fire, and the demon with it. The fire of God is the only thing that can destroy the "immortal," even demonic. I was just lucky that the jewelry store security tapes caught it all. The demon killing Stevens, and the fire burning around us. Our bodies had stayed in the store the whole time and looked frozen until the fire started. If the tapes hadn't proven my story, IA would have been far less forgiving. I mean, who would believe that a cop could call holy fire and burn up a demon. I hadn't explained the details of what I'd done. Internal Affairs wasn't big on mysticism; better to keep the answers simple for the report.

The demonically enchanted bottle had vanished on the trip from our unit to the Magical Forensics Section in the Medical Examiner's office. The containment box had just been sitting open and empty when they opened the back of the enchanted armored car. If it could help one demon climb out of Hell, then it could help another one. The clairvoyants are searching for it, but so far it remains hidden. I suggested he contact Suriel at the College and he already had, but so far no reply. If the College continued to ignore us Charleston made noise about me contacting them directly. Apparently I went pale because he stopped talking about it. Suriel I wanted to see again, and even Turmiel and Harshiel, but the College as a whole—no. Turmiel got access to a phone, because he texted me that the angels had healed Harshiel. When I tried to question Turmiel about the demonic bottle loose in our city he said he'd try to talk to Suriel, but he promised nothing. I tried to text him back, but he wasn't there. Apparently he'd borrowed the phone of this nice young lady, and that was all she knew. She did mention that Turmiel was so cute, I'd agreed and hung up.

The day I got out of the hospital Reggie came to drive me to my apartment. I'd known she was coming to pick me up, because otherwise I'd have arranged for someone else to drive me home. What I hadn't expected was that she was wearing one of my favorite outfits. The short, tight black skirt that I hadn't seen on her in over a year, with the tall black boots that she'd worn to couples therapy last time. I'd wondered then if she had just forgotten how much I loved her in the boots, but now I knew she hadn't forgotten anything. She turned around and I realized the black top was a halter, showing her tattoo of vines and flowers as the only color in the black outfit. The colors were soft and beautiful against her skin. She hadn't liked wearing halter tops after her breasts got bigger and stayed bigger after we had Connery. She insisted on wearing a bra all the time now, but here she stood in a halter top, with my favorite boots climbing her long legs, and the skirt she'd stopped wearing because she was a mother now and what if her students saw her out dressed like a hooker? I got to the makeup and red lipstick eventually, but this time she didn't get mad because I didn't look at her face first. Her smile let me know that my face showed her everything she'd wanted to see on it. "You missed our lunch and our date," she said.

"I'm sorry, you don't know how sorry I am that I missed seeing you."

She gave me that Valentine's Day promise smile. "I missed you, too."

My heart did a flip that if I'd still been hooked up to monitors would have probably brought the medical staff on the run.

"This doesn't mean we're back together; I'm sorry but I'm not ready."

I wasn't sure if my heart stopped beating for a second or just slid down into my feet. I fought not to look disappointed or to assume based on the outfit she was wearing, but it was hard. She wasn't a sadist, and to wear that outfit to pick me up and not be back together was definitely sadistic.

"I guess seeing me in the hospital just confirmed a lot of your fears," I said, and my voice wasn't normal, but it wasn't angry either and that was the best I could do.

"I'm still scared of your job, but when I saw you in the bed before the doctors knew if you'd wake up, I realized there was something else I'm more afraid of than losing you because you get hurt on the job."

"What are you more afraid of?"

"Losing you out of my life and out of Connery's life, because I'm too chickenshit to be a cop's wife."

"You're one of the bravest people I know, Reggie."

"No, I'm not, I'm really not, but I'm going to try to be."

"Thanks for driving me today."

"If I was really brave, I'd drive you to the house, so you'd be there for Connery when he gets out of preschool, but I'm not there yet."

"I understand."

"Do you?"

"No, not really, but I understand that I just got hurt on the job and that's one of your worst fears. Hard to take me home after that."

"I don't want to lose you, Zaniel."

"You won't lose me," I said.

"Did you ask the doctor if there are any physical restrictions, anything you're not supposed to do for a few days?"

"Not drive today, and not go in to work for a few more days; if I get dizzy going up stairs or doing anything to let him know, but I should be fine."

"Did you ask about sex?"

"No, I only asked about things I'd be doing sooner," I said. I fought to keep any hope or speculation off my face.

Reggie looked at me; it was a long look, and then she smiled and slid her hands down her body from the halter top to the tops of the boots hugging her thighs. She stared at me the entire time so she could watch my face.

"I don't want to assume anything here," I said.

That full, red mouth smiled like the serpent must have smiled at Eve. "I think it's time we tried out the new bed at your apartment, don't you?"

I didn't trust what I'd say, so I just nodded, smiled back like an idiot, and hit the NURSE CALL button. I stood up. "I'll go find my doctor."

"You sit down and rest, I'll go find the doctor," she said.

"I feel fine," I said.

"Rest while you can, Zaniel, because once we get to your apartment the plan is to exhaust us both."

I sat down on the edge of the bed and let her go find the doctor, because conservation of energy suddenly sounded like a great idea.

ANGEL VOCABULARY

Angelus Decantabat—the angel sang
Angelus Cantor—angel singer
Angelus Dictum—the angel said
Angelus Extium—angel of destruction
Angelus Mortis—angel of death
Angelus Natum—angel of birth
Angelus Tenebris—angel of darkness
Angelus Lucis—angel of light
Angelus Scriba—clerk secretary
Angelus Scriptor—writer who creates words
Angelus Auditor—listener to angels

BIBLIOGRAPHY

Abadie, M. J. *Multicultural Baby Names: 5,000 African, Arabic, Asian, Hawaiian, Hispanic, Indian, and Native American Names*. Longmeadow Press, 1993.

Andrews, Ted. *Animal Speak: The Spiritual & Magical Powers of Creatures Great and Small*. Llewellyn Publications, 2002.

———. *Animal-Wise: The Spirit Language and Signs of Nature*. Dragonhawk Publishing, 2000.

Anima, Nid. *Witchcraft, Filipino Style*. Indipendently published, 1978.

Bentley, James. *A Calendar of Saints*. Little, Brown and Company, 1987.

Bruyere, Rosalyn L. *Wheels of Light: Chakras, Auras, and the Healing Energy of the Body*. Atria Books, 1994.

Cunningham, Scott. *The Complete Book of Incense, Oils and Brews*. Llewellyn Publications, 2002.

———. *Cunningham's Encyclopedia of Magical Herbs (Llewellyn's Sourcebook Series)*. Llewellyn Publications, 2000.

———. *Wicca: A Guide for the Solitary Practitioner*. Llewellyn Publications, 1988.

Davidson, Gustav. *A Dictionary of Angels: Including the Fallen Angels*. Free Press, 1994.

Davis, Wade. *The Serpent and the Rainbow*. Simon & Schuster, 1997.

Dugan, Ellen. *Autumn Equinox: The Enchantment of Mabon*. Llewellyn Publications, 2005.

Farrar, Janet and Stewart Farrar. *A Witches' Bible: The Complete Witches' Handbook*. Pheonix Publishing, 1996.

Franklin, Anna. *Midsummer: Magical Celebrations of the Summer Solstice*. Llewellyn Publications, 2002.

Franklin, Anna and Paul Mason. *Lammas: Celebrating Fruits of the First Harvest*. Llewellyn Publications, 2001.

González-Wippler, Migene. *Rituals and Spells of Santeria*. Original Publications, 1984.

Grimassi, Raven. *Beltane: Springtime Rituals, Lore and Celebration*. Llewellyn Publications, 2001.

Guiley, Rosemary Ellen. *The Encyclopedia of Angels*. Checkmark Books, 2004.

Haskins, James. *Voodoo and Hoodoo*. Scarborough House, 1990.

Jocano, F. Landa. *Outline of Philippine Mythology*. Independently published, 2018.

Kelly, Sean and Rosemary Rogers. *Saints Preserve Us!: Everything You Need to Know About Every Saint You'll Ever Need*. Random House, 1993.

Lewis, James R. and Evelyn Dorothy Oliver. *Angels A to Z*. Visible Ink Press, 2008.

Losch, Richard R. *All the People in the Bible*. Eerdmans Publishing, 2008.

Mathers, S. L. MacGregor. *The Key of Solomon the King: Clavicula Salomonis*. Weiser Books, 2016.

McCoy, Edain. *Ostara: Customs, Spells & Rituals for the Rites of Spring* Llewellyn Publications, 2002.

Métraux, Alfred, Sidney W. Mintz and Hugo Charteris. *Voodoo in Haiti*. Pantheon Books, 1989.

Morrison, Dorothy. *Yule: A Celegration of Light and Warmth*. Llewellyn Publications, 2000.

Ocampo, Anthony Christian. *The Latinos of Asia: How Filipino Americans Break the Rules of Race*. Stanford University Press, 2016.

Orangutan Foundation International. *Orangutan Foundation International Homepage*. n.d. 2020. <https://www.orangutan.org>.

Paulson, Genevieve Lewis. *Kundalini and the Chakras: Evolution in This Lifetime: A Practical Guide*. Llewellyn Publications, 1999.

Paxson, Diana L. *Taking Up The Runes: A Complete Guide to Using Runes in Spells, Rituals, Divination, and Magic*. Weiser Books, 2005.

Ramos, Maximo D. *Legends of Lower Gods: Stories About Creatures From Philippine Mythology & Folklore (Realms of Myths and Reality) (Volume 3)*. CreateSpace Independent Publishing Platform, 1990.

Rasbold, Katrina. *The Sacred Art of Brujeria: A Path of Healing & Magic*. Llewellyn Publications, 2020.

RavenWolf, Silver. *Angels Companions in Magick*. Llewellyn Publications, 2002.

———. *Halloween!* Llewellyn Publications, 1991.

Reid, Fiona A. *Peterson Field Guide to Mammals of North America*. Houghton Mifflin, 2006.

Thompson, Ruth, L. A. Williams and Renae Taylor. *The Book of Angels*. Sterling Publishing, 2006.

Wilcken, Lane. *Filipino Tattoos: Ancient to Modern*. Schiffer, 2010.

Laurell K. Hamilton is the author of the No.1 *New York Times*-bestselling Anita Blake series that has sold millions of copies worldwide and created the market for sexy paranormal fiction. Anita's world is ours except that all the creatures of horror, myth and legend are real and main-streamed into society – one peopled with monsters who are all too human and humans who turn out to be the biggest monsters of all. Anita navigates the mysteries of this world while dispensing justice and living a life that could best be described as non-conventional. Laurell has published nearly fifty books and novels, including the bestselling Meredith Gentry series, as well as short stories and novellas. *A Terrible Fall of Angels* is the first book in the new Detective Zaniel Havelock series, set in a world where angels and demons walk among us. She has written in the *Star Trek* universe and in the worlds of *Dungeons and Dragons*. Along with her husband, Jonathon Green, she oversaw the adaptations of her Anita series into comics and graphic novels that were published by Marvel. Laurell is a resident of St. Louis and sup-ports many charities and links to local groups dedicated to helping animals in need and protecting the natural world.